The Chimera Virus

Dean J. Forchette

PublishAmerica
Baltimore

First printing

All characters in this book are fictitious, and any resemblance to real persons, living or dead, is coincidental.

ISBN: 1-4241-9179-3
PUBLISHED BY PUBLISHAMERICA, LLLP
www.publishamerica.com
Baltimore

Printed in the United States of America

Dedication

This book is dedicated to my wife, whose constant support and encouragement are my torch and banner, and to my son, whose separate musical visions encourage me to visit alternative realms…

And in loving memory of Marie,
'Ere I fulfilled a lifelong dream,
She winged home to Thee.

DF

Prologue

Epoch I

The asteroid struck with devastating force. Upon impact, billions of stony fragments were ejected deep into space. Aboard one no bigger than the largest common hail ball, a sampling of the viral colony clung desperately to the walls of deep crevices and interior pockets. Sadly, the bulk of the colony remained behind, its fate sealed, condemned to a dying planet. Fate had intended the errant intruder to strike a fatal blow. But for the life aboard the stony missile struggling against insurmountable odds, braving the deadly rays and powerful gravitational waves of the treacherous cosmic ocean, the long and arduous voyage to the new world had begun.

The meteoroid tumbled through the vast emptiness of space, rolling upon its axis like a die cast by the hand of some mythical god, as if the cosmos itself were the platform for an epic game of change. For eons it soldiered on, engulfed in the interstellar blackness—a common, unassuming stone, dark as the backdrop of space, absorbing the hints of starlight threatening to betray its presence. Now and then it caught a boost from the wake of a passing comet or the gravity assist of a deep, rogue planet or errant moon. Eventually the wanderer braved a distant, asteroid graveyard, seemingly tiptoeing, as if fearful of disturbing the aliens that might lay entombed on the ancient, desolate scraps. Here, powerful forces reached up from nearby balls of gas and rings of dust. The stresses arched the voyager like a hapless missile, casting it toward mysterious and unsuspecting territory. Perhaps guided by fate, more likely gifted by chance, good fortune lay in its path. Straight ahead, a comely planet of blue and green refused it passage to the stygian darkness beyond. It was snatched by a planet of wondrous beauty, hallowed by wisps of lovely, white floating mists—a world surrounded by a gaseous, luminescent shell breathing life into life. This was certainly a glorious place to call a journey's end. But here was far more than a final resting place, more than an unmarked grave for a wayfarer that had survived the ravages of space and time. Here the colony would fashion its brave new world, for this orb floated in the heavens like a mystical crystal ball predicting a bright and prosperous future. Surely, planted in this lush garden the colony would flourish. Though the landing site was cold for the moment, this was a world of promise and hope, a place of destiny for the staunch viral passengers aboard the shard of rock that had been ripped from its home and cast into the frigid and sterile wastes of the endless void. As yet, the colony could not know, but the ripples and tides of the fierce cosmic ocean had delivered it to paradise.

The stone lay frozen in the glacial wastes for thousands of years; its diminutive crew suspended in the frigid temperatures, sleeping, perhaps dreaming alien dreams, buried deeply between compacted layers of ice and slushy snow. The life within waited with the patience of the un-dead, secure in its cryogenic slumber—it waited for the warmth that would surely come. The rising temperature would be the trigger sounding the alarm, the planet's sign of good faith, offering official welcome to their new home and sanctuary.

Eventually, such a time came. The glaciers melted, the shallow, muddy waters left behind by the ice and snow receded. The drying of the crust made it brittle and much of it cracked and sank. Pockets in swampy areas pulled the sandy soil ever downward and pushed the rocky earth toward the open sky. Over the millennia the rocks and boulders peeked their heads above the ground to test their mettle against the sun, as if they feared the searing rays might be too hot against their naked domes. Yet over time they rose more and more to the occasion until, eventually, most were fully exposed, like naked bathers basking at mid-day. As the boulders heaved themselves upward they dragged their smaller companions to the surface, like sharks escorting eels along their wake. This was the time for the life within the nomadic stone to awaken, to claim its place among the stars. The light and the warmth had sounded the alarm. Although the stone was no larger than the shrew gnawing on the fungus creeping from its surface pocks and crevices, the destiny of the life it harbored was surely as big as the universe and brighter than the sun.

In addition to the light and the warmth, other signals supported the wake-up call. The strength and character of the combined gravimetric fields surrounding this world and its substantial moon had confirmed its stable nature. The rains and the favorable gasses prepared the viral tissue for the struggles yet to come. And though the warmth had washed over the colony like a magic breath and had infused it with the unmistakable hallmarks of life, and the light had guided it to the threshold of its future; it was the new home, itself, that generously offered its first true sustenance, the gift of mammalian plasma; just seconds after the colony awoke, the rodent ceased to be. The colony rejoiced in its own way at this good fortune—quietly, sedately, each member separately, yet of one accord. From that moment forward, the virus would sleep no more.

Epoch II

The golden plain shimmered under the summer sun. A thick carpet of grain swayed beneath the shifting winds, tossed about by the inland heat and the cooling breezes blown in from the great lakes to the east. Shaded breaks of dense thickets and lush fruit trees dotted the fields to the horizon. On either side heavy tree lines marked the boundaries of dark woodlands steaming off the moisture that lingered after the morning rain. A train of antelope crossed the field from woodland to woodland. Several females stepped out of the caravan to drink from the many pools, bringing their young to share the bounty. They bent low, dipping their muzzles into the shallow water. At each oasis several large bucks stood guard, hoofing the muddy soil uneasily, their ears perched high, their nostrils flared, ever wary and watchful. A leaf tumbling in the breeze or a snake parting the tall grass might elicit a sudden head jerk, a snort or a nervous twitch.

A fawn tentatively dipped its head to touch its tongue to the muddy water. As it fully inhaled the soppy scent beneath its nostrils, it caught the nearly imperceptible rustling of the tender grain and sturdy reeds surrounding the tiny pool. But already, it was too late.

In an instant the rodents were on him. The fawn leapt into the air off all fours shaking violently as if to fling them off in one bold move—to no avail. A hundred or more had covered him in an instant, leaping onto him even as he was in mid-air. They covered him relentlessly as he hit the ground, where he fought desperately to regain his footing, but could not. No sooner had he landed than his rear legs buckled. His front legs followed in short order, splaying out to the sides like broken wings. The shrews were a relentless, crazed mob, flowing over him like a dark, hairy liquid. Their whirlwind claws and razor teeth flayed his flesh. They ripped and gnawed him like a school of piranha laying claim to a kingdom beyond their familiar waters. In seconds the fawn was dead, and in less than a minute the bulk of his flesh stripped from his bones. Where the meat had fallen and the last moist fragments clung to the delicate, naked frame, the shrews continued to feast as though they had gone mad, engulfed in a frenzy of bloodlust.

Throughout the day the carrion came to feed on the remnants, but the pickings were slim, and most had gone away with only the scent or a few meager licks to satisfy them. At sundown a great, filthy buzzard perched on the scrawny rib cage, its wings embracing the bones like a dark angel. A sleek red fox, lured by the promise of an easy meal, took aim at the musty dinner prancing on its ghastly perch. Failure. The scavenger was too wary and too quick…this time. But there were rewards for the keen of eye and the persistent, like the fat rodent half buried beneath the fawn's leg bone, trampled by the hooves of the hapless creature when it had descended from its ill-fated leap. Nearly dead with a cracked spine and severed rear tendons, the crazed shrew had yet managed to consume its entire body weight in succulent entrails. The fox snatched the fat, tender morsel and dispatched it with a few quick and decisive snaps of it jaws and swallowed the tasty little critter whole.

Epoch III

The saber tooth glided along the canyon wall like a god, silently, as if its paws never actually touched the earth. This was its Olympus. Deep-gray curtains adorned the distant sky, and the breeze carried a hint of the rains sneaking over the horizon with the darkness. Night sounds from the valley began to fill the air with telltale warning messages. The huge cat picked up its pace. It would do well to find prey and make a quick kill. Instinct warned of difficult hunting in the rain. Scents, powerful and distinct just moments before would be merged or lost to the wetness, and potential prey, otherwise on the prowl, would be sheltered away.

Reaching the valley floor, the saber tooth slunk into the thicket at the edge of the wood hoping to scare up some small and tasty bit to satisfy its mounting hunger. Nothing stirred. It slunk into the woods, squeezing between two mammoth trees, creeping, each footfall measured and silent, dissolving into the impenetrable darkness like a shadow fading during a solar eclipse. All around the darkness was awash with a cacophony of night sounds, chirps and screeches, hums and buzzes, barks, hoots, and occasional growls, and with the din wafted the scents of their origins floating on the breeze. Surely, one of these clues would lead to a succulent meal and then, to a long and well-deserved sleep.

There—just on the far side of those fallen trees, within the piles of dead leaves and rotted branches, among the strewn stones and twisted logs and mounds of clotted earth, darting in and out of the many holes dotting this odd oasis—something moved, more than one—there again, and there, another, and another.

The great cat charged forward. In one mighty leap it was upon the mounds clawing at the dirt with its huge and awesome claws, tearing at the sticks and pieces of matting that layered the ground. The musk of its prey hung in the air like a bloom. The scent filled the beast with a raging hunger and escalated its digging to a frenzy. It tore and dismantled the place ever more ferociously when suddenly, without a warning that resonated with any past experience, they charged. A pack of sleek, furry beasts—enough of them to take him down—descended upon him from the shadows beyond the fallen tree. A glance to the rear confirmed as many more were coming at him from behind. And there, popping up from a hole directly in front of him, close enough that he could easily decapitate the arrogant creature, sprang the patriarch of this vicious pack.

The red fox bared its teeth and growled ferociously at the invader, defiler of its sanctuary. It stood in defiance of this brute that would dare invade its home and hunting grounds and threaten the security of its pack. Its retractable claws extended in a heartbeat, slicing easily through the packed soil and wood. Hissing and spitting now as if in the grip of a sickness, it sprang onto the back of the mammoth cat tearing deeply into the vulnerable neck muscles. Rivulets of blood streamed down the tiger's side as it bounded off the mounds. It charged directly at the pack bearing down on it squarely from the front. Leaping into the air, it struck a low, gnarled branch that exploded from the collision. Damp, stringy fibers cascaded downward and particles of wood dust filled the air like a fog. The larger shards shot in all directions. The unexpected display confused the pack just long enough for the tiger to gain a footing, to execute a tremendous leap and then melt into the shadows of the nearby trees. The patriarch lay dead beneath the rotted tree, a long, slender shaft imbedded in its heart. Its blood rained upon the ground like dreadful tears as if it had found a way to weep its last for the pack and for the precious earth beneath him, as if it had loved both more than life itself.

Epoch IV

They moved as silently as their prey—for now. Until they could track it to the lip of the valley where they hoped to chase it north, they could not risk themselves by exposing their positions, where one or more might be taken before they forced it to the place of the pit. Once there, they would rattle the bushes and toss rock and sticks, make the hooting noises and shouts of the many. Then they would drive the beast up the long valley where it would surely follow the stream up and over the rocks into the place where the climbing was impossible even for the tiger. There the god-beast would circle around and be forced down by the tribe, would be frightened by the shouting and the rattles, by the shaking of the large branches and terrified of the hunters disguised as walking trees. Eventually it would be forced down into the place of the pit where it would fall and be impaled. If it did not die, even the weakest among them would throw rocks down at it until it breathed no more, to give it peace, for it was a great spirit trapped in the skin of a beast, cursed to walk upon all fours. Did it not visit them in the dream visions? Did it not feed upon them? Had it not taken their young as gifts for its mate and cubs? Was it not their master? Had they not seen the mighty cave bear fall to its fearsome tusks?

They continued down the trail that lead toward the lip of the valley, hoping the great beast had not turned back toward its lair or followed a path away from the northern edge. No, it hadn't done that at all. The monster was there, waiting for them directly in the middle of the game trail. It was a behemoth, fully ten feet tall at the shoulder, as long as a fallen tree. It snorted in defiance and blew hot breath at these diminutive creatures that dreamed of someday being men. Its maw was a death pit, a terrifying, snapping menace with enormous daggers for teeth, which grew even longer as the creature snarled and growled viciously. Alternately pawing at the earth and sky, it released wicked, retractable claws ominously resembling the tapered rib cage of some unlucky prey. The beast inched forward, its huge muscles rippling like waves beneath its glistening coat. Slowly, belly low to the ground, it crept ever closer, surely meaning to take each of them in turn, measuring their positions and escape routes, anticipating the optimum moment to attack and cut them off. Was there no greater honor now than to run? Was there no greater glory than to huddle around the cave fires this very night, boasting of facing the master eye to eye and living to tell the tale?

Without additional ceremony, the saber tooth charged. It mowed down the first of them with its front paw. One swipe sent the proto-human flying, his backbone crushed, his flesh flayed. The others scattered; this was not the plan. Taking the great beast at the pit was a difficult matter for the most able hunters; attempting to take him on his terms in the open wood was nothing less than a willing sacrifice to the forest god. Would he be satisfied with the blood of one? At this point, they would be fortunate if that would be the case. But that is not what the saber tooth had in mind. He bounded after the nearest of them, which he rendered in two with one bite and a single shake of his magnificent head. The two halves of the apish body flew in opposite directions. The beast continued on, determined to take the others—and so it went, one after the other until the entire hunting party was lost…all but one.

Uh-Ata stumbled from the forest, alternating between limping and dragging his injured leg behind him. How he had escaped death was unclear. He remembered the huge tusks impaling his thigh and his lower leg. The bone in his shin was nearly crushed and useless. The tusk that tore through his upper leg had missed the bone; the wound was deep, but it would heal. Even now, as he hobbled from the woods it was beginning to loose some of the redness and the pain was beginning to subside.

He vaguely remembered striking at the tiger's eye with his sharp rock, and the tremendous shaking he had received for his efforts. Then he was cast into the air. Moments later he landed in the icy water. He feared the airless depths and the choking death almost as much as he feared the forest god himself, so he paddled fiercely, hard enough to keep his head above the surface. With his last vestige of strength, he dragged himself onto the bank—and then, his memory fails. When he awoke, the tiger was nowhere to be seen, which was fortunate, because he could neither stand nor walk, and certainly could not run. He may have slept long enough for a flock of crows to cross overhead and disappear over the horizon or he may have slept a full day. Who can say? Later, when he had drunk enough to refresh himself, and his leg would support him with the help of a piece of driftwood he had snagged, he made his way here, close to the place where his tribe made their refuge in the hillside caves. With just a short rest here at the edge of the shallow stream where the tribe came for water every day, just at the bottom of the narrow tail leading into the foothills, he would be able to continue on. He was eager to join the others, to see his mate, who would surely think him eaten by the forest god. When they would see him return alone, they would know the hunting party had fallen. It made him sad that they did not know the fury of this hunt and the glory of the day and the tremendous heart each had shown to their ferocious adversary. Around the cave fires, he would say more than that they had fallen and failed, and that they had been eaten. He was determined to speak of their valor and the sacrifice they had made, not just on this hunt but also on all the journeys of which he had never spoken. He would try to make their names live on, like the echoes heard in the caves of the dripping waters. He thought a long time about this, and an odd thought struck him. Though he knew Shom, Om-aga, Uh-an, Cag, and Moga were lost, he simply could not believe their spirits were not with him still. He had never thought such a peculiar thing before.

And he could not believe his good fortune; he had escaped almost certain death, and now, he was almost home. He felt different somehow. Even though he had been severely injured, he felt good, better than before the attack, stronger, more alive, more alert, more powerful. The sun had fallen far below the distant horizon, and the world now lay under a shroud of darkness. The moon, pale and indistinct behind the clouds, coursing high above the eagles' realm, seemed to twirl maniacally, as if it had looked upon the face of its brighter brother only to see a stranger there, and gone mad. Though the deepening gloom was spreading across the land like a bloodstain, he could see the distant caves clearly. The diminutive figures standing at the entrances keeping watch for the lost party were as clear to him as if they were awash in the mid-day sun. All around him the world was sharp and crisp and his head felt clear. He felt invigorated, strong and vital, and the pain in his leg had disappeared! In fact, he didn't need the crutch to help him walk anymore, so he cast it aside. Striding now without a limp or a hint of pain, with his leg fully healed, as if the tusk had never crushed his bone at all, he headed directly for the caves. He felt like a new person, a different person. He smiled a bigger smile than he ever had before and the effort inadvertently released his sabers; they slid smoothly from the front of his upper jaw to the bottom of his chin. This was new to him, and their unexpected appearance triggered the ejection of his newly developed claws from between his fingers—another powerful surprise. Yes, he felt very different because he was very different. And this land all about, which he knew so well, seemed different too, brighter, more vibrant and alive. As he drew nearer his home, he could see in each and every thing so much more potential than he had ever seen before—so much usefulness and so much beauty. It was almost as if he was seeing the earth for the very first time.

Chapter 1

Epoch V—Post-millennium

Friday, October 7, 10:35 P.M.: Kara sat on one of the enormous boulders lining the Lake Michigan shoreline. Whenever the northeastern winds kicked in and the chilly gusts slapped the chop against the stony array, the cresting wash was pounded into bits of white, soapy-looking froth. It served as a warning to everyone foolhardy enough to brave the treacherous, slippery rocks—everyone except Kara. Her footing was sure and precise, which rendered her immune to the water's obvious dangers. Here she was assured the solitude she required. And tonight, as it had for weeks, the jet stream clung steadfastly to the northlands, shepherding the cooler fronts due east, as if mindful of her reverie.

She smiled, lost in the dazzling serenity of the array of lights mirrored in the crystal waters. From where she sat all the way to the distant breakwater, the reflected stars danced with the harbor lights and the blinking signals of passing yachts and fishing boats. The moon hung like a brilliant disco ball over the shimmering dance floor. It was going to be another lovely early autumn night.

She had been restless the entire day, anticipating the darkness. Her time was near, and she was spiraling into a well of ever-increasing desire. By tomorrow morning, however, she would be feeling much better—her insatiable hunger will have been satisfied. But for now, her restlessness grew.

A subtle movement caught her eye, and she twisted her head to the left. There, on the far side of the small frontage park, the enormous masthead mechanism crowning the roof of the art museum, the Calatrava Brise Soleil, folded its wings downward like a magnificent cave bat wrapping itself in a layer of delicate, rippling membrane. She marveled at its breathtaking beauty, its audacity, the brilliance of its design and construction. She couldn't help but identify with it, as if it had been conceptualized for her alone. With the wings unfurled, viewed along the axis, it seemed to soar, a free spirit, wild and adventurous, an invincible, feral beast released upon the world—nesting here in homage to her restless self-image. From where she sat, facing the southern entrance, the structure became a sleek schooner, bounding toward the distant stars across the blue expanse of lake and sky. Now, with the shade folded snugly to the sides, as if the mast and spreaders themselves had been unfurled, it seemed docked and blocked for repairs, content to settle in and be fitted for the storms ahead; for the moment, making this port-of-call home, just as she was. Yes, for now, Milwaukee was the perfect place for a vampire with a romantic side.

She leaned forward, stretched her long legs and planted her strong, deceptively delicate hands on the cool rock. She loved the purity of it, the smoothness, its solidity; it was sure and steady, trustworthy. It felt eternal, this behemoth, and briefly, she experienced an intense sense of intimacy with it. It was as if the boulder might heave itself skyward, meld with her, and carry her to a place where she could look down on the face of the entire planet.

It was not an unusual sensation for her. It was similar to sensations she had experienced with many aspects of the natural world—to the very earth, the feel of it, the fragrance of it, to the grass and trees, to the waves beating against her feet, to the wind tossing her long, dark hair, to the birds lending a soundtrack to life, and to the skittering beasts frantically dodging the bulk of the world. It was as if the earth was trying to speak, struggling to find a common tongue in order to communicate directly with her. Generally, as she did tonight, she felt closer with nature than she felt with people, vampires or humans.

Someday, if the urge to breed became irresistible she could seek out a suitable partner at a local club. Maybe. She had several alternative ideas lurking in the wings. As things stood now, she had no interest in a family, and following the death of Megan's parents a year earlier she rarely went out. She had been far too busy helping Megan wrap up her financial affairs; plus she had finally moved out of her childhood home in New Berlin, and the search for a suitable apartment in Milwaukee had seemed like an endless and impossible task. Mostly, she had been feeling that she and the world were changing, that life was unnecessarily complicated on one hand and exceedingly trivial on the other. She just wanted to slow things down and to put her routines on pause, and to have the comfort of solitude. Even the anticipation of the peace and quiet the very idea provoked was comforting. Once settled into her new place, however, she was inexplicably dissatisfied with her newfound independence and privacy. Something was missing, and she didn't know exactly what it was. She understood what was happening to her—a transitional adjustment, of sorts. Being a vampire didn't make her immune to an identity crisis. She was growing up; she wasn't a teenager anymore, and she wasn't just a vampire, she was a woman. And she was bored with the more trivial pursuits of youth.

But she still hit the bars and clubs on occasion, mostly at Megan's urging. She acquiesced without displaying her indifference—secretly she knew it was prudent to remain in touch with the local vamp community, which was rather loosely connected at any rate. Generally the young cubs came sniffing around, as did the humans. The males surrounded the girls constantly but were seldom engaging or enticing, at least from Kara's point of view. Megan was far less averse to leading them down a fool's path for dinner or drinks now and again, and occasionally she gave it up to some particularly handsome buck. She saw no sense in denying her best friend, who refused to take no for an answer in any case. Megan seemed convinced that a bit of fun now and then was all that was necessary to put the world right.

Who was she to argue with such pure and simple logic? Besides, perhaps Megan was right. Even during this, her darkest year, she could find great solace in socialization, a trick Kara considered counterintuitive.

They had been close friends since grade school, but over the last, very emotional year had grown ever closer. Megan was her confidant in just about everything. Just about. She was human and, while they shared most of their secrets, Kara could never reveal the deeper truth. No vampire could share this intimacy with a human. Throughout the ages the vampire nation has kept its existence a secret from man, facilitated by two innate abilities of the race, the *mesmer-voice* and the *instillation*. The mesmer-voice is the ability to hypnotize, in a sense. When necessary, the vampire can cloud the human mind, exerting tremendous influence over memory and perception, but it is used as often to influence other vampires, especially those being indoctrinated into the fold, to communicate with them on a level which humans cannot comprehend, to reach deeply into their minds, aiding them in understanding new and radical ideas, helping them to focus, to expand their capabilities, to concentrate, and to keep secret the very existence of the vampire nation. This ability is closely associated with the instillation. Once these specific and singular ideas are communicated, the mesmer-voice reinforces behavior by instilling and generating within the novitiate instinctual responses to a limited set of critical circumstances. Through the mesmer-voice, the vampire nation passes its legacy from one generation to the next, safeguarding itself, instilling a fierce loyalty, not by force of overwhelming will, but by suggestion, by engendering an intense desire for the continuance of the species. Being merely human, Megan could never hope to understand these arcane concepts, and the Vampire Code, having been instilled within Kara, prevented her from revealing them or her true nature.

Still, Kara preferred Megan's company and valued her friendship above all others, male or female. Actually, whenever she and Megan had visited the local clubs, Kara had always shrugged off the attention of the males, and paid little or no mind to men. The usual fare of both simply had little to offer. Even had she been seriously looking, the scarcity of vampires would be considered a serious problem. They were far more rare than humans. Her father had once mentioned that, perhaps, one in five thousand is a vampire in developed nations. In more primitive countries that ratio dropped considerably. "That's a tough dating scene no matter how you slice it," she had remarked. "It's just as well," she had teased him. "I've got plenty of time. Besides I like women just as much as men, and I need time to figure out which way to go."

Her father would just smile and shake his head at this, not

knowing what to say, mostly because he suspected it might be true. And it was. At twenty-six, she was still as confused about life as a teenager would be. Her dad had a wonderfully loving way of making her feel that way sometimes, like a kid. He loved to remind her that she would live a lot longer than the human girls she grew up with, and that while humans were merely considered young at twenty-six, in vampire years, she was barely legal as far as he was concerned. Fathers! You've got to love 'em.

She wrapped her hands around her knee-high, leather boots, and pressed them ever more tightly against her. Her powerful calves rebelled against the confinement of her jeans and leathers, aching to be active and useful. It was time to go.

The wind was picking up a just bit, the gusts forcing her coat collar to tap urgent signals against the side of her head. Of late, it had been unseasonably warm for early October in Wisconsin, and the sudden, stiff breeze was barely a suggestion of the inevitable and bitter change to come. Perhaps, though, it was time to get back to her apartment and slip on something more appropriate for the night ahead.

The apartment wasn't far, just a few miles. It was a nice place, small, efficient, and neatly appointed with a few austere furnishing and fixtures: a contemporary leather chair and ottoman, a heavy marble end table and matching floor vase, a sleek black lamp, and a bank of miniature flood lights over a beveled mirror, a big-screen TV, nothing more. Everything in the kitchen came with the place, and she kept her bedroom in the closet: a convenient array of comforters and pillows, far more comfortable than a bed and easier to maintain. She thought her apartment luxurious, but then, she was young and understood the relative nature of the word. (She had once considered lava lamps to be luxurious!) It was enough that the living room had an incredible view of the lake and that it was quiet and secluded, lost in the myriad of identical cubicles crammed neatly into Milwaukee's fashionable East side.

In one effortless and graceful movement she sprang to her feet. She stood sentinel on the rock a moment, her tall, lithe form stark and dark against the luster of the full moon. Not far to the south a meteor unzipped the night sky, splitting the velvety darkness like a razor wound leaking flecks of golden flame. Five less remarkable streaks followed, seemingly hurrying to keep up as if fearing the terrible darkness threatened to swallow them.

Silhouetted against the jewel-encrusted sky, her five-foot, ten-inch frame appeared even taller, accentuated by the long, sleek coat that draped to her boot heels. She preferred distinctive clothing, displaying an obvious disdain for the typical Midwestern fare. She favored fashion with style or a bit of an edge—sharp Italian labels, items with expensive tailoring, name designers, and vintage pieces. For the hunt she preferred the tough and durable stuff—leathers, of course, with lots of additions, secret pockets and high-tech pouches, belts and ties around the legs, waist, arms and shoulders were a favorite. Black, always! Ammo belts were useful, as were knife sheaths and pistol holsters. A favorite was a pair of over-the-shoulder sheaths that mounted her short swords across her back, so beautifully crafted and perfectly fitted. The tiger relief tooled at the back center junction exactly duplicated the silver details on the sword handles. She even had a matching pair of earrings made, just for fun.

Whenever she had difficulty finding items at the specialty shops, she ordered from the Renascence craftsmen. (They make blade weapons, as well, and are always more than happy to accommodate the local *performance artists*.)

This customized *gear* is expensive, but she had little trouble acquiring cash whenever she needed it—vampires seldom do, and they took great pleasure in spreading it around. (Rather than hording, they had an *easy-come, easy-go* attitude about spending, preferring to put cash back into circulation, to return it to the community from which it may have been so questionably removed.) Increasing her bank role was a bonus of the hunt, never a primary motivation. At the moment, her account was fat and juicy, but, as with all good things, it never hurt to have more than enough. If she got lucky and scored a mark carrying a heavy wallet, she wouldn't be foolish enough to leave the spoils behind. She vacated the rock in one graceful, easy leap landing her twenty feet from the parade of boulders.

The edginess she had felt most of the day had returned, and she would have to deal with it soon. It had been a while since her last hunt, a full six days, and her anxiety was the direct result of her need to feed. The bloodlust had come upon her early this morning and had been building all day. Now, the hunger was beginning to grip her more urgently. She was not yet deeply in its grasp; that would come in several hours, but she could not afford to put off the game too long.

She breathed deeply, tasting the unseasonably warm and humid air. Despite the cooler evening breeze, it was still a remarkably mild autumn for Wisconsin. Tonight was a perfect night to dine out.

The moon is bright and golden new, the breeze is moist with honeyed dew, the hunger calls me to the prey, to satisfy my need today, she mused, thinking it never hurt to have a sense of humor about such things. Why not? It made dealing with her needs so much easier. The bloodlust, and the hunger, its final, most intense phase, while part of the natural order for most vampires, was fraught with their own peculiar stresses. Vampires are flesh and blood creatures, not supernatural beings, as the bogus literature and films would have people believe. Even though they are more in control of themselves than humans could ever hope to be, they have intense emotions and suffer the same psychological challenges.

The anxiety of the hunt is not mired in fear nor in the illegality of their actions. Waiting for the cover of darkness was always a minor concern, as well as the selection of appropriate prey, someone wicked and deserving of punishment. Fortunately there were plenty of thugs roaming about, ripe for relinquishing their ill-gotten gains as well as their pathetic, unsavory lives.

For most vampires, beyond the precious blood, the hunt was a necessary catharsis. For the most cunning and fearsome among them, the Bloodwarriors such as Kara, it was also intensely pleasurable. It was an addiction satisfying their most basic urges, for they relished the game as much as the taste of human flesh. Bloodwarrior vampires were simply natural-born killers.

Chapter 2

Many thousands of light-years away, near the center of the galaxy, the eternal, cosmic contest played out on a scale undreamed of by Kara, whose concerns revolved around her daily routines and the affairs of the vampire nation, at least as much as she attended to them. In that distant realm, opposing forces constantly confronted one another in the treacherous darkness of the interstellar void, and grand strategies engulfed billions of alien worlds—the stakes, literally, the fate of the entire galaxy. Jump gates, controlled wormholes serving as shortcuts across the vast, interstellar distances, were continually being introduced to remote aspects of the first primary tide and the attached spiral arm, two regions of space near the galactic nucleus. The gates were owned and controlled by the Rege'Cean Empire and seeded outward from Central Command located on the home world of its Emperor, Ne'maMegon'.

For successful expansion—trade, commerce, technological exchange and negotiations—communication with the inhabitants of distant worlds was essential. To accomplish this, Megon' utilized the Nanites, indeed, a key ingredient to his formula for success. The Nanites are microscopic, biomechanical nanoids, a cybernetic colony developed on a world populated by the Juggernauts, an ancient race of similar, macroscopic beings. The Nanites' primary function was to act as universal interpreters, although many were specifically developed for other primary and secondary tasks, as well. Size was no indication of power, and they were supremely adept at their functions. Generally, they were introduced through injection directly into the bloodstream of each new citizen embraced by the empire. They immediately located themselves in the host's primary language, cognitive and interpretive receptors where they permanently *rewired* the brain. This allowed the recipient to understand a new language even though the language was completely new and alien. There was never a need to actually *learn* an alien language. When audio signal were received, or *heard*, members of each race received those signals translated into their own language. Any adaptation required for interpretation of colloquialisms and regionalisms were made within tetra-cycles. The delay was not perceptible to any sentient species. One of the Nanite specialty functions is the ocular disparity rewiring which allows the host to override the visual discrepancies between the sounds heard and the movements of the vocalization and articulation mechanisms, such as face, jaws and lips. Without the rewiring the discrepancies were found to be most annoying.

Their creators, the Juggernauts, are a highly advanced biomechanical artificial intelligence, having memory components of crystallized metallic carbide and silica gel hyper-suspended in a microscopic gravity well. This core, or brain, is contained in a powerful, yet fully portable magnetic field, the entire structure encased in a flux-dimensional casing which neutralizes the effect on surrounding structure. Each matrix is grown, or cultured, to maximize its speed and storage capacity and to render a specific primary function. Unintended results of culturing often include compulsive personality characteristics and redundant behavioral tendencies. While each unit is a separate entity fully capable of functioning independently, they are all linked to each other by coded ion beam wave, which form an immense, intergalactic neural network. By current galactic law the whole is considered to be a complete and independently sentient being, a separate and fully autonomous entity in its own right. This megazoid, this enormous, fabricated megabrain, identifies itself through its individual members as The Union, although it admits that this nomenclature is merely a contrivance for the benefit of beings accustomed to the need for superfluous differentiation.

Each individual, each separate Juggernaut is individually mobile, equipped with exponentially self-evolving application software. Highly sophisticated beings, they function primarily as storage and data processing devices, system analysts, logicians and mathematicians, scientists, programmers, engineers, security units and consultants. They are the most highly advanced computer technicians and engineers found anywhere in the galaxy. Resembling mid-sized transport and utility vehicles more than anything else, they care nothing for aesthetics, exhibiting an odd assortment of shapes and mismatched colors, sporting features and equipment in the oddest places and jutting out in the most peculiar directions. Most have dozens of arms wielding small to mid-sized tools of all sorts, doors and hatches here and there with no discernable rhyme nor reason, buckets and baskets swinging freely, cranes and shelves, ledges and steps, sledges, coils and drop weights, pinchers and grips, hooks and drills, pokers and prods, winches and grapples, telescopes, radio and radar antennas, view screens, cameras and speakers, microphones and wave generators, radiant-collectors, lazar rifles, ion and gravity wave disruptors and even large, shiny metallic balls swinging from cables this way and that as they glide effortlessly over the surface of the silicate-paved planet scooting about on hover-glide engines. Most of the things they lug around are useless but have evolved with them over thousands of cycles. The accoutrement *viability,* the Juggernaut term for *life expectancy,* of most things is considerable enough that they simply continue to add on to themselves. In addition, they considerer it unwise to remove old and seldom-used equipment, postulating there may come a time when something that once had value may once again have value. In order to facilitate diplomatic relations, many of the latter generation Noids, as they have typically and affectionately become known, have been developed to resemble the various species comprising the bulk of the empire, reptilians, mammalians, amphibians, aquatics, and avians. The Juggernauts were not in the least reluctant to honor the emperor's request in this matter, especially in light of the initial suggestion of reptilian forms, since these were representative of their *creators.* This seemed especially energizing to their programming algorithms, and they cited a cycle recognition buffering and resolution of a memory-resident conflict, as well. The new forms are the primary diplomatic core and advisors surrounding the emperor and assisting him in his daily affairs. He finds it easier to communicate with them since they have more highly developed and sophisticated linguistic and acoustic vocalization technology that mimics biological forms perfectly. However, they retain some of their peculiar tendency to add onto themselves occasionally altering their forms in odd and, sometimes, surprising ways.

The evolutionary history of the Juggernauts is a unique and complex story, although the evolution itself was rapid when compared to fully biological entities. They were once much less sophisticated help bots of the Nosha, a race that built and programmed them eons ago. But the Nosha were rendered extinct virtually overnight by a pandemic spread by diseased livestock entrenched in their global food chain. It exhibited itself first as a fever and rash and spread rapidly to slowly disintegrate the internal organs and muscles. In only a few cycles, three-quarters of the population was decimated. Over time, the remainder ultimately succumbed to the ravages of the disease, to outbreaks of secondary plagues, and to the effects of the inevitable savagery and barbarism into which their sophisticated social structures had degenerated. In the end, their world had been driven to madness, with pockets of brutish throwbacks brutalizing each other, and they had degenerated into being cannibals. Predictably, there had been no hope.

Deprived of cultivation, the feed plant, a pungent fugal growth that had been the staple of the sandhogs, withered and died, and the virus with it. The entire biosphere had been decimated in a generation. The once brilliant Nosha had never stood a chance. But the bots survived, and flourished, and because of their clever programmers, evolved into the Juggernauts.

The standing Emperor of Rege'Ce, Sulat Tan', had been most pleased with first contact. The Juggernauts were friendly and diplomatic, and though they were peculiar to look upon and converse with, comical in their way, they had been eager to please, as they are to this very day. Emperor Megon' considers them his most trusted and valued allies and has allowed them to establish an entire city-outpost on Rege'Ce. Without the Juggernauts the jump gates would not exist, and the great expansion would never have been possible. The empire owes its very existence to them, as Emperor Megon' and his predecessors freely acknowledge. It is the will-to-power lacking in the Juggernauts that renders the bond between the emperor and the cybernoids so beneficial. They retain their status as a sovereign body, yet they maintain the opportunity to fulfill their programming, which is to serve the needs of biological entities. For the empire, it's a win-win situation. It receives invaluable assistance from these superb logicians, scientists and technicians, master planners and builders, economic and political advisors. In addition, the Juggernauts lend their expertise as military strategists. But most important to the emperor, is not what they can do or provide, but what they do not bring to the table. The Juggernauts are devoid of ego, and have no ambition. To the emperor, having them as allies was like having a god trapped within an isoflask.

Ovek scowled at the chains and shackles binding his wrists and ankles, weighing him down, tangling him like an Orturian eel weed. It was crude and insulting, being bound this way, by this mech-stuff—still the plasma-plastic restraints were doing their job, keeping him and his squad secure during transport to the prison colony on Ty. At least that's what these Tyons had in mind. Ovek had other plans. He just didn't know what they were yet.

Nol sat on the pit floor next to Ovek, his huge, muscular frame pushed up against Ovek's side. "Why don't you do something more useful?" Ovek droned at him. "Your elbow is chopping a hole in my rib cage." They both sat up straighter, forcing their backs against the pit wall. Nol stopped and looked long and hard at his hands, at the spot where he had been peeling away some of the scales from his fingertips around the short, claw tips.

"Sorry, Cap'n, got nothing else to do," he replied. But he stopped toying with his meaty fingers anyway. If anyone other than Ovek complained about something so petty, Nol probably would have killed the whining bastard without a second blink, shackles or no shackles, even with the guards watching their every move. He wasn't wired the same as most reptilians, and most were good soldiers, great and fierce warriors. Nol was something else; in addition, he could be nothing less than a crazed murderer. Ovek knew the last thing anyone wanted to do was to anger him. But that's just why he had kept Nol by his side all these many cycles. There were damn few that could best him in a fair fight. Moreover, Nol didn't believe in fighting fairly; he believed in winning. Plus, more times than he cared to remember, Nol had dragged Ovek's scaly, wounded ass out of harm's way, and it was because of Nol that Everworld was yet holding a vacancy for him. Of course, it worked both ways, and he had returned the favor in equal number. They weren't friends, not exactly. Nol didn't make friends, at least, that's the way Nol stubbornly insisted he made his way through life. But Ovek was the closest thing to a friend he would ever have and the closest thing to family he would ever know, and more importantly, they shadowed each other and constantly watched each other's backs. They placed their faith in the knowledge that there was, at the very least, one soldier each of them could always rely on to be looking out for the other in a tight spot. Cycles ago, Ovek had secured Nol's admittance to the Mercenary Quarters of the empire Army. If it hadn't been for Ovek, Nol would surely have been consigned to the Slave Quarters, never knowing one credit of profit for all the blood he'd spilled in the hundreds of battles fought to expand the empire into the outworlds. To Ovek, even more than to the empire, he swore his allegiance, and he gave his trust.

Taven, meanwhile, lay with his head slumped down, his right chin horn poking into his chest hard enough to separate his scales a bit. A small trickle of blood ran down his chest and gathered in a small pool in the crease of his soft belly. He appeared to be sleeping, but Ovek knew he wasn't. He was waiting, as were they all. Waiting for something to happen. When the time came, he knew Taven would be ready.

Guor on the other hand *was* asleep. His head was bent back and angled over the top edge of the holding pit as if his neck were about to snap. A long stream of drool hanging from the side of his mouth touched the lip of the pit and was sliding down the wall in a large wad, taking a slow crawl that promised to eventually hit the floor. Cor and Rahon were placing bets on how long until splashdown.

Beel sat with his fists tightly clinched near his neck, his knees scrunched up, merely staring at Ovek with an angry, impatient look in his eyes. He simply wanted a chance to butcher these no-good Tyons and be done with it. He didn't have Nol's overt talent for killing, although he could best most any enemy with a harsh glance, and you couldn't second-guess his enthusiasm. He was a good soldier. They all were, Ovek knew that much about them—but precious little else. He had only the briefs supplied him by Central Command.

Other than Nol they hadn't been with him very long. The others had all been hand picked by Command from various reptilian slave platoons and had trained under his command for a quarter-cycle specifically for this rescue. Sure, they were a shady lot, most of them with a criminal past, and Ovek wouldn't have turned his back on any one of them, but, they did their duty, took his commands without question, and showed him proper respect, which is all he could ask of any trooper on this kind of assignment. Of course, it had taken some knocking of horns to accomplish that, but, in the end, he had to admit, this was about as a good a team as he had ever had under his command. Surely they were the toughest reptilian troopers in their prime. They were the strongest, most powerfully built, fastest, and most aggressive. Soldiering just seemed to be in their blood. More often than not troopers from reptilian races made up the bulk of Special Forces, black-ops and critical-operations teams, assassination and rescue missions and the like. So here they were on the short end of a risky and dangerous mission, and these brave troopers deserved better than to go down to the likes of criminals and terrorists, who were the real cause of the fix they were in. And Ovek was determined to get them out of this mess.

He certainly couldn't blame the Tyons for hating him and the others. In truth, he empathized with them to a degree. He had no great love for the empire himself. War had been primarily a job, and he had been fortunate to come from a planet with a strong military, one with technology advanced enough to bargain with the empire, to join its cause as mercenaries, not as slave warriors. That's the way it worked; the empire expanded across the galaxy, absorbing system after system, accepting new worlds as technological and economic allies, or it absorbed their populations as slave armies and laborers. The warning was always given, the show of force demonstrated, the terms drawn, and the deed done, one way or the other. The outcome was always the same; worlds fell, one by one. So, what was this magic formula that guaranteed victory each and every time for the empire? Was it threat of annihilation for any world that denied it allegiance? Hardly. Dead citizens make poor soldiers or workers and burned-out worlds make for useless property. No, the answer was an old, tried and true, and very simple formula—fear and numbers—overwhelming fear instilled by overwhelming numbers. Weed out that next lone planet which was ripe for picking, and put the fear into them. It was actually very easy. One planet could not stand against thousands, or millions if the need arose. That was the key. No one knew for sure how many worlds Emperor Megonì had at his command. High technology, economic power, military might, strategic genius, all wrapped in nebular clouds of secrecy were difficult to discern because of the vast distances and the solemn oaths of secrecy sworn between the leaders and ruling class of so many worlds. Only the emperor himself and members of his High Command, at least those approved by the Juggernauts, knew the true capabilities of the alliance and his darkest and most-guarded secrets. But as much as any factor, this vast cloak of secrecy kept the alliance together, holding each world in its grip of fear and mutual suspicion. The emperor's private military police and spies were everywhere, and the jump gates were the portals that let them sneak in. Covertly attempt to defy the empire, and the gates could become sinkholes to assured annihilation. But quite often they offered opportunities, as well. The gates could be open doorways to the empire, pathways to the stars for trade, for knowledge, for glory and continuance, if a planet had something of value to offer. Without threat and the senseless loss of life, the empire was willing to bring any valuable world into the alliance, to share nearly all its highest technology except its most devastating weaponry, partner fully in trade and commerce and military might. Within the alliance, there was no limit to the heights a very enterprising planet might reach.

If a planet had forces strong enough to offer significant resistance, it might hold out for a while. The losses on both sides would be great and regrettable, but in the end, the outcome was predictable and inevitable. So why bother? Why lose so many good and brave on both sides of the cosmic divide? The empire was fair minded when it wanted to be. Sometimes loyalty was better bought than fought for, and stubborn planets were sometimes brought into the fold as limited trading partners and mercenary armies. But no one was ever being fooled—fear ruled their leaders and, despite the smiles and conciliatory speeches and high-minded ideals, terror was more often than not the true impetus behind the final signing of the treaties. It was tribal mentality and political face-saving on a cosmic scale—become a member of the pack or be the meal. Rebellion was recognized as the foolhardy business it was. The able bodied were busy enough serving their six cycles in the military, becoming so intimately acquainted with the severe nature of the empire's military discipline that none dared consider rebellion. After having served, civilian rebellion was considered either futile or unpatriotic, unless of course, one embraced terrorism, which meant being despised and hunted as a criminal. For Ovek, discipline and soldering was all he understood and favored, an option outside a legitimate system was not an option. In the most critical matters for him, choice was never actually part of the deal. Fate had simply selected the long or short path for him to die, whether comfortably serving on a planetary council or squatting uncomfortably in a holding pit on a prison transport headed for Ty.

Ovek's home world, Thacia, had been one of those worlds that, at first, chose to resist the empire. It launched an all-out assault on the empire's temporary base located on the far side of the Thacian moon, Elsane. Ultimately, the Thacians were defeated but managed to destroy much of the base and inflict heavy casualties on the troops stationed there. The base had been merely a sacrificial sandhog to the emperor. The first and only serious counter measure was a display of his primary method. His *emissaries* hadn't opened up with blast cannons or ion disruptors, discharging here and there destroying everything in sight, as one might expect an invading army might do. No. He sent a fully colored, fully decorated, military shuttle into Overseer Capital Prime. They came as a very small, very organized, elite special-operations team bearing the insignia of official governmental negotiation liaisons. They strode confidently and unopposed into the Legots' inner offices, taking hostages of the office help, computer loaders, data handlers, even hired cleaning neuters, and requested full media coverage. Then, employing genetically enhanced bio-crystallizing blade weapons that grew conveniently for them at just the right moment, they overpowered the guards and brutally murdered the hostages, ceremoniously butchering them like animals while the entire planet watched in horror. They calmly explained in great detail these simple facts to the Legots, and to the entire world: "Send your military might in opposition to the empire, fail to negotiate, do anything at all to arouse suspicion or to incur the wrath of the emperor, and imagine a billion soldiers committing a billion acts equally vile across your world tomorrow. Your elders will be boiled, their eggcrypts will lie bare, and your eggs will be crushed within the discharge chambers." Not a disruptor blast was fired in retaliation, though many had dearly wanted revenge. Most had not. Fear—fear and numbers. It's a very successful formula, and while Ovek had never had much liking for politics or politicians, and certainly had little respect for soldiers who killed the weak in lieu of challenging their equals to a fair fight, he had a great admiration and respect for tactics that work. Less than a half cycle later he had voluntarily joined the officers' training academy, secure in the knowledge that his world would continue, that his wife and egg were safe, and that he might live long enough to see his son have an opportunity to make a legitimate choice. It was a terrible compromise, but at least it was a chance at life.

The Tyons, it seemed, didn't share his view. They resisted the empire's bid for their world far too long. They simply weren't going to be intimidated. Wrong move…or perhaps they simply refused to believe, or couldn't comprehend, a so-called *civilized* power so entrenched in its own mire that it would actually carry out the heinous threats it dared to deliver. Perhaps, in the beginning of this war, the Tyons had interpreted the various threats as intimidating bluffs, terrible and horrific, but merely tactical intimidation. They had been wrong, dreadfully wrong, and they had paid for it dearly with the lives of so many young and innocent. For them, this brutal war could not last much longer. The numbers had been stacked against them, and they knew it. Thousands of Tyon soldiers had died each day while the empire's armies had expanded exponentially. Of course, all the while the empire continued to bargain for an alliance between them, hoping to quell the loss of troops on both sides, for the goal of the empire was growth, not death and diminishment, and they readily acknowledged the senselessness of the battle. All attempts at negotiation would continue at the highest levels, but, of course the fighting must continue, especially in light of the abduction of Nela, daughter of the BreAcian military High Roget, who was even now held prisoner on Ty. Every inhabitant on Ty to the very last woman and egg would be annihilated if a settlement could not be reached, especially should Nela be harmed, since she was the emperor's niece, sole heir of his brother, Roget Mena'Suel'. Such would be the horrific fate for this world held hostage to its own stupidity and stubbornness. Such a difficult lesson must be taught and learned; such an example must be made. But what waste; what a terrible waste of slaves. The Tyons were adept at acts of extreme terrorism and, though they had no legitimate chance of winning the war, they were an occasional problem for the empire, like annoying insects buzzing and biting the hindquarters of an Ovorian sand crawler. They seemed willing to martyr themselves rather than settle for an existence that would guarantee them life but consign them to servitude. The emperor considered them beyond redemption, beyond hope of being brought into the alliance as partners in his grand vision of galactic conquest. They were fit for one thing only: to be slaves. On the other hand, they would accept nothing less than absolute freedom or genocide. There was no compromise in them.

So here was one more feeble effort by the Tyons to show some semblance of strength. At this stage of the war, which for them was going so badly, every small victory was celebrated as though it were a major battle won. They knew Ovek and his crew were no band of ordinary slave troopers. These were battle-hardened soldiers, well trained, highly skilled, tough, too well armed and equipped and just too damn eager to engage. Instincts had told the battalion chief to take them alive and get them back to Ty for questioning. Something was amiss and, by the gods, he had meant to find out what it was. But he had paid a handsome price for that call. This small squad of reptilians had cost him a hundred and more of his Tyon troops, since much of the fighting had come hand to hand if the enemy were to be taken alive. These few had truly tested the mettle of his fine soldiers and forced the best from them. The truth was, one on one, his troops were no match for any of them. What was worse, if the enemy gun ship hadn't run into trouble on its own accord and run aground on that asteroid, they never would have taken them. Their captain was some sweet pilot; he had maneuvered that little fighter as if he meant to poke out the general's eye. But with superior numbers, positioning, and some clean, plasma stunner shots, the day was won. But it certainly had been hard fought.

Of course, that's exactly how Ovek's troops had felt about it too. Hard fought. The mission wasn't supposed to be like that. In and out, that had been the plan. Penetrate their space, bypass the battle squadron, get to the capital, fuzz the grid with the Juggernaut enhanced gravcom—"Just punch in this code at this vector," the techie had briefed Beel, "and push this sequence to release." Then locate Nela, rescue her, and pray to Darkworld you can get off Ty. "She's equipped with the transponder Nanites," he had told Ovek. "Locate her with this." The device looked a lot like a small ion pistol. It was too bad the Tyons thought that, as well, and destroyed it during the battle. There was just one thing the rescue team never expected. Sabotage. It seems someone back at command *wanted* them to fail!

When the jump gate had opened they were supposed to be in clear space, vectored well away from the Ty battalion position. It didn't happen that way. The gate opened, and they found themselves facing twenty or more fully armed battle cruisers. For an instant, Ovek considered opening a gate immediately ahead. No good; too many ships. The resulting detonation would have consumed them as well. This wasn't a suicide mission. Time to outmaneuver and do some damage. And then the ion bomb exploded and blew out the main drive engine, and they had to put down on the nearest planetoid they could chart. Well, that nailed it for sure—saboteurs! If they had blown out the thrusters, as well, they would all probably be no more than atoms drifting in the void by now.

And so they found themselves here, staring at their feet and betting on how long before a gob of drool hit the pit floor. They never got a chance to find out. Without warning, the transport shimmied as if being pelted by thousands of micrometeoroids and listed noticeably to the side. They felt the drive engines being scaled back and the sudden change in velocity sent a shock wave through the hull. Loud creaks and groans and a shrill, short squeal pierced the air inside the holding bay. This boat wasn't what she used to be, that was a certainty, and Ovek had a premonition that something awful was happening.

The troopers knew it too and braced themselves inside the pit as best they could. Guor, however, remained oblivious. If anything, his breathing became heavier and louder. Nol kicked him on the bottom of his boot rapidly to wake him, which was no easy matter, considering Guor's keen ability had allowed him to sleep even through a servicing by a skilled BreAcian courtesan, a gift of gratitude for this very mission from the High Roget himself. He stirred, blinked and twisted his head around, grinning a big grin at all of them in general. "What's going on?" He sniffed.

The ship banked sharply so that they all suddenly found themselves piling on top of Cor and Rahon. As they tumbled over each other, screeching and pinging noises filled the holding bay as if some menacing space giant just beyond the exterior bulkheads were running its gigantic claws along the hull. They recognized ion cannons when they heard them, and these were close, very close. A few of the blasts must have barely skimmed the hull, and some had squarely found their mark. The rotational dampeners had been blown out immediately. Fires were breaking out all across the ship, coolant was being out-gassed in an attempt to bypass ruptured lines, bulkheads were warping or showing stress fractures and ionization cracks, and some had completely buckled from direct hits. The air began to smell of greasy fumes and a thin veil of smoke drifted into the holding bay. The ship banked sharply again in the opposite direction tossing the prisoners and guards alike head over heels. Luckily the grav-units were still functioning, and inertial dampeners were online, but it was clear that this old tub had probably smuggled one too many skin-lickers to the penal colonies. More than likely all the systems would be blown out in short order. Soon, no doubt, they would all be helplessly floating about like scrubby-bubbles, popping against the bulkheads, ending their illustrious careers as bloody splotches on the pit walls.

It wasn't easy to determine exactly what was happening. The transport was being fired on, that much was clear. An alliance interceptor may have attacked them. But Ovek didn't think so. The tactics were wrong, and the shooting was way off target. Cruisers had much better locking technology and alliance trained gunners on scout ships and attack fighters were better marksmen. If the attacking vessel belonged to the empire, this boat would have been destroyed already. No, something else was going on.

There was more pinging from cannon fire and rattling from the close detonations of disruptors. Initially the transport had vibrated from the recoil of its own weapon, but this stopped almost immediately, and they all suspected the cannon had been hit. They couldn't have known it had simply blown itself off the pivot because of its inept mounting. The transport had not originally been designed as a gun ship. Before being *commandeered* by the Tyons, it had been an obsolete Zizien mining transport stolen from an alliance storage facility by the Ovorians. For a short while, they had been allies of Ty. The pit now holding the prisoners had actually been a restraint receptacle for a radioactive materials containment module. Essentially, it was a big, round hole for a big, round peg. Although it had never been intended to hold prisoners, it was convenient for that purpose. It was also well protected and, now with the profusion of disruptor and ion fire, served them well. Unfortunately, it would be useless if the ship were to be blown into trillions of wiggly, squiggly, sub-atomic particles.

When the ship leveled out again Ovek pulled himself to the top of the lip as far as the plasma tether would allow. There had been four guards in the holding area when the attack began, one near the door, one monitoring the pit, one against the far bulkhead to his right, while the other worked a terminal duty station. Grilling the latter, Ovek had gathered some useless information about the inventory database the fat amphibian had been reviewing. "Busy work!" the guard had grumbled.

It didn't matter what military you served, it never paid to volunteer, Ovek thought. This soldier was learning the hard way. Looking out of the pit now, Ovek could see the guards had been thrown violently around the room. The forward guard was sitting in the narrow hallway near the door holding the back of his neck with one hand and the side of his head with the other. The one on his right had first been tossed against the outer bulkhead then dashed headlong into the pit's outer edge. He was dead; a deep, ugly gash fully as long as his spindly amphibious mitt split the front of his forehead. The data-entry clerk in the chair had snapped his neck during one of the velocity shifts, and the guard standing watch over the pit now lay crumbled against the opposite wall like a piece of refuse; he may have been dead or unconscious.

The ship continued to shimmy from ion cannon blasts. Emergency lights kicked on, and warning flashers signaled immanent danger. The old transport had been equipped with some plasma-plastic shields, but not enough, that much was clear. If he and his troopers hadn't been on board, Ovek wouldn't have given a spit, but that boot was on another webbed foot now, wasn't it! So he chose to look for the bright side of the situation; this just might be the chance they had been looking for. Maybe this attack put the odds in their favor!

For some reason, their ship had stopped its erratic maneuvers and was set on some steady burn, a straight cruise setting. During a combat situation, this made no sense. It was a bad sign. Ovek knew there was little time. Although they were taking direct hits from relatively small-arms fire, they were an easy mark for a major strike. The culprit was probably a small, quick, easily maneuverable, attack fighter. But it was powered for one big strike only. It couldn't afford to miss its one big chance; it had meant to cripple the transport before the kill using thousands of small ion cannon bursts. This was not military. These were assassins, probably terrorists, and, it was clear, the pilot was skilled but the gunner was not. The shots were sloppy and unimpressive. This did not bode well; the gunner was handpicked under highly secretive circumstances. No good pilot takes an amateur like this unless both are expendable, and it is deemed absolutely necessary. If the major strike did not find its mark, these fools meant to crash into the transport. It was a suicide mission!

Leaning out over the top of the pit, Ovek hollered out to the guard sitting near the forward door. The fellow staggered to his feet and limped over toward him holding his oily looking hand to his oily looking head, a stream of thin, watery blood gushing from between his long, narrow fingers. Ovek pushed his hands forward. "The restraint controls," Ovek yelled, "where are they?" He nodded at the plasma discharges and plastic fibers circling his wrists. "I'm a pilot," he continued. "You need help, and I won't kill you, " he added that last bit with a big grin, feeling compelled to show some sign of good faith, hoping for the same in return. He was trying to cut through this as quickly as possible; he knew there wasn't much time.

The guard was no fool. He knew the danger they were in, and he wasn't about to quibble over the minor details. He leaned into the computer station on the bulkhead directly in front of him in the narrow hallway. "Doesn't matter," the guard yelled back over the din of disrupter fire and out-gassing. "We'll probably all be dead before you have time." He was trying hard to grin back in return.

He punched the screen on. It flickered momentarily, went dark, and then sprang to life with an audible pop. He stood silently staring at it for just an instant, then punched in a clearance code. An array of images and figures danced across it then detoured into the security-applications node. A second later he entered the release code. The energy feed was cut, and the plastic restraints immediately drifted away in wispy threads vaporizing into the air before they hit the floor.

Ovek stood up on the pit floor and gestured silently to Nol and then in the direction of one of the fallen guards. The Tyon looked dead but things are not always as they appear. Nol nodded once knowingly, and they both leaped out of the pit simultaneously. The rest of the crew followed immediately on their heels.

No sooner had Nol reached the guard then the Tyon did his duty. He was well trained; Nol recognized that much. A cichma hand ax, a circular blade surrounding the fist at the rear and fronted by two wicked mandibles, came from beneath him and zipped past Nol's belly. But Nol had fully expected such a move; he always did, and pulled back just in time. The blade missed him by the width of a scale or two. But Nol's straight right jab found its mark. His huge fist crushed the guard's large, fleshy face. The two black dots that served as nostrils vomited spurts of blood like synchronized geysers. He hadn't forgotten how soft headed these amphibians were, how delicate the bones, how soft and spongy their flesh was, or how powerfully muscled he was in comparison to these fatty, bloated creatures, and how easily he could kill them with his bare hands. He just didn't care. It had been a fair fight. After all, the guard had had a weapon, which, by the way, now belonged to him.

Fire had broken through the bulkheads in several places, and the air was getting heavy and oppressive. A yellow, acrid smoke seeped through breaches in the terminal seals and blended with the noxious fumes creeping off smoldering wires and seething metal surfaces. The poisonous mixture began its lazy glide through the room, threatening to overpower the remaining air supply. Nol draped the body of one of the guards over the computer panel in an attempt to slow the release of the deadly gases. The ion blasts had subsided now to only an occasional shot. Ovek knew the fighter would be coming around for the kill soon. Between the fumes inside and the maniac outside he figured their odds of getting out of this alive at about fifty-fifty—always the optimist.

He turned his attention to the front guard who by now had succumbed to the effects of his wounds and seated himself at the base of the bulkhead. "Can you release the forward hatch?" Ovek said as he knelt by the guard's side.

The Tyon turned a round face toward him, his bulging eyes dark and distraught. "It's no use," he said distantly. "It's gone, nothing left, computer confirms." He paused a moment to gather himself and to take several huge gulps of air. "The computer confirms the bridge took a direct hit," he streamed out. "It's gone; the bridge is gone. And this hatch is sealed, radiation protocols."

Immediately Ovek stood and turned to face his men. "We're dead drifting," he yelled. "Anyone got any ideas, now is a good time." He felt a tug at the base of his trousers.

"Help me up." The guard was struggling to his feet. Ovek propped him up in front of the computer screen. After he pushed a few of the crystals, Ovek heard a loud snap from across the room. "There, on the far wall," he pointed to his right while continuing to manipulate the console. Operating under auxiliary power, a large panel slid into its receptor housing in the bay floor. Emergency dart tubes, ten of them in a circular array! Most alliance vessels carried darts, emergency escape pods, each capable of firing a single passenger clear of a vessel in danger of going critical or crashing. They were called darts because of their shape, and because of the manner in which they landed, striking directly into the surface of the body they targeted. The type found aboard these old transports were fitted with targeting and telemetry computers for pre-set navigation, auto-thrusters for velocity control, override grip for manual, retro-rockets and plasma-plastic coils as impact dampeners, all powered by a compact biogenic battery. Normally, these relatively short-range darts were used during mining and industrial waste transport operations, not in combat situations. Combat and commercial darts were usually fitted with an ion drive. These were meant to hop only a fraction of a light cycle, not ideal under these circumstances, but they would have to do. Fortunately, with ten darts in the shoots, there were more than enough for Ovek's crew and the Tyon. That was something, anyway.

Ovek looked him straight in the eyes. "They've got one primary disruptor shot in them, and they're coming in for the kill; you know that." Ovek knew he wasn't telling this trooper anything he didn't already know. "Can you make it to a pod?"

"It doesn't matter," he replied. "You need someone to open a jump gate. I can do that from this terminal. There's enough juice in the auxiliary to fire the beam, and the spindle is located just below the dart windows. You need me here to program the jump vectors and relay telemetry to the darts. Besides," he went on, breathing very heavily now, "I'm dead already. I've lost too much." He pointed briefly to the cut on his head. The bleeding had slowed to barely a trickle, as if he had precious little more to release.

Ovek started to remove his jacket for use as a bandage but the guard stopped him with a simple gesture. "Go," the guard told him.

"Nos Po Dei," Ovek intoned with a grin. "You're an ugly one. You have a name, soldier?"

"RothEc," the guard breathed out his reply.

Ovek put his left hand on RothEc's left elbow to steady his arm and to exchange wrist grips, to properly thank him and to say goodbye. "Why?" he asked simply.

"Why not?" RothEc replied, accompanied by a wide and sympathetic grin. "You're not the emperor, and you had nothing to do with the massacre. I read the file. We're just soldiers, Ovek, on a mission."

With that Ovek turned and pointed to the darts. His crew responded without hesitation, bringing to a halt their hasty search for available weapons. The Tyon commander must have been relying on the plastic restraints to hold them, and reason supported his confidence; it has never been known to fail, as far as Ovek knew. So the guards had not been issued ion pistols or disruptor rifles. Probably because their superiors didn't trust the integrity of this old tub—at this range, an errant shot from either would blast a hole clean through the bulkhead. This heap wasn't reinforced with internal shielding, as were standard military transports. But no doubt they all had many other types of weapons secured and at the ready. However, the chamber was in shambles, and all they had managed to uncover were two chicma axes, including the one Nol had commandeered, and three jeweled mandat knives, a set of ceremonial blades patterned after various narrow phases of the

Rege'Cean moon Quin. They had been stored in one of the materials-handling cases piled next to the computer crystal array. Mandats weren't combat weapons; they were actually large cleavers used exclusively for the carving of roast sandhog, a delicacy severed cyclically at the remembrance celebration of Nosaxia. This was an extremely rare and valuable set of blades, probably a family heirloom.

Ovek turned to give his new friend one last look of thanks. He was glad he did. "You take number one," the soldier hurriedly told him." It has a transponder with an auto marker." Ovek nodded and turned, and with that, in two leaps he reached the tubes directly on the heels of his crew. Taven slipped a bundle into Ovek's hand. It was the heftiest mandat blade wrapped in a torn tunic. He slipped it into his uniform and opened the hatch to dart number one.

Guar and Taven slid into a pair of the lower darts while the others hoisted themselves by the lift handles into the center part of the array. Ovek leaned on the handles of his dart tube momentarily. "On my command, close and launch on ten." He didn't wait for a response. It wasn't necessary. He leapt into the dart. "Red up." he gave the alert signal. "Close." Their hands shot to the dart hatches as if they were a precision drill team. Quickly Ovek located the transponder control grip, set the marker and punched in the emergency frequency. Moments later he felt the explosive vibrations of the plasma coils firing the darts and pushed the launch button on his control grip.

The darts shot out of their chutes as if fired from an enormous blowgun, traveling with enough momentum to eject them from the gravitational influence of the average planetary system. In a nanocycle the darts were well away from the transport and the critical zone surrounding it. Moments later the jump gate opened directly ahead of them. It was a small gate, perhaps twice the diameter of the dart bundle, a circular pool of oily blackness set against the dull glow of ordinary space. Its surface seemed as if covered with a liquid skin of reflective waves that rolled over and under each other at odd angles and reversed directions at will, moving as if it were alive. The circumference glowed with a blue and green electro-magnetic aura that rotated clockwise and counterclockwise at regular intervals. As the darts entered, bright, pin-point discharges defined the edges but left no telltale sign, not a wake nor ripple, of the passing craft. After the darts had disappeared through the gate, like an eye looking out briefly onto the space around it, the gate winked itself shut and was gone.

RothEc leaned against the bulkhead, fingering the console, fearing his mind and legs were failing in equal measure. He worked frantically, setting the first gate directly ahead of the darts and selecting vectors for the exit gate as far from Tyon space as the transport power would allow. He searched the archives for an exit point in the outworlds, somewhere in an uncharted, relatively unknown region of space. Ancient Tyon gravimetric studies indicated a planetary system orbiting a common yellow star in the LaStigean Arm. Unverified spectrographic data indicated an eighty-six-percent probability of a Class-C habitable planet in the interior third of the system. If they were lucky, they would find it a habitable world; if not, they would be stranded in space until the marker was located. Of course, setting the marker was one thing, having the signal picked up was another thing altogether. But he was hopeful. He had little appreciation for the members of this reptilian strike team, but there was something about their commander, Ovek, something good and honorable. A noble character such as his deserved a fighting chance, and RothEc was thankful he could give him this one, at least. He set the computer to calculate the best vectors for the exit gate based on the spectrographic analysis. Then, invoking a single word of gratitude to LoPola, the divine gift giver, he pushed the activation code. He felt a low vibration from deep within the transport and a soft hum passed through the ship like a specter as the spindle released the energy discharges. Barely visible concentric gravimetric waves tore into the fabric of space opening the jump gates. Almost immediately, the clearance code indicating all darts were through was confirmed and the spindle nozzle fired the anti-proton burst closing the gates. The darts were gone.

Coming in hard and fast from the opposite end, the fighter moved into position and lined up on the derelict transport. The gunner rerouted the remaining ion crystals and forced them into the nucleonic ordnance canister. From a single disruptor cannon mounted in the nose, he fired a brilliant blue-and-white charge. A moment later, all RothEc ever knew, all he had ever dreamed, all he ever was or hoped to be, exploded into trillions of tiny, wiggling sub-atomic particles.

Chapter 3

Kara drove southwest along the lakefront into the industrial valley. Here was the working heart of Milwaukee, lined with greasy-looking haulers, heavy-duty loading docks and shipping piers laden with crates and drab, stenciled containers, commercial launch stalls packed with overused fishing rigs, and sloppy, wet stations. Further inland, during daylight, that heart was pumping dusty clouds of coal particles off the backs of busy dump trucks scurrying about like busy bees constructing enormous, black hives. As much as beer, coal was the blood that flowed through the veins of this industrial town, and the machine shops and factories comprised the sum of the parts that kept the body of this venerable old city alive. Dusty trailers and flatbeds constantly came and went, hauling everything from auto parts to quarter barrels, their cabs belching billowy puffs of dark, ashy smoke skyward, hissing and popping, clambering about like crazed dinosaurs on crack. At night, however, the valley was fast asleep, a hulking, giant patiently waiting for the sound of the first sputtering engine, the morning wake-up call signaling another day of non-stop hustle and bustle. Here, somewhere among the dirty, cement warehouses and oily, brick factories, somewhere between the mounds of coal and piles of metal scraps, among the heaps of tires and auto parts, huddled somewhere among the two-by-fours and loading pallets or discarded oil drums or behind the profusion of boxcars filled with Milwaukee's finest, she would find suitable prey to satisfy the bloodlust building inside her. She rolled down the window to suck the moist lake breezes. The sound of silence rushing from of the valley was an urgent whisper enticing her into the darkness. This was the kind of night she favored, when her mood perfectly matched her need. Tonight was a night for racing the wind. (Occasionally, although rarely, her desire was strong but her body seemed less willing, and then she hunted the lazy way—online. She would pose as a young, teenage girl cruising the chat rooms, eager to talk, willing to listen, lonely, misunderstood, looking for an opportunity to give it up. In reality she was searching for some eager pedophile to snap at the bait. Once she snagged some pathetic freak with a few lines of cleaver, impish chat, downloaded his boorish and offensive photos, she would suggest a meeting at a secluded spot, usually in the park along the lake. She always suggested a place within easy walking distance from her home. That was always a convincing yet convenient detail. The park was miles long and heavily wooded, offering ample cover and opportunity to indulge her private pleasure. They always came. They were so predictable, expecting an easy mark—and she delivered, in a manner of speaking. They were easy prey, anxious and wary, yet compelled to arrive at the appointed place despite the obvious risk. They wanted it so badly. They needed it like a goddamn fix. They felt they deserved it, as if the obliteration of innocence was some sort of fucking admirable and legitimate accomplishment. That's what they told themselves anyway. They convinced themselves of it. But the truth of it was easy enough to see. They were selfish, egocentric bastards more than willing to destroy the lives of young, ignorant girls who should have known better. She recognized it because she was not unlike them in some dichotomous way, eager to suck the pathetic, miserable life out of them, pleased to render a reciprocal justice, comfortable with her place in the world as a Bloodwarrior. Purpose. That was the essential difference, the legitimate and rational justification. It made all the difference. At least it did to her and to the Vampire Nation.

She always arrived early, making herself comfortable and obvious on a thick blanket. She often bared her breasts or sat completely naked in the dark. As they approached and caught sight of her their eagerness made them extremely suggestible—she could easily cloud their minds with a few gently spoken words, and then the fact that she was older than the juvenile they anticipated didn't matter. They would see exactly what she wanted them to see, exactly what they expected. She would spread her legs slightly too, forcing them to focus on the prize they so desperately desired.

Perhaps none of the persuasions were even necessary. Sometimes when they saw her waiting, so ready, so willing, they were too busy undoing their flies to notice her age at all, or even her face for that matter. If they had, their erections might not have been so taut, poking so near her razor-sharp fangs. The odd thing was that their anticipation was so high they usually released even as they were being consumed. It was a certainty that they didn't get exactly what they had come for—but it was close. Under her spell and the rapture of the moment they may have experienced the most intense orgasm of their lives. Certainly, it was their last. Kara's hunger was satisfied and, in a peculiar sort of way, their need was also fulfilled. And the world, in general, became a better place.)

The problem with Internet hunting was body disposal. It had to be thorough. If suspicions were aroused and records checked, the e-mail trail could be traced—although, inevitably, it would lead only to a bogus, onetime-use account. The disposal setup had to be perfect, flawless, and it always was.

For the most part, she kept the practice to a minimum since it posed the most risk, even though linking her to the scene was unlikely. And tonight, cruising the chat rooms for an hour before getting out didn't feel right.

Tonight she was in the mood for a run. And now that familiar tightness gripped her chest harder and squeezed her muscles ever tighter, and the anxiety rose in her like a sure and steady tide. She parked the car under the I-94 expressway in one of the local make-out spots. Only a few cars were parked there tonight, their occupants escaped to erotic worlds far removed from the familiar sights of the Lake Michigan shoreline. No one even bothered to peek out the windows as she slammed the door and headed west in search of a good meal.

She loved the valley; it was her favorite place to hunt. Intuitively she knew that long ago it must have been substantially deeper, with richer soil and lush with vegetation, wet and steamy, ripe with game. It evoked a peculiar sensation within her, a passion simultaneously visceral and elusive, like the memory of a vanishing dream. Tonight's hunt began, as it often did, with wild and provocative visions, images of a savage past long extinct, memories not her own perhaps, unleashed from deep within, as though they were hidden in her blood to be released only during the lust. Then, as quickly as they had entered her mind's eye, the images vanished, and her vampire's extreme clarity of vision returned. In these modern times, all that remained of the land's primitive legacy was this fifty-square-mile shallow, beaten to submission by the hand of man, denuded of its primal innocence. Few would ever guess the wondrous beauty that once graced this tranquil valley. But Kara knew; although she didn't fully understand how. She also realized that technically this land belonged to the city, to the taxpayers and to the business property owners. But she believed that during the hunt, it belonged to her. It seemed almost as if this land had belonged to her for thousands of years, as if she had hunted here long before any man had set eyes upon it. She had marked the territorial boundaries of the valley many times over with her lovely scent and anyone within it whom she deemed deserving was fair game. Tonight, she was certain, there would be at least one. She could feel it.

She had traded in her silk blouse for a black, gothic pullover with crisscross ties. Over this she had strapped on a smart leather bustier and painted on her favorite faded jeans, slightly worn at the knees and shredded just a bit along all the right edges. Beautiful. Her footgear was genuine army swamp boots topped with custom motorcycle pipe guards. The guards were black leather with sheaths on the outsides of her shins for throwing knives. They extended beyond her calves and covered her knees with shaped, jointed bridges linked to wraps that brought the guards to mid-thigh. They were laced all the way up, each main section being secured at the top and bottom with a belt sporting a custom silver buckle. In Wisconsin, this was the perfect hunting outfit for a female vampire.

In a matter of a few minutes she was a mile or more inland, running smoothly and easily, the muscles in her legs flexing and contracting like powerful, coiled springs. Had anyone been observing her—and of course she made sure no one was—they might have marveled at the sheer magnificence and grace of her movements, the manner in which she bounded effortlessly from footpad to footpad, one silent and elegant leap following another.

Vampires could easily best a human in any sport, anywhere, anytime. But the Vampire Code discouraged this since it would draw undue attention. In all activities involving relations between vampire and man, vampires were encouraged to maintain a low profile.

Kara thought about this as she darted forward, constantly piercing the darkness for the prey she knew would be lurking somewhere in the night shadows. Her nocturnal vision afforded her ten times better acuity than the most eagle-eyed human. For that reason, and a few others, she knew she had the advantage. She was lucky, blessed to have so many gifts that elevated her above the humans; and she felt fortunate to be able to use those gifts to give something to them. Humans were, after all, distant cousins to the vampire race, and it gave her great satisfaction to weed out the evil among them, helping to make the world a better and safer place for everyone. *Kind of like Spiderman,* she thought.

She raced on, her need mounting with each rhythmic step. She felt her heart pounding like a hammer in her chest, and her breath droning like distant, native drums on a tropic isle. But she felt no fatigue. She felt only the exhilaration of the hunt and the escalating euphoria of the bloodlust, and heard the first, distant whispers of the hunger calling her name. With each passing moment her excited anticipation grew, and her conscious thoughts seemed to blend with the world around her—the eternal sky, the wind brushing her hair, the full, gleaming moon serving as her guide, the open step of earth beneath her feet, the moist air sucked between her teeth, and the anticipated scent of the inevitable kill burning in her nostrils, surely, this was *life,* this was *freedom,* this was the taste of the eternal gift, the dark but certain path to the drug that satisfies like a lover's intimate touch. She raced ahead as though she had just been released from a cage. The urgency coursed through her body like an electric current. In a short while she would be desperate for a scent, and the hunger would grow to a physical pain.

She was surprised not to have spotted suitable prey by now. Usually there was some drug deal going down, some mugging or other nasty deed worthy of her attention. It would have to be soon, if not, she might find it necessary to double back, to head north just a bit. There, at the northern edge of the valley, the Potawatomi Casino filled the valley floor with its Vegas-like atmosphere and Hollywood-style comings and goings. Usually there were big crowds, big stakes, and big name entertainment—and big marks for everyone to feed on, something for everyone, including her. Of course, the huge crowd that made the casino attractive was the very thing that usually made it her second choice. A kill there was not without risk. It could be done, of course; she had done it enough times, but it was tricky. Identifying the criminal elemental was a bit more difficult under those circumstances, but experience and intuition combined to form an instinct in her, a kind of discriminating sixth sense that aided in rooting them out. In the actual attack, isolating the mark and sheer speed were key. Moving from the shadows, she could often take her prey so quickly that a witness could view the incident and not even realize that something had happened. It simply wouldn't register. The hunger was beginning to eat away at her insides now, and she decided to turn north if she didn't happen upon someone soon. But in general, she much preferred this secluded, industrial armpit of the valley. At this time of night, virtually anyone she located skulking around here would be up to no good and would probably be ripe for the picking. Besides, it was quiet and secluded here, just the way she liked it. Vampires generally regarded feeding as an extremely private and personal business. Satisfying the bloodlust was not a communal event. For her, as it was for virtually all Bloodwarriors, feeding was something of a prurient, deeply evocative, even erotic moment, consuming her in a kind of rapture, a ritual which lured the beast within to do its bidding. Lost in the frenzy of the hunger, the Bloodwarriors consumed the prey in no less a fury than an addict consumed his drug. And she needed that drug now—badly.

Just as she was about to head north, a familiar scent drifted across the grain-storage bins ahead. There, just up past that warehouse, down that dark service drive perhaps a few hundred feet...a car was parked; the passenger door hung open like a gaping mouth. A pitiful, helpless cry came from the darkness nearby. Then the silence exerted itself once again. Her retractable sabers forced their way out of their protective jackets, through the anterior vestibules at the ceiling of her gums, past her vestigial canines until they fully extended to the bottom of her chin. Her gleaming white tusks caught the glow of the harvest moon and glistened like ivory daggers in the crisp October night. Kara slinked up behind the car like a thick, dark liquid, her movements so quiet and precise she might as well have been invisible. She could see a huge, hulking body pressing down on a young girl in the doorway of an old brick warehouse. The girl continued to whimper softly as if exhausted, her frail body weighted against the hard cement porch beneath. Kara could smell the resistance and fear in her, and she could literally taste the sexual odor exuded from her unwilling body. The thug on top of her had drawn blood—he had probably beaten or cut her and was violating her so brutally now she was going into shock. But that was not the worst of it, not from where Kara stood. The girl could not have been more than fourteen years old. A slight, Hispanic schoolgirl with big, brown, almond eyes that gazed up at Kara in amazement and fear. But the fear had been stamped there long before the frail young girl had caught a glimpse of Kara hovering there with her ivory tusks punctuating the darkness. In fact, Kara wondered if she even noticed them; the girl seemed locked in a grip of terror. The beast on top of her pounded away at her relentlessly as if he were tenderizing a piece of meat. Suddenly, the girl cried loudly and pushed at him more ferociously as if with some renewed strength. Perhaps she felt a glimmer of hope, sensing an imminent rescue from this specter emerging from the shadows. The brute responded by punching her face. Kara had seen enough. She hated these monsters.

Long, slender claws sprang from her wrist sheaths out the nearly invisible lips between her fingers, the quick-twitch muscles and tendons that triggered them responded within a heart beat. Kara vaulted from behind the car, landing inches behind the brute. Leveraging off her left foot, she gathered as much momentum as her one-hundred-twenty-pound frame could muster and swung her right claw around in a wide arc. The windmill blow was devastating, catching the thug squarely at the base of the neck. Her claws sunk deeply into his unyielding, unsuspecting flesh, tearing his muscles apart as if they were overripe fruit, crushing the collarbone and severing his jugular and right subclavian vein. An explosion of blood filled the air like red streamers, covering the girl's face and hair and pumped against the brick wall. Kara's index and middle claw punched completely through his body, piercing his right lung, peeking out his neck just above the sternum. The girl's eyes were two glowing orbs in a mass of darkness fixated on the claw tip just inches from her nose, tiny spurts of blood dribbled onto her lips, which edged up ever so slowly, forming the precursor of a smile.

Almost simultaneously, Kara delivered a second blow from below. She struck upward, fast and hard, puncturing the back of his thigh, severing his leg bicep and snapping his hamstring. The claw spiked him like a medieval grappling hook. She could feel their ivory tips dig into the bone.

She had a good grip on him now and felt his body alternately go tense and limp from the intensity of the attack and severity of his wounds. She braced her feet, bent her knees slightly, and hoisted his body into the air. She spun him around and swung him sideways, tossing him twenty feet or more into the shadows on the opposite side of the service drive. She flew to the top of his car and leapt upon him as though the law of gravity had been momentarily suspended. She had looked back briefly in midair, taking a glance at the girl alone in the doorway. She had been wiping her eyes, still crying softly, breathing heavily. She would be all right for now, probably in shock, and, Kara hoped, completely oblivious to the anguished screams that would soon be coming from out of the darkness.

Kara knelt beside her vanquished prey, that only moments before had been a living, breathing, arrogant piece of work. He was the worst kind of subhuman pond scum, the kind that victimized helpless children and defenseless women. He preyed on the weak and the trusting and the innocent—and the ignorant. He had the best schooling for it, by the looks of things. He had probably gotten his degree in the school of hard knocks—mostly the ones he delivered, no doubt—and in the school of hard walls and steel bars as evidenced by the signature tattoo on his neck. Most ex-cons sported these telltale glyphs to identify the joint they had called home for...oh so many years! His type claims to disdain being incarcerated, but that doesn't seem to stop them from repeatedly committing the same crimes that landed them there in the first place, or from displaying their perverted expressions of pride. He was forty-something with lightly graying smoker's skin, sandy hair, tall and heavily muscled, probably handsome some time ago, now, just ugly—mean and ugly. He looked pathetic lying there, all torn up and twisted, with that ridiculous mask of incredulity etched into a lifetime of hatred and conceit on his face, misogynistic and violent and cruel. This had been a man of absolute evil nature. His story was all there, a pathetic epitaph painted in pain and blood, all seeping away in a dozen streams of wet refuse, his wretched legacy seeping away onto the grimy cement beneath him. With her claws retracted now, she grasped his head and shoulder. Her nostrils flared, and her mouth filled with fluid at the sweet scent of the fresh, rich nectar flowing from the ripe slices in his flesh. She bent low, hovering ever so briefly over him, savoring that last, luscious aroma bringing the hunger to its fever pitch. She opened her mouth wide and drove her tusks deeply into him. Sucking deeply, she filled her mouth with his blood and bits of meat. Anchored there by her tusks, she drank her fill and gnawed at him with her razor-sharp incisors, shearing bits of him away until her hunger had been satisfied, and until she was satisfied that justice had been done.

After releasing him she pulled a set of keys from his pocket and carried his body to the car. She meant to drive him away from the young girl who had remained in the relative safety of the doorway staring blankly at the wall over the top of the car. While Kara had been feeding the girl had been humming softly and singing absently in Spanish. Kara could not understand. Once, during the feeding, Kara had heard the girl cry out, "Thank you, gracias." It was weak, barely more than a forced whisper echoing in the doorway, but Kara knew the girl had some vague idea what had happened. Punching the car in reverse she drove about a hundred feet and stopped abruptly enough to screech the tires. Then she piled him in a heap behind the wheel, took those earthly things of value he had no use for, and rifled the car for the other things she needed—an old shirt, a cigarette lighter (though she always carried matches for the ritual burning), and an emergency flare. Moments later the car exploded in a dazzling orange and white ball of fire. The inferno drooled liquid sparks and wagged tongues of flames like a pack of ravenous dogs licking at the ashes making their escape on the wind, and tried desperately to lap up the blood draining down the narrow road into the sewers nearby. In the valley a display such as this would be seen for miles in all directions. Even at this early hour there would be plenty of late-night traffic on the overhead expressways; Kara could virtually hear the motorists pounding out nine-one-one on their cell phones, each one secretly hoping to be the first to report a minor disaster. In a matter of moments the fire department and police would be on the scene. She was certain the fire was safely contained, bounded as it was by brick buildings and thick cement holding bins, and the girl was safe enough. Soon, the authorities would find her. Kara knelt by her side stroking her long jet-black hair.

"You're all right now," she said, in a low melodic tone. "No one is going to hurt you anymore."

"I yam all right now; no one ez goinc to hurt me anymore," the girl said quietly in a quaint and childish Spanglish, her eyes glistening like two pools of liquid chocolate.

"Stay here. Soon someone will come for you. You saw nothing. You know—nothing," Kara told her.

"I no na thinc," the girl repeated.

All was as it should be. She would let the confusion and the bizarre nature of *the crime* tell its own tale. It was "always a riddle wrapped in a conundrum," as her father was fond of saying; that was a snippet of dialog he had lifted from a movie, but she never let on that she knew, and the essence of it was certainly true enough. There was always some buzz on the streets or in the media—*escaped mental patients or gang retaliations, satanic ritual killings, vicious animal attacks, vampires!* Who the hell really knew? It was always the same. In the final analysis, the media always reported each incident as something different. The more bizarre the circumstances, the more bizarre the explanation—and the more the media hyped the story. These things kept the trashy, sensational rags in business. The police were usually taxed with several hours of confused investigation and several days of follow up. Eventually the incidents were forgotten. Fortunately, for the vampire nation, in most every major city the cops and district attorneys had enough problems shutting down all the drug houses, and responding to the outrageous number of murders and domestic violence calls. The taxpayers simply couldn't afford to have the authorities chasing ghosts and hunting werewolves while the gang-bangers and deviates were roaming the streets and cruising the back alleys of cyberspace. So, without a legitimate clue about what had actually happened here tonight, this might just as well have been a tragic encounter with Bigfoot or the handiwork of an extraterrestrial. Without a backward glance, Kara slipped into the night and was gone like a shadow that disappears when the moon dims.

Chapter 4

To those outside, there exist two separate gates, the entrance in one part of the galaxy and the exit in a distant part. To Ovek and his crew there seemed to be only one gate, as if they had merely passed through a window. One moment they were in empire space; the next moment they were…somewhere else.

Ovek perused the telemetry on the small terminal recessed into the plasma-gel cushion surrounding him. RothEc had been as good as his word. The gates had opened just as he had promised. No sooner had the exit gate collapsed upon itself than the waves from the resultant gravity well triggered the quantum marker loaded into the transponder. The marker was a packet of positrons filtered through a closed-loop string coil that trickled quantum gravity waves into the remnants of the collapsed wormhole, creating a singularity-thread, a kind of subspace residue. The marker attached itself to the remnant gravity well like a magnet, marking the end of the thread, and hung there like a tiny crystal ball, its electromagnetic tendrils digging into the very fabric of space-time. For as long as the marker remained in place, the transponder, once activated, would transmit a signal up the thread back to empire space. Without the marker, the transponder was virtually useless. The distance was simply too great for the signal to be of any practical value since it would take hundreds of thousands of cycles to reach empire space. Captured by the marker, however, the energy signal traveling up the thread, like energy flowing along the length of a whip, and was amplified by undulations of sub-space currents and was released with greater force than when it had entered. Ultimately it would carry the team's identity code and could be used to reestablish vectors for new gates. With the marker set, the transponder was their only hope of rescue, and Ovek felt confident its signal would be intercepted by an allied war ship or listening post. Their mission to rescue Nela had failed; that much would be discovered soon enough, and when that happened, another team would be sent to get her out. Central Command was sure to order a general sweep of the sector in search of the missing team. When they did, he was certain their emergency beacon would be located.

Readings indicated RothEc had targeted the inner third of this system, a region occupied by a variety of suspect planets and moons, affording them an eighty-six-percent probability of encountering a hospitable world here. He'd seen worse odds. Once a suitable planet was located, confirmed by gravimetric and spectral sensors, the computer would establish heading and trajectory. In the atmosphere alignment thrusters and retros would automatically fire. Telemetry streaming would guide them safely to the planet and down to the surface. For now there was little to do but relax and wait. It wouldn't take long. The plasma coils had done their jobs. Upon ejection from the shoots they had transferred their exited energy beads to the plasma-ring surrounding the rear of the darts. The beads were trickling away, imparting more than enough energy to propel the bundle through this modest system. The darts were now charging ahead at fully one-quarter the speed of light, pushing them through a relatively barren asteroid field orbiting a common, yellow star. For the first time in quite a while Ovek allowed a bit of guarded optimism to creep in. He calculated their odds at...*damn good.*

No sooner had he settled comfortably into the gel then a port thruster fired. Ovek checked the onboard readout. Telemetry confirmed a bundle adjustment maneuver forcing them to bypass a rocky planet near the outskirts of the asteroid field. One down. He decided to skip the statistical analysis; there was no real upside to reading it, but he couldn't help thinking that the odds had just dropped to about sixty-five percent. It was just a mental reflex, a bad habit he had. He didn't really want to think about the odds. The actual statistics would probably just make him irritable. He was tired now too, and certainly didn't need the aggravation. He couldn't remember the last time he had slept. Perhaps he had dozed awhile in the pit. He wasn't sure; things were beginning to blur a bit. Now, comfortably tucked into the plasma-gel, the dart casing surrounding him like a cocoon, he was determined to get some serious sleep. He set the computer for low-angle orbital entry; atmospheric sensors would trigger the proper command codes if the readings were favorable. He wanted to guarantee enough time for an adequate visual survey of the planet before *landing—impact* was actually a more accurate description. Ideally, he was hoping to find an uninhabited world, but the possibilities were many and varied, from primordial life, to primitive intelligence, to a highly technical civilization, perhaps even a culture far more advanced than any in the empire. This was essentially an unexplored region of space; virtually nothing about it was known for certain, and he felt a little more comfortable seeing where he was going before he set foot on a planet—perhaps he was a bit superstitious, or his experience demanded a cautionary pattern and old habits forced his hand. In any event, he wanted to make sure he got a damn good look around before they touched down. He relayed the optional settings to the bundled memory cores to mimic his commands on a .001 nanocycle delay along with orders for the troopers to get some rest. Finally, he relaxed, closed his eyes, and pinched off his ear slits, allowing his body to relax and his mind to drift as if he were riding a wave which carried him aloft, floating on the inaudible buzz of the onboard computer vibrating through his secondary dorsal receptor.

He awoke to the sound of the alert buzzer assaulting his ear wells. The dart was tearing through the ionosphere of a suitable target planet. Looking out the portal, Ovek spotted the boundary of deep cobalt blue turning to violet, then teal, all floating on a lush sea of fluffy white and translucent aquamarine.

"Nos Po Dei," he whispered. "We've run headlong into paradise."

Retro-rockets and declination thrusters had slowed the darts considerably, but they were still coming in fairly hot. The retros fired again just as they passed from daylight into the deep shadow of the night side. Glowing in the darkness, they resembled a chance meteor shower, which was probably quite spectacular, but not an uncommon occurrence on most worlds. Ovek opened one of the flare nostrils on the nose of his dart, rotating it one hundred eighty degrees. Looking out the portal at the planet's surface, he could see a massive, dark feature delineated by a gossamer network of twinkling lights connecting intermittent bundles of sparkling arrays. Civilization—rather advanced. But sensor readings also indicated destructive levels of chlorofluorocarbons high in the atmosphere, radical disintegration of the protective ozone layer, and residue levels from the burning of fossil fuels high enough to be lethal to hundreds of races they had encountered. This was a civilization in transition, technological infants. Such civilizations were generally more dangerous than either primitives or very highly advanced cultures. Here in the outworlds, ion drives and biogenic suspension was generally unknown. Interstellar space travel was usually found only in stories for children and in the songs of poets, and the harsher reality was that such beings had a tendency to use lethal force first and to make fundamental inquiries afterward. They had a tendency, also, to regard visitors from other worlds as carriers of exotic diseases and to *extract information* about *alien invaders* through vivisection. The idea of having come all this way to end up on the examining table, merely odd, scientific curiosities didn't sit well with him. He didn't bring his team all this way only to have them splayed like wild urshocs, to have their organs stuffed into preserving jars, their brains bloated in foggy, acrid liquid and scrutinized through the walls of hideous magnification bottles.

However, the darts were not second-launch vehicles, so this planet was their only choice. Once on the surface, they were here to stay until the rescue team's arrival, and Ovek meant to keep his team alive until then. He knew that would be a more difficult task on this world, where the mere sight of *aliens* would be cause for alarm. Once again, the odds were shifting, and not in their favor. Still, his troopers were tough and resilient. The darkworld knew they were the best and he was sure they were more than a match for any adversary. Of course, Ovek was too good a soldier to underestimate anyone or anything they might encounter on this fledgling world. The first rule of engagement is to know your enemy—and he knew at least one critical detail already; creatures capable of destroying utopia are capable of anything. The inhabitants of this world were fools, and fools were dangerous. Once they landed, the team would have to be especially vigilant.

During the last three hundred cycles, virtually all emergency darts had been designed and fitted by the Juggernauts, therefore, they were highly sophisticated and reliable. Since the moment the bundle had exited the shoots to the time it had entered the atmosphere, all protocols had executed exactly as expected. Retros and thrusters were firing at regular intervals, slowing the darts, lowering their altitude, and adjusting velocity. The sensors and computers were narrowing the range of available landing sites, analyzing the ratio of natural to constructed structures in order to identify relatively secluded areas. They were busy analyzing suitable flatlands for soft soil near sources of fresh water, monitoring air traffic patterns, population densities, topography, geologic activity, radiation, radar, infrared, x-ray and radio telescope scans, and a host of other priorities. Looking over this world and the data streaming from it, Ovek studied the massive amount of information to be processed. Based on visual analysis alone, however, he knew there were numerous impact sites. Alternating between the readings and corresponding sightings out the portal, Ovek marveled at the pristine open grasslands and inland lakes, the lush jungles and forests, the deserts and flatlands, the lively, winding rivers and magnificent mountain ranges. While the planet was generously populated, it did not appear to be overrun, as was the case with many worlds he had seen. This surely was a gifted world, with a bounty of natural resources. Rich, fertile soil, and clean, clear oceans blanketed more than half the planet. Everywhere the land seemed blessed with water as if Nos Po Dei himself had cried his last tears of joy at the making of this secret corner of the universe. Ovek had seen many worlds of rare and wondrous beauty, and this was one of those uniquely gifted islands, a jewel lovingly set into the dark, rich fabric of space.

At the specified altitude, the command codes fired adjustment retros on all the darts putting his in the lead and kept the squad locked on him. Wherever his dart finally put down the others would automatically follow. Everything was executing according to protocols, and he was confident things would continue along that smooth and steady course. They were close now and, once again, he allowed his optimism to soar just a bit.

Too soon! Without warning he felt a vibration shimmy through the dart—source unknown—and he didn't like a mystery. It was just peculiar enough to make his neck scales stand on end. He checked the computer, but the screen gave him no clue. All functions were nominal, although the vibration was beginning to scramble the screen somewhat. They were in the lower atmosphere now, and impact protocols automatically sent a charge from the battery to the dampening trigger, further expanding the gel around him, and not a moment too soon. The vibrations were increasing, and even with his head firmly wedged in the expanded gel, his head still managed to rattle a bit. Peering through the portal, he checked along the length of the dart in order to locate the source of the offending vibration.

From that angle, he could just see the top of the transponder housing protruding from the hull. The lip of the housing was mounted with ordinary zip bolts. That didn't seem right! Ovek wasn't all that tech minded, but he knew that zip bolts were interior fasteners, not exterior. The explosive sealant in the bolts must have held up well in the vacuum of space or surely he would have been killed the moment he had exited the shoot. The pirates who had originally stolen the transport must have been in a real hurry putting together their emergency escape plan, and they hadn't been too particular about it. They had been very sloppy, or ignorant, or desperate, take your pick. After fitting, when the computer had confirmed the transponder connection, it simply never complained about the nature of the mountings, which was purely mechanical, and evidently, no one had ever checked. Just prior to loading the darts, the bolt heads had probably been spray-coated with plasma-plastic to reduce the effects of friction. As with most space vessels, the more energy applied, the stronger the plastic becomes. But the bolts were beginning to rise up, probably due to lateral friction and improper mounting. This was not good. Ovek could see the bolts jiggling, slowly spinning as they rose from their mounting sockets until caught by the mass of sealant holding them to the inside of the hull. Here, beneath the bolt heads where the metal had not been coated, they were heating from the intense friction, beginning to turn white hot. They were being eaten away, the rushing air trailing a slender stream of sparks behind, the loose sprinkle creating a dazzling display as superheated metal followed the dart like the wake of a runaway comet. The transponder began rocking violently in its shallow well. The thought of losing it, as much as the vibration, set Ovek's teeth rattling. At regular intervals powerful gusts caught under the lip and yanked at it with a mean and urgent intent. The violent tugs threatened to wrench it from the well altogether, and with each lurch Ovek thought the bolts would disintegrate. He kept his eyes fixed on the transponder, hoping it would hold a microcycle longer; the darts were nearly on the ground. He checked the computer but the vibrations had scrambled the programming into a mass of unintelligible gibberish. The screen flickered a mad, intermittent array of calculations and images. A nanocycle later it zipped at breakneck speed through various applications and data lists.

At this point, he had no idea if his command codes were any longer a priority. For that matter, he wasn't even sure if he was still with the team or if they had already landed according to secondary protocols. They were far to the rear and out of his direct line of sight. Besides, the flare of the burning zip bolts was nearly blinding. He doubted he would have been able to see them in any case. All he could do now was hope for the best, put his faith in the Juggernaut programming, and pray the transponder would hold to the well. It didn't. Even as he watched, it made one last desperate attempt at escape, as if it had been held prisoner too long and was being too severely tortured by this alien atmosphere. The posts had finally burned away, and what little remained of the heads disappeared into the glowing wash trailing behind the dart. Looking back, Ovek could see the transponder rocket downward toward a structure nestled in a large agricultural field. The dart was relatively low, and Ovek made a quick topographic image of the place in his mind. The field was bounded on the near side by a lighted roadway and on the far side by dense woodland. There was a similar structure adjacent to the first, well lit, probably a dwelling, with tall, reed-like foliage bordering the far sides of the field. There was a ravine of some kind on one side. If the dart kept on a straight path, he felt certain he could make his way back. Looking forward, he spotted a great expanse of water, a huge lake or ocean coming up fast. By his calculations, his trajectory would carry him beyond the shoreline. It was not difficult to figure out what had happened. When the vibrations had reached a critical point, it had caused the computer to go offline. Prior to that, protocols had meant to land him near the water. When the programming had scrambled, it had locked him on an impact point somewhere out to sea. He hoped the dart would not come down too far from the shore. He was a good swimmer—most amphibians were, but not that good.

Chapter 5

Megan McClurie sat on the old, weathered stump that marked the midpoint between her house and the pumpkin field. Here, where the dim bulbs of the quiet frontage road could not reach beyond the shadows of the house and barn, the sky was awash with a dazzling display of twinkling, pastel stars, a kind of bootleg Van Gough that was hers to admire whenever the cloudless sky accommodated. She bounced her heels against the chipped, brittle bark to match the rhythm of the music playing in her head, the music inspired by the stars blinking above. She sat tap, tap, tapping until another piece broke away revealing the lighter, peach-colored wood beneath, just as she had been doing since she was a little girl. Soon there would be nothing left to chip away.

Though the evening was unseasonably warm and she would love to stay up admiring the evening's celestial canvas, it was after ten-thirty, and she was getting very sleepy already. The day had been long and arduous, and boring. Selling military surplus offered very little in the way of excitement. Having been on her feet all day, catering to the special needs of would-be survivalists preparing for Armageddon and soccer moms outfitting their junior scouts for weekend camping excursions, she was ready now for a really good, well-deserved night's sleep. She took a deep breath of the unusually warm fall breeze, scanned the magnificent vista above her once again in the hope of instilling the stuff of pleasant dreams and headed for the door.

Suddenly, out of the inky blackness, as if someone above had fired a signal flare, an amazing shooting star sailed over her head. It seemed so low that she might have stood on her tiptoes to reach up and grab it! For a moment it glowed as bright as the summer sun, yellow and white and orange, frizzing sparks like a whirligig on the Forth of July. Quickly she made a wish. Surely such a spectacle carried special powers from the heavens, bringing the magic of the stars with it to grant her heart's desire. Maybe she would never see the surplus store again. Behind and off to the side were a group of other shooting stars, not so bright and beautiful, but very lovely all the same. She had never seen meteors so close and low before, so bright and colorful.

Reaching for the door handle she heard a faint whistle coming from high above. She backed away from the house quickly in order to get a better view. Peering over the barn, she spotted another meteor approaching from the west, dropping at a sharp angle. She couldn't actually see it; this one was not a blazing ball of sizzling sparks as the others had been. It was invisible, a dark, shapeless mass that blended into the black, velvet curtain of sky behind it. Rather, she saw its tail, long, thin globules of heat trailing behind it as though the very air were being channeled through a scalding tail pipe.

The meteor looked as though it was going to hit the old barn for sure. But it didn't. Instead, it skimmed the roof and plowed into the pumpkin field about a hundred yards or so from the house. It made a heavy, dull thud in the soft earth, not a terrific explosion as Megan had expected; she had quickly plugged her ears and ducked the moment it slipped past the barn. There were no flames or sparks, no smoke, nothing but the sound of a truckload of dirt and rocks and mud being flung back, and a soft hissing sound. A cloud of fine dust rolled away as if the thing had just slid into second base, and some steam rolled up for a minute or two. The breeze breathed gently over the field for a moment, then all went quiet and still.

Megan didn't move; she simply stood there looking out over the field, looking at the spot where the thing had landed. She stared at it for quite a long time. Finally, she approached it very slowly but stopped after walking only a few feet. She stared out at the place for a while longer, then decided to leave the visitor alone. It was much too late, much too dark, and far too eerie out here to be poking into peculiar things falling from outer space. "I'll do that in the light of day," she said aloud, staring out at the field. "I'll do that tomorrow. Maybe." She had seen a movie once in which an old man poked a similar meteor with a stick. A huge glob of raspberry jam inside had eaten him instead of the other way around. Megan knew she wasn't the brightest jewel in the case, but she wasn't about to be overpowered by a dull rock. She turned and headed for the house.

Saturday morning, however, the sun had barely beaten her out of bed when she was up and eager to collect the meteor, providing she could locate it buried beneath all that mud. She didn't bother getting dressed. She simply threw her robe over her pajamas and topped off her ensemble with high fishing boots. Plodding across the field, she could see the spot marked by a long slash cut into the earth like a fresh wound. Soppy pumpkin mash had seeped into the gash like a thick drool. Chunks and bits of pumpkin lay scattered all about. Most of them had been smashed, and much of the pulp had been boiled into a loose, stringy web that covered the area like a sweater that had come unraveled. The firmer gourds had been kicked outward for a hundred feet or more leaving colorful trails behind. At the far end of the trench Megan saw something buried in the mound of mud and stones and pumpkin debris that the meteor had shoveled there. Only a bit of it was exposed at the base of the pile, just where she had hoped to find it. She thrust her hands into the mud around the thing, the bright morning sun having burned away her earlier trepidations. Her concerns over hungry, oozing substances had vanished into the bright October sky, leaving an unabashed enthusiasm in its stead. Bracing herself with her feet against the mound, she pulled the wad of dirt outward. It resisted only momentarily, protesting with an audible sucking noise but, to her surprise, the earth released the meteor rather easily. The object was caked with mud, which she peeled away, revealing a surface scratched and scorched. The thing was no larger than a coin purse and much lighter than she anticipated. It felt much different from what she expected, also, smoother and sharper, with crisp, well-defined edges. She had expected a heavy rock or laced with metal, pitted, with sharp, jagged edges. This was not like that at all.

She frowned as she looked at it, noting the smooth red lens set into the indentation on top and the tightly braided silver wires dangling from the bottom. There was a narrow shelf surrounding the base with six tiny holes drilled into it. Clearly the box had once been screwed onto some larger object. She felt rather disappointed. The promise of finding a genuine meteorite had been dashed in an instant. This was merely a part of an airplane or helicopter; probably an emergency light; that's all it was. She dropped it unceremoniously into a small burlap bag she had brought and shuffled back to the house. On the way she lobbed the sack into the back of her pickup with the other useless junk she filed back there slated for the parts bin stored at the deer cabin.

If she saw or heard anything on the news concerning a plane crash or landing emergency she would call the police to inform them about the light. Otherwise, she thought not to make a bother of it; she would simply keep it. She doubted she would ever have a practical use for it, but, she thought, if something just falls out of the sky, common sense dictates that it's not a good idea to simply toss it away.

During breakfast Megan perused her book of Greek mythology. While it contained a lot of poetic and romantic passages, which she enjoyed, it seemed laden with accounts of bloody battles and arcane geographical references, and she often found it necessary to reference dull and complicated charts depicting lineages of gods and adventurers with odd names and peculiar attributes. After a time she couldn't remember who begat whom and who were gods and who were mere mortals. She didn't know the good guys from the bad. Who were the heroes? Who were the villains? It was all so complicated. Some of the book was quite beautiful; most of it was very tedious, but she was determined to get through it. She was determined, in fact, to finish all the books she had failed to read while in high school. She had kept them all in a large garbage bag in the hall closet, and she was thankful she had been smart enough to do that. (Although she realized now there probably was something telling about her choice of storage container.) She was tired of being *functionally stupid* as she rather critically described herself. She was severely disappointed about never having gone on to college—more, accurately, about not having the courage, for never having even tried. But the truth was, at the time, she had been so insecure as to convince herself that she simply wasn't smart enough. She believed she hadn't been good enough even for a junior college. Now she discovered that graduating high school with a low C average had gotten her nowhere, fast. She was fed up with her dead-end job, fed up with feeling inadequate, with feeling everyone was so much smarter. She was just fed up with being the dumb, pretty farm girl.

But it was all her fault, and she knew it. She had barely cracked her books the entire four years. She couldn't help feeling it had been wrong to reward her sloppy attitude. Sure, she had desperately wanted to graduate, at the time imagining her high school diploma as a vehicle to a world of independence and assured success. Now, as a full-fledged adult, she saw it as a kind of magic carpet, merely a fanciful illusion which had carried her nowhere, imprisoning her in a province of personal failure. She sincerely wished *the system* had sent her a recognizable and substantial wake up call; it should have kept her rooted in place until she had earned the right to travel the highways and byways of the real world. Her high-school diploma had earned her nothing but the opportunity to clerk mounds of surplus military gear, a dubious opportunity taking her nowhere—very quickly.

The thing that really boiled her eggs was that, deep inside, she knew she wasn't actually stupid. She had simply been lazy. She hadn't really applied herself, not to the work and to the things that would have made a difference, although she had seriously applied herself to the things that mattered at the time—like boys and having fun. It wasn't that she had been loose...well, yeah, she had been. All right, she still was occasionally. She had grown up a daddy's girl, spoiled and used to getting her own way, and giving in to her immediate needs. After coming of age, quite often she needed it immediately. But at least she played safe, and she was very particular. She could afford to be. She had been a lovely girl then and was certainly a beautiful woman now. Splashed with ribbons of shimmering amber baked in by the summer sun, her long, strawberry hair cascaded down around her heart-shaped face like a waterfall of precious metals. Her solid, Irish heritage blessed her with small, regular features, creamy, lightly freckled skin, and crystal, dewy, green eyes. And her body—(well, she knew!) it was five feet, six inches of pure C-4. When she moved the parts that needed to shimmy left and right did so with precision; the parts that were supposed to jiggle up and down did so with perfection, and the parts that were expected to remain absolutely still did not move. In that particular realm of womanhood, she was especially blessed and always in complete control.

Now, struggling with the conclusion of the Trojan War, her attention wandered as she pondered the enormity of the task—the challenge of completing all those books and the work sections at the ends of the chapters. If she could just get through them, if she could just learn the things she should have learned back then, perhaps she could find the courage to quit her crash-and-burn job and get her ass into a real school. It was all about confidence and integrity, and about the respect for herself she had never earned and therefore had never given. At age twenty-six she felt an urgency rising in her; if she didn't accomplish the task soon she might never actually have the courage to return to school, even though, at the moment, she had no idea what academic path to pursue. "I need that," she whispered; "I need that bad." She sat back, considering her grammar for a moment. "I need that badly," she corrected herself.

Finished with her studies and the dishes, she prepared for her busy day off. This included tuning in to her favorite premium cable channel and tucking her pajama tops neatly into the bottoms to avoid elastic attack, putting up her feet on the coffee table, and checking her cable lineup screen before switching to local news.

She considered visiting Allen later in the day. He was often home, working in his studio. Since he lived only a short distance, it was easy for either of them to pop over for a quick beer and to play poker or to watch the Packer game. Of all the boys she had been attracted to in high school, she had wanted Allen the most, but they had never made love. They had never even kissed, not romantically—not on the lips. Of course, she had wanted to, sometimes, mostly when she fantasized, when she touched herself. But he had always been going steady with this girl or that, not always the prettiest girls, but pretty enough, usually with someone brainy, and for that reason, he was the one guy that truly intimidated her. Eventually, however, they found common ground through their mutual friendship with Karasel

Knight. Upon discovering his kindness and sensitivity, she learned to appreciate him more, and her desire for him grew in kind. But eventually their friendship blossomed as well, and with it the idea of a romance with him began to diminish. She enjoyed the simple pleasure of his company, the ability to simply converse with him about things that mattered, to be able to take brief road trips and detours along life's highway without the proverbial sexual speed bumps impeding her progress. She didn't, and couldn't have this kind of relationship with any other guy.

Besides, the realization that he was far too intelligent never abandoned her. He never came on to her and he talked freely about the girls he was dating, especially when she would talk about guys she was seeing. They were comfortable with each other purely as friends. All three of them were, actually, she, Allen, and Kara (whom she also enjoyed fantasizing about on occasion). They all seemed to genuinely need each other; they each embraced their trio as an ideal friendship, a *fellowship* Allen called it—(he espoused romantic and antiquated ideas like that; that was part of his charm). But whatever one might call it, their friendship was a gift, and they all cherished the very idea of it, the idea of having friends the others could count on. It was rare for women to find a straight guy who could fit that bill—Allen was that kind of friend for her and for Kara. It often baffled Megan that he would devote so much of his free time to two women that he wasn't romantically involved with, but she didn't think much beyond that. They were friends. Good enough, mystery solved. Kara often joked that she had him hypnotized and that someday she was going to have his baby. "Great," he had said. "I'm ready to donate my sperm right now!" And he winked.

"Wonderful," she had replied, and handed him the empty beer glass. "Fill 'er up!" They had all laughed about that. They all knew nothing was ever really going to happen, because Kara wasn't his type either—and that was a certainty! She was too strong, too independent. She was too much power wrapped up in one woman for Allen. (Actually, she was almost too much for any man to handle.) Allen did have a huge ego, and he needed a distortion mirror of a woman to balance his personal view of himself. He needed an equal and an opposite, but decidedly not a superior. (Kara could probably best him at everything from thumb wrestling to tackle football.) He needed someone soft and demure but not weak of character, someone smart—but not too smart—someone beautiful but not obvious, someone proud but not vain. He had ample opportunity, that was a certainty, and she was sure he would find her eventually, probably sooner than later.

She decided if he wasn't too busy today, maybe they could get together for lunch and spend the afternoon together. He would probably be interested in hearing about the airplane thingamabob and examining the spot where it had crashed. Maybe he might even want to take a look at the piece of junk. He was a just a guy after all—crap like that fascinated men. But simply because it was her day off didn't mean Allen wasn't busy. Often he worked on Saturdays. Having his studio at home, he regularly sacrificed his weekends to meet tight deadlines. (She had discovered soon enough that simply dropping by with her bikini and an invite was not a very good idea. He could be extremely focused when he needed to be.) Maybe she would invite Kara over, although she was a little reluctant to call her this early. She had called just after the meteor shower, but Kara must have been out. Megan knew she would probably want to sleep late today. Every now and then Kara would insist on her privacy, not wanting to be bothered for a few days stretch. It happened at regular intervals and was annoying to Megan. But friends do what friends must, and she had learned to accept Kara's idiosyncrasy as an acceptable tradeoff for the love and kindness Kara had shown her over the years.

Kara was her best and, truthfully, her only true girl friend. She had other friends, to be sure, but there was a snide, undercurrent of intellectual superiority blended into each and every one of them evident in their language, in their vocabulary and innuendo. Most other women seemed to go out of their way to make sure she felt inferior, and they seemed to take a guarded pleasure in her discomfort. She felt it might be they were somewhat envious of her obvious good looks (which she felt was unfair since she did not flaunt that aspect with them.) Kara, on the other hand, never would have had such a concern since she was the most stunning woman Megan had ever seen. In fact, it had been their mutual complement to each other that sparked their initial friendship in their freshman year, admittedly a superficial and inauspicious start to a lasting friendship.

But it was still going strong. Now that they were adults, with jobs, they went to the clubs occasionally or *partied* at Megan's old farmhouse—well, they would have a few drinks and watch TV (Megan stopped smoking pot years ago, and Kara never touched it).

Every year at Halloween, Kara helped decorate the huge frontage garden with corn bundles and scarecrows and whimsical jack-o-lanterns. When the snows came they made snow giants all around the house and barn, and more often than not Kara was there for Christmas Eve. Every fall they would spend weekends at the deer cabin just for a get-away. Often they would just hang out, talking about nothing in particular, just girl stuff, laying in the soggy hay bales poking at the decaying old skeleton that once was a real barn, and Kara never talked down to her. Megan felt as if they had been friends forever, though much closer, much deeper friends after her parents had been killed in that horrific crash on their way to Chicago. (It had been her father's first real vacation in so many years she couldn't recall, and he had refused to fly anywhere because of the risks posed after 9-11. The car was much safer, he had said, and, besides, he might want to backtrack to Gurney and make a day of it at Six Flags. They had never made it past Racine.) For a while after she was a mess, and Kara handled most of the funeral arrangements and even helped to settle her financial affairs. She had negotiated the business contract to divide and lease the land to the corporate farm and promised to help Megan find a new, affordable apartment when the time was right. It was simply impossible for her to farm the land on her own. No matter; she didn't want to be a farm girl all her life anyway. The taxes on the property were outrageously high, and it made more sense to sell the land eventually rather than try to hold on to it. More than likely she would have to relinquish her home soon for the same reason. The land, the old farmhouse, and the barn were all simply too much for her. Losing her parents had hit Megan hard, but it seemed to draw Kara closer to her, strengthening their friendship.

She hoped there was something more, something much deeper and more meaningful to their relationship. And then, there was that enticing spark of physical attraction…Kara was dark and mysterious with exceptionally long, lustrous raven hair, a perfect nose, pouting lips, and hypnotic, steely eyes that had the uncanny ability to exhibit spectral shifts depending on the changing light or her changing mood. She was lovely and exotic beyond words. Megan, on the other hand, had always had that high-school-cheerleader appeal, and it had served her well, especially when she and Kara were together. Megan knew there weren't two men alive who could possibly resist either of them. But when guys approached it had always been Megan who hooked up and Kara who made excuses to go home alone. So Megan thought it might be just a matter of time until Kara "came on" to her, and she was already determined to let Kara know it would be all right. If Kara felt that way toward her, if friendship was destined to turn to love, then Megan was willing to help her explore those feelings. She was certainly willing to explore those feelings she had for Kara. She had admitted as much to herself not long ago. She didn't know how far those feeling might carry her.

Until recently she had never focused her attentions on another woman, although the thought had crossed her mind now and then. But Kara wasn't just another woman—it was Kara, and that made all the difference in the world. It would be an adventurous journey they could travel together. But for now she was content to allow their friendship to simply blossom and grow with both of them nurturing and encouraging it in their own way. Megan continued to enjoy the attentions of men as she always had, so allowing Kara to control the game was not a problem. She could afford to bide her time; the ball was in Kara's court. Megan was just waiting for the serve.

Chapter 6

The darts zipped from the sky like automatic weapons fire, hissing and steaming as they pierced the dark waters, disrupting the sparkling, choppy surface with a boiling scar as if chunks of the moon itself had fallen. They dove at a severe angle dragging a wake of vaporizing water and bubbles thirty feet or more into the murky depths. Eventually, they leveled out and began their gentle ascent to the surface. As Ovek's dart rose, the gel surrounding him relaxed. He moved from side to side, spinning his craft this way and that in order to catch a glimpse of his surroundings. Even in the tumultuous darkness he could see a few of the others twisting in their wakes, streaming upward toward the light of the moon guarding this great sea like a watchful eye. No sooner had the darts broken the surface than the troopers released the hatches. The frigid water rushed in as they flung themselves out of the rear portals. In no time at all the slender vessels filled, upended and shot like torpedoes straight to the bottom.

As the spent pods disappeared into the depths, the crew followed Ovek toward the shore, gliding quietly to avoid drawing attention, but briskly enough to keep the numbing cold from penetrating their bones. Fortunately, they had not landed as far out to sea as Ovek had feared; he could easily see the lights of land vehicles stopping along a high bluff overlooking the shore. (As things stood, it would still be a challenging swim even for him, and he considered himself one of the strongest swimmers of the group. He was certain Guor's limits would be severely tested.) The sight of the darts streaming through the night sky must have caught the attention of local inhabitants who would naturally be curious about missiles falling from the heavens, disturbing the waters of their peaceful sea.

Perhaps to these natives this was an omen (whether good or bad who could know?). Either way, they were gathering on the rise, their lights beaming like wide, curious eyes, slicing the darkness to place the exact spot where the rocks had dropped from space or to determine if the sky itself were falling. (Again, who could tell?) Regardless, while these interlopers were examining the waters with their spot lights, the troopers could not swim directly to shore, instead they were forced to swim at an angle, making their course longer and more tedious. But it was necessary; even without a briefing from Ovek—they all knew it was essential to remain unseen. Finally, they neared the base of a long, stone pier. Taven was the first to reach it, having pulled ahead of Ovek by a full hundred strokes or more. He was by far the strongest swimmer, having served eight cycles on TennuPe, a world populated by the aquatics. His wife, Didra, was once a TennuPean security officer in the council chambers of Soled, the primary governing citadel in Ocion Prime. There, they had swum together most every day, and he had developed a particular strength and love for it. He pulled himself easily onto the pier, which served, evidently, as a breakwater for a huge, stone structure built directly into the side of the bluff. He lay quietly until the others caught up. They grasped the edge eagerly and rested, satisfied to merely bob up and down in the water. Here and there small channels interrupted the pier where a metal grating was set into the stone, and metallic cages attached to the outside of the walkway encased valves and pipes which fed directly into the water at regular intervals. Nearer to the huge, stone building, where the pier met its squat, rectangular base, a high chain link fence affixed with barbed spires separated the plain, stone fort from the sea, as though protecting the structure from marauding pirates. Warning placards depicting lightning bolts were fastened at various intervals all around the fence. Obviously, these signs warned of high-energy output. Similar glyphs were used on many worlds for this very purpose. Ovek ordered Taven back into the water just as a searchlight atop one of the square towers beyond the fence lit up the pier. Near the corner of the structure's base, where a wooden platform reached out to the stone pier, a thick, dull-colored door squeaked open. Two figures quickly emerged. The first was a hairy quadruped that attempted to charge ahead recklessly. It pulled and bucked at the harness fixed to its thick neck, rearing on its hindquarters as it bounded forward, yanking at the arms of the biped holding it in check. The beast was a vicious-looking mammal, with long fangs and powerful muscles that betrayed its duties as a guard or attack animal. It seemed eager for the kill, and its humanoid master had all he could do to keep the monster from ripping the strap from his grip. It pulled so hard at times he was forced to run behind momentarily or be dragged into the boards. The eager beast stopped suddenly at a thick wooden post protruding from the water that knocked into the pier now and again as the waves jostled the flexible platform about. He relieved himself on it…copiously.

While it did, the team studied the taller figure highlighted brightly in the search beam. He was an unremarkable, formally symmetric mammalian, biped humanoid, who was perhaps two or three heads shorter than Ovek, of medium musculature and bone structure. In most respects quite ordinary and similar to any number of species encountered on hundreds of worlds. (Surely it was no coincidence that most of the lower classes invariably seemed to be mammalian and that a great percentage of the backward fringe planets and outworlds belonged to these hairy, *tert* primitives.) This one wore a uniform of the same, indistinguishable dull color as the door, the only bright spots being the colorful insignia patches on the cap, breastplate and shoulders, patches reminiscent of their own unit identifiers. And he wore a side arm. This was to be expected for a guard at such a facility and didn't pose a problem, as they were well out of sight, except that Guor had the misfortune to fall asleep at that very moment. (Perhaps the swim had been too much for him, and he simply passed out from exhaustion; it's difficult to know.) But regardless, he lost his grip on the side of the pier and went straight down as if some unseen denizen had pulled him into the depths. No one noticed; he didn't make a sound when he went under, and they were all too busy observing the hairy intruders. They discovered his predicament only when he resurfaced, sputtering and coughing and generally thrashing about as if caught in a tangle of Orturian eel weeds. Taven immediately threw an arm around Guor's chest and covered his mouth and squeezed, forcing the liquid out his nostril slits in two long, thin streams, as if the water had been fired from aqua-guns. The guard's hand-held beam played over their heads onto several stumpy logs lashed together by a webbing of twisted, gossamer string that floated by lazily; a small aquatic creature, snared by the wire, flopped in and out of the choppy water in a desperate attempt to escape its tiny, island prison. The furry monster growled and yakked his displeasure at their intrusion, all the while straining at the leash as if it would gladly make the long leap to reach the tiny morsel and devour it whole. The guard clicked his light off, jerked his beast under control and headed back to finally disappear through the heavy, creaky door.

Close. It would be best to steer clear of these fortresses, which were clearly military installations, perhaps nuclear weapons storage or manufacturing facilities, always heavily guarded and under surveillance. It was either simply their dumb luck to have landed near one of these highly fortified facilities, or more likely, this was an extremely warlike world on which the proliferation of nuclear weapons had gotten ridiculously out of hand. Regardless, they had managed to draw the attention of the guards protecting the perimeter, soldiers with orders to fire upon any intruders unable to offer proper identification. Except for an enemy command post, this was the worst possible place to be at the moment. If captured, there would be no negotiating. They would be assumed to be terrorists—alien terrorists at that! Who knows how these primitives dealt with such situations? Ovek had no intentions of finding out.

He signed for them to move on, quietly. They wadded silently to the shore adjacent to the pier and in short order the search beam went dim. Once there, they dragged themselves into a thicket of trees along a seamless, stone wall that separated the pier from the wood. It was fully twice as tall as Ovek and topped with a tangle of fortification wire. It was a toppled monolith running the length of the pier, past the fence, cutting headlong into the bluff that extended from their position well past the spot where they had spotted the vehicles parked when they had first surfaced. The place was dark and well protected from prying eyes, and though it was still dangerously close to the fortress, it seemed an unlikely place to be patrolled.

They were tired now and hungry. Not a one of them could remember the last time they had eaten a decent meal.

"Well, Cap'n," Nol offered, "you sure put on a show up there."

"I know." He paused, wishing he had something better to report. "I lost the transponder. The mounting was bad, and she ripped out of the holding well." There were a few grunts, and they shook their heads, but they seemed less than surprised, considering the way his dart had lit up. Actually, they had all guessed the truth even before he had told them the bad news. Nevertheless, they broke into a chorus of chaotic whisperings following his announcement. He waved his hands in front of them and whispered some reassurances in return, or so he hoped.

"Look, I'm fairly certain I know where it went down, and I think that with a bit of recon we can locate it. Now—it'll be tricky. We'll have to move by night, rest and stay hidden during the day. We want to avoid their population. We don't know this race or their capabilities. The last thing we want is to engage them. Remember, it's just us against an entire planet. Those are not good odds. Our mission will be to get the transponder and activate it, nothing more. If the transponder is damaged we need to fix it. Beel, that will be you; you're the closest thing to a tech we've got."

Beel nodded his affirmative, but discomfort was written all over his face. What little he knew of tech devices he had learned in the last few detri-cycles at Central Command. "Don't worry, it's in a pretty tough housing, and it didn't fall all that far. I doubt it was even damaged," Ovek reassured him. "I'm more concerned about one of the locals making off with a souvenir. Once we activate it we'll establish a base camp and wait for the rescue team. The mission has failed. Central Command will want to know why. They will make another attempt and send sweeper teams to do reconnaissance in an attempt to locate us. They'll pick up the signal." Ovek was confident that someone back at command was going to want some answers.

"What about somethin' to eat, Cap?" Guor said offhandedly. "Got any ideas?"

"I wish I had a disrupter. I'm sure I could disrupt something tasty out of these waters," Taven said.

"Maybe the locals are tasty," Nol snorted.

"Funny," Ovek said, aiming a half smile at Nol. "I spotted plenty of agricultural fields before splashdown. If we're lucky we'll find some crops for easy picking. But we may have to steal something from a local storehouse or residence. Later we might be able to take some game. We'll have to keep our eyes open for opportunities." They all understood, and they translated in their head—it would probably be a while before they saw a decent meal. "But our first order of business is to get some rest. There's plenty of dry foliage here. Cover up and keep warm. We've got the trees and the stone wall here for wind block. We'll move when the moon is high. Till then, get some shuteye. I'll pull watch. I got enough rest in the dart."

They nodded in unison, eager to rest, each of them, even Taven, unwilling to admit just how taxing the swim had been. They lay back, scraping dry leaves over themselves, padding down, hoping to sop up the water dripping off their uniforms. Guor had barely covered his legs before he fell back with an audible thud. In short order the sound of his breathing hissed rhythmically through the thicket, broken occasionally by the buzzing of some passing insect or the hooting of a nocturnal hunter. Taven, Cor, and Beel lay for a while admiring the gigantic, mountainous moon before sleep overtook them. Nol and Rahon rested quietly, peering now and then between the trees, ever wary of the dangers that might be lurking in the shadows of this alien world. Good soldiers admitted to being afraid; for them, fear was a necessary part of life. The manner in which they faced it was the issue. The best soldiers used fear like a defensive weapon, keeping them edgy and vigilant.

As planned, they moved up the bluff when the moon was directly overhead. On top, the tree line ended where a road cut through the wood. On the opposite side was a clearing, and in the distance, the woods continued. That was their target. Ovek was certain the transponder had fallen on the other side of that woodland. He ordered them to halt, wary of having to traverse the clearing where they were sure to be as obvious as fire slugs in a Tyon bog. He surveyed left and right, checking up and down the road carefully. It looked deserted: the vehicles that had stopped earlier had disappeared. It looked safe to cross.

"Nol, you take point, Cor, you've got the rear." Ovek gave out the assignments. "Three stride spread." He touched Nol's back and his point guard took off. Rahon darted out in short order. Beel followed, then Guor. Ovek positioned himself in the middle and shot across with Taven on his heels. Cor took off directly behind. Ovek had just reached the other side when two blaring beams unexpectedly lit up the road. Taven jumped like a Cruvian cave spider toward the shoulder, but Cor, caught in the middle of the road, turned intuitively in the direction of the charging vehicle.

Although it was well into the night, Kara was wide-awake after her hunt and not in a hurry to head home. The kill had been exhilarating, transforming her wistful restlessness into an adventurous spirit. She was fairly rocketing down Lakeshore Drive, the long stretch of winding road spurring her onward like a beckoning finger. The drive here was a perfect offering for her mood, with its magnificent presentation of regal pines, sturdy oaks, and battalions of snowy birch trees set against the vast expanse of lake and endless sky. The water sparkled like a vast carpet of diamonds from beneath the bluff to the distant horizon where the myriad reflections of the moon merged with the twinkling stars.

She admired the view for a moment, for just a second or two, enraptured by its poetic beauty. But it had been a moment too long. Rounding a gentle curve, she turned her head in time to see a figure standing directly in the center of the road, not more than fifty feet ahead. She slammed on the brakes and swerved to the left. Fortunately, he made a tremendous leap, clearing the car by inches a moment before it would have struck him. He landed in the gravel on the shoulder of the road. Kara stopped a hundred feet or more beyond. She had been moving far too fast, and had he not jumped, she was certain he would have been killed. Although, watching him leap through the air, she wasn't sure what she had seen. It was built like a man, tall and husky enough, but he, or she, probably had been wearing a costume. Only, there had been something particular and disturbing about the costume, something about the ultra-realistic way the muscles moved when he had jumped out of the way. She had caught only a glimpse, for just a second, but long enough to notice the huge, coiled muscles rippling beneath the surface of his skin as he bounded into the air. Once he moved, he had been quick and agile, not slow and clumsy, as she might have expected. What was he doing out here at this time of night? And why the costume? Halloween was three weeks away. She could feel her body go on minor alert, but resisted. After all, she had nearly run him down and needed to find out if he was all right, to offer him assistance if he needed it. Pulling the car to side of the road, she had taken her eyes off him for only a moment. She sprinted to the spot where he landed in the dirt. If nothing else, she was sure the fall to the ground would have injured him. The gravel here was loose and sharp. But he was gone. She looked along the small ravine below the shoulder but he was nowhere to be seen.

Perhaps her mind had played some trick on her. Maybe she had simply been caught up in the exhilaration of the moment. No, she had seen him, and there, lying on the ground at her feet, was the proof. Many of the stones were smeared with his blood, and near the edge of the grass dozens of droplets formed a trail leading into the field. Kara dabbed her finger into a tiny pool and brought it to her nose. She dropped her hand to her side and frowned. She cocked her head to the side and looked for quite a while into the woods toward the direction the blood spatter pointed, toward the direction he had presumably disappeared. She stood looking out over the clearing because she didn't understand. She couldn't. She had never smelled blood like this before, and it had surprised her. She had fully expected it to smell human. It didn't. But it wasn't animal blood either; she was certain of it. It reminded her of iguanas and crocodiles and other reptiles she knew well, yet, it was different. There was something odd about it. For a moment she entertained the notion that it may have been cloned or engineered because it had an artificial air about it. It was puzzling, and it confused her. She tried desperately to define the nature of it, to characterize it in a way that made sense. While attempting to make the puzzle piece fit into her rational world, she noticed the tiny stars twinkling among the stones at her feet. She captured one on the end of her finger. It appeared to be a small fish scale, fine and delicate, reflecting and refracting the light of the moon into a miniature spectral display. She puffed at it and watched it flitter away to disappear as if it had simply dissolved into the air. Fishing in a full body costume! The scenario seemed more and more bizarre. Each clue made the puzzle more complicated. She smelled the dab of blood again. The unusual scent overwhelmed her; there was something mechanical in it, synthetic. But it wasn't mixed with the blood. It was part of it, part of its genetic make up. Her senses were keenly developed and her instincts precisely aware of the nature of things.

There was no mistake. Even if the blood had been manufactured, the technology to create it simply didn't exist; that much was certain. She wiped the blood onto her handkerchief and put it securely in her back pocket. Suddenly, as if a button had been pushed, the word popped into her head, the missing piece her mind had been searching for. The word most people fear to think and dare to say. Certainly, no one seriously entertains such a thought. Yet, the blood, she thought, the very nature of it, the smell of it—so *alien*. She didn't want to entertain that notion either. Yet, historically, her race was thought to be on equal terms. Humans considered vampires to be fanciful beings, yet her race has co-existed with man for millions of years. Throughout the ages, through cunning and vigilance, their secret has been safeguarded, hidden in plain view, woven into the very fabric of popular culture. Popularized in legend and folklore, in literature, film and urban myth by humans and vampires alike, the historical nature of vampirism has been explored, mostly inaccurately, for centuries. Perhaps aliens have lived within both cultures in exactly the same way, keeping their existence secret through some clever mechanisms of their own. Perhaps they have been among Earthlings for a long time. How was she to know? This was certainly not the first close encounter. This was merely the first she had ever had. Of course, the evidence of those encounters was usually a few fuzzy photos, or worse, fuzzy memories of remote abductions and weird examination. But surely, this was different. The blood evidence she possessed was not under scrutiny by unscrupulous technicians for a quick buck and instant publicity. There was no examination by parapsychologists whose notes would ultimately become a book attempting to proselytize a gullible public.

Her lab was simply an unassuming mind, a fresh slate, conducting a comparative analysis utilizing the considerable knowledge of the blood of man and animals, the smell of it, the very essence of it. No, this blood belonged to something other than human, and it was from no animal that ever existed, nor was it the blood of a vampire. Something strange and mysterious was happening—something that mocked the natural order of things, and it piqued her curiosity as if the hunger had been renewed. It suddenly occurred to her that she couldn't do anything about it by standing at the edge of the road staring across the field. She removed her long coat and dropped it into the darkness of the ravine, determined to follow him and get to the bottom of this mystery. In just a few seconds she crossed the old football field and disappeared like a mist between the trees.

It wasn't long before she heard him moving west through the woods. He made as much racket as a dozen men. She stopped and cocked her ear in his direction. He was trying to be cagey, watching his footfalls, avoiding branches and thickets, balancing atop the fallen trees, moving across the soft earth and mosses and along the narrow streams that cut through the woodland here and there. But she thought, considering that she was tracking something that didn't actually exist, it may as well have been a dragon for all the noise it was making. And then the obvious struck her. This was not one person she was following. Why had it taken her these precious minutes to realize this perilous fact? Fool that she was! She was following the trail of a group of these creatures, for now she had no other word to describe the nature of her prey—except that fearful word, the word that kept sticking in the back of her head, *alien*. It stabbed at the back of her brain like a sharp stick.

It wasn't just the weirdness, the impossibility of it that bothered her. What was it? She mulled it over as she slunk on. The peculiar nature of the blood bothered her. Moreover, it frightened her. She had never actually been frightened before. Not like this. No man or beast she had ever encountered was truly a match for her. She had always been the superior, and supremely confident during an encounter with any prey. But this was uniquely different. She recalled again the size of this creature and his armor-like skin, so taut yet supple. The short, leather kilt he wore exposed thighs as massive as the young trees surrounding her. His leap had carried him from the center of the road completely to the shoulder. The arc of it was tremendous. She would have been capable of it. But from a dead stop, no human could have done it. Impossible! Finally, she didn't get a very good look at his face; there hadn't been time. But she had seen enough to know he had been wearing a mask, or so she had thought at the time. Now, she realized what it was nagging at the back of her mind, why she was frightened. If he hadn't been wearing a mask, what was she following exactly? If there were more than one of these *creatures* up ahead, what was she getting into? If they were as powerful as she was beginning to suspect, perhaps she needed to formulate a plan before running headlong into their midst. This was not the first time Kara had ever thought about death, but it was the first time she had ever thought about her own.

They were up ahead about a hundred yards when suddenly they came to a dead stop. Kara dropped to her knee to listen, her ears perked to reveal the footfalls of a spider if it came to that. There was only a deep silence, broken now and again by whisperings that might have been mistaken for tiny whirlwinds stirring the fallen leaves. Resting on her fingertips, head up, sniffing the air, every muscle at the ready, her eyes cut keenly into the stygian darkness. All her instincts, every fiber of her being telegraphed subtle messages of life and death. There were none of the usual night sounds or common woodland activities. There was no cry of a screech owl or the scurrying of rodents rooting out beetles along their favored trails. Not a fox or raccoon stirred. Not a bird flittered. The air itself seemed to be standing still. The tree branches froze in place as if to render themselves inconspicuous, anticipating something awful happening in their midst. It was as though the bizarre creatures ahead frightened the earth itself. Everything she knew about stalking her prey triggered some primal instinct deep within her and she moved forward ever more cautiously, more stealthily, like a great cat protecting its territory from a marauding cave bear.

Nol stopped at the edge of a clearing cut into the wood. Here the tree line bordered a gravel road that divided the profusion of oaks and pines and widened into a large circular area appointed with worn, wooden furniture and grated, open air stoves. Ashes and charred remains of dark, caked fuel were heaped in casual piles nearby and littered the gravel surrounding the cooking pedestals. Several pieces of recreational equipment, probably intended for children, stood on the far side of the clearing. The designs and function were familiar, the common features found on most of the worlds they had seen. All seemed quiet here, and the clearing offered an ideal rest area, but they couldn't afford to stay long.

"It's clear here, Cap'n," Nol reported. "I'll check the stoves before we move on. Maybe there's something edible in one of them."

"Okay, but make it quick. There's also a receptacle on that end," Ovek pointed to a large wire basket near one of the wooden tables. "Maybe there's something in there that will hold us." Ovek took Cor aside while the team conducted their search, checking under tables and benches, scouting quickly and somewhat desperately for anything that might offer a bit of sustenance.

"Were you hurt when you took that dive?" Ovek asked.

"Not much, Captain. A few cuts and scrapes. I'm fine."

"I'm just concerned about infection. Sooner or later we're sure to encounter something the Nanites can't handle. There seems to be fresh rain water on some of the tables, better clean those wounds as soon as you can." Cor nodded.

"Do you think the local spotted you?" Ovek asked.

"Briefly, Captian…a female, I think. I got a pretty good look from my belly, and then low crawled it out of there as quickly as I could," Cor admitted.

"Did she follow?" Ovek looked concerned.

"No. When I hit the forest she was still standing there. She was curious and thinking. But a female, alone in the dark, it ain't typical, Captain."

"Well, I hope you're right. All the same, we don't know enough to be sure. Keep sharp," Ovek warned.

"Aye, Captain."

During their reconnoiter, Guor found the only prize. The basket had held several plastic bags of grain bread. Though dry and brittle, the slices were still edible, a welcomed feast to the hungry soldiers. Within minutes they consumed the first bag and nearly finished the second. "Perhaps we should ration some for later, just in case," Ovek said. He was confident they would soon locate a better supply of food and that they could easily have eaten it all, so it was more of a suggestion than a command. However, they all seemed satisfied and agreed. Guor tied a knot in the bag and slipped it into his jacket.

Feeling refreshed, they were determined to reach their destination by dawn. Ovek pointed in the same direction they had been headed. "Straight on, same spread, move out," he ordered. Nol proceeded on point as before, slipping between a table and the swing chairs into the woods beyond. They all followed in the same order with Cor taking up the rear. Passing the last table, he dipped his head for one final sip from the shallow pool of water clinging there. While he drank, he noticed a slight movement at the far end of the clearing. It was almost nothing, almost imperceptible, but it was enough, the slight shifting of something large, something potentially dangerous. He stood up very slowly, purposefully accentuating his full height and turned his back to the spot where the intruder was hidden. Reaching into his jacket he slipped his hand into the Chicma axe handle. He expanded his muscles, flaring his back while holding his fists firmly to his hips. He held his head low and relaxed, the axe turned edge on, offering his opponent no appreciable view of it. His neck scales bristled at the thought of battle and the glory of the inevitable outcome.

Cor feared no one. Ovek may not have wanted to engage these locals, but the battle may have come looking for him, and he was ready. Then ever so slowly he turned, the axe cleverly hidden behind his thigh. There, standing at the edge of the clearing, was the female he had seen at the road. Even in the pale moonlight he recognized her thick mane of dark hair, the tall lithe form, her proud, regal stance, that steadfast, unflinching glare. But he sensed something of a hesitation in her, as well. She stood as if frozen, unsure of what her next move might be. Of course that was understandable; surely, she had never seen the likes him before. These natives seemed excessively curious, which might just be her undoing; he couldn't simply let her walk away. She would be sure to file a report with local authorities. She represented a threat, one that could seriously compromise the mission. But he didn't want to harm her either. He considered taking her hostage. She looked young, fragile, and was probably untrained in the ways of war. It would be an easy matter. He needed to make a decision and to do it fast. He was falling behind the rest of the crew. In a heartbeat he made his choice. He couldn't let her go. He would let the captain decide. Ovek would know what to do with her. He would simply subdue her, knock her out, and carry her along, an easy matter from the looks of things. Returning the axe to its hiding place within his jacket, he began his slow approach. In that moment he realized it might not be quite as easy to overpower her as he had thought.

Making her way to the edge of the clearing, Kara stopped at the picnic area. She could see her quarry hunched over one of the picnic tables. She knew now for a certainty that her imagination had not gotten the best of her. This was a strange creature indeed. He was dressed in a dark leather kilt and wore boots with straps that wound around his leg, past his knee and fastened to a wide leather band at the base of his thigh. The kilt was secured with a metal-linked belt. Tucked neatly into the kilt, he wore a heavy, collarless shirt with several flapped pockets, which emphasized his huge, muscular chest. Over this, he sported a short, dark jacket decorated with colorful patches and insignias on the shoulders and chest and on the long, arrowhead collar. It was unbuttoned at the front but stayed neatly in position, held firmly in place by posts built into the metal belt at the hips.

His skin was covered with a mesh of fine scales like those found on a fish or a lizard. It moved and undulated over his rippling muscles like chain mail. He stood up slowly, turning his back to her, fully six and a half feet tall, broad and powerfully built, weighing perhaps two-hundred fifty pounds. He was, by all standards, a tremendous specimen. She couldn't help admiring his huge shoulders and broad back, his slim waist, his massive thighs. But as he slowly turned around, it was his face that she found truly amazing, that captured her rapt attention. It was fearsome and beautiful all at once, truly alien. It struck her now. It hit her square in the face in an instant, the reason she had been so uneasy at first, then so afraid, terrified actually. It wasn't for herself, for humans, or for vampires (which might be usurped as the strongest race). She was afraid for all life on Earth.

The enormity of what might be happening here overwhelmed her. For the first time in her life she felt the lethal combination of fear and panic. Up to this moment she had not dared believe her suspicions could actually be true. Yet here he was, standing a mere forty feet from her. An alien being. Clearly, he did not belong. So, she simply stood somewhat stunned, just staring at him. He had deep-set eyes and sharp bony ridges wrapping round his brow circling the sockets, down his cheeks to his jaw culminating in two blunt horns at the base of his chin. At the very top center of his forehead a bony horn protruded outward about six inches. From it extended a flexible membrane, like a fan dividing the head into two separate halves until it tapered and disappeared at the base of his neck. The scales of his face were so fine as to be almost imperceptible, and he had virtually no ears. Two small slits in a modest, shapely, mound served as a nose and his thin, even lips jutted forward on slightly muzzled jaws. She thought that if dinosaurs had not been replaced as the dominant species on Earth, this creature could very well have been one of their descendants.

He stood very still observing her as well, sizing her up, she thought. Perhaps he had no ill intent. After all, she had almost run him down with her car. She had almost killed him, not the other way around. There was no reason to suspect he meant her any harm. She was about to speak him when he began moving toward her. Suddenly, she saw the weapon in his hand—there was no mistake. It was a wicked, circular blade with split forward teeth, the whole of it shaped like the mandibles of an insect, the razor edges curving round the sides, his hand fitted neatly into the recessed back end. It was so thin and compact that it had been difficult to spot until he brought it fully into view. Such a weapon could do a lot of damage in any direction. In the hands of a skilled combatant, she had no doubt such a weapon could be lethal. A sure and powerful blow could decapitate her in short order. Instinctively, her body reacted. In an instant, the animal in her was fully awake, every sense fully aroused, every instinct peaked, every muscle on alert, her entire being in survival mode. Even before he had completed his second step, she was high in the air on the downside of a parabolic arc descending directly onto the spot where he would be in the next microsecond. Her claws and fangs discharged in midair, translucent in the moonlight, glowing like miniature light sabers.

She caught Cor completely off guard. He had not expected so benign a creature to be so swift, so aggressive, to move like a vicious animal. He was surprised, too, by her physical transformation. She had literally become more bestial and primitive. It stunned him momentarily. He froze in place, his axe at the ready, and he braced himself for the inevitable strike. In mid-flight she twisted sideways. Cocking her leg back, she snapped her foot forward catching him squarely in the chest. The force of the blow staggered him. He swung the axe uselessly at the air as he flew backward, lifting him fully off his feet. He landed on his back next to the table. He would not underestimate her again. With a forward whip of his legs, he was immediately on his feet. He advanced quickly, with an underhand cross-body slice, hoping to catch her in the neck, but she would have none of his clever tactics. She leaned far back, spun around following the trail of the blade, then caught him flush on the side of his head with a spinning roundhouse kick that sent him reeling. He realized much too late that his left side was fully exposed, and he paid dearly for that mistake. Continuing her spin, building momentum, Kara delivered a devastating punch just below his rib cage, and he went down. Her claws punctured his lung, and his chest heaved as if he were drowning. The blood shot from his mouth like an evil curse. How he managed to hold on to the axe he didn't know. No sooner had he fallen to his knees than Kara struck again. Her fist landed squarely on his neck just to the right side of his jaw. Her claws ripped through to the other side popping scales off his neck, which wafted to the ground like silvery snowflakes flittering in the moonlight. Backing away, she yanked the claws out in one clean, swift motion.

She stood staring at him, watching him die. She realized suddenly that she had been fighting blindly, instinctively. While the kill had been in self-defense, it seemed almost a knee-jerk response, as if she had panicked. She had felt an uncharacteristic hysteria, mild, yet tangible, distinctive and disturbing, a feeling she had never known before. Certainly, she had never experienced this sensation during the hunt. The short battle had been exhilarating, but the kill had not been satisfying. Without the incentive of the bloodlust or the intense desire of the hunger, she took absolutely no pleasure from it. Her assessment, however, was premature. Cor was far from dead. He stood up slowly, twisting his head back and forth, stretching his neck, poking and scratching at his wounds with his short stubbing claw tips. Without taking his eyes off her, he spit a tremendous spray of blood and defiantly spread his arms out before her, the Chicma axe still firmly in his grip. He spread his legs wide and moved in a small circle around her, looking for some advantage. She was fast, faster than anyone or any creature he had ever fought before, and she was far more powerful than he could ever have suspected. Those hidden claws between her knuckles, how very clever! And her fangs certainly looked formidable. What a fool he had been to underestimate this changeling!

Kara had fought some tough and dangerous opponents in her life, but no one like this, although, having wounded him, she was confident of the outcome. He was skilled, but not her equal, although, he certainly was resilient, and she realized the importance of dispatching him quickly.

Should he make good his escape, he would die a slow and painful death. The wounds she had inflicted would be fatal over time—that was a certainty. She wanted to end it, now, quickly and painlessly, without that axe removing anything she'd rather keep. She feinted in. He didn't react. She faked a left blow to his chest. He swung a combination cross body block and counter strike with the axe. She anticipated his move by jumping into the air even before he swung. A full twist put her in perfect position, fully eight feet over his head, zeroing in on his back. He had never even seen her leave the ground. The ax sliced only the air where she had been. As if by magic, it seemed, she had disappeared. Before he had time to consider how she had outmaneuvered him, she dug her fangs deeply into the back of his neck, severing his spinal cord. Briefly, Cor caught a glimpse of Ovek bounding across the clearing, a mandat knife flashing in his hand, its jeweled handle sparkling like the tearful eyes of Murva, his wife, overjoyed to see him coming home again…and then she was there with him, his beloved, taking his head in her hands, her gentle, loving hands.

Catching a glimpse of Ovek, Kara's immediate instinct was to escape with her kill, to secure it at safer ground. Gripping Cor tightly in her jaws, she began dragging him across the clearing, but Ovek was narrowing the distance quickly. He would be on her in a moment. She spotted the knife, which he held back and away, edge up, typical of combatants supremely skilled with the blade, and sighted more dinosaur men directly behind him. She was outnumbered, and soon she would be outflanked. She opened her mouth wide, dropping Cor in a disrespectful heap. She gazed down at his wretched body, which only a moment before had been a proud and powerful warrior. The very sight of him shocked her system, driving her adrenaline level down a notch. As if emerging from a dense fog, the stark realization of what she had done overwhelmed her. She hadn't followed these creatures only to kill this one. She hadn't come looking for a fight or to make enemies of them. He had misunderstood her intentions and that misunderstanding had cost him his life. She had only been curious, mystified and fearful of the possibilities his blood represented. But fear and mistrust by both of them had lead to bloodshed and death. Now she regretted that it had come to this.

She should have stayed hidden, observed him from the shadows without betraying her presence. But recriminations seemed senseless at the moment with this pack bearing down on her. Considering their mad advance, they seemed hell bent on revenge. They meant to kill her, and she would be hard pressed to defeat so many of these monstrous brutes. How could she explain that it had been in self-defense, that her instincts had simply taken control, and things had gotten out of hand? They seemed to be in no mood to listen to reason. Besides, she had no way of knowing if she could communicate with them. She knew the only thing to do, the best thing to do, was to run. And so she did. She dashed quickly into the woods, retracing her tracks as quickly as her powerful legs would carry her. Gliding swiftly over the undergrowth and between the densely packed trees, she recalled her reactions the moment she had seen the weapon in his hands. Immediately, as the fight had begun, she had felt an immediate exhilaration, much different when the thrill of the hunt urged her onward and dispatching her prey rendered so much satisfaction.

It was as if her animal nature had completely taken control, as if the feral beast within was in command. Such a thing had never happened to her before. Perhaps the creature, the very *idea* of him, provoked a fear that had unleashed a part of her she had not dared release before. Perhaps that fear, more profound than she had previously been willing to acknowledge, was the very worst or very best part of her; she didn't know which. Certainly, the moment of the kill had been thrilling, but the lingering aftereffects, the memory of that thrill, was frightening. She doubted she ever wanted to feel that good and this bad ever again.

She ran for about a quarter mile when exhaustion overtook her. Her eyes grew heavy and her head fell forward as if a great weight bore down on her. At first she thought that tracking them and the unexpected battle had taxed her more than she had realized, but the metallic aftertaste in her mouth was an alarming and bitter reminder that she had swallowed far too much of the alien's blood and that she might be infected. Taking it had been another reckless mistake. It had been foolhardy to allow the animal frenzy to usurp her better judgment. Of course, it was foolish now to think she had any say in the matter. Normally she was not so careless, but nothing she had done tonight since she had spotted the creature in the road had been typical of her. It was as if the very smell of the blood had set her on a course of wild abandon. Something in it had compelled her to reckless action, like a bloodhound relentlessly pressing forward.

Now, ironically, a generous quantity of that blood seems to have infected her, stopping her dead in her tracks. She simply couldn't run any longer. She felt dizzy, fearful that she might soon faint in the open. She could hear them on her trail, perhaps a hundred yards behind. Soon they would spot her. She scouted a tall, ancient oak, and quickly leaped to a high, gnarled branch, kipped her hips up and around until she secured a foothold. The effort was exhausting, and the infection was draining her strength so rapidly she feared she might fall from the tree at any moment. Making her way upward, she quickly wedged herself into a deep crotch in the massive trunk. She was certain they would be unable to see her from the ground and hoped they would not think to look for her in the trees. Here, she was determined to rest. She felt she had no choice, actually; the nagging weariness in the back of her head was overpowering now. Surrounded by a dome of branches and early autumn leaves flittering in the uneven breezes, clacking softly like distant wooden chimes, she closed her eyes and drifted into a deep, dreamy sleep filled with peculiar sounds and visions of fantastic vehicles skimming over shimmering glass surfaces, then…

She was running on all fours across the open pampas. The wind stroked the black fur between her ears, across her head and down the length of her back. She felt the coolness comb through her thick coat and flow along her skin. The machines were far behind, but they were gaining on her. They had appeared out of nowhere. The world had been hers, barren, save for the deer running in herd up ahead. They disappeared into a thicket, which exploded into a dark cloud of flying lizards that blotted out the sun. See turned to look again. There were thousands of them. Quick, darting things with pinchers for teeth and wings like tiny oars. Their legs were wrenches tucked under them as they skimmed the surface like angry, terminator wasps intent on taking her apart. She pushed harder with her powerful hindquarters, digging her claw deeply into the hard soil for greater traction. But they were relentless, nearly upon her now. She roared and flashed her tusks in anger. But they ignored her warnings. She could feel the gusts of their churning wings now pushing the fur against the grain, forcing it to stand in on end. She flicked her tail at the lead machine in a mad attempt to knock it from the sky. But she missed. It was buzzing over her now like some flying carnival car run amok, forcing its vice-like claw around the back of her skull.

She forced her eyes open, and slowly the buzzing drifted into the distance as if the squadron of crazed machines had exploded into a starburst and flittered off in separate directions over the horizon. Her mind went quiet, and her body was still and relaxed, and she felt them even before she heard them. Tiny vibrations through the tree betrayed their presence below. She peered cautiously down along the trunk. Five of them were spread out beneath her, checking the ground, the thickets, the low-hanging branches, parting the grasses with their boots, sniffing the air. Clearly, these were experienced and clever trackers. But they were unaware of her ability or they would be checking much higher in the trees. The tree she had chosen was much older and larger, slightly separated from its neighbors, its branches much too high for these aliens to reach with their best jumps, and Kara assumed they thought such a leap would be impossible. She had chosen the perfect spot to make her ascent. She could hear them speaking their peculiar alien language, all pointing at once in various directions. One particularly commanding creature, large and powerfully built, was directing the others. He was very thorough and systematic, and when he stood in the spot where she had jumped to the branch, he did look to the tree. Clearly, he dismissed the idea. Eventually, he gathered the group around him for a meeting.

She was hoping they were going to give up the search. He pointed in the direction from which they had come, which harbored good news for her, since she was still very tired. Suddenly, in the middle of a sentence, she was amazed to hear a few words spoken in English! And then more! Suddenly, she understood everything he was saying.

He was speaking perfect English, as if he had lived in the Midwest all his life. At first she heard him say "his body" and "take him back." She heard him very clearly and distinctly. Next he said something about "the field and eating crops" and "We have to get there before dawn" and "We can't allow revenge to jeopardize the mission." Then he said quite distinctly, "We need to find the transponder before it's taken by one of the locals. We shouldn't have allowed ourselves to be sidetracked like this. It was a mistake. He's gone. It happens." Finally he said, in the most military way, "Pack it in and move out," and pointed again toward the west—directly west, directly toward Megan's farmhouse. Then she passed out.

She was awakened at dawn by the rays of the sun filtering their way through the tree branches. All around her was the animated skittering of birds and squirrels busy collecting their meals and winter's horde. The frightful creatures chasing her earlier were nowhere to be seen. She ran swiftly now, almost effortlessly, feeling refreshed and rejuvenated from her sleep. She was not happy about having engaged these creatures and having needlessly made enemies of them, but she realized her instinct to follow had served her in the end. If she had understood the leader correctly they were headed for Megan's farm. They were on some sort of mission, looking for something, the transponder, that much was clear. And, to a great measure, she had unraveled the mystery of the peculiar blood. As bizarre and tragic as this situation had turned out, at least that part of it had been solved. But she knew there was so much more to it. This entire episode had left her with a bad and very eerie feeling, and though a few questions had been answered, a multitude of unanswered questions still remained.

By the time she reached the road, she estimated it had been about two hours since she had first taken to the tree. If they followed the creek up through the woods into the park and on to the edge of the cornfield, they would happen upon Megan's farmhouse soon. She thought it might take them about two hours on foot. They were moving in unfamiliar territory, after all. She figured she still had time to beat them there. She gathered up her coat and headed for her car, debating whether to tell her father about all that had happened. She had put the sample of the alien blood on her handkerchief specifically for that purpose. Now, however, she had serious misgivings about going to him. She loved him dearly, and this was clearly a very dangerous situation, not that he wasn't a tough old prowler, but she was not convinced that getting him involved was a good idea. He didn't need this kind of stress. Physically, she knew, he could still best virtually any man or beast. But ever since she had found a place of her own he was more distraught than ever. This had less to do with the bloodlust and her hunting on her own than with the clubs she frequented and potential suitors he imagined. So, he was more than happy to have her around as much as possible. Being a single father had been hard on him, and the strain of it all had taken its toll. After Kara's mother left, the only thing that kept him sane was his work. He owned the Knights Veterinarian Clinic in New Berlin, just west of Milwaukee, which was actually more of a front than a genuine business, since the care and treatment of animals was more a hobby now than a vocation. He enjoyed their company, and it gave him great pleasure to minister to their simple needs. He was valued and respected far more in the vampire community as a research scientist. Vocal and insightful on issues pertinent to the council, indeed to the Vampire Nation, he also served, on rare occasions, as a doctor treating vampires with unusual and, generally, severe injuries. (He once recounted an incident in which a young male had been severely injured during an encounter with a rather vicious, and somewhat unstable, cocaine dealer. The short-lived dispute had ended with the business end of a sawed-off shotgun pressed against the vampire's face. A single, deadly discharge removed a sizable portion of his skull, including most of his right cheekbone and lower jaw. The blast had also caused some unusual brain damage that created a conflict between the neural transmitters and the viral repair activities. Normally the essence would fully restore damage of this significance, regenerating bone, muscle tissue, and neural-vascular activity; even the regeneration of entire limbs was common. But in this case, even though eighty percent of the higher brain functioning had been restored, some critical aspect had not, and the difference severely impeded the repair work. Portions of the cheek, jaw, and the entire right tusk would not regenerate. Applying his considerably advanced techniques, Dr. Knight was able to give the young cub almost an entirely new face and restored, not only the tusk, but the jacket within the sinus cavity, the vestibule, and the tooth's mobility, as well, a rather remarkable accomplishment.)

Because of Kara's fondness for animals, as well, her father employed her as his assistant. But in truth, it was merely a token job allowing her to come and go as she pleased. The office was small, and the business was slow. She knew he was more than grateful to have her there, and she reciprocated those feelings. Besides, she especially loved handling and learning about exotic animals, which hardly seemed like work at all. In fact, she sometimes returned the entire amount of her paycheck in the form of birthday or Christmas gifts. She felt the job and the checks were mostly for official appearances anyway. He seemed so lost without her at times, bravely alone, yet so obviously lonely. While vampires are superior to humans in so many ways, they often share similar emotional problems, and marital troubles are no exception. Kara's mother had been far more a big-city woman with aspirations of becoming a star of stage or television, while her father was content with a modest, small-town life in the Midwest. Consequently, they had gone their separate ways when Kara was eight. Her mother had moved to California, and Kara had not seen her since nor heard any word of progress concerning her career.

Her father had been severely depressed for years afterward and had poured all his love and energy into his research and work and, of course, his life with Kara. For him these things had been a joy and solace, and he found genuine fulfillment in them. Kara knew this was because work and his relationship with her filled his life with meaning, with a sense of accomplishment and fulfillment, with continuance. Vampires live much longer than humans, but they are not eternal, as the bogus literature suggests. Now, having thought things through, she decided not to tell him about all that had happened today. He would worry about her far too much. His life was stressful enough. It hardly seemed like a good idea to add to his burden. His weakness was that as a father, perhaps, he loved too much. He may have been a powerful vampire and a brilliant scientist, but, emotionally, he was a train wreck.

She thought it might be best to contact a padder, a politically and socially connected vampire. They are extremely ambitious, with influence and numerous contacts to the world of politics and industry, who generally aspire to a council position, which is a vampire holding an influential position within the human population. The Vampire Nation itself has no actual formal structure or political party, but those in positions of power within the general population are held in great esteem, nonetheless, not because of their ability to influence or institute change among humans, but because, as in any culture, their drive, organization skills, intelligence, and willingness to serve hone these same skills for their culture. Padders can usually introduce a vampire in need to a local council member. And she was in way over her head...maybe. But there was that stubborn, independent streak in her to deal with, as well. First, she would check on Megan, and then consider whether or not to contact a padder. At least she had a plan—sort of.

While the team tracked the intruder, Guor had gone about the sad business of fashioning a litter to carry Cor's body. Now that the team had reassembled and Cor had been gently loaded onto it, Ovek spoke a few words about his sacrifice, but urged them to focus on the mission. The priority was to reach their destination before daylight and find a safe haven from which to conduct their recon. They were behind schedule now, and he meant to get them back on track. Nol took the forward position once again with Beel taking up the rear. Taven and Rahon carried the litter. They worked their way due west to the edge of the forest where it was bounded by a shallow river. It ran along a narrow ravine bordered by dense reeds and thickets, thick willows, and tangled, thorny trees. On the opposite side the land was open and flat, appointed with public benches and a dark, narrow roadway meandering through the green. The river turned westward here, heading in exactly the direction Ovek was leading the team. As long as it guided them toward their destination, he decided to travel along the bank. In the distance several bridges cut across the water, their dark, round tunnels promising ample cover and safe passage under the roads. Besides, the river guaranteed a ready source of fresh water.

The sun was just peeking over the horizon as they approached the third bridge. No one spoke, but they shared the same thought. Ovek knew it all too well: the inhabitants of this planet were not at all what they had expected from the looks of things. Sure, it was a typical transitional civilization, sophisticated and cultured in a technologically crude manner. They had seen hundreds of worlds like this. But the inhabitants seemed far from typical. They had been stunned by the brutality of the attack on Cor. The level of savagery was more than equal to that of a black ops strike by the emperor's negotiations task force, as the emperor euphemistically called it. While Ovek, especially, wasn't particularly proud of the emperor for those kinds of tactics, they did serve the greater good. But here, without reason, this savagery had been tantamount to murder. It served no purpose. True, the creature probably had been terrified of Cor, but it seemed odd that she had tried to carry his body away, as if to keep him for a trophy. He was certain, too, when he had first returned to the clearing, that she had been trying to consume his flesh. It was a haunting image that he found impossible to erase. It disturbed him in a way he didn't want to acknowledge, not even to himself. It made his scales stand on end and his blood drain from his primary regulatory chambers. It was an image that reminded him of sleep visions he had had as a fledgling—weird, terrible visions that forced him to wake up screaming in the middle of his sleep sessions.

Now they were only six against an entire planet of these crazed, barbaric monsters. Also, it had not escaped their attention that Cor's axe was completely clean when Taven had retried it. There was not a drop of blood on it. Cor was powerful and skilled with the blade, yet this delicate, nubile had handled him as though he were newly hatched. Resting now under the bridge, staring down at Cor's body, Ovek knew his thoughts reflected those of this team. They were all seasoned soldiers. Each had seen countless battles, yet he, as they all did, still knew the fear of death. Moreover, none was willing to sacrifice his life needlessly, especially to the likes of the ghastly beasts inhabiting this peculiar world. It was a soldier's job to kill the enemy, not the other way around. Being a good soldier and doing the job well meant staying alive. A dead soldier never completed a mission, but sometimes, like Cor, they contributed in ways civilians found difficult to understand. Sometimes, by dying, a soldier helped the team to recognize exactly what they were up against. In certain circumstances, to a soldier, fear and the discipline to overcome it are the only things that truly matter. Death is the constant reminder of that supposition. Cor's death exposed the true nature of the inhabitants of this planet, opening a window that revealed a danger far greater than the troopers had anticipated, and the fear within each of them had risen because of it. These aliens were savages and barbarians, out of step with the level of technology they possessed, and there was something unsettling in that. The troopers would have to match their fear with equal resolve. Looking down at Cor's body now and knowing how easily this mighty warrior had fallen, they each swore that the next body lying at their feet would not be one of their own.

Far to the right of the river was an area packed with dwellings and storage facilities. It was crisscrossed with roadways on which several vehicles moved rather slowly. Occasionally one would traverse the very bridge under which they had hidden themselves. They recognized the sound and smell of internal combustion engines. Their use was generally phased out on transitional worlds and banned on fully allied planets, incrementally replaced by higher technology until the planet's ecosystem was in harmony with the empire's purposes and standards. Hover engines developed by the Juggernauts were the most commonly employed form of ground transport utilized by the empire. Nol broke the silence just moments after one of the vehicles rolled past. "These brutes would be better off with some ion drives," he sneered. They just stared at each other knowingly, nodding their agreement.

Checking downstream, Ovek noticed a thicket of dense, short trees and shrubs. Most everything was the color of dried blood, tangled and leafless, surrounded by coarse, unruly grass. Contrasting them, were the narrow white trees like severe, disciplined sentinels standing in formation at the edge of the bank and formed into a battalion running far to his left. Though he had viewed the land only briefly, he was certain this was the type of woodland he had seen in the glow of the flaming dart. They were close to the spot where the transponder had detached. He was sure of it. The water under the bridge was not deep; it would reach to their thighs at most. Crossing here would be fairly easy, and the odds were good that breaking from under the bridge at double time would secure them in the woodland before another vehicle crossed the bridge. Though the star was nearly over the horizon now, and they would be caught fully in its glow, he decided it was worth the risk. He laid out his plan. "Once we reach the cover of the wood," he said, "we'll continue straight, sticking close to the river until we locate the field. If we're lucky, we'll spot the buildings shortly after."

They traversed a narrow trail through the woods until a deep, crystal pool that had formed in the pocket of an abandoned quarry interrupted the river. Its mirrored surface reflected the overhanging trees and the sheer cliff walls set off around the circumference. They made their way around easily, walking along the wide, sandy ledge surrounding the water. Here and there weather-worn logs and sawed-off stumps were placed strategically around the perimeter for seating. Clearly, the locals pulled aquatics from these waters. This was good to know. The river was much smaller at the point where it fed into the quarry, no more than a steam. Here, at the juncture, fresh water bubbled from deep within the ground and joined with the stream to flow headlong toward the center. Eventually it spilled out over the far edge, cascading out and down over the rocks at the exit point to make its way toward the sea from which they had come. Making their way upstream, just beyond the quarry, they discovered the field Ovek had seen from the dart. Checking to the right, the crop stretched to a clearing in which only a single dwelling stood in the distance. Much further, packed uncomfortably close together, many more appeared vague and diminutive. To their left, a thin wire fence separated the stalks of a dry, brittle crop from the riverbank. Gazing over the field, they could see the two structures just as Ovek had described them, one old and weatherworn, the other kept in better repair. The older structure was probably used for storage, the newer one was probably a dwelling, probably occupied. Fortunately, both were isolated, out here, seemingly, in the middle of nowhere.

"The quarry is our base camp for now," he instructed. "We'll split into teams, keep watch from the wood, locate and recover the transponder. Meanwhile we need to discover if anyone is in the dwelling and if there is food here. And check it; no one leaves." They understood. The loss of the transponder meant sure death for them all. Taking this base was critical. Anyone attempting to leave must be engaged. Anyone resisting was to be killed. Fighting would be hand to hand to the very last if necessary.

Ovek and Nol scouted the field while the team tended to Cor.

Rahon and Beel dug a suitable pit in the side of the quarry while Taven and Guor gathered rocks to disguise and seal the entrance. It was a poor substitute for the fused glastine eggcrypt in which he would someday rest on his home world of Egania, but for now, it would serve.

"There," Ovek pointed to a fresh scar near the center of the field, "that looks like an impact trail in the soil. I'm going to chance it." He proceeded to low crawl to the near end of the track where the soil had been pushed into a semispherical mound. He rummaged through the soil, digging furiously, unearthing nothing. He returned moments later empty handed. "It's gone," he said, "but the footprints around the spot tell the story. It's as I feared; someone discovered it." It was difficult not to let some disappoint register in his voice.

"What's the game then, Cap'n?" Nol raised his bony eye ridge.

"Odds are the transponder is inside the dwelling. We'll go in after dark. For now we grab some food and get some rest."

"What about resistance?"

"It's a small building. I'm thinking two, maybe three at most. Perhaps we can catch them asleep. I'm hoping we take hostages and that no one will get hurt. These creatures are tough but, if we can take them by surprise, I think we can do this without bloodshed." Ovek tried to sound optimistic. They weren't really armed for a major skirmish, and at the moment, this wasn't a combat mission. They were in survival mode, pure and simple. But considering the aliens' natural defenses and tactics, their long, cycle-like claws, their deadly fangs and the dreadful way Cor's opponent had gnawed on him, doubt about his plan clearly showed on his face, though he tried his best to disguise it. Nol's expression mimicked his; neither of them seemed convinced. Knowing the transponder was in the hands of the enemy meant, inevitably, it would probably have to be recovered by force. Deep inside they both knew that blood would be spilled, and more than likely Cor would not be the last to die. But Nol nodded eagerly as if the plan were airlock tight. Without another word he went about gathering several of the large, orange gourds scattered about. Beel and Taven joined them shortly after. Ordering them to stand guard, Ovek and Nol returned to the quarry to join Rahon and Guor, which brought the entire team up to date on the situation and the plans for the night's mission. The chicma axe made quick work of the vegetable. The meat was tough and stringy but flavorful and altogether satisfying. There was plenty in the field, and it was a relief knowing there was a ready food supply nearby.

Suddenly, Beel broke into the clearing near the edge of the pool, a piece of the orange rind dangling from his hand. "We've got company," he said in a loud whisper. The troopers moved as one. From the edge of the woods Ovek could clearly see the vehicle and the occupant who had emerged from it standing at the doorway of the dwelling. There was no mistaking her tall, nimble body, the peculiar alien garb, the long, dark, flowing mane. The female who had butchered Cor had made her way to this very spot, although she looked somewhat less formidable in the light of day. But her manner was sure, if not wary and guarded, her movement quick and decisive. She looked around cautiously as she made her way quickly to the short stairway. She seemed to be sniffing the air. This was a trained and clever adversary, to be sure. All plans had to be abandoned. Her arrival changed everything. They had to make their move and make it quickly.

Somehow she had learned something of their plan, and Ovek meant to put an end to her deadly meddling here and now. He split the unit into three groups, sending Beel and Guor behind the ruined structure to come at the dwelling from the opposite side. Taven and Rahon would approach directly from the left. He and Nol would come around from the right through the reed field. They didn't have time to do the recon Ovek would have liked, but they could see a door on the left and another where the female had been standing just moments before. This was not the way Ovek wanted the mission to play out. But surely, she was here for a purpose. Her arrival here was no coincidence. They had to get inside and pacify the situation. They could not allow these creatures to set up a defensive posture or contact reinforcements. This fragile-looking creature may be a primitive brute, but she was no fool. She was outnumbered and likely to take the appropriate measures to even the odds. Also, it had not escaped Ovek's attention just how easily she had eluded them in the woods the night before. She was clever as well as deadly, and he would not underestimate her as Cor had done.

It took a moment for Megan to answer. She always turned the TV up much too loud. The amplified volume of Schwarzenegger's commanding voice and Silvestri's driving music literally rattled the heavy door. Finally, still wearing her pajamas, she opened up in the middle of the third barrage of knocks, a coffee mug the size of a coconut dangling precariously from her finger.

"Hi," she said cheerfully. "I was thinking about calling you."

Instinctively Kara snuck a furtive glance toward the road and the wood, then fired an all-too-obvious look over her shoulder for good measure. "What's wrong?" Megan inquired. She had never seen Kara look quite so anxious before.

"I'll tell you in a minute," Kara responded quickly, although, in truth, she hadn't a clue what to tell her. "Let's get inside." With that she shuffled Megan back into the house and locked the door behind her. "First, turn the TV off and get dressed." She knew her only recourse now was a really clever lie. "I'm in a lot of trouble, and I need your help." This was a good start. That much of it was true. "There are some people after me, and I need your help." Now she was winging it. The truth was about to be stretched a light year or two.

"Should I call the police?" Megan looked puzzled. Surely, Kara could have done that herself.

"No, this is kind of a sensitive situation. I don't want the police involved. I need a place to hide, and I really don't want to be alone. I thought perhaps we could stay at the cabin for a few days, until this all blows over?" Kara thought if she were vague enough Megan would be eager to learn more and hurry a bit. She had no doubt from the start that Megan would come with her. It was just a matter of how quickly she could get her moving.

"Sure, just let me get a few things together."

"Okay, but please hurry. I think they were following me."

"Oh," Megan looked worried. "All right, then, I'll just take my purse and..."

"Do you still have your guns?" Kara interrupted.

"Well, my dad's .38 and a shotgun." She answered calmly enough, but her eyes went wide at the question. "I sold the hunting rifles. Now that Dad's gone, I don't think I'll want to go much anymore. But I did keep the .22 for targets and for those fucking squirrels that keep jumping on me out of the woodpile. I stored that at the cabin."

"Which do you like, shotgun or pistol?" Kara asked coolly.

"Well," Megan responded readily, "it's easy to do a lot of damage with some well-aimed buckshot."

"All right, give me the .38. How are we fixed for ammo?" Kara called after her as Megan dragged the gun box from the kitchen pantry.

"Take a look," Megan said, opening it. Her dad was responsible for the contents. He had carved two careers out of a single passion, the love of his country. He had been a good soldier and a smart cop. But the passion came from being just a country boy at heart. Like most typical Wisconsinites he loved the outdoors, fishing and hunting and the like, and he was accustomed to surviving in the rough—and he believed in always being prepared. There was enough ammo in the box to keep Butch and Sundance holed up for a week.

Megan cradled the shotgun, loading it while Kara removed the holster from the leather harness. Standing in her pajamas holding the huge rifle made for a comical picture despite the gravity of the situation, and Kara fought the urge to beam a nervous smile in her direction. Instead, she focused on her equipment, unbuckling a few straps that secured her pipe guard and fixed the holster to her shin. She loaded the revolver and resolutely snapped it into place, then distributed a handful of shells into the various zippered pockets of her bustier. With the shotgun firmly in her grip, Megan didn't seem quite as frightened as she had a moment before, but, had she known the nature of the adversary eying her farm with firm and desperate resolve she may very well have been, and quite likely should have been.

"Before we go I wanted to ask if you found something today..." Kara's query was cut short by a sudden, earsplitting crash. The front door exploded from its hinges and somersaulted into the far wall.

Nol rushed in through the gaping hole where the door had been. The oak slab hit the dividing wall and bounced straight back, nearly clipping him at the knees. He leapt into the air, attempting to avoid the ricochet. The edge caught him in the foot, slowing him down momentarily. Megan's eyes went wide as she caught sight of Nol bounding toward her and Kara standing at the dividing arch near the kitchen. Nol shortened the distance in huge, bounding strides, his head fan brushing the ceiling on his last jump. Megan stood transfixed, holding the shotgun tightly, angled toward the ceiling. Then, as so often happens when in battle mode, time itself seems to slow down. Kara instinctively turned to head him off but heard the sound of Ovek's fist bursting the back door jamb. She saw him an instant later rushing in the back door on the far side of the kitchen opposite Megan. This was the leader, the huge one she had noted giving commands in the woods. Striking, powerful. Clearly he was the one she must deal with.

"Megan, the gun!" she yelled. Her voice felt thick and distant, as if coming from someplace vaguely remembered. Yet, this short reminder was all she had time to say. Nol was descending upon Megan like a titan from the heavens. Megan pumped the twelve-gauge and planted her foot, aiming the gun at the center of his chest. But even as she brought the butt of the rifle level with her hip, Nol spotted her aim and twisted to his right. A shoulder roll and some quick footwork carried him out of harm's way. The sudden blast filled the air with buckshot where he had been a split second before, disintegrating a chunk of drywall into airborne grit and powder.

Although the vampire code discouraged revealing her true nature, the rule applied to normal, daily circumstance. This was hardly it. If she and Megan were to survive this attack, something had to be sacrificed. Kara feared it would have to be her secret. She would try to prevent that if she could, but she doubted it. She went for the .38.

The revolver found its way into her hand before she was halfway over the top of the table. One powerful leap had catapulted her directly into Ovek's path as he cut diagonally across the kitchen, the .38 aimed ominously at his left eye as Kara lighted directly in his path. Kara was fast, and the gun recoiled slightly as she let loose a round aimed squarely at his head. But Ovek had been in this position many times and leaned far back before her finger could twitch against the trigger. His boot snapped hard against her right bicep flinging her arm backward. The revolver discharged a second time, sending another round uselessly into the ceiling. A small drizzle of plaster rained down onto the center of the table. Allowing the momentum of Ovek's kick to augment her pivot, she brought the revolver around in an attempt to target his chest. He spun quickly, landing a roundhouse kick to the side of the gun. The blow sent it reeling over the kitchen table and down the hallway toward the utility door.

Kara was a skilled fighter in her domesticated mode, but unless she transformed into full vampire form, she would be no match for this trained killer, and she knew it. And things were about to get much worse. Megan was pumping away with the twelve gauge, keeping Nol at bay as two more of these odious creatures pounded their way through the utility door even as Kara glanced at it. From the corner of her eye she saw Beel's massive boot crash through the front door on the far side of the living room. They had surrounded the house and were now coming at them from all sides. Her pupils began their involuntary dilation, and the lubrication levels at the entrances to her interior canine vestibules increased dramatically. Her adrenaline levels were increasing with each microsecond; her heartbeat was rocketing out of control. The very air around her became crystal clear. The dust particles seemed to drift by more slowly.

The creatures seemed heavier, more sluggish, offering her an opportunity to plan a strategy, to gather her thoughts. She could hear their breath inhaled and expelled between the deafening blasts of Megan's gun as her ears softened and extended, their fine silken hairs reacting to the sensitive changes in the air around her. Her secret was about to be revealed. Survival instincts were taking over, and now there was no sensible reason to put a stop to it. Kara spun around again and side-flipped onto the table. In midair she threw her arms back and unleashed her claws. "Megan!" she screamed out in a hissing cry. Bewildered by the bizarre events unfolding around her, Megan threw Kara a momentary glance. But her bewilderment only deepened at the sight of Kara standing on the tabletop, holding one of these gruesome creatures at bay.

Powerful white tusks protruded from her upper jaws to the bottom of her chin. Long, iridescent claws like scimitars protruded from her knuckles as she stood defiantly against the creature slowly circling the table. Her veins appeared more prominent, as if her skin were paper-thin. Her fairy ears protruding through her dense black mane were covered with a soft, snowy down. Her muscles seemed slightly larger, more refined and delineated. Her calves filled her slacks to their absolute limit. Her shoulders and arms exhibited a shapely bulk, which only moments before had not existed. She was Kara, yet she was no longer the woman she had been just moments before. She was primitive and bestial, terrifying and beautiful all at once.

For Megan, at this moment of crisis, each detail seemed crisp and clear. Seeing Kara up there on the table sent a chill though her but boosted her confidence at the same time, even though she couldn't comprehend what was happening—none of it. All she understood was that Kara was trying to protect her. She focused on that, embracing it for whatever degree of comfort it might bring.

Kara reached out to her, encouraging her to jump onto the table, and she was more than happy to oblige.

"Watch my back," Kara told her. "I'll take care of the big one."

Seeing his chance to move in, Nol made a leap at Megan's feet as she cleared the table's edge. He was greeted by a sudden swipe of Kara's claws as she turned her attention once again to Ovek. The Chicma axe flipped out of his hand, striking the wall behind him. He slid under the table holding his bleeding cheek, blinking wildly in an attempt to clear his vision. He recalled the speed of this changeling and recognized the foolishness of his move. He flung himself free of the table in order to reclaim the axe and regroup on the opposite side of the wall. He successfully retrieved the axe but nearly lost his foot from a tremendous blast that annihilated a chunk of the dividing wall just as he rounded the corner. He flung his head around in time to catch a glimpse of Megan crouching next to Kara, pumping the rifle in order to refill the chamber, an extremely satisfied expression frozen on her face.

Kara stood up, sizing up Ovek, weighing her options. He stood his ground, doing the same. At this point, none of them seemed eager to make a decisive move, but they had the advantage, and she knew it. She and Megan were trapped, two against many, with limited ammo—out maneuvered, outnumbered, with nowhere to run! The odds were with these dinosaurs. Maybe it was time to bargain? Perhaps Megan had this transponder, and it would be a good idea to simply give it them. But Kara doubted she had it. How could she have gotten something belonging to these aliens? Besides, it might be wise to be cautious in that matter. There was too much mystery surrounding these creatures and their missing device. If Megan did have it, perhaps it was best to keep it, and this was hardly the time to discuss such matters. No. Negotiation, at this point, was probably not an option. Besides, Kara had killed one of them. More than likely, discovering her here was reason enough to kill them both. They didn't need any greater motive than revenge. Well, they would not find her to be easy prey, and to take Megan they would have to take her down first. Perhaps the best thing to do was to prove the age-old adage that *offense made the best defense*. With two more of these brutes coming up the hallway and yet another coming through the living room, it would be prudent to dispatch them in short order. She and Megan were *not* going die at the hands of these monsters.

Having heard the gunshots, Taven and Rahon quickly scurried into a room midway between the outer door and the kitchen. The room was large enough with ample cover but the hallway was narrow, and immediately they realized their strategic disadvantage. In an attempt to move forward, they could be easily picked off one at a time. They would have to wait for a more opportune moment to advance. Megan used the opportunity to reload. Then, standing boldly in the center of the table, she pumped and unloaded on Taven as he brazenly offered his arm and shoulder to her from around the corner of the doorway. A few of the pellets tore into him, but not enough to do any real harm. It was merely a test of her resolve, and her aim. Most of the pellets simply tore up the side of the hallway wall. But the action had answered Taven's question.

"Kara!" Megan screamed, but far too late. She let loose a round that blew a hole in her ceiling above Taven's head. His mandat knife zipped past Megan to dig deeply into the fleshy part of Kara's shoulder. Megan winced involuntarily as she reached up quickly to draw it out. Kara barely flinched. She hadn't even noticed until she felt the slight tug and the momentary spurt of blood that trailed down her back. She turned, her purple-and-yellow eyes fixed in a blank, cool stare. The jet-black pupils were monstrous oval pools that narrowed into long, vertical slits as she settled on Megan's face. Whatever her kinship to humanity, that line between man and beast in her continued to blur, continued to spiral out of control. Normally, when the bloodlust was upon her, when tracking or during combat, her instincts asserted themselves, and quite often she felt the animal rise within her. But never like this. At this moment she could see only through the eye of the beast. Her thoughts seemed projected to her mind as a series of rapid images only. She understood more than reasoned. She was aware of the combat in which she was engaged and of protecting the life of a friend she loved but she did not *consider it*, she only *felt it*. This was her territory and these invaders, these interlopers, had no business being here. Their very presence was an insult to her authority, to her claim of supremacy over this place, to this land and the life it harbored. She could smell their insolence. And she could hear their footfalls, their breath sucking and discharging, the faint, sticky clicking of their nostril slits as they opened and closed from the exertion, especially the one whose face she had lacerated. She could hear their voices, spewing confused simultaneous whispers, or now and then a loudly barked command.

Everything still moved in slow motion, thick and ponderous. Had she been on the table for seconds, minutes? It was impossible to know. She was lost to the beast, guided by some imperative within the Chimera virus which had been aroused by the arrival of these beings, its genetic memory incited now to complete awareness. She could feel it like a separate life within her blood, communicate with it, direct it, mentally command it to supplement her for additional power and endurance. She had never experienced such control, yet she had never known such slavery to the agent that made her vampire.

Megan spun, pumped, and fired down the hallway toward her bedroom where Taven and Rahon were secured. As she did, Nol made a quick rush and retreat past the arched doorway. She turned toward the movement. He dove past the door again in the opposite direction like a target at an amusement park. Kara knew his rapid, unexpected passes were meant to check their positions. Megan thought they were showboat maneuvers and told him so. "Fucking showoff," she sneered through the doorway. She punctuated the epithet with a blast fired directly through the wall.

Nol scrambled to take cover behind the sofa, blood pouring from a plaster-covered wound on his shoulder. All the while, Kara never allowed herself to lose track of their leader, the big one circling the table. He had a mean-looking knife tucked in he belt but seemed content to keep his hands free for the moment. No doubt he meant to strangle her with his bare hands and to brag about it later. This group struck her as a race of barbaric, macho bastards. She could easily envision them sitting around their camp fire swapping war tales, exaggerated stories of their murderous kills, heroic lies to elevate their pathetic lives to some level of imagined greatness. This tale, the story of how they managed to best these two devil women, would probably find its way into their lore.

Kara, however, had other plans. She had no intention of allowing herself and Megan to become mere anecdotal characters in the annals of these primitives. She did a forward flip combined with a full twist off the table to land squarely behind him. He hadn't expected the move. She pulled her arm back in mid-flight and delivered a devastating blow the moment she hit the floor. His reflexes were quick, and he launched himself forward in time to receive only a glancing blow to the back of his head. Blood was draining down his back, but the wounds were not deep, and she had missed the sensitive nerve tendrils at the critical juncture where his head fan merged with his spinal node. He knew, however, she would attempt another strike with the other claw at any moment. However, the table was directly in front of him. He had a nanocycle to decide—if he launched himself under it, he might come out the other side and take a gun blast in the head from the female standing directly over him. He couldn't risk that. He had only one sure move, and he took it. He dropped to his left knee. Kara's left arm swung over his head in a wide arch that would have decapitated him. Kicking back quickly with his right, Ovek intended to wrap his leg around Kara's ankles and sweep her onto the floor. The maneuver would allow him to address her face to face again, at least. The tactic worked, sort of. Before his leg could drop her to the floor, she went straight into the air, laying her back flat against the ceiling. She meant to land on him like a flying denizen. He grabbed a kitchen chair by the leg and sprang upright. Swinging in a broad arch as she dove down, he cracked it across her chest. She paid little attention to his puny defense. The chair exploded into an array of shards and chips that seemed to float in the air like autumn leaves. She snatched one of the larger slivers in midair, spun quickly on her heels, and threw it like a dagger at the creature coming through the front door. Beel heard a distinct popping sound as the wooden spike severed his rib. He ducked behind the wall lest more of these darts should be tossed his way.

Megan bounded off the table and fired several volleys as a curt reminder to the monsters in her bedroom that she hadn't forgotten them. There at the corner near the pantry was the box of ammunition. She reloaded, stuffing in as many rounds as the gun would hold, then marched directly up the hallway. She fired a round that took a huge bite out of the door jam. She heard them scuffle away. The entire march down the hallway, however, had been false bravado. She had no intention of going in there after them. She bent down and scooped up the .38 which had slid nearly within their reach, then ran back to the table, around to the right, directly behind Ovek. There was nothing fake about this maneuver. She had an easy shot at him, and Kara was moving on him from the opposite side of the room.

Ovek knew this was a dangerous situation. If the changeling behind him fired the weapon he would be killed. Should she suddenly transform, as the other had, the two of them could easily tear him apart. The mission plan had not worked. The intruder had forced his hand, and the result was a disaster. The entire mission was in jeopardy. If these fragile-looking country dwellers were skilled and ruthless combatants, then this entire planet must be populated by natural warriors. He had heard rumors of worlds on which the inhabitants were so gifted in the art of soldering that they were indoctrinated into the planetary military at birth, and served for a lifetime. This surely must be such a world. The unit had met their match, in this battle, at least. Perhaps, for now, a retreat and regroup was in order. They needed a better plan. But even as these thoughts flashed though his mind, Megan circled behind him, bringing the muzzle of the revolver level with his head. As she did, she skirted sideways, making her way toward a set of keys dangling from the convenience hanger near the door. She could do more than simply hold a few of them off! She could be the means of their escape! If she could just get to the keys! Kara began edging ever so slightly in the same direction.

But Ovek, backing up now toward the open archway, desperately attempting to keep tabs on them both, could easily determine their intentions. He couldn't let them escape, not without knowing the location of the transponder! Ovek was certain it was hidden somewhere nearby. Besides, if they escaped, surely they would return with reinforcements. The unit would never leave this planet alive. This was their only chance. He had to take a chance. "You can't leave," he told her. Taven and Rahon heard Ovek's voice, peered out beyond the doorway and made their move. Ovek snared Megan's arm as she turned and made a sudden dash for the door, hoping beyond hope she wouldn't send a round squarely between his eyes. Ovek squeezed tightly enough that she dropped the revolver at his feet. Megan screamed and brought the shotgun around. Suddenly Rahon darted around the corner. Seeing Megan's gun coming to bear on Ovek, he threw his mandat knife at her head, but his aim was low and it passed fully through the base of her neck instead. She dropped the shotgun, struggling feebly to remove it, but fell unconscious even before she could get a decent grip on the hilt. As if an ill wind had blown her directly in front of him, Ovek found himself face to face with Kara, her breath like a perfume inspiring images of flowers laid to adorn the eternal egg.

Kara felt a rage explode within her. Time itself was reduced to meaningless conjecture, as if the universe were turned inside-out, and the reality of movement which is the very essence of its passage, the measure of what was, and is, and what will be...was gone. Nothing moved. In less than an instant of a moment she could have killed them all. But instinctively she knew it was mere illusion and focused her attention on their leader. When she had heard him say, "You can't leave," and a moment later she saw the knife impale Megan, her mind went completely numb, as if an oily blackness had swept across it. Her purple irises floating in iridescent pools of glistening blackness were pinpointed with minute yellow orbs, and her breath reverberated in deep, audible hisses. Her ivory skin seemed to glow of its own accord, and her tusks glistened with the sheen of viral essence. She snapped her claws outward, displaying their full ten-inch deadliness, bent her knees, and threw back her head tauntingly. She hissed and spit at him like a wildcat. Circling slowly round him momentarily, she suddenly launched herself at his throat. She was a dreadful storm, moving like a terrible, unexpected gale. One moment she was eyeing him keenly, the next moment she was on him, her fangs sinking deeply into his neck, the familiar and awful metallic flavor of his blood filling her mouth. She released him and bit into his neck again near the back, shaking her head, hoping to snap his spine. He would pay dearly for killing Megan; she would make certain of that. But even as she clutched and bit down on him, she saw Megan's arms and legs flail, her fingers twitch, and she heard her heart beating faintly.

Kara opened her mouth wide to release her grip on Ovek. The necks of these beasts were so thick and the muscles so powerful she was wasting time bleeding him this way. Perhaps he was dead already. In any event, she was determined to end it. She leaned back, drew her fist even with the side of her head, intending to skewer his heart and be done with him. However, instead of delivering the deathblow, she was forced to divert her attention to the shotgun staring directly into her eyes.

Nol felt he had something to say about this upstart changeling thinking she was going to dispatch the captain so easily. No sooner had she sunk her teeth into him than he had crossed the room in a few swift leaps and a shoulder roll. A moment later the shotgun was in his grasp. She bit down on him again, and he pumped the rifle for good measure. He was sure a perfectly good cartridge ejected from the chamber would be effective, and he was uncertain, now, if the weapon had ammunition but, at this point, a bluff with this antique was a better tactic than doing nothing at all. She leaned back anticipating she might attempt a third strike on the captain's helpless body. He squared off directly in the middle of her face.

Kara grabbed the barrel of the shotgun and twisted it sideways forcing his finger hard against the trigger. The explosion shattered the glass cupboards above the sink, filling the air with flecks of sparkling detritus. She moved swiftly, then she seemed transparent, as if made of smoke. There was a flurry of motion as the .38 disappeared from the floor and the keys jingled momentarily, whisked from the wall as if by a ghost. The captain lay alone on the floor bleeding and breathing heavily, his legs struggling independently to bring him to his feet. As Kara moved past Nol, her claws cut a wake so close to his face he felt a breeze in the wet blood on his cheek, but before he could bring the barrel around to bear on her, she snapped a kick to the underside of his jaw that sent him tumbling back into the living room. He staggered to his feet, but not before she had retrieved her fallen comrade and had vanished like a spirit god returning to the woods along the river. Nol understood, and he felt he was beginning to understand her. She was in command of this territory. The troops here were her responsibility. She would not leave one of her own in the hands of the enemy. Admirable. But it didn't change his feelings about this alien. Eventually, they would have to kill her.

Summoning all her strength, Kara scooped Megan's body up into her arms. The adrenaline was still pumping madly within her, and she struggled to maintain absolute control. A part of her wanted desperately to stay behind and kill them all. But she opted to snatch the keys from Megan's hand and slip out the door. Spotting Guor coming round the house, she made a beeline for the pickup. A side snap kick to his midsection sent the lumbering beast reeling into the barren tomato garden lining the rear of the house. One tremendous leap carried her over the truck. She settled Megan gingerly into the passenger side. Another leap and a full twist brought her back to the driver's side just as Nol and Rahon pushed their way through the battered kitchen door. As she started up the engine, she heard a loud report and felt a barrage of pellets rip a honeycomb into the side of the truck. A second later she was driving wildly, headlong through the corn stalks toward the creek, leaving a giant gopher trail in her wake. She tore through the fence with an audible ping, across the shallow water, and up the steep bank into the field beyond. As it sped away, weaving left and right, the alien troopers stood dumbfounded, watching the top of the black Chevy cut its erratic swath through the tall stalks. Ovek was among them, holding his neck and breathing hard but standing tall and strong nonetheless. They were gone. But they had been forced to leave in haste and that was something anyway. Perhaps this disaster wasn't quite as disastrous as he had feared. He turned to face his team. "It's difficult to say how much time we have. At any rate, there's nowhere else to go. We had better start looking," he rasped out. "It has to be here somewhere."

"How you holdin' up, Cap'n?" Nol asked, although, because Ovek was on his feet, he knew the answer he would get.

"Fit enough, I suppose," Ovek replied, rubbing his neck. "But the darkworld take her! She nailed me pretty good."

"Well, she didn't hit anything vital," Nol noted. "You're as ornery as ever."

"And I hope to never get over it," Ovek managed a half smile. "But you don't look so good," Ovek said, pointing out the lacerations on Nol's face and the pellet holes in his shoulder.

"Just pride wounds, Cap'n. Never did like a good fight without somethin' to brag about back on homeworld."

"Yeah," Ovek intoned. "I heard that." Then, looking in the direction in which the truck had disappeared, he smartly displayed two horizontal fingers in front of his chest. "I'll rightly give her this, though," he said with some resignation. Nol immediately recognized the sign, *two* victories scored for the opponent. Ovek would not grant her number three.

Chapter 7

Saturday, October 8, 6:37 A.M.: Allen woke early, earlier than he should have considering the time he had finally gotten to bed. He had worked tirelessly on a project for Harley-Davidson until nearly midnight, and when finally he hit the sack, he was sure he had tossed and turned until well past one before fatigue finally tricked him into something resembling a fitful sleep. He sat up and snapped the alarm to the *off* position even though it wouldn't activate for another hour. The volume was set extremely loud as extra insurance and the unanticipated peak noise that interrupted him when he forgot this minor ritual usually caused him to respond with an annoying knee-jerk reaction. On more than one occasion the sudden "mystery music" had given him an instant headache.

He shuffled to the window and threw open the curtains. The scene that greeted him through his bedroom window was actually worth the early wake up—a glimpse into a mythic pantheon. The sun's crescent sliver was barely visible rising from the depths of Lake Michigan, its blazing arc just crowning the hazy horizon fanning delicate rays outward, gifting the earth with translucent feathers of gold. The black veil of night still clung desperately to the heavens, vaguely studded with the delicate remnants of stars that were fading like dissolving jewels in the advancing glare of the rondure Prometheus. He watched the orb forge steadily upward, melting the curtain of deep purple into a soft azure. The blazing eye of the god glared at him through the open curtains of his bedroom. It seemed to question and implicate him with its unwavering stare—*why the hell are you awake so early this morning? what's going on with you boy?*

What was this accusation all about? Why did he feel so uneasy? So unsettled? He certainly wasn't losing any sleep musing over the project; it was moving along rather well. He was quite sure it would be completed ahead of schedule, *today* in fact, which would allow him a well deserved vacation, a few lazy days commuting with nature and a couple of six packs stretch out in a sturdy bass boat on Nagawicka. The weather seemed unnaturally warm and the pike were probably still in thirty-foot water. Perhaps that was the answer to his restlessness, the weather; it was just too damn nice to waste on sleep. Since he was up, he may as well hustle up a decent breakfast and get into his studio to wrap things up.

Actually, it didn't take a lot get him motivated and he never indulged in the art of procrastination. He enjoyed his work. For him, corporate design wasn't a job; it was a contest, a cerebral sport, like fishing. Of course, the contest was not man versus a fish; it was man against himself, besting his last, greatest achievement, but a competition all the same. The angler played according to the rules set by nature; while the designer adhered to parameters dictated by the needs of the business, although the creativity inherent in any project allowed him flexibility and interpretation, at least, during the development stages. That's when he reeled them in. In finalizing the work, the game became a bit more brutal, like a contact sport. The rules became more rigid, and the client, acting as the official, became more demanding. But then the game afforded him the opportunity to make dazzling offensive and defensive maneuvers, to score impressive goals and ultimately to win the coveted prize. And wasn't that the point. After all, the high score, represented by a huge purse, was really the goal—besides a job well done, of course.

He was *good*, the best young designer around. More often than not his preliminary work needed little selling and his final work rarely required much alteration. As a free-lancer he specialized primarily in corporate identity program development, logos and symbols, manuals, signage, ambient architectural enhancements and related marketing materials for new and expanding business. These projects usually involved working with corporate professionals of relatively high level, department heads and vice-presidents. They weren't always real bright, but they were polite and decisive, and they were good listeners; and because of Allen's excellent reputation, his outstanding portfolio, his obvious good looks and charm, he was well received and well treated…and well paid, for this neck of the woods, anyway. He had already made enough money to nearly pay off the mortgage on his new suburban home. For him, it was the perfect place to work. It was spacious with a light, airy interior; the main living area exhibited a thirty-five foot high cathedral ceiling. A circular doorway opened onto an ultra-modern kitchen and the dividing wall was adorned with tall, vertical mirrors adding even greater depth and volume. Just opposite, a natural stone fireplace sliced the pristine, ivory expanse like an avalanche, the natural theme reinforced throughout the room by the giant stone vase, the rough pottery, marble table and matching entertainment center. Outside the front window a hundred-fifty acre pastoral flatland dotted with reedy thickets, young oaks and crab-apple trees served as a virtual private wilderness. In spring and summer rabbits and ground squirrels were everywhere and the crickets were as riotous as *Them* from the sci-fi movie. Before a storm, the kind that forces the clouds in thick and low, turning them white and yellow at the edges, brown and dirty where they hang overhead like an old carpet flapping in the wind, moving slowly like a vaporous slug, the birds gather there like a profuse ribbon blotting out the sky and rattle the widows as they race toward the shelter of the woods just beyond the open field. The house was situated right in the middle of Megan McClurie's farmland. Megan's parents had built it, but their untimely death had forced her to sell it to him. Other than the seasonal farming, there was little activity around him, which suited Allen's sensibilities perfectly.

During the dog days of summer the cooler lake breezes generally kept the wispy clouds at bay, gracing the coastal skies with a perfect pallet of chalky pastels in the morning, and in the darkness the spray of stars sparkled like a slice of freshly split quartz. There were none of the annoying city lights here, nothing to obscure his personal view of the heavens. Only last night, during a break from the work, a meteor shower as beautiful as God's tears slipped from overhead and slid into the lake. He could have sworn they were so close they threatened to drip down onto his roof. It was the most spectacular meteor shower he had seen in quite some time.

He loved this house, the look and feel of it and the location; it felt like living in the country, but was actually close enough to the city that he never felt isolated from the business community he served, never felt removed from the night life surrounding the university. It didn't take long to get to Miller Park or the art museum, the music festivals were held along the lake just minutes up the parkway. And living here in his boyhood haunts kept him close to his friends, and kept him grounded. For now there was comfort in the order and simplicity of the familiar.

Admittedly, he felt a little guilty when buying the home from Megan. After all, her parents had built it knowing the land and the home would someday be part of her inheritance. But she had confessed to Allen that the taxes would be a burden and that he actually would be doing her a huge favor by taking it off her hands. The time simply was not right for her to assume the responsibility. And of course, it had been a perfect opportunity for him. He hadn't even bargained with her. She was too good a friend; he hadn't wanted to take advantage of her or jeopardize their relationship. The thought of haggling with her seemed like trying to low-ball his sister. It just didn't seem right. Besides, the price was right and they both knew it. And now they were neighbors. It was an ideal situation, at least in his mind, for additional reasons he never mentioned. Things were going well for him and someday he might move on. There was always the possibility. The place was perfect for now and he loved it, but if things went his way, someday he might take one of the swank studio apartments in the Third Ward. And if things were going well for Megan, perhaps she would want to reclaim the home for herself. He would make her an offer she simply could not refuse.

After breakfast he made himself as presentable as necessary for the day, which meant a pair of jeans and a tee shirt, and marched himself into the studio to finish the project. The print promotions for the opening of the new Harley-Davidson showroom were finished. The television leads and all the showroom display designs were completed. All that was left was some minor tweaking to the executive promo-packs and some application designs for free advertising specialties. He probably could finish before noon if he put his mind to it.

His studio was located off the south side of the kitchen, just down a short, narrow hallway. It was a generous work area featuring several state-of-the-art computers, a scanner, rail-mounted digital camera, a light table, drafting cabinets. Glass shelves on the east wall contained dozens of new and vintage graphic tools, some of which he used regularly, some of which had gone the way of the eight track since the invasion of computer graphics. Covering nearly the entire north wall was a set of massive sliding glass doors. The electric blinds covering them offered perfect control over the natural lighting and the track mounted halogens overhead were independently controlled by remotes affording him command over changing conditions. The doors opened onto a modest patio where he often played cards or barbecued. He would leave the doors open so that the whole house would fill with the rich, magical aroma of honeyed bratwurst and butter-brushed sweet corn. Often in the evenings, he and Megan and Kara would just sit around downing a sixer of Milwaukee's finest; just taking it easy. Sometimes they would have a luau or order tons of Chinese and play board games or charades. He enjoyed corny, old-fashioned fun like that, and he knew Megan, especially, enjoyed those things, as well. He was certain it reminded her of the happier days when her parents would stage simple parties for the girls during sleepovers, and Kara enjoyed anything that made Megan happy and allowed her to kick back and simply relax for a while. She was always on the go.

His home was enigmatically warm and comfortable despite its austere appearance, being appointed, minimally some might suggest, in modern and ancient Japanese décor, which suited Allen's temperament and taste perfectly. Professionally, he wanted clients to immediately glean something of his understated sense of style. Often, even before they looked at his portfolio, he could tell if they would hire him. It was a gift he had. He could see it in their face, read it in their eyes. And it was even easier if the account exec was an attractive woman; sometimes he could tell as he opened the door to let her in. But to be sure, if the client was willing to hire him, he never took the job unless he was absolutely certain he was right for it. He had his ethics. He had the talent and he knew it, so if the project came with some fringe benefits in the form of a warm and fuzzy with lovely long legs, so much the better. He wasn't a company man, so conflict of interest was never the issue. But professional pride was always a primary concern and he insisted the deal was made before any plans were laid, so to speak. And he had been very busy over the past five years or so. With his reputation he knew he could probably make a lot more money out on either coast where the contacts were more lucrative, and perhaps the fringe benefits might boost his personal life to measures he had never dared dreamed. But he wasn't that ambitious. He had admitted that to himself already. He had modest needs, really, and modest goals. Success to Allen Dakota was just *good* money (it didn't have to be great), good friends, a good beer, a good woman *someday,* and not having to die of some god-damned stress related illness long before his time. Success was the road he was on. So he kept his eyes focused straight ahead, which at the very moment was on the patio doors. He was just about to swivel around and snap on the computer when, from out of nowhere, Megan's truck roared across his patio. First, it crashed headlong into the tangle of miniature trees and stumps which lined the east edge, tossing stones and bits of shattered pottery in every direction, then it reared up on it haunches like a fierce, black demon. It flipped a heavy oak table against the house and then landed hard, bounced several times flattening the barbecue grill into the cement. All the while the tires were spinning wildly, grinding at the metal until it fired the grill toward the rear of the truck like a missile. He twisted his head to the right as he watched the truck disappear along the side of his garage, making its escape toward the street. By the time he was able to focus on the spot where his grill had been, the patio was a nightmare, reduced to a haphazard array of crushed and shattered memories, and in an instant, for a brief, panicky moment, he had a premonition that his life was coming undone. Though he was not superstitious, for hours afterward he was unable to rid himself of the odd notion that the truck had been possessed, that Kara had not been in control of it at all; it seemed as though an evil spirit had commandeered it. He couldn't help feeling its appearance had been an omen, a portent of dreadful things to come.

Chapter 8

The pickup raced westward on interstate ninety-four. Kara continually urged the speedometer over the limit, tempting fate, keeping a watchful eye for the highway patrol. This was a dangerous situation. A simple speeding ticket could lead to disaster for them both. How would she explain Megan, who lay unconscious on the seat beside her, an exotic, jewel-encrusted blade buried deeply in her neck? All hell would probably break loose. They would dispatch an ambulance or the Flight-For-Life helicopter and rush her to the hospital, which would be the end of her for sure. She was alive now only because Kara had applied a dab of vampire saliva to the wound. The viral essence had displayed its recuperative powers immediately, slowed the bleeding to a trickle, and then stopped it altogether. The hospital staff, for all its expertise, could never understand that, for all intents and purposes, Megan was already dead. Should her connection to Kara be broken, she could not last the day under any circumstances. Kara would be arrested on a number of charges; at least, they would try. She would be forced to fight and make her escape…to become a fugitive; she could never allow that to happen. So, she drove quickly, but cautiously, ever mindful of those tricky speed traps. She knew them all; she had sprung each of them with her Lexus at one time or another, and she slowed to the speed limit at just the right moments and pounded the accelerator when she was in the clear. One lucky break this morning, there weren't many cars on the road. The truck was a dog in heavy traffic; otherwise she would be grinding the gears for sure. They were making good time and once secured at the cabin Megan would be her old self again…and more.

The instant Megan had fallen Kara realized how much she would miss this vivacious little imp. Megan was the perpetual sit-com of her existence, without her the familiar day-to-day routines would pass like droll, sad dramas. Megan added the laugh track to life, and for Kara, as much as for anyone, the smiles and the laughter obscured the evil and the ugliness she saw on a regular basis. The Bloodwarriors saw more than most vampires; it came with the territory. Megan was the buffer between her dichotomous realities, between the visible, mundane world of humanity and the veiled, perilous world of vampire vigilantes. She and Megan were kindred spirits sharing the quiet intimacies of life, more often than not managing the day-to-day burdens that gathered one upon the other. She listened, and never complained when Kara needed time alone. Megan cared; without pretense or effort, Megan's faithfulness defined the nature of their friendship. There were certain aspects of Kara's behavior and routines, even physical characteristics, which others might have questioned, but Megan did not. (Her eyes were so incredibly sensual and luminous, like the eyes of a panther hiding in the deep shadows. They were almost too wondrous to be human; they might have been plucked from an angel or a god! Megan never seriously questioned this rare and exotic gift; she merely whispered compliments, as if it might be sacrilege to overanalyze such singular loveliness. During workout sessions, she had often watched in rapt fascination as Kara executed some clever martial arts maneuvers; she was astonished at her strength and agility—and she clapped. That was all. And she knew about the dominatrix clothing and the collection of peculiar weapons, and more than once she had discovered blood on Kara's clothing where it should not have been.) Because she had faith; and deep insight, she knew Kara was different, and special, and whatever secrets existed, there could never be any true evil attached to them. She never trespassed into *that* sacred territory; she respected Kara far too much to dig too deeply. That respect endeared Megan to her far more than anything else.

In that awful moment, the moment Megan lay at her feet, Kara *felt* the tragedy of it far more than she had *considered* it. She felt it deeply.

From the moment the battle had begun she had continued to retreat from the world of logic and reason. She was being guided by instinct alone, prompted solely by the animal aspects within her. When Megan lay dying at her feet, those impulses, which now were only a jumbled memory, had become a conflux of instinctive urgency—*remove your mate to a place of safety…nothing else matters…save her…do all that is necessary*. Now that she was able to reason it through, she realized that nothing had changed. She felt that same urgency and her decision stood firm, and she was headed exactly where the imperative had compelled her…to the cabin.

Finally, it came into view. The twenty-eight miles had seemed like a million, and it had been a difficult drive. The truth was, she had never been very good behind the wheel of the truck. She hated stick shift, it was just one of those damn things she could never get use to.

"You just have a mental block," Allen had once said. "It wouldn't be a problem if you didn't have such a bad attitude." It was good thing he had been smiling at the time or she might have poked him in the eye.

"Yes I do," she fired back, teasing him. "But if I have to have a problem, an attitude problem is the best kind to have." But of course, he was right.

Earlier today, her reckless maneuver through his yard had been the first serious incarnation of that problem. She remembered having been airborne momentarily and the horrific sound of crushing metal. At the time however, she had been attempting to keep Megan from tumbling to the floorboards, and she had been rattled from the events of the morning. From the moment she had sped away, images of the lizard men and the battle had flooded her mind. Flashes of their scaly, horned-ridged faces and finned heads had dodged in and out of her mind's eye as she weaved through the cornfield and into Allen's yard, across his patio and onto the street beyond. She realized in some vague and unsympathetic way that she had done considerable damage to his yard, but she wasn't sure exactly what that had been. Anyway, she was confident she could straighten it out with him another day. Right now her only concern was Megan, barely breathing, weak and pale, lying in a fetal position on the seat beside her. She had lost far too much blood and the vampire first aid Kara had administered earlier would not hold her to this world much longer. She needed serious intervention. She needed the infusion.

It was shortly after nine when the truck found it way to the end of the long gravel drive and stopped at the edge of the clearing. Kara eased Megan out and rushed across the frontage lot toward the cabin. The real estate sign was ensconced in the yard like a grave marker, an unwelcome omen mocking Kara upon their arrival. She gave it a kick as she ran past, sending it skidding across the lawn to disappear into the maze of straight pines and cedars. Megan wouldn't be selling the cabin now; she could keep it since money wasn't going to be the worrisome issue for her it used to be. Kara would see to that. In the past, it would have been condescending and presumptuous to help her too much, to rob Megan of her humanity, of her right to grow up facing the challenges and triumphs that are her birthright. It would have been wrong not to allow her to overcome the adversities which life placed before her. But now, things were different, and they always would be from this day forward. Cradling Megan in her arms she threw the cabin door open and hurried inside. She knew what had to be done. She couldn't let her go, not like this. Someday, if she chose to leave, that would be the way of things, but as Megan hovered now near the dark horizon, she needed a chance and a choice. As things stood now, she had neither, and the odds were she would not live to see the setting sun. Kara could feel her slipping away even as she carried her toward the bed. She had simply lost too much blood and her fragile body was failing. Kara could feel her body turning colder and hear her heartbeat grow faint and more distant as though she had been tossed over a precipice, falling into an endless pit. She couldn't know if this is what Megan would choose, but there was no more time to consider the question; it had to be done now or Megan would be dead in a matter of minutes. She loved her too much to simply let her go.

The cabin had been vacant for months and the dark, lifeless interior encased the chilly air like a tomb. The fireplace was a barren, black cave littered with scraps of charred wood and dirty powder. There wasn't time to build a fire so she simply pulled back the blankets and lay Megan on the bed. She undressed quickly and dropped her cloths in a heap on the floor and hesitated for only a moment, contemplating the implications of what she was about to do. She desperately needed to know that she was doing the right thing, that ultimately Megan would be grateful and love her for it. But she couldn't know for sure; she could only hope. She could only trust her instincts and keep faith in the deep and intimate friendship she and Megan had shared these many years. Quickly, but very carefully, she undressed Megan and lay next to her, pressing the full length of their bodies together. Megan was a glacier, the iciness so intense her flesh chilled Kara to the bone. Kara wrapped herself around her, gently rubbed her arms and thighs, her shoulders, her cheeks and brow. Their feet touched and their legs intertwined. All the while Kara poured more of her warmth into her, surrounded her with it. She messaged the small of Megan's back, her buttocks. She spread her legs and pushed into Megan, pressing the warmest part against her, praying the moist heat would penetrate deeply enough to keep the spark of life within her. She covered Megan's mouth with her lips forcing hot breath into her. She pressed her hands hard against Megan's breasts, squeezed and kneaded, urged the blood to move through her; pushed against her chest, encouraged her heart onward, nurtured it, willed it to grow ever more distinct. Finally, when the time was right, when the heartbeat felt strong, her body warm and dewy, her chest heaving in a deep and regular rhythm and her hips pressed urgently upward, Kara wrapped her hands around the jeweled hilt and, in one swift, bold motion, pulled it from her throat. A spurt of blood shot onto Kara's face. Megan had so little to be wasted and Kara's mouth covered her neck quickly. Ever so gently, she lowered her fangs from their vestibules into the long, deep slit the blade had left behind. The glistening fluid coating them helped slip them in. She lay beside Megan for a long time, working her fangs gently, embracing the life within her as it slowly returned in the form of soft caresses from Megan's finger tips, the tightening of her arms, the fluttering of her eye lids, her soft moans and incoherent whispers. Eventually Megan opened her eyes and stared at her. She wasn't fully conscious, only vaguely aware of her surroundings. Her mind drifted in and out of her familiar world, trapped somewhere between the ambiguous realms of knowing and feeling. With Megan's lovely, blue eyes fixed on her, Kara felt her body push hard, and her arms cling more tightly. Then she fell into a deep sleep once again.

Finally, once Kara had released enough of herself into Megan, she slowly retracted her fangs, held her in her arms and kissed her cheeks. It was done. She would live. In fact, now that she had been transformed, she would live much longer than if she had remained merely human. Her entire life now would be forever changed, bonded to Kara in a manner beyond human understanding. It was a bonding that would assume its true identity based upon a mutual acceptance and embrace. Call it a pairing, a kinship, or a sisterhood. They would choose, over time. Their mutual trust and respect, their friendship or love would determine the nature of their bond, eventually. Megan was Kara's responsibility now; she was Kara's shadow vampire. It was a serious proposition, especially for Kara, and a wondrous, lifelong gift for them both. Should Megan's love for her never blossom, they might still share a lifelong friendship, and that alone would be enough. They were comfortable with one another, and that was a foundation upon which Kara could easily build. Megan was the only woman, except for her mother, with whom she had ever shared any intimate details of her life. As a child, those details had been the joys and the fears of a child, and her mother had been there for her to share in them or to dispel them, at least for a while. As an adult, those details were the daily concerns every woman has and secretly shares with her best friend. And Megan was always there for her. Now it would be possible to share *everything*. The burden on Kara's shoulders had been lifted. There was only one obstacle, one fear. Megan might be unable to accept her new life as a vampire, horrified by its demands and come to despise it, or worse, she might despise Kara for forcing it upon her. She wished deeply that such things didn't matter, but of course, they did. She understood all too well the gravity of what she had done. If Megan could not appreciate this singular gift or would be unable to embrace the code of silence imposed by the instinctual imperative, then it would fall upon Kara's to dispatch her. The thought of it broke her heart.

Time was as precious as any of the supplies they were likely to discover inside the house. Not a moment was to be wasted until the transponder was located. Ovek immediately assigned Guor and Rahon to perimeter guard and set the remainder of the unit searching both structures. Searching inside the house, he happened upon a cabinet stocked with medicine and wraps. He found a tube of clear salve that smelled like an antibiotic and there was plenty of clean white cloth in the various cabinets. They had sustained a number of injuries, but nothing life threatening and this medication would suffice. However, it wasn't the wounds that had Ovek worried, it was the sickness that occasionally rushed through him like waves of heat rising from a desert floor. Not only was he beginning to feel sick, but also a noticeable depression was beginning to settle in. If only they had been able to take the females hostage! The fighting had been intense but neither side had been eager to take a life. Something had gone terribly wrong after Taven had thrown the knife. He had thought that she was about to fire the weapon, but taking her down had been a fateful mistake. It had forced the one in command, Kara, to step up the attack. Retribution. Ovek understood her feelings. They had felt the same about her attack on Cor, and they had reacted in much the same way. Perhaps the females were solders, perhaps not. But when Megan had fallen, Kara had reacted with a fury and a vengeance that spoke volumes. Revenge. If they were soldiers, this day's events hadn't been a part of any duty they had signed up for. This wasn't a part of a mission. She and her companion had simply been living their lives when the troops had invaded their territory. They were merely protecting themselves and the world they knew, and her companion had paid the ultimate price. Retribution had not been an obligation nor had it been a reasonable option; it never is, not for a soldier, and not for Kara. But it was her right, and Ovek knew he deserved having been defeated. And he admired her for it.

"Perhaps, if we can locate them, we might negotiate for the transponder," he suggested to Nol. "Perhaps, we came in a bit hard because of Cor. Maybe his death was an accident."

"An accident?" Nol fired back. "She tried to eat him, Cap'n."

"Maybe that's only how it looked. You might have thought the same about her attack on me," Ovek was thinking out loud now, talking more to himself than Nol.

"Maybe."

"And I wonder why Megan didn't change, you know, the fangs and the claws. Kara certainly seemed substantially faster and more athletic, as well," Ovek continued.

"Maybe she didn't need to," Nol replied. "She seemed to be doing well enough with this pop gun," he said tapping the shotgun wedged like a sword in his pistol belt. "Or maybe at the moment she couldn't. Who knows?"

"You could be on to something there. Maybe it takes a lot of energy to transform; maybe she was tired, or sick. It's even possible she lacked the necessary training. There's so much we don't know about these creatures. But whatever the reason, we might be able to use it to our advantage." If they couldn't find the transponder they would need every legitimate tactical advantage they could find to survive on this savage world, and he was determined to discover all he could.

They spent the bulk of the morning searching to no avail. The barn held nothing of value. There were large, soggy bundles of dank grasses, some worn agricultural equipment and a heavy, rusted toolbox. A search of the yard and field turned up no fresh digs, no place where the transponder was likely to be buried. They investigated each room of the house thoroughly, in each cabinet and drawer, in, under and behind each piece of furniture. Nothing. They checked for fresh patches in the walls, broke open every locked container, opened and emptied every box and bag large enough to hold it. They tapped the walls with a small hammer searching for secret compartments and felt for loose floorboards, combed every inch. Still nothing. By late afternoon, standing amidst the clutter they had created, Ovek had a simple and sad epiphany. He called off the search and gathered his crew in the living room.

"They never intended to keep it here. This is why they were armed when we arrived and why they made their way toward the back. They were expecting us, and were about to leave. It was in the vehicle," he announced. "It was in their escape vehicle." He slammed his fist into his hand. "It was outside all the time! We could have just taken it and walked away."

Perhaps Guor was just pleased to be off his feet but, as he lay stretched out on the sofa, he couldn't help but laugh. Instinctively, they all knew Ovek was right on target and began snickering at their folly. All except Ovek, who marched from the living room into the kitchen swearing at himself for the fool he had been, because he had not thought to check the vehicle, and because he realized just how much Cor's death had affected his judgment. Retribution—the thought of it, the desire for it, was a curse that poisoned his mind the moment he had first laid eyes on Kara, and he had allowed his desire for revenge to affect his plan. Once Kara had arrived he had thrown caution to the wind and gave no further thought to other possibilities. There were alternatives; there were other tactics he should have considered! What was it about the sight of this alien female gnawing on his fallen comrade that had put such a deep-seated fear into him? He had seen so many things in this universe—so many atrocities, so many lives lost, so much destruction, so much hated, so much pain and suffering. This had not been nearly as vile. Yet he had allowed it to affect his judgment. That was a mistake, and only he was to blame. It had been by his command. If they would end up stuck on this rock, they would surely die here unless they could find a secluded place to live out their lives. On this out-world the existence of aliens was unknown. The inhabitants would be incapable of accepting them, and these locals were simply not the hospitable type—hostile was the more accurate description. At the very least, it was time to begin developing alternative plans. The farm would make a suitable base of operations for the time being if no one came snooping around. His worse fear, that a force of locals might return immediately, had not happened. Since no one had come during their search, Ovek guessed that Kara had not reported them to the authorities. (Local authorities generally responded immediately or not at all.) That fact alone was curious, but welcomed. They needed whatever good fortune could come their way. He realized how badly he had messed things up for his troops, and he meant to make things right. He meant to keep them alive.

On the offhand chance that he was wrong about the transponder, they continued to search halfheartedly but divided their time and duties between cleaning up the mess they had made, repairing the doorways, securing all available weapons and taking inventory. They found the farm to be well stocked and took the time finally for a well-deserved meal. There was a generous supply of frozen meats in a cold storage locker, some packaged vegetables and plenty of delicious and colorful liquids. Their first real meal was lavish and they ate and drank their fill. Later after reviewing their stock, Ovek estimated they could easily hold out for ten to twelve days with modest rationing and far longer if they harvested the gourds from the field. They had running water from the taps, electrical power and were likely to discover many more valuable resources. He recognized the phone as a local communication device and removed it from its mounting. He hoped anyone attempting to contact the farm would assume the residents were simply unavailable. It was a weak ploy, but not knowing local protocols concerning such matters, it was the best he could do. Other than this minor concern, the farm was quickly becoming an ideal base. Once again, the odds seemed to be shifting in their favor, at least on this score. Here they could recuperate and formulate a plan. It was something. It was hope. It seems they had found a home on this distant world, for a while anyway.

Allen wrapped up the project around noon and attached the files to his client email. He had hoped to finish earlier but had been delayed by the cleanup following the monster rally stunt executed earlier. Kara and Megan must have been doing some god-awful celebrating this morning. Sober people generally drive on the road. He could scarcely believe she could tear across his yard that way, as though she had been given the green light at a tractor pull. He had caught the briefest glimpse of her behind the wheel, just enough to see that she looked completely out-of-it. It wasn't like her at all. She wasn't a heavy drinker and he had never seen her party in the morning. In fact, he hadn't seen her tie one on since their graduation party. Even then it wasn't the kind of bender some of the other kids had gone on. He remembered she had maintained enough control to keep his hands out of her pants, and that had been a real eye-opener since he had always believed that once he had charmed a girl enough to kiss her and get her bra off inevitably she would go all the way. But Kara had disproved that boyhood theory in a heartbeat. Ever since then, how could he help but love her from afar? But the truth was he was content to be just friends. There was an unspoken pact between him and Kara and Megan that he could not bring himself to violate. He valued the honesty and insight of these two lovely women, and he valued their trust. When he was with them he felt no pressure; the sexual tension was eliminated, even though they were the most desirable women he could imagine. There was a comfort in their circle he found impossible to define. He could just be himself, just a guy to talk to and he didn't have to be anything more than a good friend—and it was easy because he knew Kara and Megan loved each other. It was a wonder they couldn't see the gift each of them secretly hid from the other. It was so odd that nature obscured on the inside what was so obvious from a distance. Sometimes, it just made him laugh.

He considered simply going to the cabin to find out what all the celebrating had been about. But he decided against it. If they had gotten stinking drunk last night and had partied into the morning, they must have had a good reason, and a very good reason for excluding him. He smiled at the thought uppermost in his mind and the sensual image in provoked. That certainly would be a cause for celebration. If that was it, he was happy for them. But a few contradictory ideas nagged him throughout the afternoon. It seemed odd that Kara hadn't stopped when she had plowed onto the patio. The situation had been dangerous, plus it was unlike her to be so thoughtless, and it was just goddamn odd. More importantly, considering Kara's ineptness with the Chevy and the stupidity of it all, he was genuinely concerned about their safety. By seven that evening that nagging thought had turned into a full blown worry and he decided to call, but neither of them were answering their cells. He convinced himself that was a good sign and decided to stop worrying. They were big girls and could take care of themselves. He made one more call to the farm just in case and was surprised to find it busy. He went to the window to check across the cornfield. Sure enough, faint lights filtering through the curtained windows staring out of the side of the farmhouse flickered now and again as if someone were walking past them now and then. And he was certain Kara's Lexus was parked in the driveway. He thought it odd that neither she nor Megan had called or stopped by to offer an apology or an explanation concerning their earlier antics. The more he thought about it the more it bothered him. This just wasn't like them. Damn it! He had better things to do on a Saturday night than to bother with this. But he had to admit it, his feeling were hurt. Screw it! Why not just stop by to find out what all the excitement was about? Besides, once he was there, maybe they would invite him to make a night of it. Of course he might be barging in! Of course his ego was hurting just a bit! Of course it might be a mistake! It wouldn't be the first one he'd ever made.

Beel sat on the sofa nursing his bandaged rib playing with the buttons on the TV remote, flipping from channel to channel. Nol and Guor bellowed each time he switched channels or pushed an information button. Several times the TV blinked on and off in rapid succession, the sound went dead, and a programming loop was displayed with an arrow spinning round and round for no discernable reason. Finally Nol popped the controller out of his hand and a minor scuffle for control broke out between them. Nol was the victor. He was able to get the set on track settling on a station presenting a variety of short stories with laugh tracks and news reports featuring maps and videos of local weather conditions and forecasts. They knew, however, not to pay too much attention to the local communication services in general. Traditionally, on alien worlds it was virtually impossible to distinguish fact from fantasy through the entertainment venues. It fact, it was dangerous to do so. Even news broadcast were often parodies in disguise. Humor, including the mocking of stark reality and the twisting of bleak and dark events, was a psychological coping technique common to relatively advanced and sophisticated worlds. Watching and listening to these devices might offer some superficial insight into a culture, but it could not be trusted to offer truthful insight into its nature. Gaining false information about an adversary was more dangerous than gaining no information at all. Ovek was especially mindful of this and was wary of giving credence to information gleaned from the TV. The situation had become far more complicated than necessary and his judgment had already been compromised. But the TV did offer a welcomed diversion and he felt they all deserved some R-and-R after the many hardships they had been through these last few cycles. So toying with the remote awhile, he joined in to witness Conan's victory, and even enjoyed the culturally enlightening scenes of these mammals enjoying sexual intercourse. Their method, he noted, was not dissimilar to most bipeds scattered throughout their sector. He found it peculiar and fascinating that the female changeling Conan coupled with was not unlike Kara in most respects, dark and mysterious, and deadly. The viewing fun came to an end when they heard a rhythmic tapping, Rahon's signal that an intruder was approaching. Ovek pulled the plug. The lights went out and everyone assumed defensive positions. They hugged the floor and concealed themselves behind the heavy furniture. Peeking out from Kara's vehicle, Rahon held up a finger and pointed toward the road. Then he pointed downward and twiddled his fingers forward, indicating that one individual was approaching on foot. Ovek ordered Nol though the kitchen door to support Rahon. He sent Taven out the back door to circle around, behind the intruder. Everyone else was to hold positions near the windows. On his mark they moved as one. Ovek jumped to the door, a flood lamp and cichma axe at the ready.

Allen was certain that a few minutes earlier the lights had been on in the living room. Now, as he approached Megan's side door, the house was dark and it appeared deserted. He opened the outer door and raised his fist to knock, but hesitated. Perhaps he *was* intruding. If they were avoiding him they must have a damn good reason. Perhaps he might ruin some sort of surprise they were planning. Perhaps that is why he hadn't been let in on the secret. He realized that intruding would be a very selfish thing to do. All in good time, and this was not it. Just back off. He had other friends he could call, and there were plenty of clubs in the Third Ward that would be hoppin' tonight, loaded with college babes full of spirit and alcohol and attitude. Somewhere out there a pretty young thing was whispering his name and (because Saturday was "free mimosas for anyone in a skirt night" at most bars) by ten o'clock she should be fairly shouting, and it shouldn't be tough to find her.

Just as he turned to leave he spotted the hasty repair work to the door jam. He put his hand to the top for a closer inspection, then ran his hand along the length of the jam noting the severe damage to the entire length of it, as though the door had been violently ripped from the hinges and brutally hammered back on. In fact, the hinges and the splintered jam itself were secured with a battery of amateurishly pounded nails. Some were hammered in crooked with their pointed tips peeking out of the jam at odd angles; many overlapped each other as if they had been fired in with a machine gun. The wood around the hinges had been so severely damaged he thought he might easily pick them out with his fingers. As he pulled on one, the door suddenly burst open. Allen twisted his head around. A blinding light cut into his eyes like a razor, the intensity nearly knocked him off his feet. The nail came loose and slipped from his fingers. The spotlight hit it as it zipped through the air like a silver bullet nearly striking Ovek between the eyes. He twisted sideways thinking it was a dart of some kind. Nol hit Allen like a freight train, delivering a crushing blow to his mid section that sent him lurching backward. Everything went black and he couldn't breathe. He heard the door slam and some peculiar voices. A blow to the back of his head paralyzed him to his knees. Then he saw a dazzling display of meteoric lights, similar to the display he had seen the night before but a million times more beautiful, and felt his legs buckle beneath him. He had intermittent encounters then with a dense mist and odd voices and glimpses of weird anime characters moving through the fog.

When he awoke he was gagged and bound to a chair in the middle of the living room. In a flash he realized why Kara and Megan had demolished his patio and why they had been in such a hurry. They hadn't been drunk or celebrating, they had been running from a nightmare, one that was alive and walking upright like a man, a nightmare that looked as though it should have been basking on a rock or clinging to the inside of a wire cage.

Nol grabbed Allen by the hair and sneered and laughed a hideous kind of laugh. It didn't take long to convince Allen that these creatures were as peculiar as they appeared to be. As they chattered and moved around he could see these were not elaborate masks and body suits or men covered with clever make up. In the movies, special effects can make such things appear very real. But in reality, he knew, such things are not so easy to create, at least, not so close up. And these creatures certainly smelled like the genuine article. The more he looked at these peculiar creatures the more he wished they weren't real, and the longer he scrutinized them the more real they became. The very thought of it hurt his head that much more.

He twisted his head to discover more of these bizarre creatures lurking about. From his vantage point he couldn't tell just how many were in the room, let alone upstairs or beaming down at the very moment all over the farm. The few he could see were sitting around nibbling on ham sandwiches and chips, drinking soda and beer or milling about the kitchen as if they actually belonged here on this planet. It was comical in a surreal way, until the big, ugly one nearest him began jabbering in that peculiar language. Then the panic set in more deeply.

"What now, Cap'n?," Nol asked. "He's breathin' hard and I think he's gonna' pass out again."

Ovek rubbed his neck a while, starring at Allen. "He came looking for the females, assuming they were here. Now he knows differently." He paused, continuing to rub his neck. "But he might know where are. We need information, and we need it fast." He turned his back to Allen as so that Allen might not see his face, careful not to give away any clue of his intentions. "Scare him. Don't do any real damage. And whatever you do, by Nos, don't kill him," Ovek ordered. "And Nol," he added, "watch him real close." Ovek didn't want any mishaps. This hostage was the only lead they had.

"Beel, Guor, locate an injector, " Nol called across the room. He turned to face Ovek again, who was resting his head in his hand, pressing his bony ridge tightly into his fingertips. "You all right, Cp'n?" Nol asked Ovek. "You're looking a bit yellow under the ridges."

"I've been better. Just tired, I guess." He rubbed his head unwilling to admit the pain he was feeling, and that it was continuing to mount. He sat at the kitchen table, poured a tall glass of water and stared at Allen. A lot depended on how they handled this hostage and on the information he could provide. He hoped Allen would not prove to be as deceptively troublesome as Kara had been.

In short order Guor returned with an enormous tackle box filled with a tangled assortment of fishing line and leaders, hooks, bobbers and lures. Here was more recognizable gear, which diverted Guor and Beel into long orations about the length of some aquatic creatures they each had caught on distant worlds. Nol interrupted their reverie with a mild obscenity and an annoyed look. "Ah, oh yeah," Guor said, reaching into the tackle box. "I saw this thing. It ought to do." He placed a small plastic bottle topped with a hypodermic nozzle into Nol's hand. Allen's head snapped up at the sound of Nol's approach. The brute was holding a torture device in plain view—in a manner of speaking. It was a small plastic bottle, a squeeze-hypo used to inflate rubber worms. Although its needle was only three-quarters of an inch, it could be excruciatingly painful if poked into a sensitive area—like him. He felt his eyes go wide at the sight and his body squirmed involuntarily, but the utility tape holding his arms and legs to the chair was unforgiving and the heavy chains wrapped around his hands seemed to get heavier. He was sure this huge bastard was enjoying every second of his discomfort. He wanted to believe that he could endure any torture, and once he was free of these restraints he would repay them for every second of agony they were about to inflict. But the truth was, he had no experience to support that bold contention. Actually, he had a very low pain threshold, which he had thought was a good thing. A low pain threshold, he held, served as a survival mechanism and was a substantial evolutionary advantage. If an individual recognizes injuries or illnesses early, one is more likely to retreat or seek treatment sooner, and therefore, increases the odds of survival. It had always made sense to him. At the moment, however, having a low pain threshold seemed to put him at a disadvantage. Seeking escape was one thing, being unable to escape was another. He sat staring at Nol trying to divide his attention between the fiend's insidious grin and attempting to rectify the painful failure of his evolutionary theory. It suddenly occurred to him that, should he find a way to free himself from his bonds, he wouldn't have the slightest idea how to defend himself against one of these monsters in a fair fight. He could box, a little, but he hadn't done that in quite a while. None was under six feet and the brute with the bandage on his throat stood nearly seven. Fighting only one of them would have been suicide. He had no chance against so many. Eyeing Nol as he drew nearer, he could feel the sense of complete and abject helplessness rise inside him. Each weighty step foretold of the dreadful and horrific experience to come. Each weighty step vibrated up the chair into Allen's chest. He felt as if his heart were about to burst with each heavy footfall. This was it. He knew nothing he could do either now, or later, was going to make a difference. He was going to suffer and die, and there wasn't a damn thing he could do about it. Moreover, he would never know why they had tortured and killed him. He couldn't understand—their language sounded like Japanese being spoken by drunken Norwegians. As Nol stood before him now, the hypo in his hand and a wicked grin on his face, nothing made sense anymore. Allen's entire universe had been turned inside out. His eyes grew wide as the creature crushed the bottle and rammed the needle into his own forearm. Easing up on his grip, he filled the bottle with his blood. He pulled it out and blew on the spot briefly, casually flicking away a few small scales that had broken loose. Then, with absolutely no introduction or ceremony, he plunged the needle into Allen's shoulder and injected the blood into him. Allen had never been a coward, although he had never been tested under any kind of extreme circumstances, and he had never been particularly squeamish. He had never considerer himself a sissy either. But when Nol popped the hypo into him and he watched the blood disappear into his body, he fainted in a matter of seconds. He woke up feeling dizzy with a buzzing at the back of his head. He had no idea how long he had been unconscious. Nol was sprinkling him with water from his claw tips and laughing uproariously, a bit too raucously it seemed to Allen. This guy seemed to be having way too much fun.

"How ya' feeling, trooper?" Nol asked. "Translators working yet?"

"Yeah, yeah, I feel all right," Allen replied, trying to act and sound a lot braver than he felt. Mostly, he was happy just to have the gag off his mouth and to have the needle out of Nol's hand. Perhaps now, Allen thought, he might get some answers. He didn't require lengthy explanation about why he could suddenly comprehend his language; the crack about the translators explained it well enough. Apparently the injection had introduced a sophisticated linguistic technology. That's all he really needed to know. He was eager for answers to questions with greater relevance—like, who were these guys and where did they come from, what the hell did they want and how was he going to get out of here alive? He decided his best defense, and his best chance of survival, would be a strong offence, a show of bravado.

"Who are you guys, and what do you want?" he demanded to know. At that moment he panicked, fearing the answer might be, "We come from a galaxy far, far away," or " We seek out new life and new civilizations." Because Nol stood directly over him, trepidation surged through his body like an electric current. He envisioned him raising his hand and saying further, "Take me to you leader!" His panic heightened. The beads of sweat emerging from his forehead felt like a troop of ants marching across his head. He bore down, looking deep within himself for the strength not to laugh, hoping Nol would not kill him should he be unable to control himself.

"Shut up!" Nol fired back quickly, in a most unambiguous tone. He zipped the tip of a mandat knife very close to Allen's eye. "I will ask the questions. You will answer. If I don't like your answers you will lose valuable body parts. Am I clear?"

"Very," Allen said. And he meant it.

"And don't try your changeling tricks on me, or those long, pretty teeth of yours will be the first to hit the floor; got it?"

Allen figured this last statement hadn't translated well because he didn't have the slightest idea what the brute was talking about. But it didn't matter, considering the look in Nol's eyes. Thankfully, the bigger one intervened.

"Nol," Ovek said, moving slowly between them. "I have some questions for our guest." Then he turned to face Nol. "But stay close and keep that blade handy," he said in a way that offered Allen no comfort whatsoever. Allen looked up at the behemoth towering over him. He scrutinized Ovek's huge, muscular frame, his thick neck, the fine camouflage of scales, the bony ridge surrounding his face, the horns jutting from his chin and forehead and the rigid fan adorning the top of his head. He realized how peculiar and alien these creatures truly were, and it suddenly occurred to him that they would never let him go. They could never allow him to disclose their presence here. Wherever they had come from and whatever they were doing here were deep and dreadful secrets that no one could be allowed to discover. These animals could not risk his leaving here alive. Any hope of survival he may have entertained since he awoke was dashed by the look on Ovek's face.

In that moment Ovek's strategy was set, he could read his captive as easily as reading a data screen. He was terrified. He was not a soldier; or if he was, not a very good one. He certainly had no intention of dying for his comrades or his world, not if he had an expectation of a reasonable alternative. All Ovek need do was convince him that once they had the transponder they would leave, and life on his world could go on as usual; convince him to cooperate and neither he, nor anyone else, would be harmed. Even though his head was spinning and the thing he wanted most was a good night's sleep, Ovek was determined to stick with the interrogation for as long as necessary. Considering that he was feeling worse with each passing moment, he hoped it would not take long. The scare tactic had worked perfectly; now, a pacifying gesture of some kind seemed appropriate.

"Nol, perhaps we won't be needing that blade after all," he said. "I think we can come to a reasonable understanding without it, don't you?" He looked to Allen, who nodded with noticeable relief.

"I'm sure we can," Allen replied. He suspected Ovek's tactic to be nothing more than a ruse but felt better with the knife out of view and with Nol sitting quietly on the edge of the sofa. And he liked his tone, his easy manner and the hint of a promise it conveyed, like a faint glow on the horizon, suggesting this latest turn of events might lead to his eventual release. It hardly seemed likely, but it was a glimmer of hope, and at this point, Allen was accepting any measure of it he could get.

The interrogation began with introductions, and for both of them, proceeded slowly into the night with ever deepening disclosures and a search for common ground. At the end of it, Ovek had gotten the information he had wanted most after convincing Allen that all they were interested in was having returned to them that which was rightfully theirs. No one was to be harmed. They all listened and leaned a lot about Earth and its inhabitants, but Ovek was skeptical of much that he had to say. He found Allen as obstinate as an Agurian mud hog. Time after time the hostage claimed to know nothing about Kara's changeling abilities, and he adamantly denied such abilities in himself or in any other Earthling. He admitted only to finding such ideas laughable. His stubbornness defied all logic because they had witnessed the evidence with their own eyes and discovered bits and pieces of the changeling history on the TV. This was an undeniable combination. While the stories may have been fictitious with romanticized and diverse plots and details, the general history of changelings on Earth was clear. As usual, on this planet as on so many others, entertainment bore only a superficial resemblance to reality. But Kara herself was the quintessential proof of Allen's deception and his denial, then, had been an overt lie. But it was powerful evidence that Allen would not yield in this particular area, even though he knew his life was at risk. He was protecting a sacred trust. To Ovek, this indicated the changeling nature was so significant that these Earthlings would do anything to protect its secret, even die. The various stories seemed to support this conclusion. From what he could tell, it had some connection to their religion, or perhaps it did long ago. According to some of the legends, it was a taboo subject at one time, confined to the darkness, shrouded in mystery, the metamorphosis affected only in the most personal and intimate of circumstances. Usually there were overt sexual overtones associated with various rituals following the change that included sadomasochistic bloodletting. Occasionally it provoked violent behavior, acts that probably occurred during a documented period of widespread superstition and inquisition. Such repressive epochs are common throughout the galaxy, for often behaviors and customs that evolve quite naturally often become shunned or ostracized, forced into a world or moral ambiguity, or labeled as evil. They become feared, interpreted as spectral extensions of the darkworld exerted into the corporeal universe. It sometimes takes hundreds, even thousands of years on some worlds, to break these ancient taboos. The changeling capability was once probably an aspect of a morally reprehensible practice, a remnant characteristic of a despised and loathsome subculture now embraced. More than likely it took millennia for these creatures to gain control of their urges and become master of their ability. It would be useless to pressure Allen concerning its resurrection and its advocates. Where this taboo or ancient religious conviction was concerned, he seemed steadfast, determined to take its secrets to the grave. He might even gladly be a martyr to its cause. On this score, Ovek understood and admired his courage, even though it was a bit maddening and, for the longest time, he had appeared to be just plain stubborn. But in every other aspect of the interrogation, Allen had been most cooperative. He had been willing, even eager it seemed, to talk of his planet, the good of it, the bad, its wonders, his perspectives on its progress and its setbacks, the history of war and oppression, of victory and triumph, its first small step on the lunar surface and the tiny vehicle carrying humanity's vision to another world, its disappointments and despair, its greatness. He had answered mundane questions about his work and favorite foods, to queries concerning technically complex military secrets, about which his knowledge had seemed extremely limited. Considering his occupation, about which he seemed glib and assured, Ovek had not been surprised by his lack of knowledge in more crucial areas. But one thing was clear, Allen was intelligent and courageous, cultured and highly educated, an extremely rational and a logical being. If he was typical of these Earthlings, then they were a peculiar and contradictory combination of ruthless beast and sophisticated being. They represented an extraordinary evolutionary experiment, a successful union of deceptive physical prowess with highly advanced intellectual potential. Their current development coupled with the changeling ability made them excellent candidates for membership in the empire, either as partners or as slaves. The emperor would decide following an incorporation study, a cost benefits analysis and strategic planning review conducted by his Juggernaut advisors. Of course, during the interrogation he had said nothing of this. He assured Allen that the information would serve only to keep his troops alive long enough to locate the transponder, allowing them to return to their home world. It took awhile, but he finally gained Allen's trust and he pried loose the thing he wanted most to hear. "Yes," Allen said with some degree of enthusiasm, "I think I know where they might have gone—probably up to the deer cabin."

"The deer cabin—and where exactly might that be?" Nol suddenly had become very interested.

"Not far from here, in the woods up in Waukesha County," Allen had replied with that shaky tone returning to his voice. Ovek had won him over, but Nol still scared the crap out of him. "It's less than an hour's drive."

"Would you be willing to take us to this deer cabin?" Ovek had asked. "I promise you, all we want is our property; no one is to be harmed."

"You'll let us all go?" Allen had asked sheepishly.

"We're not interested in you hairball," Nol had fired in, his stubby claw hovering close to Allen's eye. "All we want to know is if you can get us there, without pulling any of your animal tricks."

"Sure, at least I can get you close. I know the general vicinity. I was there only once," he had said. He glanced sideways at Nol, confused as usual by his cryptic references.

"Good enough," Nol had grumbled. "Get us close then. She

shouldn't be hard to find; I won't forget her scent anytime soon." He had grinned.

There had been something about the look in his eyes, something maniacal, that made Allen fear for the girls, that made him regret mentioning the cabin. There was something kind and honorable about Ovek, something that resonated with Allen's sense of humanity. But this other creep, Nol, had all the charm of Freddy Kruger, and there seemed nothing humane about him. "Just don't go all Godzilla on the place, all right?" Allen blurted. He knew it was weak, but he had felt obliged to express some bravura. It was the only thing thugs like Nol truly respected.

"Sure thing, trooper," Nol replied. He leaned in to Allen's face. "I'll go easy on her," he sneered. Nol hadn't understood the *Godzilla* reference, not exactly, but he had gotten the gist of it.

With that final exchange, the business end of the interrogation was over. Ovek added a bit of small talk, but only to reassure Allen that he had done the right thing. The questioning had continued well into the night and they were all exhausted. They needed rest and since Allen promised to play a significant role in their plans, Ovek felt it was time for a sign of good faith, yet he couldn't take any changes that Allen might have second thoughts. A bit of psychological manipulation seemed in order.

"You know, Nol wants to assure your cooperation by removing your feet to guarantee you won't try to escape," Ovek said, wrapping up their conversation.

"I won't; you know that," Allen said. He glanced over at Nol, who glared at him, his fingers toying with a nasty-looking circular blade.

"I think I can trust you; I hope so, for your sake," Ovek said. "Nol will be looking for an excuse to carve you up," he said; but he thought, now, at least, Allen would be much more comfortable with the accommodations they had planned for him that evening.

It wasn't the Hilton. Nol chained him to the pipe under the bathroom sink and threw a few blankets and a pillow into the bathtub; he also left him a generous supply of ham and several slices of bread. It was a confidence game. Ovek had won him over just enough to get the information he had required. Now it was about building a trust that would escalate their relationship into something

Allen would view as mutually beneficial. The way to do that was to bring him in, make him a part of a larger universe, a part of something more exciting and dramatic than the humdrum world he knew. Ovek had him pegged; Allen was a civilian who feared being torn from his comfort zone, but a romantic who secretly harbored a deep and perverse desire for adventure. Such an opportunity just might be the tool to use on him, to bend him to their will. Tomorrow they would execute phase one of a plan to retrieve the transponder and Allen would be the key to its success. But that was for tomorrow. At the moment Ovek felt as if he was being sucked into a black hole. His head was on fire from his neck to his fan, and his muscles ached from his rib cage down to his ankles. It had been a long day, for him and for his troopers, and he was exhausted. So, he called for lights out and ordered Nol to post the first guard. The sickness he was feeling was just fatigue; he was convinced of it. Tomorrow he would feel much better; the plan would unfold and the mission would get back on track. He had no doubt about it; with Allen's help, the odds seemed to be in their favor. There was a variety of ways to utilize hostages, and not all them involved butchering innocent civilians in cold blood—he tried to shake the horrific images of the Legot's offices from his mind. He headed off in the direction of the master bedroom but never remembered actually getting into the bed.

Chapter 9

The transponder sat in the middle of the table like a diminutive toaster, without slats for the bread, at once oddly familiar, yet peculiar and creepy. Megan half-expected it to sprout legs and skitter into the shadows. The girls stared at it awhile, pondering its deeper significance. Kara recognized it as part of a communications system, but didn't know its precise function. She was certain of only one thing, that it was vitally important to the aliens, recalling that Ovek had spoken urgently of it to his team while searching for her in the woods, and she said as much to Megan. "We might have saved ourselves a lot of trouble by simply giving it to them," Megan offered. Of course, at that time she hadn't known they had been searching for it.

Now, for Kara, a few key pieces of the puzzle had snapped into place after learning that the device had fallen out of a meteor shower. She had assumed the aliens had broken into the house to take revenge for the death of their comrade at the picnic grounds. Now she realized she had been mistaken. Perhaps had she known this cursed thing was in the truck she might have connected the dots and considered using it as a bargaining chip. Perhaps. But she was uncertain that simply handing it over to them would have been the wisest thing to do. "Evidently this was important enough for them to risk exposure. If it is part of their communications system, with whom do they wish to communicate, and why?" she wondered out loud.

"Good questions," Megan said, chewing on her lip, "I think we should talk about it over breakfast." If there were definitive answers, which she doubted, they could wait, a short while anyway; first and foremost, she was famished. For some reason her appetite was running wild. She felt as if she hadn't eaten in ages. "I'll see what we have in the cupboard—powdered eggs and milk, pancake mix, Spam—" Megan said excitedly, "and coffee, I know there must be coffee here somewhere." She was flittering about like a hummingbird.

"That sounds fine to me," Kara replied, pleased to see her so animated and in such good spirits. She was probably suffering some delayed shock, from the battle, the wound, and was still reacting to the initial stages of shadow transformation, but handling everything very well, indeed. Kara sensed her excitement; she knew that on some level buried deep within, Megan understood how dramatically these recent events would alter her life. She could feel the novitiate's resurrected spirit—her heightened confidence and enthusiasm, her alertness and attention to detail. They seemed to be communicating on an intuitive level now, as though their minds were linked by an invisible, empathic umbilical. "You had better make a big pot," Kara said. "We have a lot to talk about."

"I know," Megan said cheerfully.

She had been thinking exactly the same thing while opening and inspecting the various boxes. In addition to the questions she had about their bizarre attackers, Megan was more eager to explore more personal matters, primarily Kara's startling arcanum, her bestial metamorphosis. Also, she had a few questions about the events following the battle. She had no recollection of their escape, of leaving the farmhouse or traveling to the cabin. She had only a vague memory of momentary pain, a feeling of weakness and vertigo, of falling from a great height, of suffocating and floating on cool breezes. It all seemed to happen in a barely-coherent, monochromatic dream which she had drifted into and out of throughout the night. She wanted to know exactly what had happened after she had fainted. The last thing she recalled was reaching for her keys and nearly making it out the kitchen door. She wanted all the details. When she and Kara had awakened early this morning, naked, basking in the warmth of each other's embrace, Kara had given her only the most cursory answer, explaining she had been near death and had needed to be warmed quickly.

Kara had seemed more apologetic than necessary and so Megan had kissed her cheek assuring her it had been the right thing to do. Besides, if Kara hadn't insisted on going out to the pickup to check for supplies, Megan would have been content to have her simply stay in bed. They had been warm and cozy wrapped around each other and she would have been content to have that last much longer. Now, sitting at the table, staring at the transponder, they could each sense how urgently they needed to talk, how necessary it was, but how difficult it was to know where to begin.

Before preparing breakfast and tackling the issues facing them, they decked themselves out in more cabin friendly clothing commandeered from the generous stockpiles stored on the utility shelves. Megan donned new Autumn-wood hunting pants, a red plaid shirt and wilderness boots. She fondly remembered buying the outfit as a birthday gift for her father only a few years ago. Kara selected camouflage fatigues and kept her military swamp boots. The uniform had belonged to Megan's father, as well, probably one he had worn in Vietnam. All the clothes were a little big on them, but they were clean and warm and the roominess made them all the more comfortable.

Kara offered to help with breakfast, but Megan would have none of it. She was far too energized to share the duties, preferring to have Kara just sit back and be served, and serve she did; Megan laid out a splendid meal. She piled mounds of scrambled eggs and toast and pancakes on their plates and fanned out slices of fried Spam like playing cards around the edges. They topped off the meal with coffee and a box of little golden crackers shaped like fish. While they ate, Kara explained about nearly hitting one of the aliens with her car and following them into the woods, everything progressed from there. Their conversation continued nonstop into their busy workday, which saw them ridding the cabin of the winter's drifted ash and trampled, crusted mud.

Throughout the day they shared their thoughts and bonded, the way women are fond of doing while puttering with guns and knives and ammo and taking inventory of available food and bottled water, blankets and linens, candles and oil and emergency supplies, all of which was boxed in generous amounts for weekend getaways. The conversation lasted the entire afternoon and all through dinner. Eventually, the evening sun peeking through the top of the window signaled a moment of quiet reflection, and they sat silently awhile, holding hands. Megan kissed Kara once passionately, just because the cool light striking the side of her face made her look so very lovely, like a depiction of Helen, whose beauty was said to rival Aphrodite herself.

For the most part, Kara had done most of the talking while Megan had listened, perplexed at times, fascinated at others, often rendered speechless by revelations nearly as alien as the creatures that had fought. To discover that vampires have lived among humans for thousands of years was astounding. However, all the common lore cushioned the peculiar notion somewhat, and the recent vision of Kara's startling transformation rendered the concept very real and palpable. But Kara's admission that she had killed, viciously, freely, so many times, was equally amazing, and difficult to fathom. She explained the Bloodwarriors' activities as a form of vigilante justice, killing only the evil and perverse. But was it murder? Did such a question have meaning to vampires? Was the human predilection for adherence to provincial notions of right and wrong, good and evil, actually relevant? Were culturally naive philosophical perspectives on such matters of any import to creatures of such vastly superior capabilities? Should individuals of an advanced culture bend to the self-righteous moral prerogatives and imperatives of an inferior one? These are questions that had been explored and debated by vampires for an eon or more, and still there were no definitive answers. They merely did the best they could, coping with life by adapting their urges to serve humanity in the most non-intrusive and least damaging way possible. It was the best they could do, for now.

To Megan, there seemed a poetic justice woven into the fabric of their crusade. In popular literature and media, there has always been a deep prejudice against vampires and their perceived nocturnal activities, a kind of kill-first-and-ask-questions-later attitude toward them, an attitude which would wholeheartedly be embraced in reality, no doubt. Certainly, the first human impulse would be to kill them, or at least, to try. Humans would no doubt experience the worst of that impulse. That course might be inherently shortsighted on two counts, similar to the eradication of a black widow by squashing it between your fingers—you're quite likely to suffer its venomous bite and, simultaneously, you would purposefully be destroying a superb and useful predator of bothersome, even deadly, pests.

Unfortunately history has irrevocably linked vampires with evil and Satanism, and deemed them worthy of our disdain, suitable only for destruction—much like spiders. Considering this skewed predilection on the part of humanity, vigilantism, especially the ruthless and relentless type practiced by the Bloodwarriors, seems a reasonable posture. The prey has always been a member of the unscrupulous social fringe dwellers. These unsavory characters, perpetrating their seedy business in the dark, shadowy places, were always considered to be the ones most likely to discover the existence of vampires. It was logical, therefore, that they should serve as the primary source of sustenance. After hearing these arguments and thinking it through, Megan was forced to agree, and she recognized that, of the various alternatives available to the Bloodwarriors, considering their severe bloodlust, vigilantism was actually a most honorable and benign path to follow. She was, however, amazed by the depth of Kara's addiction, by the pitiless viral taskmaster within, driving her to a relentless hunger once every seven days. Its drug-like power and hypnotic nature evoked rich and terrible images. Megan's mind swam with bizarre visions of Kara pinning her quarry like a crazed panther, draining his blood and stripping his flesh. It was frightening, yet sensational and provocative all at once.

Kara told her as much of the history of the vampire nation as she knew, holding back only some of the more specific and intimate details; that would come later. It was well into the evening before they came full circle, once again discussing the battle and the details that finally lead them to the cabin. The day had been momentous for Megan whose provincial life had never before been touched by adventure or danger. As events had unfolded, she hadn't thought consciously about them; rather she had allowed them to flow through her like a river, touching her, but never overwhelming her, never flooding her central core. Now each second began to crystallize, from the moment she had first marveled at the breathtaking beauty of the meteor shower to the instant the blade had whistled through the air and pierced her skin. All the recent, startling revelations began churning in her mind like a boiling fluid, all rebounding against one another in their struggles to dominate her consciousness. Breaking the surface like a huge bubble that had forced its way though a thick, hot soup was the realization that Kara had been able to keep her wondrous secret so effectively all these years. Suddenly, as if the burners had been turned up, her mind boiled over with so many questions she barely knew where to begin.

But it was late, and the cabin was getting cold. So first they gathered armfuls of split pine and birch from the enormous stock already piled along the side of the cabin and built a mammoth, roaring fire. Then, tossing their uniforms aside, they embraced within a mound of pillows and comforters spread out on the floor. Their array was cozy and warm and would have suited an emir. Within it the physical and emotional bond between them was consummated with a sharing of intimate, hidden secrets while their spirits wafted to the realm of goddesses where they fused into the essence of a single being. After a time they lay back, their bodies spent and relaxed, both nestled in the blankets and pillows as if floating in a sea of foamy cream. They lay quietly for a time until Megan broke the silence with a sudden, errant thought.

"I don't understand the change. How you do it?" Megan asked distantly, looking up at the ceiling as if she expected the stars to answer her.

"I suppose it's like blinking or smiling," Kara replied, fully understanding Megan's puzzlement. "Extending my tusks and claws comes naturally. And all the neural and muscular control is second nature to me, like changing the shape of my ears or directing blood to muscles where I need it most. None of it seems peculiar to me."

"You certainly are stronger and faster than I ever imagined."

"We have denser muscles than humans and millions of more capillaries. And adrenaline affects us in a peculiar and beneficial way. It increases our concentration and awareness; it enhances our senses; gives us greater endurance, makes us more resilient, and self-confident—and more cunning."

"It must wonderful. To be so powerful, I mean, to be so strong, to be so sure of yourself, to know that you are a part of a great and historic legacy. To be—" Megan hesitated, "to be *somebody*!"

Kara smiled knowingly. She sensed Megan's instincts sharpening and her intuition, weaving itself into the fabric of her queries and observations. Soon she would be able tell her the truth—the wonderful, perhaps the terrible, truth. "Being vampire doesn't make you somebody. We all have a responsibility to be the best we can be. Each of us must cultivate ourselves to our full potential, whether we're human or vampire. You are and always will be a bright, beautiful, and sensitive woman, Megan, and you were a wonderful human being," Kara said, looking deeply into Megan's eyes, hoping to see some precognitive gleam. "But I hope you will be pleased with your new life. I hope you will be happy as a vampire. It's not always easy."

"I think I will be," she said, a smile as perfect as an orange peel slowly curling up under her nose.

"How long have you known?" Kara asked.

"I only suspected. I've felt a hint of it most of the day, as though you've been whispering to my heart." Megan's smile grew even larger.

"How do you feel?" Kara asked.

"I feel wonderful" she replied, smiling. "In fact, I feel better than I have for a long time. I feel as good as—as before Mom and Dad died," she said.

"And as time passes, you'll feel even better than that," Kara reassured her. She put her arm around Megan and held her tight. "I will be there to make sure of it. Besides, there is so much you need to learn."

"And right now there is so much I want to know, so many questions I want to ask."

"But I have one for you first," Kara said. "Are you afraid?"

"No. Not if you stay with me," Megan said sincerely. Kara smiled in return. "But I am worried about the bloodlust and the hunger." Megan added, "What if I am unable to kill? How will I survive?"

"Well, there is so much I've held back. Perhaps you've asked the most important question first," Kara replied. "Often, shadows never experience the bloodlust; you may never be compelled to take a life. Yet, you will reap the benefits of the essence all the same. You'll be healthier, stronger and faster, more cunning, more resistant to disease. You'll heal more quickly from injury and live longer. But there may be many vampire characteristics you will never exhibit. It has always been this way; each shadow responds differently to the virus. My father's shadow studies suggest this is because subtle mutations within the strain have occurred over the millennia. In purebreds the mutations are nullified by the complex hormonal changes within the womb. The creation of shadows naturally bypasses this critical staging period."

"I see," Megan said, digesting this latest bit of news. Surprisingly, she seemed somewhat disappointed. "You mean I may never be able to transform? I might not grow fangs or claws?"

"Some shadows can; others cannot."

"When will I know?"

"Hmm," she hesitated. "The length of time is difficult to know; a lot of body chemistry and genetics are involved; it differs for each person, but the difference will be a matter of days or weeks, so you'll know soon enough. You seem to want the transmutation. Is it that important?" Kara was surprised by her desire for it. She had lived with the ability all her life; for her it was as natural as growing hair, and while she understood the fascination, part of her was mystified by Megan's enthusiasm.

"I think it is so fiercely beautiful!" Megan replied, "When I first saw you on the table, so powerful, so majestic, I couldn't help being a little jealous. I want that. I want to look like that; I want to feel like that. And if I develop the bloodlust, won't I absolutely need it?"

"Yes, you will, and have no doubt; the genetic and hormonal response to the virus that causes the bloodlust will stimulate the growth of tusks and claws to help you accomplish the necessary tasks. Developing the bloodlust is a virtual guarantee that you will eventually transform," Kara assured her. "But you may very well experience transmutation without developing the bloodlust. Understand this, naturally born vampires and shadows alike do not absolutely need human flesh and blood to survive. That's a myth. The bloodlust simply compels some to seek it out, but very rare meat is sufficient for survival. The bottom line is this: most vampires are capable of transformation and experience some level of bloodlust, but are never actually compelled to seek out humans. My mother never took a life. However, a minority of vampires, those who know the severe hunger and experience intense bloodlust, called Bloodwarriors, are born with a taste for humans, and we regularly seek them out."

"You are a Bloodwarrior," Megan said slowly, nodding her recognition.

"Yes. The bloodlust is a potent and formidable specter within us. It offers commanding power, but great responsibility as well. For thousands of years, for as long as our history has been handed down, the harvesting of evil humans has been known as the Bloodwar. It is a complicated history, documented only in tales passed from generation to generation, shrouded in mystery and wrapped in a veil of legend, but it is a fierce and compelling story, a legacy of which I am proud to be a part," she said, her gray eyes graduating from blue to purple as they reflected only inadequately the pictures visualized in her mind's eye.

"Someday, perhaps on an evening not unlike this one, cold and damp with a full moon peeking through the window, we'll snuggle in front of a blazing fire drinking…" Kara paused for some comic effect and adopted that heavy Hungarian accent, "vine," she said dramatically. She paused then and smiled with a faraway look settled upon her face, as if watching some great drama play out before her.

"Seriously," she mused, "someday I will tell all I know, all that my father told me. It is truly a majestic epic, a tale of warlord kings and vast armies and empires fallen, a chronicle of fierce vampires on dangerous quests and vanquished demons, a story of evil slayers who faced unspeakable, and wicked humans who betrayed, not only the gods, but their fellow man." The words floated from her mouth like musical notes and seemed to dance the short distance between their faces. They flowed into her mind and spread out in waves of color forming pictures of serene pampas and crystal steams, of deep-blue lakes and distant, rolling hills. Lush, dense forest lay at the feet of the smooth canyon walls that rose up around her and dark, foreboding thunderclouds rolled overhead. She could taste the wind and the promise of rain, and she felt like running. As if from high on the canyon wall she could hear Kara's voice like a deep, throaty purr and could feel her moving on the comforters as though she were pawing nervously at the ground. She saw them then, enemies all around her, wolves who transformed into men who became knights brandishing huge swords held outward like protective crosses. There was a confusing array of rats and bats in caves, of dark, ruined castles, of naked warriors armed with sticks and impossible creatures dead these ages past. She shook her head.

"Won't you tell me tonight?" Megan begged. She didn't want the magic to end. She rubbed Kara's thigh and blinked her long eyelashes displaying that sad, puppy-dog look, purposefully overdoing the flirtation. She knew she wouldn't get her way.

"No. It's a long story, and I still need to tell you the vampire code, and that will keep us up long enough tonight."

"The vampire code," Megan repeated sternly. "Sounds serious."

"Well," Kara continued, "it's important. The code is the unwritten law that governs the Vampire Nation. It buries itself deeply into the unconscious mind and integrates itself into the instinctive behavior of purebreds and shadows alike." Suddenly Kara's voice became a soothing trill, humming like a rhythmic Buddhist chant. "Listen with an open heart, and embrace the code for much of it will have meaning for you now. The future will determine if there is a Bloodwarrior hidden within you, and the hunger will demand a test of will and a sense of honor. The code will be the guide you carry inside. Now I will instruct you, and at the hour of your need I will protect you. Listen and remember." Megan lay spellbound, mesmerized as the words flowed from Kara's lips like glittering effluent from a magic wand. They were not many and appeared simple and straightforward, yet each aspect of the code held an underlying import, and Kara revealed their mysteries each in turn. But overall, she stressed the importance of simply understanding their intent, of recognizing their spirit, and the importance of abiding by them. So Megan opened her heart and her mind to the vampire code and embraced it. In this manner told and remembered from that night, it would be forever instilled within her:

One. Man is the only prey. Only the evil among man is to be taken. He who is without pity, without remorse, is for eating. The procession of evil is endless; the supply to satisfy the hunger, eternal. The virtuous shall not be hunted.

Two. The feast is the prize, not the goal. Evil is the beast that slithers through the hearts of men. The goal is the extermination of the beast.

Three. The quarry belongs to the blood-letter. No one may challenge for the flesh of fallen prey.

Four. The essence is bound to man alone, through logic he reigns, through reason he commands the beasts, through hope he aspires to fly with angels. The essence was the enigma; the question was the mammal. The answer was man.

Five. The vampire shall not reveal his superiority over man.

Six. The vampire must not disclose his true nature to man.

Seven. Only the man beloved receives the essence; thus a shadow is extruded from the master. The advocate protects and mentors, and shall render justice onto the fledgling who wanders from the path.

Eight. Mating shall be vampire to vampire. This is the way. The shadow shall be the dispeller of despair.

Nine. All justice shall be swift and merciful.

Ten. The ethical and moral concerns of the Vampire Nation are beyond the realm of man.

Eleven. The Vampire Nation asserts its moral superiority over man and stands in judgment.

Twelve. The Vampire Nation serves man and the evolution of good. It harvests the wicked, yet assumes no stand in war, in terror, in organized crime, in government, in police action, or the making of laws which rule man.

Thirteen. A vampire knows allegiance is to the Vampire Nation alone.

"Render justice." Megan noted of number seven, "That means you would have killed me if I had freaked out today?" It was more of an indictment than a question, and by the look on Kara's face she knew it was dead on.

"Yes," Kara replied; "we have been vigilant in keeping secret the existence of the Vampire Nations for thousands of years. Dispatching shadows who are unable to accept or adapt is simply part of that safeguard.

"But it doesn't happen often because the virus alters the neural receptors to respond favorably to the mesmer-voice," Megan theorized.

"Yes. And the virus alters the vocal capacity and speech center to allow for the intuitive development of mesmeric capability, as well," Kara explained. "Adaptive evolution; it's a wonderful thing. Unfortunately, as with all evolutionary leaps, there are hits and misses, favorable and unfavorable mutations that pop up now and then. Consequently, there are some who simply do not adapt and must be dispatched. It has to be done. However, from what we've been able to piece together, it happens infrequently. You must know, though, if you were one of the rare few, I can't think of anything that would hurt me more."

"Kara, I don't know where life will take us now, whether we will be friends or lovers, but I hope you will always love me. Only time reveals fate, or at least, the truth that lies hidden deep within us. But I know this for certain. I will never betray you nor do anything to cause you harm."

Kara hadn't cried since her mother had left for California all those many years ago. She prided herself on being in control, at least on this score. But she put her head on Megan's shoulder now and cried large, crystal tears, which cascaded like lush rain drops until Megan's shirt was soaked and matted against her skin. She felt Megan's hand against her head, stroking her hair, pressing the long, jet strands against her back. She cried until her breathing settled into a deep and even rhythm and only a few silent sobs escaped in staccato waves. Megan's hand answered her signals with loving pats and soothing rubs, and occasionally her lips brushed Kara's ear.

"Everything is fine. You did the right thing," she said. "You did the right thing." Once, so softly she was unsure if Megan had purposefully spoken the words or if they had unconsciously hitched a ride on a sigh, like a whisper in the wind she heard, "I love you, Kara." Kara's tender embrace and warm, moist lips answered silently in return, and Megan sighed again. Kara knew then the voice she had heard had been the eternal echo in Megan's heart and her shadow would be more than just a friend.

Finally, Kara cast her a small, embarrassed smile. "Thanks. I guess I just needed a good cry," she said, wiping her eyes with the bottom of her shirttail. Then she broke into a blue-ribbon smile. "It wasn't just the virus talking, was it?" she laughed. "Because I need you so very much."

Megan matched her smile, and the tears welled up in her eyes. Kara was only partially joking about the viral influence on emotions, because it did create a mild euphoria by re-engineering adrenaline receptors in the brain. Apparently, the gradual readjustment to the effects of adrenaline made it easier for the novitiate to accept his or her new life. As far as anyone has been able to determine, this is probably the actual reason few shadows have actually been dispatched. The transmutation feels good. But Megan's admission, she believed, had nothing to do with receptors, with adrenaline, with the virus or any aspect of the transmutation. Kara believed it hadn't developed overnight or come from a place within her that had changed or grown in the past twenty-four hours; she believed it had come from a place where it had been residing for a long time, waiting for the right moment to find its way out, seeking a clearly defined trail and signals that gave it permission to be released. The euphoria of the transmutation and the intimacy of this moment was the opportunity Megan had been waiting for. That is what Kara believed. That is what she hoped. That is what she chose to embrace.

Extremely tired now, they settled in looking forward to a long sleep into a late and lazy morning. Kara piled a generous supply of logs into the old stone fireplace, stacking them neatly into a great pyramid. She watched momentarily as the glowing embers reached out to the fresh logs, caressing the virgin wood with tenuous fingers. Then she crawled into the tangle of bedding to snuggle against Megan, who was breathing deep and steady already, sounding an endless procession of contented sighs. Kara thought she was fast asleep, but she opened her eyes suddenly and spoke through a sleepy yawn, "So, what do we do with that thing on the table?" Kara propped herself up on her elbow for a moment, thinking.

"We'll bury it," she said. "We'll bury it where they can never find it." They both lay entombed in the pile of blankets and pillows with that empathic current connecting them like an electric charge, entertaining a similar thought, their common instincts sounding a warning that it wouldn't do to keep the transponder in the cabin much longer. They both knew it would be best to be up early, to bury it at first light—so much for sleeping in.

Chapter 10

Sunday, October 10, 6: 00 A.M.: The morning brought no relief. Ovek's head was splitting, his wound was throbbing, and he could have sworn he had aged a hundred cycles overnight. The skin under his eyes was puffy and had faded from the usual soft teal to a smoky yellow. The fine scales from the top of his ear wells down to his shoulders were turning gray and flaking off. His joints ached, and a sharp cough cut deeply into his chest. Worst of all his stomach felt as though it was twisting around his backbone. He was hungry, but the thought of actually eating something sent a lump up into his chest. The night had deceived him, robbing him of the rest and relief it had promised. He had slumbered fitfully, dreaming intermittently of flittering, hairy avians and of battling a monstrous beast, a fearsome permutation of man and wolf. He knew now, with a deadly certainty, that Kara's bite had infected him, and that he was in serious trouble. Worst of all, he knew his command was in jeopardy.

Yesterday, no matter how strongly he had pressured Allen, his captive had remained steadfast in his ignorance of Kara's changeling abilities. He seriously doubted that he could break that resolve today. If he couldn't get Allen to admit that the changeling capability even existed, it was useless to press him for an antidote to the changeling bite. Threats would be useless; that much was certain, and torture was out of the question; they needed his willing cooperation to get to the cabin. He simply had to hope the illness would not prove lethal. One thing was clear, though; he was likely to get a lot worse before he got better, and the thought of it nearly sent him spinning out of control. It wouldn't be easy to deal wit, but he would have to find a way. They were counting on him to develop a plan to get them off this outland rock, and he wasn't about to let his team down now. *Tough it out,* he thought; *tough it out.*

Throughout the day, Allen remained confined to his improvised cell. He found it reasonably comfortable; they gave him enough to eat, and he had ample opportunity to move about. The chain was long enough and split near the end to lock his wrist and ankle, enabling him to reach every corner and to lie easily in his makeshift bed. Guor dumped a generous pile of books and magazines on the floor and, when he asked, Ovek allowed him a large marker and a pad of paper so that he might make some sketches.

"Count all the sheets," Ovek told Guor. "I want every one accounted for." It was simple concessions like these that Ovek considered vital to keeping Allen pacified. The primary concerns of the day were being mapped out in the kitchen, which, for the moment, had been converted into a situation room. The plan was a simple one. They needed a vehicle large enough to carry them all to the cabin. Allen would play a significant role in securing it and driving it back to the farmhouse.

"I think I can handle it, Cap'n," Nol volunteered. "These Earth rovers appear simple to operate."

"No," Ovek said, "the controls look simple, but we don't know enough about regulations. There are too many unknowns, too many variables to deal with. It wouldn't do to be singled out by the local authorities for an infraction. Far worse, an accident would be disastrous. We need you and the vehicle back here in one piece. So, you're taking Allen. Besides, I want a dry run to see how he handles himself before the trip to the cabin tomorrow. Give him space—just enough to tempt him."

"Aye, Cap'n," Nol conceded, "will do." The plan was set, but it was mid-afternoon by the time it was finalized, and the effort had taken its toll. "You look really bad." Nol observed. "Maybe you should get some rest, Cap'n."

"Not yet," Ovek replied, "but soon I will pad the nest for a short while. I need to be geared up for tomorrow."

"I've seen you tore up some, Cap'n, but nothing like this. Just what is it anyway?"

"I'm not sure. It's either an infection or a poison," Ovek replied. "Either way, Nol, if it's fatal, you have to be prepared to take command; you know that."

"I know." Nol bobbed his head slowly. "I'm ready, and I know what has to be done, Cap'n," he continued, "but you know I never wanted command this way."

"I'm sure of it."

"I'd rather see you go down to disrupter fire than scale away like this."

"There's a sweet sentiment, Nol." Ovek smiled. "Thanks."

"You know, Cap'n," Nol said, "the more I think about it, the more convinced I become that these Earthlings would make a formidable slave unit. Their combat and survival skills are outstanding—natural weaponry, physically and mentally disciplined, intelligent, and technologically literate. I think it our duty to file a strike report on this planet."

"As much as they worry me, I'm inclined to agree with you," Ovek replied. "But I believe their changeling ability is their most valuable asset, and I would like to see them brought in as partners, not slaves. As ambassadors and special ops troops their natural abilities and instincts would prove most useful. They're raw; they would need extensive training, and the empire would be faced with a massive disciplinary challenge. But it is doable. If we get back, strike that...*when* we get back, we'll file the report and make the appropriate recommendations."

Ovek headed for his quarters in the master bedroom, leaving all the preparation details in the capable hands of his second in command. The promise of sweet oblivion guided his dragging feet to the foot of his bed, where he collapsed in a heap on the tousled surface. Nol headed up the stairs in search of the perfect tool to accomplish the task planned for that evening. He discovered it nestled in one of several large chests stuffed into the walk-in closet. It was secured with a pair of long, flat runners intended for traveling over snow, hidden under an assortment of helmets, which might easily have passed for special-ops gear. It was a superbly designed weapon, a compound bow with an attached ammo-mount stuffed with deadly metal-alloy arrows. It was light and compact but amazingly powerful. The arrow tips were multi-faceted blades, chicma sharp, intended for hunting beasts of considerable size and strength, or it may have been designed as a weapon of war.

It had a beautiful golden insignia stamped on it, representing a fearsome, hairy beast with long, sharp teeth and deadly talons; quite possibly it was a ceremonial instrument for the ritual killing of fellow changelings. Perhaps it was intended to deliver a death more honorable and spiritual than that dispensed by firearms or other more conventional methods. Here was another find indicating a history of Megan's combat and weapons expertise. The more he discovered about her, the more he grew to appreciate this Earth woman who favored the use of weapons over her changeling abilities. He wasn't sure why, but that appealed to him; there was just something about females with blasters and blades! He sincerely hoped she had survived her encounter with the mandat knife. He had assumed her dead at first, but now, he very much doubted it. He had a feeling about her and about these changelings in general. They were tougher than they looked. She was like her bow, deceptively powerful. Holding it now, it felt like an extension of her. It seemed to pulse in his hand as if he were clutching her beating heart. He believed that personal possessions, such as this weapon, transmitted signals through space and time, which revealed truths that could be communicated in no other way. Only soldiers who have faced a common enemy or who have met each other in mortal combat know the language and hear its voice. Only they can interpret its cryptic symbols.

He savored the exquisite weapon with his hands, enjoying the feel of the molded grip, the clean, sleek lines of the re-curve, the even glide of the draw and the sudden tension of the pulleys. The weapon spoke in a sensual whisper, and he understood. She was alive, this vixen gladiator. Great warriors do not fall to a single blade. Nol smiled, revealing the short, pointed teeth on only one side of his mouth—he knew, for good or ill, they would meet again. Just as fate had crossed their path with Kara a second time, so too, he believed, it would bring him face-to-face with Megan once again. She would either dispatch him with a display of tactical skill, or he would outmaneuver and kill her, perhaps with the gun in his belt, the very bow in his grasp, or in hand-to-hand combat. In any event, it would be a glorious fight. He would be proud to die by her hand or to deliver her a proper soldier's death, to ensure she relinquish her spirit to the battlefield.

He would kill her quickly, without shame or suffering; she would not bleed out and die a cold, miserable husk like some hapless, wounded animal. Soldiers deserved better; they deserved the benefit of a swift and honorable death. Hadn't he always felt exactly the same toward Ovek? Surely, it would have been better had Kara killed him right there in the kitchen. It was difficult to watch him deteriorate like this, as if his remaining days were an unheralded battlefield, and he was falling in slow motion, silent, invisible blades piercing him, cutting unseen wounds, bloodless, leaving only the wretchedness of his body and the dark *inevitable* etched upon his spirit. It seemed that tomorrow could not come quickly enough. If Kara would not negotiate for the transponder, which he thought likely, the battle would ensue once again.

When it did, he hoped she would do the honorable thing and kill him quickly, mercifully. Poisoning a soldier was demeaning, especially one of Ovek's caliber. It was an ending and a legacy he didn't deserve. If Ovek was one step closer to Nos tomorrow, and Kara would not send him honorably on his journey, Nol thought, perhaps he ought to do it. As a lieutenant in service of the RegeìCean Empire it was wrong and seemed dishonorable; but as Ovek's friend, as someone who understood the captain better than any reptilian alive, it was not only the right thing to do, it was the most honorable. Certainly it would be better than having the captain rot like a piece of forgotten meat.

It was heart wrenching to look at him lately; he had the pallor of a limb left behind on the battlefield. It would be an act of kindness, a sign of true and abiding friendship. He and Ovek had never seriously spoken of such a thing, but he knew the captain would consider it his duty to deliver him a soldier's death, to send him to the chambers of Nos Po Dei a true hero and champion of Thacia. How might Kara interpret such an action? Might there not be some serendipitous fallout? Perhaps a truce might be considered; she might be inclined to consider his request for the transponder. It was clear that Kara believed Ovek had thrust the blade into Megan, and she might interpret his actions very favorably. So, if it had to be done, it might be made to work in their favor. Nol knew being in command sometimes meant making the truly tough decisions. Perhaps fate was testing his command abilities, and this was an opportunity in disguise. He folded the bow, slung the carry case across his shoulder, and headed down the staircase.

One step at a time, he told himself; there was no sense in burying the captain while both his feet were still planted firmly on the ground. Besides, though wounded and sick, Ovek was still in command and a skilled soldier, and Nol was well aware he was a formidable threat to any opponent even when flat on his back. Besides, Nol wasn't prepared to give up on him yet; he knew the captain wouldn't be giving up without a significant fight. After all, it was Ovek.

Just as the sun settled beneath the horizon the captain slipped into the room with Allen. The plan was in motion. Without a warning he popped the hypo into his shoulder and injected him with a healthy dose of orange juice. "Sorry, Allen," he said.

"What was that?" Allen grimaced, rubbing his shoulder. "This sneak attack is starting to wear thin."

"I need your help, and I need to make sure you won't run or put up a fight. It's just a precaution," he explained. "I injected you with a slow poison. Very lethal," he lied.

"You gotta' be fucking kidding me!" Allen blurted out, his eyes wide. He was turning white.

"Don't worry. It's very slow acting—standard military issue, made especially for deterrent situations. There is an antidote, and there is ample time to deliver it. And it's painless."

"Yeah! Why don't you pump a little in yourself! You look like a goddamn zombie—seems to me you'd be better off dead!" He was practically foaming at the mouth.

"Settle down. I understand you're upset. Look, everything will be fine. I made a promise to you, and I intend to keep it. No one is going to die. All you have to do is help us get to the cabin. The injection is just a bit of encouragement for you to keep your end of the bargain. We need a large vehicle to get us to the cabin, and I need you to pilot it. Can I count on you? I promise you, the antidote will be waiting for you when you return. You have my word."

"All right," Allen said, resigning himself to fate. There was nothing he could do about it anyway, and he knew it. "How long do I have?"

"You have more than enough time; don't worry."

"You want me to rent a truck; is that it?" It was something of a hedge.

"No. I know that would seem the easiest way to handle this, but I just can't let you talk to anyone. You might panic and say the wrong thing. It's too risky."

"What do you want me to do then?" Allen could feel his stomach descending somewhere to the vicinity of his lower intestine.

"I want you to help Nol commandeer one, " Ovek said.

"You mean you want me to help him steal one," Allen replied peevishly.

"No. It's merely a temporary situation. When we leave, we won't be taking the truck with us," Ovek said. "You can return it if you like. Surely, Allen, you can see the logic in that."

"I suppose. Besides, I guess I don't have much choice. But damn it, Ovek, what makes you think Nol won't kill me out there and eat my bones for breakfast? You've seen the way he looks at me," Allen complained.

"He looks at everyone that way. It's his nature," Ovek replied. "But his job is to obey orders, and his orders are to secure a truck with your help and bring you back unharmed."

"And if he doesn't?"

"I'll kill him, and he knows it." With that Ovek considered the conversation at an end. He turned and marched out the door.

At nightfall they would put the operation in motion. They would travel north by foot keeping the farmhouse in view. Past the farmhouse the narrow frontage road ended abruptly some two hundred feet beyond the edge of the wood, which virtually guaranteed no one would be traveling it by night. To the west, a natural prairie owned by the Pacific Northwest Railroad faded to the horizon. It was bordered on the north by a corporate tree nursery clustered with sapling pines and junipers. The virtual isolation was ideal.

The three of them, Nol, Tavon, and Allen, would make their way past Allen's home to the boulevard, and there wait for a suitable vehicle. Allen would flag it down, feigning an emergency of some sort, just long enough for Nol and Tavon to incapacitate the occupants. It was a simple plan; even Allen felt confident about its success and his part in it, and it fit in nicely with the escape plan he was developing. He was no one's fool, regardless of Ovek's high-handed speeches and sincere gestures. From the looks of things Ovek wasn't likely to be in charge much longer; whatever was causing his illness would probably kill him before ever reaching the cabin, putting Nol in the driver's seat. That prospect alone would have set Allen on this course of action, but the fact that none of these aliens had realized how well their voices traveled through the pipes in the old farm house had been a major oversight.

Allen had heard every word they had said about incorporating Earth into their empire and making Earthlings slave soldiers in their unwitting army. It was a hideous, unthinkable prospect. Once Ovek had explained the evening's mission to him, he began to hatch a plan of his own. He had resolved to play along with their scheme and wait for the right moment, then make his escape. They would never reach the cabin and, if all went as planned, would be stranded in the woods to be hunted down like the animals they were. Although he wasn't a killer by nature and didn't quite know how to go about it, he had to take a few of them out in the process, primarily Nol. He would have to bide his time, keeping his eyes open for just the right moment. He could afford to be patient, at least to a point. His knowledge was his leverage. They needed him; their ignorance was their weakness, and he would use it against them. He just had to hope that once his plan had been executed he would be able to make it back to the farm and administer the antidote in time. He wasn't the heroic type, but he was logical, and considering that the entire earth was at risk, he knew, realistically, the antidote hardly mattered.

Chapter 11

Rich surveyed the room one last time, pleased with all his work and attention to detail over the past year. Everything was ready; everything in its place. The room was complete, secure and self-contained, waiting for *her* to arrive. The bed's steel posts were permanently rooted to the cement floor. The small refrigerator rested squarely on the food storage cabinet in the far corner, which made for a convenient and compact kitchenette. An austere, ivory table and matching chair sat adjacent the cabinet forming a quaint dining area. It had been a shame to anchor then into the cement. But they would belong to her, as well, and be equally permanent, so there was a poetic irony in destroying the portability of such valuable antiques. The sink, the vanity, and toilet were all to the right. A floral-patterned screen slid along a semi-circular track mounted high on the wall above the toilet. It was a questionable and generous addition to the bathroom. There was no practical need for it because she would be alone, except for the time he would spend with her, of course. (Although it would increase her sense of privacy it would prevent his being able to view her through the various peepholes he had situated in the walls, and he would probably not be able to capture her using the toilet on video. So the screen was definitely a negotiable item. If she gave him any shit he would rip that fucker down.)

Near the opposite corner was a small office desk displaying a compact CD player with a generous supply of contemporary favorites and a sleek, expensive laptop. Of course, no Internet applications or connections were included. Above the desk was a permanent storage container with an attractive, slide-away face cover. It was attractive and would allow her to keep things organized and uncluttered. Across from the bed a diminutive, potted tree gave the room life and a sense of the outdoors. A wall fan generated the breeze simulating wind rustling the leaves. It was pointed directly at the tree for that very purpose. He liked that sound—he was sure everyone did—it made his heart feel young and carefree, and he knew she would appreciate his thoughtfulness, his sense of poetry and romance.

Beside the tree, a TV was bolted to the top of her dresser. It boasted full cable access that would allow her to enjoy all the movies on his premium stations, even the porn. He was sure she would love that enticing feature. Although she would have no control over the channels, he was sure she should be pleased with the selections he would make. After all, he wasn't required to provide any entertainment. He had included it out of kindness, as he had the Fold-n-Glyde treadmill that stood in the upright position in the near corner. It wouldn't do for her to get lazy and out of shape. It came equipped with the E-Z Glyde pads on the feet for handy repositioning. It would be a simple matter to slide the unit in front of the television and get a decent workout while walking through an episode of *CSI* or running through a round of *Jeopardy*.

The walls were still mostly bare. There was only the large, shatterproof mirror over the bed, which rendered an illusion of a room larger than the meager twelve-by-fourteen-foot reality. It reflected a pale violet block of wall, the jagged, meandering outline of the tree, and the studio lamps set in the track along the ceiling. All in all, it was quite a handsome place. He could easily live there himself—almost. It was still somewhat drab and lifeless; it lacked personality. Once she was secure, she could dress the place with décor that pleased her, put up posters or pictures and scatter stuffed animals about, make it feminine and pretty the way women were good at. He wanted her to make the place her own, to reflect her individual style. He had painted the remaining walls neutral beige for that very reason.

Similarly, the dresser drawers were still empty. It wouldn't do to have the wrong size or color undergarments, although eventually he would supply several pair of black panties with lacy edging; perhaps a crotch-less pair or two. He was confident she would find those exciting! He would get her some push-up bras and assorted lingerie, as well, white and virginal, and some sheer and black, and very naughty. Maybe he would sneak in some leather items and a battery-operated gismo just to round things out. Once he knew her better, more intimately, he would be able to plan further ahead, anticipate her needs more adequately, and, in general, make more decisions for her. Perhaps she would be into the really kinky stuff like ball gags and whips; maybe she would beg him to slap her or piss in her mouth, or push the needles in just a little deeper. After all, it had been a long time, and who the hell knew who she was this time!

Time, yes. It was all a matter of time. He pushed the light switch in and out rapidly and turned the dial left and right to check the dimmer. All was in order. Standing in the doorway, he ran his hand along the outer wall, letting the rough, cool bricks play against his fingertips. A coarse granule broke loose, and he rolled it slowly around and around imagining her nipple between his fingers, the hardness of it exciting him to erection until he crushed the tiny stone into a fine powder.

Soon. Soon all his hard work would be rewarded; all he had dreamed of these many years would become reality. He wouldn't be forced to live without her, and his lonely, bitter life would come to an end. He could admire her at his leisure, enjoy her company whenever the mood struck him and satisfy his intense need whenever it arose. In the past few months he had seen her often, though only briefly. She had been difficult to spot since she had reverted to the clever disguises. She was coy and smart, a few of the many things he loved about her. Sometimes, she had been a blond with long legs and large breasts that bounced with a musical rhythm when she walked in high heels. He knew this disguise well; she always made the mistake of wearing the same style of tight, cashmere sweater that displayed her tits like targets with their tiny bulls-eyes centered for perfect aim.

Often she became a brunette, displaying a sassy, club-culture cut with multi-colored highlights. She sported modest breasts and wider hips with this look. She created an illusion of shorter, more powerful legs, but was completely unafraid to display a lot of fleshy thigh beneath those sexy, leather minis.

Occasionally she was a redhead with a cute, little overbite and nerdy, little black glasses. Sometimes she looked like a teenager, sometimes very mature, at other times she was thirty-something; on rare occasions she looked like a child. She was shrewd, always different, yet always the same. He was looking forward to stripping away the disguises, to laying bare the real woman, to revealing the truth, to exposing the sexy, filthy bitch beneath. He knew that is what she actually wanted, what she needed. He needed something equally fundamental; he needed her to realize just how much she loved him.

And he wanted something equally selfish, to make love to her whenever the madness overpowered him. It would be as if he owned a private place in heaven, to be able to caress and kiss her, to feel the warmth and smoothness of her skin against his, to feel her moist lips on his body, to know the thrill of releasing himself on her whenever that need forced him into her arms. Most of all, he wanted her scent on his hand, to know the deep, honey musk of her moistness clinging to him. He crossed to the opposite side of the room and jerked the chain and U-bolt anchored to the wall. It resisted his most ferocious pull and protested with a raucous clank. He caressed the steel-linked dog collar and heavy-duty lock hanging on the hook next to the toilet.

Soon he would whisper her name as he came inside her. He wondered if she would resurrect one from the past or, like some clever genie, blink up a new one for this latest encounter. He hoped, no, he knew, this would be their last encounter. Whatever her name this time, he looked forward to whispering it, repeating it night after night after night, until she acknowledged her love for him and whispered his name in return. He knew with a deadly certainty it would happen. He walked back to the doorway, took one more look around, turned out the lights and headed upstairs leaving her room to rest comfortably in the shadows of his basement. Now, all that remained was to find her. Again.

He had first met her in sixth grade. Her name had been Janice, though she had since changed it many times. She was neither the prettiest girl in class nor the only one sprouting nubile breasts; nearly half the girls in class laid claim to those juvenile bragging rights. But there was an aura surrounding her as if she were capable of hovering above ordinary human girls; she seemed to glow with a soft, violet light that pulsed in exact rhythm with the rise and fall of his chest and the beating of his heart. He couldn't explain it. She was blessed with brilliant saucer-sized eyes, and an easy smile that displayed her row of upper teeth like a bright, crescent moon. Her long, red hair funneled down her back to her waist like a southwestern tornado. She had a sassy Scottish face with skin as pure as newly-driven snow, perfect upturned titties that matched her nose and, how her mom ever let her get away with those short, pleated skirts and lacy white panties, well, who knows!

He wished now that he had never fallen in love with her, but more precisely, he wished she had ultimately paid no attention to him at all. But she had. In school, she had mostly ignored him except for the usual, casual greetings, but then, one evening as he was walking home from the movies, crossing the baseball field, he happened upon her lazily strolling directly toward him. The light overhanging the infield illuminated her unexpectedly, separating her from the shadows like a conjured spirit, as if he had wished-upon-a-star and his fondest dream had come true. They exchanged a few words and a brief, awkward moment. Then, suddenly, as if reality itself had waved a magic wand, they were on the side of the hill in the outfield, serenaded by the leaves swaying in the breeze, buried under the cover of darkness and a blanket of stars, and his finger found its way inside a woman for the very first time. She hadn't even touched him, but it didn't matter. It was enough that he had felt up a woman, slipped through the wetness of her and enjoyed the comfort of her warm secret refuge.

True, he had fumbled and poked around her lower abdomen for an inordinately long time until she had finally decided to take matters into her own hands and guide him down between her thighs to a point were things mattered most. But once there, he felt he was master and was quite sure she appreciated his manly, instinctive expertise. Her whimpering and spasms seemed a testament to that assumption. So he was certain, the true and steady course of his life had been set because he had found true love. But Janice seemed to see things differently. She talked with him more frequently at school but was loath to mention anything about that night on the baseball field, let alone about their lovemaking. He asked about being with her again, about "doing something" together, but she always had a noncommittal answer at the ready.

When they entered seventh grade things went from bad to horrible. She flat-out told him to leave her alone. Then one of his classmates bragged about being with her one night at Mary Ellen's house, about being pushed into a closet with her and how she went down on him. The betrayal was more than he could bear. He passed her a scathing note in class a few days later telling her exactly how he felt about a girl who could do such a thing, and how much he hated her for it. But he also let her know how much she had hurt him and how much she had meant to him, because he still loved her and he knew, no matter what she did, he always would. When she turned to look at him with those huge, dewy eyes his heart melted, and his mind screamed for her to beg his forgiveness.

It hurt all the more when she put her finger to her mouth in a poorly executed attempt to disguise her girlish laughter. It cut into his heart like a razor and, even now when he closes his eyes and envisions that lovely, cherub face with its mocking grin, the wound opens and bleeds again. A few weeks later her family moved to Wyoming, supposedly. Her father allegedly had a health problem that forced them out of Wisconsin. However, Rich knew it was all a ruse to go underground, to remove their daughter from the circles of her familiar world and its overwhelming temptations. Because of the note he suspected it was to ensure he never find her. In any event, he knew they had never left the state; in fact, they had never ventured far from Milwaukee. He had not been deceived, because he easily recognized her when they met again, despite all her surgery.

It was on a particularly warm summer day; the temperature was in the upper nineties. He was walking lazily down Wisconsin Avenue scanning the posters trying to determine which of several theaters he might select simply as an excuse to spend the afternoon in a dark and cool refuge. Suddenly, there she was, window-shopping. To be sure, he didn't recognize her immediately; her makeover had been so clever and complete. But her unmistakable signature would be written and displayed later that day. At that moment he merely experienced a sense of her, a sensation not unlike déjà vu. Perhaps her pheromones triggered a recognition patterned imprinted in his brain. Perhaps she simply used the same soap she had used back then. Who could say?

But it didn't matter because it was quite clear she had set the trap, and he had sprung it like a yearling hare. Why? Maybe over the course of these seven years the guilt had been eating away at her. Maybe she was ready to make amends. So he introduced himself just as if he had no idea who she was and gave her every chance in the world to make things right. They spent the remainder of the day together, and even before the movie was over he had kissed her. He felt the passion in her supple lips, in their slight and easy parting and in the way the tip of her tongue searched for his, tasting his mouth as if he were a delicious dessert. By the time they finished their dinner he realized how much he still loved her. But later that evening in the dark shadows of the trees near the yacht club, with his mouth pressed firmly to her breast, his finger exploring deep inside her, as he guided her tentative hand around his mammoth erection, he ejaculated onto her blouse the instant her fingers brushed him.

Actually most of the fingers that touched him were his own and he suspected that is what she found so very humorous, which embarrassed and infuriated him all the more. But there it was, that signature laugh. He recognized her now, beyond all doubt. His instincts had been dead-balls on. She may have changed her name to Christine, but it was Janice; he was certain; she smelled the same, she tasted the same, and she laughed the same as before. He whipped his finger out of her and left her lying there, her legs spread, her blouse dripping. What did it matter? She had humiliated him for the last time. He promised himself to never see her again. But even as he zipped himself up and walked away he doubted it was a promise he was likely to keep. The very smell of her on his hand, which he was loath to wash for several days thereafter, was testament to that sad fact.

Afterward she began stalking him. He acted as if he didn't notice. He wanted to observe. She would take odd jobs to be near him, biding her time, looking for the perfect opportunity to take revenge it seemed. Each time her disguises were more clever and elaborate, the wigs, the glasses, the accents and makeup. Once she must have spent an entire day in a tanning salon because she was so dark and exotic she looked as though she had been in Mexico the entire winter, unbelievable attention to detail, and why? Torture. Where once her goal was merely to tease him, now all her scheming and effort were dedicated to a more sinister goal: punishment. She would smile and bag his groceries or ring up his sandwiches, and be as pleasant as could be. From behind the bar she would lean over to display deeply fabulous cleavage and slide his beer in front of him as if they were perfect strangers.

On the street she would sometimes turn her head slightly, just enough to identify herself, then with a winning smile and a matching wiggle be on her way. At the movies she would sometimes sit behind him and chatter with her girlfriends about her "boyfriend" just to irritate him, as if he would ever let on that he were seriously jealous. No, he was too good at the game to be suckered into that ball-crushing trap. Sometimes at the beach she would walk by and kick the tiniest bit of sand on him just to get his attention, never look down, and act as if he hadn't been lying there at all. But the one, single most powerful weapon she had in her arsenal to fire at him for walking away from her that night was the single-shot verbal-blast cannon, and she used it lavishly against him, she consistently said *no* whenever he asked her out. If she really wanted revenge, he was willing to give her the opportunity, because deep inside, buried in a place he couldn't reach, he had a weakness for her that plagued him like a reoccurring canker, and he was willing to accept her back into his life faster than he could undress her in his mind. Time and time again she brought him *this fucking* close to saying *yes*, only to shoot him down for no apparent reason.

Then, one day she simply disappeared; he never caught the slightest glimpse of her again, leaving him surrounded by women whose disguises were dull or repulsive, or just peculiar, disguises that, when stripped away, revealed neither Janice nor Christine nor any of the few dozen other personas she had adopted. One of those disguises was an austere pair of black glasses underscored by an expensive silk scarf. These masked a snobby, foreign aristocrat who subjected him to a virtual eruption of arcane words; the illusion was a woman so vastly superior he could barely tolerate being in the same room with her. For a while he encountered a string of this type milling about Milwaukee's fashionable East side and hobnobbing in the various new clubs and restaurants being established in the renovated Third Ward.

Some disguised themselves as artists or writers, personas of impressive, creative talents; but these disguised harpies loved their meager gifts more than the thrill of being in his arms. He quickly grew tired of stripping away their masks to reveal the cold, lifeless women beneath. All he accomplished was to reveal their hidden disdain for him and to expose their reluctance to invite him inside their secret, private place, that warm and luscious opening to the ultimate truth. If he could touch that part of them, open that doorway and step inside that world, they would not have been able to hide from him; they would have been revealed. But their stubbornness prevailed, and their evil natures denied him access. Just as Janice had, they all played the temptation game, the game of hopes dashed and wishes unfulfilled, the game of *desire,* which aroused him to a marble hardness with nowhere to prove his tool equal to the challenge.

Sluts! Bitches! Every one of them! But by ripping away all those disguises, he had revealed women for whom he felt no desire, women who were less than nothing, women who weren't even that fucking interesting. Most enlightening of all, he revealed no one worthy to leave their scent on him. One day, he had always known, when his preparations were completed, he would find *her*, allow her to wreak her petty revenge if that is what her heart demanded, then he would make sure she would never go away again.

Finally that day had come. He knew the timing was right; the very night all preparations of the *guest* room had been completed he had seen a sign in the sky, a blazing omen of good fortune announcing her arrival. Like a laser pointer from heaven it guided him to her location, toward the east, somewhere in the vicinity of the Oak Creek power plant. The small, surplus delivery truck had been ready for months. He had made sure it was always in tip-top shape, running smoothly as could be. The fake plates would go on just before he pulled out of the driveway. The tape, the ropes, the music equipment bag, the locks and refrigerator box were all tucked neatly in the back, waiting patiently. He had painted over the big, yellow logo on the side with brown paint to match the bulk of the truck. It wasn't a perfect match but it would do. He didn't plan on keeping the truck anyway; he was only going to use it this one time. It's the only reason he bought the ugly, old thing. Afterward, he'd give the inside a cursory rinse, just in case she managed to leave her scent or some other telltale sign behind. Then he'd sell it.

He ate dinner an hour later than usual that evening to avoid those nasty hunger pangs while on the road. The fewer stops he was forced to make the better. He stuffed a few energy bars into his pocket and snatched a water bottle from the fridge in case his search for her ran longer than expected. Just as the world began to turn dark he strapped the survival knife to his chest, grabbed the plates, and slipped a .45 into his belt. One way or another he wasn't coming back without her. A few minutes later he fired up the truck and backed out of the driveway, committed to his final date with destiny.

Allen strolled along the curb toward the oncoming traffic, feigning a casual interest in the bits of trash and leaves matted into the gutter as if searching for some windblown treasure, but he was intently focused on the headlights of the cars and trucks rolling down the avenue. The traffic was light; it usually was this time of night, especially on a Sunday evening. He reached his marker point then hastily retreated to the beginning to repeat his stroll, passing Nol and Taven, who were hidden in the field at separate checkpoints along the route, prepared to converge on the truck when he brought it to a halt. So far the ten or twelve vehicles that had passed were unsuitable. Most of them had been compacts or sport-utility-vehicles. He thought he had walked the route thirty times or more and feared a truck might never come along when Nol gave the signal. "This one will do."

Quickly Allen squirted the lighter fluid onto his gloved hand and the sleeve of his field jacket. Then, with a neat pop of his thumb and jerk of his wrist, flicked the lighter open. He clicked the wheel with a single, even stroke and lit up his arm like a torch. He jumped out in front of the oncoming truck like a crazed maniac, spun around, waving his arm about this way and that mimicking the stunt men he had seen so many times in the movies. He kept the flames away from his head to prevent his hair catching on fire, but other than that he knew there was little danger. He was far more worried the truck might run him down or that the driver might pull around him and simply pass on by. But the flames did the trick; the truck came to a screeching halt fully ten feet in front of him. When it did, he fell to the pavement burying his arms beneath him and lay still and silent as he had been instructed. He had done his part, and rather well, he thought. Nol and Taven would have to actually take the truck; that was their job. He had to admit he was looking forward to seeing the look on the faces of these poor bastards when they caught sight of the truck-jackers. When all this was over, he would take great pleasure in explaining everything: the kidnapping, why they had been held prisoner in his home, and especially the crucial roll they had played in saving the world. Right! No doubt they would think him a complete lunatic; probably have him arrested anyway. But he would deal with that when the time came. Besides, he thought, a solid glimpse of Nol and Taven would go a long way in supporting his story. Plus Kara and Megan would be there to back him up, as well.

Slowly, cautiously, Rich stepped out of the truck. He didn't know whether to feel annoyed at this turn of events or thankful he hadn't run over this asshole with an IQ equal to the current time, which, for him, was leaning somewhere between late and fucking late. "Come on, crack head, get your ass out of the street," he barked. He had seen addicts do weird things before but this was the first time he had seen one set himself on fire. He nudged the prone figure with his foot while sneaking his hand inside his coat, gripping the handle of his .45. The man lay as if dead, even though he had seemed lively enough just moments before. The fire was out and he looked perfectly fine. Something was not right. The hair on Rich's arms stood on end. The very air he breathed seemed electrically charged. Suddenly, he felt like a caged animal with an irresistible urge to claw his way out. Every instinct told him to run, to leap into the truck and pound on the metal until he was far from this dreadful spot.

Something was happening here, something awful, something he was never meant to be a part of. This wasn't his destiny; it wasn't part of the plan. He knew there were weird and dangerous people *out there*, junkies and thugs who would nonchalantly kill for your shoes or a debit card, serial killers and perverts who collected victims like plastic cups, animals disguised as humans who thrived on humiliating other men and inflicting pain. No one had to remind him about the tidal wave of twisted creeps flooding the planet; he knew the likes of them all too well, and he had vowed to never fall victim to any one of them. Yet here he was standing in the middle the road, having been suckered by one of the oldest cons in the book, with two hooded figures approaching from the left and right prepared to deliver the coup de grâce.

He could not understand how or why fate had conspired to destroy all his plans and trash his labors to make a mockery of his destiny with Janice. What would she do or be without him? Rich had once heard that just before you die your entire life flashes though your mind. You relive all you've done, the good and bad; you revisit all your fiends, make amends to those you've hurt and seek their forgiveness, appraise your list of regrets and accomplishments, consider what might have been, and even formulate one final coherent and consistent philosophy. Most believe that at that moment each of us seeks spiritual enlightenment and forgiveness. But Rich barely had time to consider that much-debated philosophical supposition, let alone actually have time to ponder any of these individual notions.

All he could think of before he died was how beautifully the light reflected from the arrowhead as it entered the center of his eye. Slightly out of focus, a split second before the arrow drove through his brain, out of the corner of his eye, he caught a glimpse of a grotesque, grinning dinosaur. But he knew it was only a mask. As his legs buckled, his last thought was not about God or philosophy, about heaven or hell or the deeper meaning of life. It was not about a cleansing of his soul or a sincere wish to go back to right all the wrongs he had done, or to relive a past that had failed him. It was one clear, simple thought, a truth, a revelation about Janice and their final rendezvous that he had planned so carefully. He had to give credit to her final act of revenge, to pay homage to her victory over him. What an ingenious trick she had pulled! What a very peculiar and very clever disguise!

Nol rose slowly from the edge of the field and stood silently for just a moment. He was decorated in alternate bands of light and dark vertical stripes that camouflaged him superbly within the dense reeds. He stretched his legs, forcing the feeling to return to his numb legs, then jogged directly toward the driver hovering menacingly over Allen. He locked the nock of the arrow into the bow and signaled to Taven, who jumped to his feet and similarly began his approach. At the prearranged distance, the troopers slowed to a brisk walk. Nol pulled back on the bowstring and, barely taking aim, zipped an arrow directly toward the driver's head. He didn't seem to notice the troopers at all; he was too busy expressing his annoyance with Allen. Upon the release of the arrow, however, his attention was diverted, and his complaining stopped immediately.

The arrow slapped him in the right eye, cracked through the back of his skull and stopped abruptly just before the feathers disappeared into the bloody well of his socket. He stood swaying for a moment, one hand inside his jacket, the other flailing about, opening and closing as if to grasp some imaginary object floating in space just in front of his face. His mouth continued to articulate a litany of grievances, but the only sound was the hissing spray ejecting from his eye and the plinking sound of the larger droplets striking the pavement. He stumbled a few meandering steps, then teetered back and forth until Allen reached out to grasp his ankle. He fell forward, his face landing squarely in the center of Allen's back, forcing the arrow ever deeper into his skull. Allen rolled away quickly, unnerved as the fellow's head plunked onto the pavement like a ripe pumpkin. The side of his head lay flat on the road, a drizzle of blood and white foam oozed from his mouth and arched away as if he had expelled a world-record, slow-motion spit. Allen stared at him for a moment, transfixed. It was extremely unsettling. He had never seen a dead body before. Setting himself on fire had been child's play compared with this grisly sight. This poor sap had morphed from living human being to dancing zombie, from jack-o-lantern to roadkill in a heartbeat; it was all too much.

"Ovek said no one was to be hurt," he hissed at Nol as he pulled himself to his feet. "What did you do?"

"Shut up and get the keys," Nol hissed back at him. "You should be happy there was only one human in the truck." Nol already had another arrow in the bow, the string pulled back slightly as a warning; if Allen was going to use his changeling abilities, Nol knew, now would be the time. But Allen looked again at the body lying at his feet and just nodded his head. He seemed more inclined to stick with the plan despite the killing. Besides, he had that poison to worry about. Nol knew the threat of dying a slow and painful death was probably keeping him at bay. All the same, he purposefully reflected the overhead light off the arrowhead directly onto Allen's face, allowing the glittering star pattern to play from one eye to the other and back again.

Allen stooped to check the driver's pockets—a wallet, a hanky, a few candy bars, nothing unusual. He didn't open the wallet. He had no desire to know the guy's name or anything personal about him. The guy's blood and bits of his brain were seeping under the soles of his shoes. What more did he need to know? He rifled through the coat pockets as well and spotted the .45 tucked neatly in the dead man's belt. He hesitated a moment. It would be a bold move. If he took it, if it was discovered, there was a good chance this thing could get him killed. Should he risk it? He took a surreptitious glance at Nol who had hurried around to inspect the back of the vehicle and then at Taven who was vigilant in his lookout duties. He eased the gun from the belt and slipped it beneath his shirt. The last pocket in the man's jacket held the prize. "Got 'em," he yelled out, a little too loudly he realized, as he rattled the keys.

"All right," Nol said as he came around the truck on the driver's side. "Now, open the back door and I'll throw him in." Just then he stopped, stared down a moment, then, leaning over, buried his hand beneath the driver's coat. Allen's heart shot up into his throat. What had he missed? The ammo belt? Allen heard a snap, and Nol's hand came out wrapped around a wicked knife with a blade resembling an evil grin. "Looks like you missed this, trooper." Nol's grimace matched the blade as he brandished it in front of Allen. "Too bad."

"And just what would I do with it? Kill all of you?" Allen said sarcastically, though secretly he breathed a sigh of relief; his patience with Nol was beginning to wear thin, and his annoyance was beginning to show. He was still afraid of him, of course, but with something of a plan in the works, he had a bit of hope, which bolstered his courage. "What would be the point?" He ventured, "Ovek promised to let me go once you've got your precious transponder. I expect him to keep that promise, unlike what you've done here tonight."

"Look, I couldn't take the chance. This human was too angry. I thought he might morph, and when that happens, you humans are far too dangerous. I had to kill him." Nol flipped the knife keenly around in his hand and threw it smartly at the telephone pole. The blade spun rapidly and buried itself deeply into the wood, a perfect strike from thirty feet away.

"There you go spouting your wild theories again. I'm not even going to bother arguing with you," Allen replied. "But I'll tell you this much; he didn't deserve to die. Not like that. He was probably a good man. He had a life, and you destroyed it. And the lives of all the people he has ever touched have been changed forever. You think about that, Nol."

But Nol wasn't inclined to think about any of it. He hoisted the guy over his shoulder as if he were a sack of spent ordnance and then tumbled him into the back of the truck. Taven leapt in and pulled him further to the back, into the shadows. The clank of the doors virtually screamed, *Out of sight, out of mind.* But even as Allen walked to the front of the truck, despite his minor diatribe, he couldn't help wondering why the guy had found it necessary to travel this lonely country road packing a .45 and a mean-looking bowie knife. It seemed an odd thing to do. What had he been up to? As he boosted himself into the driver's seat, Allen decided, it no longer mattered; whatever the reason, fate had seen fit to lay a valuable weapon in his hands, and he had the dead stranger to thank for it.

Nol hopped into the passenger seat and stared at him. "Look, it's done. It makes no sense to worry about it now. You worry about your hairy skin and getting us to the cabin so we can get off this rock. Keep your eyes forward, soldier; that's all you gotta' do."

"All right," Allen said. "But you had better hope no one comes looking for him."

"From where I'm sitting," Nol shot back in an ominous tone, "*you'd* better hope no one comes looking for him." Then his mood changed abruptly. "But I wouldn't be too concerned about it, We should be long gone before anyone even notices he hasn't shown up for dinner." He displayed a silly looking grin then, which Allen considered all the more ridiculous and surreal, stretched across the face of a dopey-looking lizard, especially since the insidious creature had so senselessly killed a man. Nol waved his thumb repeatedly past his shoulder. "Now, get us back to the farm before this human starts stinking up our truck."

Allen parked in the back next to the kitchen door. Nol snatched the key from him, and he scurried out, eager to get inside to receive the antidote, but before he reached the door he felt Nol's powerful grip on his shoulder. "Not so fast," Nol barked. "I want a word with you." He first turned his face to Taven as he scrambled out of the back of the truck; he seemed to enjoy making a tense moment last that much longer. "Bury the human in the field near the edge of the wood," Nol instructed, "and take Guor with you. Put him deep. I don't want any vermin digging him up—at least not until we're well away from here." He put his huge mitt on Allen's shoulder, his stubby claw's digging in slightly, even through the heavy field jacket.

He reached out with the other hand, palm up. "All right," he droned, "hand it over." Allen's eyes went wide and, though the air was brisk, he could feel the sweat trickling between the hairs on the very top of his head.

"What do you mean?" he replied. But he knew exactly what Nol meant.

"You don't think for a moment I'm going to let you keep it, do you?"

"I doubt I would ever use it anyway," Allen said. And that was certainly the truth. "I suppose it was foolish of me to think I could get away with it."

"That's right," Nol replied more emphatically. "I told you, when we get in the truck, hand over the lighter!" He had no intention of allowing Allen to burn the farm down while they were all asleep. "And the fluid, too."

"Oh, oh, yeah," Allen said as casually as he could. He fished around in his field jacket, realizing how close he had been to revealing his secret.

"All right," Nol said, releasing him. "Now get inside. I'm sure Ovek will be pleased with this vehicle. It seems more than adequate."

"And I'll get the antidote as promised?" Allen asked.

"When the time is right, you'll get it," he said rather curtly. He turned Allen around and pushed him gently toward the door. "By the way, you did a good job out there, trooper," Nol continued in a more evenhanded tone. "It's not a soldier's job to be kind, Allen," he said. "It's a soldier's job to get things done; that's what I did. That's what *you* did. I appreciate that."

This human may not have been one of the regulars, but Nol felt it might be a good time to get in the greater habit of recognizing the deeds of troopers under his command. Allen may as well become part of that regimen. Besides, sooner or later these humans were destined to become part of the empire's army and would be become regulars in due time. He may as well become comfortable with incorporating them into the command structure. But without a doubt, he thought, if anyone under his command ever questioned his actions again, Earthling, Thacian, Tyon, even RegeCeon elite, he would gut them on the spot. So, having expressed his appreciation, Nol promptly escorted Allen back to his makeshift prison.

"You'll be reporting to Ovek now, I assume," Allen said as Nol closed the bathroom door.

"I'll let him know we were successful and that you were helpful," he replied.

"I need that antidote."

"I'll remind him," Nol replied lazily.

There seemed to be little urgency about the matter, at least, it appeared that way from where Allen was standing. *Nol might not feel that way if the poison were coursing through his veins,* he thought. Though the house had been filled with only an eerie silence, he returned only a moment later, filling the doorway like a living barricade, his arms crossed in a most resolute manner, stoic and humorless as usual, delivering a message from the commander; at least, that was his story. "Ovek will give you the antidote tomorrow morning just before we head out to the cabin."

"But he promised it to me as soon as we returned with the truck!" Allen fired back.

"No, he promised it would be here, and it is." Nol smiled. "Keep your britches on, trooper; you have plenty of time. Besides, if we give you the antidote now, then you have to spend the night in chains again. Do you want that? Think about it." With that, he locked the door and banged his way down the hallway, his heavy footfalls faded toward the kitchen, then stopped abruptly. Through the pipes Allen could hear, very clearly, the squeal of the kitchen chair as Nol parked himself at the table. At least Nol had not bothered to search him or even bothered to take his field jacket. He had gotten a lucky break on that score.

Moments later he heard more squeals as others joined Nol in the kitchen, then the sound of muffled voices and laughter, which grew louder and more distinct as the night wore on. The refrigerator door opened repeatedly and he could hear very clearly the hiss and pop of cans being opened—soda perhaps, but beer, more likely. The animals were having a party! It was a goddamn celebration! Nol had just skewered a man, and they were celebrating. Why was he surprised? From their vantage point, he and all the other *Earthers* were the animals. Perhaps he should be grateful they did not have a taste for human flesh, or he might well find himself out there on the table with them as part of the celebration. He lay there with his head to the wall listening to the general reverie, the laughter, the talk of the evening's adventure of which he had played a significant role. Actually, as the evening wore on he did begin to feel a bit left out. Then, suddenly, he heard his name, quite distinctly. There was mention of the fire, the ruse he had used to stop the truck, and some laughter and some accolades praising him and how well his trick had worked.

All in all he felt quite pleased about it. Then the mention of the poison grabbed his attention and the raucous laughter echoed off the walls as if the party were right there in his cell. He heard the entire story about how it, too, was all a ruse, a trick to guarantee his cooperation. There was no actual poison, no antidote! The ersatz poison was actually diluted orange juice. With the disclosure the laughter became an insane din. He didn't know what to feel. Relieved? Angry? Amused? Humiliated? He felt confused more than anything else. Whatever trick they had used to force him into their scheme, he had done their bidding, bravely and honorably, and he had done it well. It was the first time he had ever done anything truly adventurous or harrowing in his life, and, while he wasn't pleased that it had cost a man his life, he was pleased that he had performed well under pressure. He had even come away with a weapon of his own. That spoke volumes about his resourcefulness, and he was proud of himself. So, he wasn't quite sure why their laughter upset him. He knew only that he didn't like it.

He took the revolver from his coat. He had never owned a weapon or fired one. He wasn't even sure he knew how to operate it. The only clue he had were scenes from movies and television. He inspected the weapon and thought the safety was off. He pointed it toward the ceiling and, grasping the slide firmly, pulled in back briskly and released. It slid back smoothly and cleanly, making a crisp, solid snap. He was sure a round had been loaded into the chamber. So, he was good to go, and he had heard enough. This new information about the poison didn't change his plan one iota. It fact, if served to strengthen his resolve. In truth, it was one less thing he had to concern himself about.

Poison, indeed! He laughed at himself and shook his head. How foolish of him not to have seen through their charade. Wasn't it a classic old gag? But there certainly was something about a needle being pushed into your arm accompanied by a serious threat that forces part of the brain to go completely numb, and your brain to remain fixated on the reality of it all. The thought that it might be a trick never even crossed his mind. Well, he would continue to play along with the gag, and use the relative freedom it bought him to get a good night's sleep, free of the annoying chains that had clinked and clanked throughout the previous night. Now he could pick and choose his moment. Now the joke would be on them!

Chapter 12

Sunday, October 9, 6:00 A.M.: The sound of the curtain flapping in the early morning breeze evoked a hazy, eerie vision—*an apparition that evolved from the blinding staccato flashes that filled the air all around and slowly morphed into a man who, in turn, transformed into a woman and continued to morph into a succession of anthropomorphic beasts. The unearthly figure, inverting a pair of broadswords and displaying them like sanctified crosses, raced along a treacherous mountain path on a magnificent white steed. The stallion reared and pawed at the sky, knocking stars from the heavens as if plundering jewels from the ceiling of an ancient citadel. A long, crimson banner locked firmly into a leather grommet at the horse's flank writhed like a sinuous dragon in the wake of the magical steed whose hooves never actually touched the earth. The herald, emblazoned boldly in black and gold in the center, depicted a rearing tiger battling an eagle and a dragon from above, and from beneath, a huge python coiled up the hindquarters. Below the snake, a shark made its desperate escape from the flag's lower border, its tail and dorsal fin trailing into nothingness. The banner bled a stream of deep red mist as the hero raced to the end of the trail near the summit, toward the edge of a sharp precipice giving way to a bottomless chasm. As if death was only a myth, the mounted figure gave a tremendous leap at the streaming clouds, directly at the rising sun.*

Slivers of light flashed intermittently through the edge of the curtain as morning fought its way through the maze of pines and cedars beyond the outhouse. Megan squeezed her eyelids to defend herself from the intrusive, stinging beams and stretched her arms into the disheveled bedding, looking to find Kara beside her, to wake her with a sweet morning kiss. But Kara was gone, and her hands fell instead upon a cool and empty hollow. She pushed the tousled blankets and pillows aside and forced her eyes open.

Kara must have replenished the fire during the night. Long, lively flames danced in the fireplace, bidding her good morning with their friendly popping and crackling. She buried her face in the blankets and breathed in deeply. Kara's scent, which lingered, was not as fresh as she would have hoped. Her best guess was that she had been gone more than two hours. The transponder, too, had disappeared from the table. It wasn't difficult to guess why Kara had snuck off. But why not do this task together? She couldn't help feeling a little hurt, a little left out, but she knew Kara had her own way and her own reason for all things. All the same, it was the first morning of her a new life, and it would have been comforting to have Kara's by her side. Besides, two hours seemed excessive for hiding such a tiny thing. She should have been back by now. Perhaps something had gone wrong. It wouldn't hurt to go out and have a look around. Besides, she felt edgy, cooped up as she was in the cabin, though she had been there little more than a day. She felt as if she needed to run free for a bit, and she knew the fresh air would do her good. Her neck certainly wouldn't be a bother. During that single day it had healed almost completely. Only a faint, pink scar remained, a battle trophy that would vanish altogether with the help of her new regenerative powers.

Hurriedly, she jumped into her boots and pulled on her hunting jacket, then virtually flew out the door. The crisp air surprised her face like a miracle. She sucked it in as though breathing was a new experience. Tilting her head to the sky, she sniffed, attempting to discover the direction Kara had gone. A faint, reminiscence wafted through the air from the south, a blend of Kara's natural scent and a suggestion of her perfume. Rather than shout the direction, it whispered, offering a hint to the trail she must follow. Megan stepped into the mist sneaking beneath the tall pines, each footfall carefully placed, cautiously following the narrow trail that disappeared into the early morning shadows. There was no readily apparent need for stealth, yet she felt wary, mindful of the unseen and the unknown that might be lurking in the hazy gloom, clinging like a dragon's breath to the soppy forest floor. For the longest time she moved along the foraging trail ignoring the wobbly opossums and chatty squirrels that crossed her path. She was tempted once to follow a large buck and doe to see where they would hide, simply because she felt the urge to run and to satisfy her curiosity, but she kept to the trail. It was faint and irregular, a trail peculiar to the logic of the earth it traversed. It meandered according to the idiosyncrasies of the deer and the fox. It twisted and turned in a way humans find annoying, deviating from the obvious and easy, paying homage to the lager oaks and elms offering a bounty of succulent moss and fungi, giving access to places where the tastiest morsels grew, and to cubbies where smaller rodents took refuge.

It detoured through tangles of young black spruce and crossed narrow steams. It snaked through havens of dense pines stinking of formic acid exuded by red ants and through cathedrals formed by the branches of heavy elms and the interlocking tendrils of creeping ivy. It wandered through occasional uprising of rocks and stones where snakes and lizards hid and shed their skins, but inevitably, it wound ever southward. Here, alone in the deep woods, moving through the thick foliage, Megan felt a peculiar sense of purpose, and oddly at home. She felt *the change* coursing through her veins just as Kara had predicted. She sensed it in her very nature, as if her mind was reaching out to the earth and to the shell of life surrounding it, and she felt that life reaching out and touching her in return. She knew the virus had incorporated bits of DNA from every host creature and was now passing characteristics from those creatures on to her. She didn't know a great deal about genetics, but she knew enough to understand that the change was altering her at a fundamental level, transforming her in a way that, she trusted, would elevate her beyond the mere girl she used to be, advancing her, evolving her, making her smarter and stronger, making her better, forever. She didn't know the exact characteristics that would become dominant in her; no one did in advance. In life, that was the way of things for everyone.

For most people, it was of problematic import—Will I be fat? Will I be tall? Will I go bald? But for a shadow, this ambiguity was a more pragmatic consideration. There was a huge difference between downing a plate of steak tartare and draining the blood of some thug. Purebreds were more predictable, exactingly so, Kara had said. It had to do with the intimate compatibility of estrogen, hormonal secretions, and the molecular structure of the virus. That predictability was certainly a blessing for them, or for their parents, at any rate. All their senses were heightened, and they almost always inherited the morphing gene as well. A genetic anomaly, now and then, would not, but these were extremely rare. The primary variable within them was the bloodlust; some suffered it little, some had it to a maddening degree. The Bloodwarriors experienced extreme bloodlust, or, more accurately, those who experienced it instinctively sought training as Bloodwarriors, which channeled their rage and desire into a beneficial and noble cause. Well, where fate had taken Kara, so it might lead her. At least, that is what she hoped.

So far, Megan noticed her sense of smell had improved dramatically, and her eyesight was becoming razor sharp. From where she stood, she could easily spot a ladybug sitting on a speckled leaf twenty yards away. For nearly an hour she had been moving quickly, yet she was still fresh and breathing easily. Her stamina had definitely improved. She clenched her fists, forcing the blood to her fingertips. Her grip felt powerful, as if she could crush a rock with her bare hands. This newfound strength was probably an enhanced response to the adrenaline her body was creating. The very idea that she was changing excited her and heightened the effects of the drug. It was as if life itself, sensing and experiencing it so completely, was making her high. Most satisfying of all, she didn't feel undeserving. She felt as if she belonged—in this world, with this body, with this mind. She didn't feel like the dumb farm girl any longer. "It feels right." Megan whispered to herself. "This is the way it was meant to be," she continued as she pondered the heavens, as if she could see the stars beyond the wispy clouds and canopy of blue, as if she was remembering a past long dead and a place far, far away.

Finally, after leaving a shallow valley cluttered with thorny crabapple trees, she rounded a low rise dominated by poplars and cedars studded with a rocky outcropping where the deer scrape the mud and youthful irritation off their antlers. There she caught Kara's stronger scent. It was crisp and pure and unmistakable.

"Megan?" She heard Kara call out. Continuing over the rise she spotted Kara in the valley below, walking leisurely toward her. She was dressed from head to toe in the camouflage field gear and had a regulation army-drab pack strapped to her back, the stub of a short, military shovel sticking up over her head. and a matching pistol belt wrapped around her waist. In it she sported several army survival knives, a World War II bayonet, and the mandat blade she had pulled from Megan's throat.

"What are you doing out here?" Kara asked. "You should be resting."

"I thought you might need help, that you might have been hurt." She knew neither of these excuses sounded convincing but, at the moment, they sounded better than the truth, which was that the final vestiges of her decaying insecurity had compelled her to come.

"How did you know where to find me?" she asked. "Never mind," she retracted the question virtually without a pause.

"I could feel it, Kara," Megan said, coming close enough to touch Kara's hand. "I mean, I felt closer to the earth and to you, in a way I never knew I could feel. I simply gave myself up, allowing the wind and the earth to guide me. It's hard to explain. But of course, I don't need to explain it to you, do I?"

"No, I understand," Kara said, smiling. She leaned forward and kissed Megan's cheek. "But you needn't have worried. I'm quite all right."

Megan realized Kara was being kind and was letting her off the hook. "I suppose I felt abandoned. I thought we were going to bury it together," she confessed.

Kara's steel blue eyes peered deeply into hers, her dark brows narrowed slightly, her dangerously beautiful features, made more stunning by the diffused light flickering through the dense leaves, playing against the morning shadows, mesmerized Megan into a serene dreaminess. She spoke softly but deeply, intensely, emphasizing each word, stroking Megan's flaming hair against her cheek. "I would never abandon you," she said. "We are bonded by blood and by love. We are sisters of the essence, and it is my duty and privilege to have you walk this path by my side. The essence is the spirit of your life, and I am the guide, your protector, teacher, and faithful love. We are allied by a truth and a power spanning eons of time to form our family, and our union is strong. Never doubt that, and never forget. You will *never* forget." Her voice was a deep, resonant bell being struck softly, ever so softly, again, and again.

"I will never forget," Megan whispered. The words echoed deep within, her heart embracing them as if opening to a personal angel, the neurons racing across freshly spawned synapses, embedding them in the newly developed creases generated by the essence where the instinctual actuators and hematogenous memories are stored.

Kara smiled then and, still holding Megan's hand, invited her to sit on a huge branch lying beneath a mammoth hickory tree. "I only wanted to protect you. I thought it best you not know where the transponder is buried. I'm not sure it's the right call," she said. "All I know for certain is that they wanted it badly enough to kill you for it. If they should get their hands on it, I fear they would kill many more—vampires and humans alike—and that this is larger than either of us, so the fewer people that know the location of their device the better. That's why I went alone."

"I understand," Megan said. "I know you're struggling with this, that you're looking beyond this tiny forest, beyond this city, this country. Last night I saw something in your eyes I had never seen before, fear and sadness, and I sensed so many conflicting emotions in you."

"Yes," Kara replied. I suppose all my life I've feared loss in one form or another, and loneliness, and now, recently, I've feared for my life and yours. Now I have a new fear, a trepidation I have never known, a fear for the entire world, for the future of humanity, and for the vampire nation, a fear for the future of Earth itself."

"Do you think these aliens have that kind of power?" Megan asked.

"I think they come from a place where that kind of power exists," Kara said. "And I think they mean to bring it here. That's what has me worried. That's why they want the transponder so badly."

"Are you sure they can't get to it?" Megan hissed in a whisper, as if something beyond the trees might be listening, her eyes wide, her adrenaline running wild, riding the wave of Kara emotions. "You're sure!"

"I'm sure," Kara said, nodding slowly. "It would be difficult, even for me." *And it would be,* she thought. She explained how she had carried the shovel only as a contingency, in case the marsh to the south was not as compliant as she had anticipated. But it had been more than accommodating, yielding a wide expanse of black ooze near the reedy shoreline, a virtual bed of quicksand, probably ten feet deep or more. She had tossed the transponder from the shallows; it had been sucked down slowly as if being eaten by the odious muck. It sounded reassuring, still, there was something slightly ominous and tentative in Kara's voice and body language that Megan sensed, subtle signals she transmitted. "Why did you bring all the weapons with you?" Megan asked.

"Well, let's just say the woods can be a dangerous place." They forced a smile together at that, and then Kara slipped the mandat knife into Megan's hand. "You hold on to this," she said. "It rightfully belongs to you now."

"It's beautiful and terrible," she said slowly, admiring the handle, sliding her fingers along the flat of the crescent-shaped blade.

"Yes, and don't worry." Kara tried to be reassuring. "We'll practice with it now and then. Your reflexes and strength have probably all improved. You'll make quick progress, I'm sure. I just hope you never have to use it."

Megan tucked the knife into her belt as they began their climb up the short rise. "It will be well past nine by the time we get back to the cabin," Kara said to her. "I don't know about you, but this morning air does wonders for my appetite. I could eat a horse trainer!" She laughed. Megan rolled her eyes and shook her head. "It's an old vampire joke," Kara said.

The sun was beginning its advancing intrusion over the horizon, threatening to destroy the cover of darkness as the troopers gathered at the rear of the truck. They wore hooded coats and sweats and mismatched trousers, opting for Earth clothing rather than their uniforms. "When in Rome," Allen observed.

"What?" Guor asked.

"Nothing, it's just an old Earther saying. It means, 'You look great.'" Allen stretched a fake smile at him.

"Just trying to keep warm," Nol broke in. "It's not a beauty contest." He wrapped the chain around Allen's wrists and dropped a lock through the looped end.

"I can't drive with this thing on!" Allen protested.

"You can, and you will," Nol scowled.

Allen looked to Ovek, who was crawling into the back of the truck. He looked like the warmed-over dead, and if looks were any indication of his mood, Allen wasn't certain a petition was worth the bother.

"Ovek, would you tell this brontosaurus I can't drive with chains on?" he said. Clearly, Ovek was in no mood. Apparently, he had his hands full coping with the pain and the sickness and preparing for his confrontation with Kara.

"Allen, just do as Nol tells you," he said. "We just need to get through this. He's responsible for you, and so he calls the shots. Clear?"

"Clear," Allen said. It was also clear that the only reason Nol hadn't bashed his head in yet was because Ovek was still alive. Oh, right, they needed a lift to the cabin. Then the bashing would begin! He turned and headed toward the front. "I'll start the truck," he said, fishing in his coat pocket for the keys. Nol closed the back doors and headed to the passenger side while Allen used the opportunity to slip the .45 into the left pocket of his field jacket. It was annoying with his hands linked together. Nol had allowed him about fourteen inches of play between his wrists so that he could drive. Still—fucking chains!

"Why is this necessary?" Allen asked, holding his hands in the air. "Didn't I prove myself last night?" He actually thought that he had, and that he deserved more leeway, but more importantly, he feared the shackles might interfere with his plans.

Nol looked him squarely in the eyes, a hint of a smile curled under the two slight slits that served as a nose. "You did fine last night, but keeping in sight of the farm is one thing, driving into unknown territory is another. I'm not an idiot." He looked to the front suddenly and his voice became mechanical as if reciting from a manual. "A soldier's obligation is to escape. This would be your best opportunity. I know it, and you know it." He pointed the shotgun directly at Allen's face. "So, make your move, outworlder." He grabbed the leader chain draping from the side of Allen's right wrist and locked the far end to his own wrist.

"You're forgetting, Nol, I'm not a soldier. Besides, I need that antidote," he countered.

"I think you're afraid Ovek is not going to make it and that you're never going to get that antidote. Fear makes a trooper do desperate things, stupid things. That's all I'm sayin'." Nol settled back as Allen pulled out and headed up the frontage road. "Well, you had better pray to your gods that Ovek takes a turn for the better." He threw Allen a wicked grin as they turned onto old Highway Double B. "Now, you say we can get to there by taking country highways and back roads all the way?"

"Yes, it will take a little longer, but it will be safer. I mean, just in case the cops are looking for this truck."

"These 'cops,' they're heavily armed?" Nol asked.

"Well, they're not packing phazers if that's what you mean. But they have pistols and rifles and, personally, I wouldn't enjoy being caught in the cross fire," Allen replied, pulling the seat belt around his shoulder. "But they will pull the truck over if the driver isn't wearing a harness."

"All right," Nol said. "Get us there, then, and avoid the cops."

"Nol?"

"Yeah?"

"Do you think Ovek will die? Soon, I mean? He promised me the antidote once we get to the cabin, once he has an opportunity to talk with Kara."

"Well, like I said, get us there." His words had an ominous fatality to them. He didn't seem to care at all about the antidote, even had there been a need for it. And by the looks of things, Ovek would be lucky to survive the day. The die was cast, if Nol assumed command there was no way in hell Allen would survive. The escape plan was his only salvation and the unanticipated chain was merely an added wrinkle that required it to be tweaked just a bit. He would deal with it when the time came. And it did moments later, a few miles south of their destination as they approached the Bark River. When it did, his stomach dropped into his lower intestines. The enormity of what he was about to do nearly overwhelmed him, yet he remained firm in his resolve. Besides, once he spotted the bridge, he didn't have much time to reconsider. He swerved to the right. It required only a quick jerk of the wheel to aim the truck squarely at the tip of the guardrail.

A few safety barrels detonated instantly, ejecting sand in every direction; the plastic remnants tumbled over the bridge and down the embankment like giant orange rinds. The edge of the railing dug deeply into the front bumper, ripping it in two, devoured the radiator and ate its way into the engine compartment. The vehicle jerked like a lassoed steer. The rear wheels lurched six feet into the air and crashed to the ground, bursting like cheap balloons when they hit the pavement and dirt. The impact flung the top of Nol's head into the windshield, his bony fan punched through the glass like a dull knife shattering the glass into a cracked and foggy mass. The airbag exploded in Allen's face as he fumbled for the gun, but the crash left him dazed momentarily.

Finally, he managed to wrap his hand around the revolver and get his steering hand back on the wheel. That was the best he could do for the moment. The truck's landing had brought the rear right tire down off the shoulder, far off the embankment. The truck had pitched downward, looking for solid ground on which to light, but there had been none. The angle was too steep; the ground sloped away from the shoulder for twenty feet or more. By the time the wheel touched anything resembling solid ground it had already been too late. It had come down hard on the rear wheel, forcing the truck far to the right, ripping the guard rail out of its mooring. The spring action of the rail snapped the front of the truck upward and back like a helpless tortoise. It rolled once down the embankment where the ground leveled off, hit a small rise, and sprang into the air like a jackrabbit on a thistle. It fell to earth with a clunk and a cacophony of metallic rattles. Then it simply rocked back and forth and bounced up and down several times until finally settling quietly in the shallow flat well off the side of the road.

Clumps of earth and stones, dust and leaves, and man-made scraps scattered high into the air as if a bomb had decimated the area. Fragments of all that had been lifted skyward began pelting the earth all around, pinging the truck and rail and the road for a moment or two. Then all was quiet.

Gathering his wits, Allen searched Nol's coat pockets for the key, but came up empty; the brute was just too big and heavy to be moving around. He was wasting time. In desperation, he pressed the muzzle of the .45 against the leader chain. He turned his head and pulled the trigger. A spattering of melted foam pelted the side of his head as it was ejected from the hole where the bullet ripped through the padding of the seat. The report was deafening; his ears reverberated painfully from the blast. He brought his hand to his face, working his jawbone just below his right ear. It was an invitation to an instant migraine, but at least it had worked! His wrists were still linked by the heavy, steel bracelets, but he was free of Nol, and that was more than enough. He looked over at him, slumped forward, his bloody head punched into the broken glass. "Should have buckled up, Nol," he admonished him.

Allen jumped from the truck. There wasn't a second to waste. Any moment now, the troopers in the back were sure to come storming out. He ran to the front, hopped over a piece of twisted, buckled railing and headed east as quickly as he could. It was at least thirty yards to the woods. He covered the distance in world-record time. His first thought was to reach the nearest road, perhaps hitch a ride. He desperately wanted to get some real distance between himself and the truck. But something was eating at him, something Nol had said toward the end of the interrogation. He had bragged about never forgetting Kara's scent and only needing to get near the cabin to locate her. At the time, Allen had thought it merely a boastful exaggeration. Now, he wasn't so sure.

After learning more about them he had come to realize that these were trained and gifted trackers who, in addition, may have instincts and attributes Allen could only guess at. Perhaps they might actually have the ability to locate Kara from only a few miles. The more he thought about it, the more credible it seemed. Unfortunately, while the bridge had been his best opportunity to make his escape, it was also close to the cabin, dangerously close. But was it close enough for them to catch Kara's scent? Could he risk that? Even before he asked himself the question and postulated the ramifications, he had known the answer and formulated a generalized response, hastily outlining a course of action quite different from his original plan.

When he darted out of the woods onto the adjacent road about a mile due east, he turned north and headed directly for the cabin. He had to warn them. He had brought these cursed aliens here; if there was even a remote chance they could locate Kara he had put her and Megan at great risk, and perhaps was risking far more. He thought about stopping a car to elicit help, but listened briefly to the sound of that petition in his head. At best, he would be fortunate to be taken for a complete lunatic. More than likely anyone ballsy enough to offer him assistance would call the cops faster than he could say, "Close encounters." He would have a very interesting story to tell about alien abduction, and have a grand time explaining his chained wrists, the handgun, the truck, which might be empty by now, and his participation in the murder of an innocent truck driver. He doubted he could get anyone to help him in any event. He probably looked like an escaped convict and felt as if a thousand eyes were peering at him from every direction. His clothes were a mess from trampling through the undergrowth and he was bruised and battered from the buffeting he had received during the accident. He looked conspicuous and he knew it.

Certainly, he would make better time on the road, but realized it was a bad idea. Now that he had made his decision, it wouldn't do to be spotted by the police or someone else who might report him. Though it would slow going and, perhaps dangerous after the autumn rains, he opted to abandon the roads in favor of the swamp and the woods beyond. He broke into a jog over the left shoulder, down the low rise and disappeared into the towering reeds and cattails marking the southeastern boundary of Willow Marsh.

Nol braced his huge hands against the dashboard and forced his head out of the shattered windshield. His crown horn was uninjured, but the fan sloping down the center of his head was lacerated severely in several places near the front and top. The sliced cartilage hung limply to the left and flopped and bobbed as he moved his head from side to side. Bits of dust and grass continued to drift to the ground like nuclear fallout and rosy, watery blood still dripped to the floorboards from the small pool that had gathered on the dash beneath his chin horns. He had been unconscious for only a short while—long enough, however, for Allen to have made his escape! He should have known the poison ruse would not fool him for long, but was surprised at how quickly he had managed to sever the leader chain. This Earthling was proving to be most resourceful, an admirable quality in a soldier sworn to serve the empire, but not so desirable a trait in an adversary—or a hostage!

He unlocked the remnants of chain from his wrist and gathered up the shotgun, which had found it way under his seat. He headed for the back of the truck to check on the team, apprehensive about the report he would have to deliver to Ovek. Allen had been his charge, and he had allowed him to escape, even though such a move had been anticipated. Curse it all to the darkworld! It had been a trainee mistake. He had grown complacent and underestimated the enemy. Ovek had warned him many times! Things were not always as they seemed. Now he would have to face up to his mistake. Worse, this would surely jeopardize their chances to reach Kara and retrieve the transponder.

The gravity of the situation hurt him far more than his wounds ever could. Except for the lacerations on his head and a few bumps and bruises, he wasn't badly injured. His thick, muscular frame had withstood far greater battering than this puny attempt to kill him. Rounding the far end of the truck he found the doors hanging open and Rahon and Beel already out of the truck. Rahon sat on the grass rubbing his head and rotating his shoulder, while Beel leaned back pushing his palms into his tender ribs. Even before he could hoist himself onto the truck's rear landing, Ovek stumbled out, followed by Guor and Taven. Ovek was groggy and nearly fell onto the grass at Rahon's feet. With his hands on his knees, breathing hard as if he had just run a great distance, he threw Nol a curt command.

"Report," he ordered.

Nol hesitated, but only for a moment. "Prisoner escaped, Cap'n, crashed the truck, knocked me out cold, and made off into the woods, looks like. Couldn't have gotten far." There, he had gotten the words out. Complete. Concise. Accurate. No excuses.

"By Nos!" Ovek cursed. "What else can go wrong?"

"Should we pursue?" Nol asked. So far so good; at least Ovek hadn't gutted him on the spot. He deserved nothing less, and he knew it.

Ovek stood silently, looking north, as if he hadn't heard the question.

"Cap'n?"

He stared at Nol. "How you holding up?" he asked, pointing to Nol's head briefly.

"I'm fine, just a minor fan wound," he replied. "How does it look?"

"You look—good," Ovek replied blankly.

"Yeah, yah, look real nice," Rahon chimed in.

"I look better than your sister, and that's a fact," Nol shot back at Rahon.

"I meant, has the bleeding stopped?" he asked. "I'm no good to you if I pass out along the way."

"It's fine," Ovek said, "and I want a check on everyone. Is everyone all right?" he asked around as loudly as he could. They all grumbled in unison, which he accepted as verification that no one was hurt beyond some minor scrapes. They'd all seen worse than this many times over. Ovek turned his face northward and peered into the dense woods beyond the river, as if his eyes were penetrating the deep, misty shadows.

"Cap'n," Nol broke into his reverie. "I say again. Should we go after Allen?"

"No, we'll head over the bridge and into the woods on the other side. We need to get out of sight," Ovek said. "We're heading upwind. I have a hunch."

"About what?" Nol asked.

"About Allen," Ovek replied as if it should have been obvious. Ovek turned his head again and looked to the sky. "You smell that?" he asked.

"All I smell is smoke," Nol replied, "far off." The light went on! And perhaps the crisis had been averted.

"Exactly." For the first time in the past few days, Ovek smiled. He couldn't help feeling the odds were in their favor once again. "Let's head out."

Nol ordered Rahon on point and they crossed the bridge at a brisk pace in a three-meter spread. They made it all the way across without incident except for encountering one small vehicle about halfway. But it zoomed by without even slowing. The driver barely looked at the hooded parade jogging down the road and never paid the slightest attention to the battered truck abandoned at the bottom of the embankment.

Ovek gathered the troopers around once they were safely ensconced in a shallow valley deep in the forest, well away from the truck and any curious travelers or authorities that might discover it. If he was correct, the cabin was not far ahead. By his reckoning, they could make it there before the morning was half spent. He was sure Allen was attempting to get there before them, to warn Kara that they were near. He was confused about exactly why Allen had broken faith, but all that mattered now was getting to the cabin first, to give negotiation a legitimate chance to succeed. He knew he had handled the siege on the farm poorly, that a greater good might have been served by preventing either of the girls from being harmed.

Considering his mounting illness and the fact that this mission was problematic at best, he realized now that enraging Kara had been a bad idea. Diplomacy might have been the smarter approach in securing the transponder; at least, it would have been worth a try. But what was done—was done. He had to deal with things as they were. Wishful thinking was for children and fools and for civilians whose positions held no life-and-death consequences. He had made mistakes, and he thought the troopers should know—he took full responsibility. But though he felt as if he had been condemned to the punishment chambers of the darkworld itself, he was committed to getting them out of this mess, and thought he saw a way, and to that end outlined his impromptu plan.

"Nol will take a team along this game trail directly north. My guess is that it leads directly to the cabin. We had been traveling for quite a while, and I doubt Allen wanted to travel far on foot in order to reach his destination. He will have brought us fairly close. So you'll be moving quickly in order to beat him there. That means leaving me behind. I can't keep up. I'm feeling the effects of the infection, and I'm not up to it," he explained. "Secure the cabin, but do not engage. Keep out of sight, and make sure Allen doesn't gain entry. It's imperative that he be retaken. We need him as a bargaining marker. Guor and I will catch up as quickly as we can. Then I'll go in and negotiate with Kara for the transponder. If I can convince her that all we want is get off this Nos-forsaken rock, I'm sure she will listen to reason."

"I think I should go in with you," Nol said. "What makes you think she won't try to finish the job she started back there at the farm?"

"Allen's a male—he came to visit them, remember? I think his life is more valuable to them than you know. I think Kara will listen, especially when I make it clear we're desperate to leave. Besides, it's a chance I'm willing to take," Ovek replied. "I have to go in alone. I need to send a clear signal, a sign of good faith—it's a negotiation not a confrontation."

"And if she kills you?" Nol asked.

"Then you've got your first command, lieutenant," Ovek said.

Chapter 13

Sunday, October 9, 10:17 A.M.: Finished with breakfast, Kara relaxed at the table, fidgeting with her second cup of coffee and the snub-nosed .38. The weapon had performed admirably during the fight but deserved a routine cleaning and inspection, at the very least. It was a welcome relief having an excuse to simply sit back and think things through, to consider their options. Perhaps it was time to recognize that they were in over their heads, that the discovery of aliens among them had grave implications, and that they needed help. Megan sat across the table assembling the vintage .22. Her father had always broken it down before storing it in the case. He always lovingly rubbed the stock with orange oil and cleaned the metal components, as well. She pushed the slide bolt into position and aimed the rifle toward the ceiling. She cocked the bolt, enjoyed the smooth, sensual action of the glide, and slid it forward once again. She pulled the trigger. Laying the Remington down gently, she ran her hand over the handsome, polished wood. "So, what should we do today?" she asked, fixing the Mossberg scope into position and rotating the locking levers.

"We're going to see my father," Kara replied. "I should have asked for his help in the first place."

"What can he *do*?" Megan realized it was a probably a stupid question. Things were so complicated; she knew it was impossible to know.

"I'm not sure," Kara admitted; "however, you should know now that he is a gifted scientist and a powerful Bloodwarrior, highly respected in the vampire community. For years he's been encouraged to take a seat on the nation's council, and he has a lot of connections. He'll know what to do about these creatures, or at the very least, he'll know someone who will."

Megan brought the rifle to her shoulder and, aiming out the window, checked the sighting. "I hope so. It's a pretty wild story, though; I hope he doesn't think we partied a little too hard," she said, "considering the proof is at the bottom of a swamp."

"Honey, our veins are loaded with proof," Kara reminded her, "and I have the blood sample on my hanky, as well."

"Oh, yeah, I forgot about—Kara!" Megan cut herself short. She sat perfectly still, the rifle frozen to her shoulder.

"What is it?"

"I spotted someone moving between the trees," she said. She lowered the rifle as Kara jumped to her side, ushering her away from the window.

"Who was it?" Kara asked.

"Hard to tell. I only got a glance," she replied. "Big, wearing a hooded jacket, maybe a hunter."

"Big enough to be one of them?" Kara asked.

"Yes."

"Load up," Kara told her. "Now!"

Once again, Nol thought, Ovek's instincts had been dead on. The game trail had led the troopers directly to the cabin, just as he had predicted. There was no doubt Kara was inside, and there was a good chance Megan was with her. The vehicle they had used to make their escape was parked not more than thirty meters from the front door. Upon their arrival the troopers immediately began running reconnaissance about the perimeter, checking entrance points and possible escape routes, noting signs of activity, and keeping general watch for any incursions, especially keeping watch for Allen. Beel constantly assumed a wide, circular patrol around the cabin, keeping a sharp lookout for signs of him. Taven kept a steady eye on the back door and on the tiny shed nearby while Nol and Rahon crossed in a continuous pattern that took them from the corner of the cabin to the edge of the road, always staying under cover of the woods. Everything was quiet.

"Maybe we should just go in and *take* what belongs to us," Rahon said to Nol as they met halfway through their duty route. "Besides, far as I'm concerned she deserves to die for what she did to the captain." Nol stopped and put his hand on Rahon's shoulder.

"I've thought about it," he said. He knew Rahon would never disobey orders but thought it best to enlighten him. "I don't have much faith in this *negotiation* the captain is planning, and I doubt Kara will give up the transponder in any case. But the captain was the one bitten, and she may have an antidote to offer. He may be able to wrestle that from her, at least. We need to give him a chance."

"And what about Megan? How does she figure into this 'negotiation'?"

"We don't even know if she's still alive. But I hope to Nos she is," Nol said.

"Why? These Earthlings are only for killing or slaving as far as I can tell," Rahon replied.

"Because, ya big mammal, Ovek is right. We *could* go in there and kill 'em, or try. And what if we did? Where would we be then? We'd be stuck on this Nos-forsaken rock fighting these changelings endlessly until we're killed or captured. They might be the only two Earthers who can get us out of this space hole. I hate to admit it, but as much as I would like to see this Kara dead, we need her."

"And Megan?" Rahon asked wryly. He noticed Nol's face soften a bit when her name was mentioned.

"We need them both; they're our only hope," he said.

Suddenly the front door burst open and two camouflaged figures sprang out heading directly for the pickup. There was no mistaking the ribbons of fiery red streaming behind Megan or Kara's rich, raven mane. Their uniforms came as no surprise to Nol, who had suspected all along that they were soldiers, probably members of an elite anti-terrorist unit. (Nol was just beginning to realize that the spotting team they had observed from the water shortly after landing was probably not the curious and benign on-lookers they had assumed them to be. Most likely warring nations regularly infiltrated each other by air, and these sentries had reported an incursion to the local military authorities. Kara had probably been alerted and ordered to investigate. It had either been dumb luck that the transponder had landed on Megan's property or, more likely, virtually everyone on this planet, at some time or other, was required to serve in the military. No doubt, the device had been reported to Kara, as well, and she was following up on that report when the team had interrupted. From the onset, it appeared as if they would be easy to overcome, but the girls proved to be highly trained and very skilled professional soldiers, adept at subterfuge.

It was no wonder it had taken him so long to figure all this out! Now more than ever he wanted to return to the empire and file that report.) As he drew nearer, he could see that Megan appeared well healed and strong, and he was pleased, and rather surprised, at her amazing recovery. Nol gave a shrill whistle, alerting Beel and Taven to the situation. They broke into double-time which brought them around the far side of the cabin in short order. Breaking into a run directly behind him, Nol urged Rahon toward the truck. He hated this type of command decision, the kind involving containment. He certainly didn't want to kill either of them, and simply wounding them might prove just as difficult and risky. He couldn't do either, nor did he want to, but he certainly couldn't allow them to escape. He also had to defend himself and his troops, and these changelings had proven themselves to be fierce and clever. It was a tough situation and he had precious little time to make a decision. As little faith as he had in the tactic, he decided to stand as proxy for Ovek in the negotiation, provided he could get them to listen.

At that moment he severely wished Ovek were there to handle the duty. Bargaining and pacification simply weren't on his list of specialties. The darkworld knew, he had only one true talent, killing. He had never attempted anything resembling a peaceful negotiation. But he had to try. The last image he had of Ovek was of a warrior who resembled a mere shadow of his former self, a shell emptied of the majesty it once held. He seriously doubted he would ever see his friend alive again. Nol knew if he did not attempt the negotiation it might never come to pass. Nearly cutting the two figures off halfway to the pickup, Nol grabbed Rahon by the shoulder, forcing him to an abrupt halt. Holding the shotgun in his left hand he forced his arms up in an unmistakable gesture of surrender and ordered Rahon to follow suit. They both stood as if allowing themselves to be taken prisoner. Kara and Megan stopped near the pickup and stared at them in amazement. Nol stooped slowly and lay the shotgun gently down at his feet and kicked it toward the center of the clearing. It was the only concrete gesture he could think of.

"We need to talk," he said. "There has been too much fighting and too much bloodshed already."

"And whose fault is that?" Kara shot back.

"You have something that belongs to us. We just want it back, that's all," Nol said plainly. "Once we have it, we'll leave." He saw no reason to skirt the issue. They either had it or they didn't. By being direct he would force them to be as well. He would know she was lying if she denied it without wanting to know more details. Also, other, more pragmatic questions should be weighing on her mind, and he would look for a hesitation, a moment of genuine confusion. If, indeed, they had the transponder, they would realize that they held a powerful bargaining chip. They would have an edge, and they would know it. If they remained confident and defiant, he would know for certain. If they didn't have it, and they knew there could be no true negotiation, their mounting desperation would begin to show soon enough. The die was cast. He had made his play early. It was all he knew. He hoped it would be enough.

They stared at Nol and Rahon, sizing them up. Beel and Taven stopped short at the far side of the clearing near the edge of the woods, waiting for some sign from Nol. Kara turned her head toward them for a moment.

"We just want it back," Nol repeated. "Then we'll go."

Kara looked as if she didn't like the odds and was sizing up the situation. She turned her face toward Nol and Rahon and shot a quick glace again back toward Beel. That was the moment of hesitation Nol had been looking for. There was no confusion, no question about the *item* they wanted. They had the transponder! They had it, and she was thinking the deal over, weighing their options and assessing disengagement strategies. Nol looked at Megan, who had her back to the truck, looking first to the pair on her right, then to her left, all the while playing her fingers against the trigger of the rifle which she had pointed in Rahon's general direction.

He had to admit; she was a remarkable trooper, looking rather handsome gripping that long, polished weapon. He bobbed and weaved his head slightly and split his hands further apart hoping the body language might encourage her to intervene. He felt there was a connection between the two of them. He knew there was. After all, she was much as he was—when he was a younger reptile, before the empire had enslaved his world; just as he had been, she was headstrong and defiant, wanting to cut her own path, to do things her own way. She wasn't a follower, she didn't like being controlled, but she did need a mentor, someone who would not tell her what to do and how to do it, but rather, teach her the correct way to live, how to be. One brave warrior to another, surely she of all Earthers understood he would prefer the old ways, when soldiers met on the field of battle to face each other eye to eye. When the prize was there for each to stake a claim against, and the victor walked away with pride and package in hand, and the vanquished was laid to rest in a place of honor on the battlefield to find a glorious place prepared in Everworld. But she didn't intervene. Perhaps she couldn't. Kara was probably the ranking officer, and it would have been improper for Megan to open negotiations. He would just have to offer Kara a little more incentive. Unfortunately, he didn't have any. "We just want to get off this Darkworld space-hole. We just want to go home," he offered.

"No, they don't!" Allen yelled as he raced out the front door, a pistol pointed directly at Nol's chest. "They're planning to enslave all of us, all of Earth."

Click. That was the only sound his weapon could manage. He had never considered that he might not have more than the single bullet used to severe the chain. He continued across the clearing, tossed the pistol aside, and flung himself directly onto the shotgun. He rolled once and sprang to his feet, gripping the weapon in both hands. The shotgun discharged once, sending a few pellets into Rahon's shoulder. The bulk of the grouping zipped harmlessly past his head.

As Allen raced across the yard Nol and Rahon dropped their hands. *Curse Allen!* Nol had thought, *this fumbling Earthman is about to ruin our chances.* Just before Allen discharged the shotgun, Nol had given the signal, a twist of the wrist and a point. Rahon had snatched the cichma blade cradled in the hood hanging behind his neck, stooped slightly and twisted the blade around his left side. As Allen had risen, Rahon had let loose with a deft side-arm toss that had decapitated Allen even before he had been fully upright. His body had continued to rise, jerking with spasms and spurting blood from the stub of his neck like a geyser. The shot released at Rahon's head had been fired from the hand of a dead man. The blast forced Allen off his feet to splay flat on his back. His head shot forward over Kara's feet toward the truck and spun in tiny, wobbly circles in front of Megan like a sloppy, discarded melon. The earth women had seen and heard enough, and Nol knew it. Negotiations seemed to have ended early.

Near the cabin the trail widened and the going got a bit easier. Ovek could see its rough log walls and treated timber roof intermittently through the brigades of tall pines and birches. A gray, aromatic smoke streamed from the mammoth stone chimney along the west wall, a steady breeze bending it due south. A wry smile returned to his thin, cracked lips. He may have been sick and exhausted, and he may have been dying, but at least he retained a proper sense of perspective, and he could enjoy the moment. His instincts had served him well. He patted Guor lightly on the back while pointing ahead. It was all the celebration he could muster as they continued their slow and steady pace. The long trek was nearly at an end. Perhaps, if the negotiation went well, he might find time to rest in their cabin, he thought. Maybe they all could. He was hopeful. Nos knew, at the moment, he had enough trouble simply putting one foot in front of the other.

"Captain, someone's up ahead," Guor whispered as he pulled Ovek behind a huge tamarack. Ovek aimed his stubby claw tips toward his own eyes then down to the ground and finally outward toward the intruder. Guor immediately obeyed the silent command. He went belly to the ground, did a surreptitious low crawl just beyond the tree to the edge of the trail and sighted down the trail out to the cabin. He returned to Ovek a moment later. "It's Allen," he said, "sneaking into the back of the cabin."

"Help me up. We've got to hurry," Ovek said.

"Beggin' yer' pardon, sir, but your more likely to kick open the gates of Everworld if you start rushin' things," Guor replied.

"It doesn't matter," Ovek rasped, "we've got to hurry." He was certain Allen wouldn't have risked an escape unless he had been convinced the poison tactic had been only a ruse. That meant he knew more than he had let on, and he was dangerous. "All Darkworld is about to be unleashed."

Whatever had happened to Allen to embolden him must have been profound and certain. At least, that's the way Kara saw things. He wasn't a man given to flights of fancy, and he wasn't careless or prone to macho heroics. He was pragmatic and logical, and he planned and calculated everything he did. The impetus that had moved him had been profound, had stuck him with a sense of grave urgency, and had made him desperate. There was no doubt in Kara's mind he had been speaking the truth. His warning still echoed in her ears as his head rolled past her feet scribing a bright, ruby trail resembling alien text written across the pale ochre grass. Even before it stopped spinning her long, scimitar claws ejected, her tusks fully extended and her entire body prepared for battle. She squeezed her fists so tightly her nails cut into her palms. She did a small pirouette to gain momentum, threw her leg up and around as a counter balance flipping herself sideways directly in front of Nol. Immediately upon landing, she delivered a hard, straight right punch at his head. He barely had time to get his hands up. He was lucky. Her claws impaled his left forearm. She attacked again with a deft left uppercut. Again he countered. She pushed her translucent blades fully through his right forearm. They stood facing each other, each struggling to force the other to the ground, standing toe to toe, becoming an exemplar of *an irresistible force meets an immovable object*.

He was big, outweighing her by at least a hundred pounds. She was smaller, but faster and more agile, and deceptively powerful. Using his weight and leverage, he tried twisting her sideways, attempting to dislodge her claws from his arm and to simultaneously toss her aside. She stood her ground and spun quickly in the direction of his driving force, never allowing him to gain proper leverage. Failing at the maneuver, he tried to leverage her arms back that he might force his fingers around her neck. She adjusted her stance again in an attempt to push him over but he anchored himself like a loaded coal freighter. This time, he refused to move, so she decided on a dramatic chance of tactics. To do so, she would need to disengage. She attempted to pull her claws out of his arm, but he twisted inward, which brought his stubby claw tips that much closer to her neck. Each time she jerked her hands back he twisted his arms, which kept her locked onto him. His boot suddenly went up into her midsection, and he tumbled over backward. Kara flew into the air as he kicked her upward while he rolled onto his back. As he catapulted her away her claws released, and she retracted them. The blood squirting from his arms followed her through the air like laser fire. She did a double flip into a shoulder roll, landing her ten feet from his position. When she turned he was on his knees reaching up for the shotgun Rahon had tossed to him.

Kara dove high to her left, shooting her arm forward, swimming upward as if the air was a liquid. She brought her knee up, and her right hand dropped to the .38 tucked in the holster on her boot. Nol snared the shotgun with his left hand and gave it a deft, one-hand gravity pump, then attempted to level it at the spot where he thought Kara would be in the next micro-second. Kara pulled the revolver and fired as she brought it level with her knee. The pump grip exploded in Nol's hand, and also disintegrated his two smallest fingers. The weapon fell at his feet, the blast having reduced it to a piece of useless scrap metal. Kara discharged a second round even before she hit the ground. The bullet passed cleanly through the fleshy part of his muscular thigh. A flurry of scales flittered into the air around his hip. A moment earlier he had meant to use the shotgun merely to wound her. Now, he knew that time had passed. Both shots she had fired were a clear signal that she meant business. He was still alive only because she had fired on the move. The shotgun had saved his scaly hide the first time and a desperation shot tagged him low the second. Dumb luck, that's all that separated him from Everworld. He had to face facts; they all would. If Megan wouldn't help them, the transponder was history. As for Kara—she was about to *become* history. The concept of negotiation was about to take on an entirely new meaning. Nol reached into his jacket and wrapped his fist around the handle of his cichma ax.

Megan had never seen anyone killed before. She had seen dead bodies, of course, at her parents' funeral. But it had been easier to look upon the colorful, waxy figures lying in repose as mere placeholders, visual aids simply representing the larger-than-life personas already enjoying their eternal vacation. She had never actually seen anyone die. Except in the movies, but that had never been like this, raw and tangible, moist, with spray that wet the skin and a smell of blood that made the mouth water. And she had never heard the true sounds of death. It had always been a rather quiet episode on the screen, except for a moment just before, perhaps. Sometimes there was a screech, a scream or a crescendo of some intrusive music to alert the audience, warning the squeamish to turn away. But there was no warning in real life. One moment she heard Allen's vehement protest, and the next, all was silent except for the soft, sickening sound of the blood spurting from his arteries and the tiny droplets whispering all around like a gentle, summer rain. His last, full breath was expelled from the top of his severed esophagus in a gurgling, gaseous flagellant that bubbled in the crimson pool gathering in the stump above his shoulders. She heard the dull thud of his body strike the ground, followed by the clop, clop, clop of his head bouncing across the lawn, watching in horror as it rolled and spun to a slow, anticlimactic halt. Without warning, the true face of death had been exposed, and she had heard its eerie call. But no sooner had his body hit the ground than she decided that the next head to roll would be sprouting horns and a scaly fan. She decided the next kill would be by her. She brought the .22 to her shoulder and fired a round directly into Rahon's back as he tossed the shotgun to Nol. A puff of scales fluttered into the air between his shoulder blades as the bullet struck his scapula. He turned to face Megan, laughing as if she had told a clever, little joke. He marched toward her, laughing even louder as she cocked the rifle and fired another round directly at his forehead. The bullet barely penetrated his bony ridge. He snorted as he twisted the rifle out of her hands and punched her in the side of the head. Then, with a quick forward snap of both open palms he pushed her forcefully against the truck. The combined blows to her head and chest nearly rendered her unconscious. Everything went black momentarily and she couldn't breathe. She slid down the side of the truck and dropped to her knees. Rahon balled his bony fist and, squaring it up with her forehead, drew back his arm in order to deliver a devastating punch. He meant to end the fight with this upstart quickly and decidedly.

Kara immediately jumped to her feet and leveled the .38 at Nol's head as he reached inside his jacket. But she was unable to fire the shot. Taven had brought the bow for this mission, and he let loose an arrow from thirty feet away that impaled her in the back of her hand. The revolver fell uselessly to the ground. At that moment, she expected Nol to attack, but he ran toward Megan instead. She watched him curiously while removing the arrow from her hand. Gripping the shaft just above the arrowhead, she pulled it until the feathers passed completely through. Nol wrapped his hand around the bicep of his fellow soldier and stayed him from punching Megan. It was clear he was protecting her. More than likely, he wanted her alive to lead them to the transponder. It didn't matter. She knew nothing that would be of use to them anyway. Besides, it was time to put an end to this nonsense. Kara had made her decision the moment they had butchered Allen. She meant to kill them all.

She moved forward slightly into the center of the clearing, stepping over Allen's fallen body, attempting to move out of the edge of the shadows cast by the pines bordering the yard to the east. She wanted the glare of the morning sun to frame her. It still hovered low enough that it might grant her a slight advantage. She stared hard at Taven, who was loading another arrow into the bow, and at Beel who continued to advance, but she also kept a wary eye on Megan at the same time. Rahon stooped to retrieve the rifle wrenched from her hands and tested the cocking mechanism. Kara stood defiantly in the center of the lawn, ejected her talons, and roared her contempt at the lot of them. Her tusks gleamed like crystal shards, the viral essence glistening in the sunshine. She perked her soft, fuzzy ears to fine, elongated points and jerked her head quickly from side to side. She pawed at the ground with her boots tips as if marking the territory in front of her. Beel advanced steadily along the face of the cabin, pulling a wicked US Army hand ax from under his heavy, field jacket.

Taven stopped abruptly and drew back on the bow. He aimed directly at the very center of her chest. At the same time, Rahon jerked the rifle to his shoulder and pointed it at her head, hoping to tag her in the way Megan had tagged him. Kara's sized up the situation in an instant, her instinctual behavioral mechanisms kicking in as if energized by remote control. The neurons rocketed across her synapses to form a coherent plan of attack and a variety of defensive counter measures. She would spin once, quickly build momentum and loop into the air in a long arch that would bring her down on top of Rahon. Her talons would sever his jugulars on the sides of his neck. She would snatch the rifle from his hands and, using the butt end, ram it into the front of Nol's face. She probably wouldn't kill him but the blow should knock him unconscious. Megan was coming around, so she probably could get into the truck and start it on her own while Kara fended off the other two.

The ax was not intended as a precision fighting weapon, the balance was poor and it would be a long throw for Beel. She would take care of him last. Taven was another matter. Her best bet was to flip and cartwheel toward him making for a difficult, moving target. When she got within arm's reach, killing him should be a relatively easy matter. He wasn't quite as large as the others, not as powerfully built. She noticed he never cared to get very close to an adversary, preferring instead to stay his distance. Close-quarter combat skills were probably not his specialty; she would use that against him. Sheer aggression would give her the distinct advantage. She would come at him with everything she had. And she would show him no mercy. Actually killing Beel might prove more difficult. Once he was disarmed, she would have to find a way to use his massive bulk to thwart him. He was more rotund than his partners, muscular but barrel-chested with massive shoulders, a thick waist and thighs. Speed and agility would be the key to his defeat. The tactic she had used against Cor at the picnic grounds might work well against him. She would confront him head on, go up and around, attack him from behind. If all went as planned she might land her tusks in the back of his thick neck before he ever realized she had left the ground.

She began her pirouette the instant she heard the twang of the bowstring. But her impromptu plan went awry when her leg would not respond, and she fell to one knee. Rahon's shot passed over her head and pinged harmlessly off the metal McClurie placard nailed to the front of the cabin. A sharp, searing pain shot up her leg and flared into her hip. An arrow stuck her firmly in the neck, driving to its midsection, where it stopped abruptly, centered perfectly above her shoulders. The arrow was firmly seated in her as though she was a living weathercock. She wrapped her hand around the shaft with one hand and grasped the blade lodged in the back of her thigh with the other. Taven released another arrow before she could pull on either and pinned her left arm to her side; it tore fully through her bicep and dug deeply into her lung. She tried desperately to rise on her good leg but fell, as Rahon fired another round that tore through her shinbone.

She went down on both knees. Another arrow caught her between the ribs angled just below her left breast. She felt the blood well up into her throat. She heard the whoosh of the ax as it sliced the air, but her only move was a feeble roll to her right side. It wasn't enough. Beel had anticipated her only option and had released a long, desperation throw. He had gotten lucky. The ax pounded her squarely in the upper right shoulder, and she went down for good. Another arrow found its mark in her leg, then, from a mere ten feet Taven zipped one into her back while Guor pulled his mandat knife from her leg. "This isn't going to rot with her," he said, unceremoniously yanking it out of her.

"But this is," Taven said, pounding an arrow into her leg at close range.

"And this," Rahon sneered as he fired a bullet into her back for good measure. She jerked once and lay very still.

Megan had watched the entire scene unfold, confident that Kara would prevail. Upon thwarting Nol's attempt to shoot her with the shotgun, Megan knew Kara was running on all cylinders, and that she was not likely to allow any of these brutes to leave the clearing alive. But that confidence was dashed the moment Guor crept around the cabin and tossed the mandat knife. She had been focused on the others and had never seen him coming. For a clumsy-looking fool he certainly could move quickly and quietly. One moment she was poised and ready to strike, the very next, she lay helpless on the ground, a mere target for their cruel amusement. It was more than Megan could bear. The tears streamed down her checks as they tortured her.

Kara lay in the center of the lawn like a downed fawn. Rivulets of blood streamed from her wounds forming dozens of tiny crimson pools, as if a bouquet of roses was blooming all around her. Assured she was dead, the aliens simply walked away to gather around Nol, who held fast to Megan's wrists. Rahon cocked the rifle once again and forced the barrel against her forehead. "Make a move," he warned her. He looked to Nol who simply nodded, knowingly. They both knew what was at stake. Only Megan was unaware they would never shoot her now. She was far too valuable a commodity, but they had to bluff. Killing Kara had been a credible start.

"Watch her like a greetch," Nol said as he released her arms. "If her teeth begin to twitch, pull the trigger. Where's the cap'n?" he asked without hesitation. Guor looked to the cabin

"He's inside resting. He barely made it. We followed Allen through the back door hoping to intercept him, but the captain collapsed once we got inside. I made him as comfortable as I could." No sooner had Guor finished than Ovek appeared at the door. He looked cycles older than he had yesterday and had lost even more weight. His skin was yellow, his eyes sunken and dark, and scales flittered off him as he staggered forward down the steps. Guor ran to help him, acting as a crutch, and it seemed an eternity before they joined the group gathered near the truck.

"There was no other way?" Ovek asked, surveying Kara's body.

"No. I was close to making a deal, Cap'n," Nol said, "but Allen interfered. I tried. But we have Megan, and I think we might find her more willing to help us now."

Ovek pushed the gun barrel from Megan's head and took her chin in his hand. "I'm dying," he told her. "Please, let me return to my world, to be interred with the eggcypts of my ancestors," he pleaded. "We never wanted any of this." He looked toward Kara and forced his sad, steady gaze deep into Megan's eyes once more. "Whatever Allen told you, he was wrong."

Megan matched his stare with resolve and a deep vehemence she never knew existed. She knew very well all that was at stake, and she developed and hatched her plan in a heartbeat. "You were fools to come here. All you had to do was check the barn. Your little device is hidden under the floor boards beneath a heavy tool chest," she said. She had never been a good liar but she put every ounce of acting skill she had into this one big lie.

"Did you check under the chest?" Ovek turned to Nol.

"No," Nol answered. "We only looked inside."

"Is it possible?" Ovek rasped.

"Yes," Nol admitted, angry with himself for not being as thorough as he might have been.

Ovek turned to Megan once again. "All right. Then we're getting off this rock, and you're going to help us further. Do you understand?" he rasped. She nodded. "I want you to operate this vehicle and return us to the farmhouse. Once we have the transponder you're free to go. You can return here and dispose of your dead. But right now, the security of my team comes first. Do you understand?" he repeated. She nodded again. "Good," he said, out of breath. "Megan, I'm sorry it had to happen this way," he told her as he opened the door and ushered her behind the wheel.

Nol hopped into the passenger side while Beel, Rahon and Taven piled into the bed. The tarp on the floor would make for convenient cover while on the road. Guor gently pushed the captain from behind while Beel took his arms, easing him up into the truck. He looked as though he was about to tumble head-over-heels across the tailgate.

Suddenly, Kara pushed herself to her knees. The viral essence had been at work long enough to overcome the effects of the more serious wounds and to return some mobility. The initial shock and pain was subsiding rapidly. She jumped to her feet while simultaneously reaching under her left breast and grasping the arrow protruding from between her ribs. It was the one that seemed to be bothering her the most, making it difficult for her to breathe. She gave it one quick jerk and whipped it tip first into the ground at her feet. Without hesitation, she launched herself in a long, looping arch toward the far end of the truck. In midair she dislodged the ax from her back, deftly flipped it in her hand and swung as she passed up and over Guor. His head flopped at a ninety-degree angle like the top of a Pez dispenser, and his body slipped to the ground like a torn bag of dirt. A gush of blood spurted skyward and rained down into the truck bed soaking the stunned troopers. While not as graceful a landing as she was accustomed to, Kara was able to pivot and jump quickly enough to snag Ovek's leg before he could hoist himself inside.

She dragged him to the ground like a wounded gazelle. She was on him immediately and her tusks found their mark. She buried them as deeply as possible into the back of his neck. While shaking him mercilessly with violent jerks of her head, she grabbed his trousers and hoisted him level with her chest. His lower leg repeatedly slapped the ground as if he were a flimsy, stuffed animal. The shaking forced the arrow from her lower leg. She tried pulling her left arm away, but the arrow there was stubborn, keeping her arm pinioned to her side. The effort was made all the more difficult by Ovek's continued struggling. Even in his weakened condition he was still huge and powerful. She squeezed her jaws together more tightly until he finally breathed a heavy sigh and went limp. The blood poured from his neck in a long stream marking their trail as Kara backed up toward the cabin. The troopers watched in horror as Kara dragged her prey back to her lair. Nol was half hanging out of the cab, holding the rifle on Megan but his attention was focused primarily on Kara. The troopers waited on his command before launching themselves from the truck, but Nol was quick with a cautionary signal.

"Hold!" he shouted. "He's dead. Ovek's dead already."

"I know. But we can't leave either of them behind," Taven said.

"We won't," Nol said. "I've seen this before on the field of battle, with creatures of tremendous fortitude. This is her last, desperate attempt at life. But she's lost too. No one can survive those wounds. Let nature take its course. We'll get the transponder and come back for their bodies when she's dead. She won't last the day," he assured them. They all watched sadly as she and Ovek disappeared within the shadows beyond the cabin door.

"Now drive," he told Megan. "That's an order."

Megan was more than happy to oblige. She put the truck in gear and pulled up the frontage road, thankful to leave this sad, secluded battlefield behind, relieved to be rid of its gruesome reminders of the horrors of warfare, at least for the moment. Allen had said the aliens planned to enslave the entire Earth. If that was true, and she had no reason to doubt it, then Kara's instincts had served her well. She had made the right decision, the best decision possible. Surely, this little battlefield was but a microscopic prelude to the worldwide catastrophe that would ensue should the aliens order a full-scale invasion. Instinct had told Kara the entire Earth was in danger. She knew, and she probably saved the earth by hiding the transponder. Now it was up to Megan to save Kara. When these animals discovered the transponder was not hidden in the barn, they might return before she could fully heal. Kara was tough, but they had overcome her once when she was at her best. There was no telling what they might be able to do to her in her weakened condition.

The smart thing to do was to comply with their demands. She needed to get these creatures as far away from Kara as possible, to keep them away for as long as she could. Of course, there was always the chance they would kill her immediately when they discovered the transponder was not beneath the floorboards as she had promised. The only thing hidden there was her high school diary, mostly detailing her sexual misadventures, exploits which she had desperately kept hidden from her parents. Once they learned the truth, she would swear to these monsters that Kara had told her it was hidden there, but that she must have lied to safeguard the truth. Realizing the transponder could never be found, they probably wouldn't harm her. This lie was actually quite near the truth, and Nol would see the wisdom in Kara's tactics. At that point, killing her would gain them nothing. Besides, they would need someone to replenish their supplies and taxi them to a permanent place of safety once they realized there was no going home, and if none of this occurred to them she would conveniently suggest it to them when the time came. At least, that was her plan.

Nol pulled his hood up around his bony head to shield him from view. The others buried themselves beneath the heavy tarp. "Stick to the back roads," he told her, "and keep the speed down. We wouldn't want any mishaps on the way back, would we?" It really wasn't a question at all, and sounded purposefully menacing. But she was certain he had no intention of killing her, not now anyway, not while she was driving. However, she knew one thing for certain; a bullet in her arm or leg from the .22 would be a painful reminder of who was in charge at the moment. So she drove with extra care, keeping her speed well under the limit and slowed considerably while passing the fleet of squad cars parked near the bridge on Willow Drive.

Chapter 14

Ovek lay on the floor at the base of the fireplace. A thin line of soft, pink foam gathered between his lips trailing into a pool of dark crimson that had drizzled onto the floor beneath his face. He coughed several times and forced himself to a sitting position but immediately dropped to the floor. He forced himself up uneasily. His hand instinctively shot to the back of his neck, to massage the pain away and try to force some sensibility back into his head, but his hand slid across a slick layer of blood. He tried desperately to remember what had happened, but couldn't. He had been climbing into the truck—he remembered that much—beyond that, nothing. He realized he had lost a lot of blood. He felt very weak and, literally, very close to death. The darkworld knew, he should be dead already considering the nature of the adversary standing sentinel over him—although he was amazed she could stand at all considering the severity of her wounds and the number of arrows protruding from her.

One of them penetrated fully through her neck and another pinioned her arm to her side. As she paced back and forth, studying him, he noticed yet two more, one sticking out of her back and the other buried deep in her leg. She was drenched in blood from head to toe. Most of the blood was hers, but some was probably his and the troopers, no doubt. Nonetheless, she certainly had taken quite a beating, and he was certain that any less a trooper would be dead already, or splayed out flat on her back contemplating her eternal place in Everworld. But the fact that she seemed as fit as if she had not been scratched at all was a testament to her toughness.

These Earthlings were an extraordinary breed, he thought, and it would be the emperor's good fortune should they be amicably brought into his service. Ovek held onto his hopes that he might yet be instrumental in making that happen, as remote as that prospect was beginning to seem. Though severely injured, she moved gracefully to the sink and poured water onto a cloth from a plastic bottle. She approached as if there was absolutely nothing wrong, the arrows jiggling a bit as she walked. She looked somewhat comical, but the seriousness of her wounds seemed all too obvious. He wondered why she wasn't dead. The shaft through her neck looked especially ominous. Under different circumstances he might have laughed at such a sight, but he couldn't. He was confused. Besides, it hurt too much to laugh.

Kara knelt beside her hostage and handed him the water bottle. She covered the back of his neck with the wet cloth. "You've lost a lot of blood," she said.

"So have you," he quipped.

She stared at him for a moment. "Aren't you worried I might just kill you in the next few minutes?" she asked.

"Seems to me you would be doing me a favor," he said.

Kara had known the moment she had snatched him from the truck that he was no longer a threat to her, and she never meant to kill him from that moment on. She only wanted to quiet him. She had cut off the flow of oxygen to his brain to render him unconscious. It was much easier to take a hostage who was not resisting. Ovek was the leader of this alien vanguard, and she was sure they would do anything to get him back. She could use him to bargain for Megan. She had been outnumbered and knew they would probably get away before she healed enough to challenge them all and Megan could be freed. Ovek had been her best bet.

"You should know, it was *your* bite that poisoned me," he said, surprised she didn't know he was already dying. The exertion of uttering long sentences forced him to stop and rest after each one now. Any utterance longer than a few words forced him to breathe heavily and made him cough violently. Swallowing was becoming more difficult, as well.

The light in her eyes went on immediately. She knew exactly what was happening to him.

"The Bloodlust Rhyme," she said.

"The what?" Ovek asked, surprised by her nonsensical reply.

"The Bloodlust Rhyme" she repeated. "It a little poem my mother used to recite to me before bed when I was a little girl. It explains exactly what's happening to you," she said—a little too cheerfully—it seemed to him.

"Explain it to me, then," he said.

Kara sat quietly a moment. It had been a long time since she had heard the rhyme. She recited it to herself first just to make absolutely certain she remembered it properly.

"It goes something like this," she told him:

Never bite a snake
For it will be stricken,
The same for a frog
A gecko or chicken.
If perchance you do
The essence will curse,
And the beloved chameleon
Will surely get worse.
You may give it a taste
But never too much,
For the priceless you waste
Too precious the blood.
Surrender a cup
For a time to survive,
Though a river of blood
Won't keep it alive."

Ovek looked at her, a quizzical look pasted on his face. "Well, what does that *mean*?" he asked.

"It's a warning about the lethal nature of the virus. In short, it's a warning about the dangers of biting any creature other than a mammal, and obviously, you're not a mammal. Of course, that rule doesn't apply when the other creature—that means you, Dino—is the aggressor. You attacked us, remember?"

"Don't remind me," Ovek shook his head. "I'm beginning to realize what a serious mistake that was." He paused just a moment.

"And Cor," he said sadly, "he attacked you in the woods? I ordered him not to engage."

"He had a blade, and he made a move toward me," she replied, "but, now, I'm not sure. I was spooked, and I may have overreacted. I don't know."

He nodded. "Fair enough. I'm sure tracking the likes of us hadn't been on your to-do list that night. Things happen." He sat quietly a moment, looking at her, but not seeing her, not really. She knew it. "His name was Cor Amam. I didn't know him long, and we were not all that close, but he was a good trooper, and he never disappointed me," he said, stretching his dry lips into a hard, straight smile.

Kara gazed steadily at him and nodded knowingly. It was difficult to lose someone, even someone you had known only a short while. Obviously, that was something both of them understood and could agree on. She couldn't help feeling a mounting empathy for this peculiar soldier. If nothing else Ovek was an honest and honorable creature. That meant a great deal to her. "I wish you hadn't stabbed Megan," she said. "I would never have lost my temper and targeted you the way I did."

"Well," he said, "for the record," he paused, "I didn't stab her." Again he stopped to take a deep breath. "One of my troopers threw the dagger."

Kara looked into his eyes and saw the truth buried behind them. They looked so pitiful, dark and sunken. The young, piercing eyes she remembered so clearly from their first encounter were gone. Thick, dry yellow folds, which seemed to age him a hundred years, had replaced the bright, moist green skin that once surrounded them. The bright golden orange irises and deep chocolate pupils had been replaced by dense shades of sickly gray. Suddenly Kara straightened and placed her hand on his shoulder. She looked even more deeply into his eyes. She spoke evenly, her voice deep, and melodic. "You are going to help me, and I will help you in return. We are going to form an alliance, you and I. You understand? We are going to help each other."

"We're going to help each other," he said, as if it were his idea.

"First, you will help me remove these arrows."

"I'll help you remove the arrows," Ovek said.

"Good," Kara said. "Let's do that now." One by one Ovek gripped the shafts as she pulled away, dislodging each in turn and dropping them at her feet. When all four had been removed she gathered them up with a distinct air of disdain. She hurled them sharply like tiny javelins, three at the planks crisscrossing the ceiling and the final one into the centerboard of the canoe suspended above her head. Then she stood over him, her arms crossed resolutely.

"Now," she said firmly. "Tell me, why are you here, and how did you get to Earth?"

Megan inspected the tub and realized she was locked in the very room in which they had held Allen captive. The indentation on the pillow made the memory of his head rolling around in the yard all the more sad and creepy. A few magazines and some lingerie catalogs were scattered on the toilet tank, a platter with a half-eaten piece of toast lay on the floor next to the sink, a glass stained with milk sat nearby, an unopened chocolate bar, extra socks and tee-shirts were stacked neatly in the corner, all echoes of a life never to be fully heard again. But she would always remember his frequent and comforting advice and hear his voice in her mind. She had loved him once, like a brother more than a lover, when all was said and done. The truth was that he had been too smart and too sophisticated for her. She knew it. That made romance between them impossible, and she assumed he had loved her more like a sister.

They were true friends, and there was nothing more valuable. The horror of his death would stay with her always. She vowed to hold the memory of it as inspiration and a source of inner strength. Alien creatures may have butchered him, but there were similar brutes native to this planet equally cruel and insidious, and she was beginning to understand that the strength and courage to face them and to dispose of them was certainly within her. It was there. She felt it stir the moment Allen had fallen, and if fate opened that singular path to her, if the bloodlust would grace her with its strength, she would nurture it, force it to blossom to its fullest.

She sat on the floor with her head against the tub waiting for the hammer to fall. It wouldn't be long before the monsters discovered the diary and nothing else beneath the tool chest. Her confidence in her plan was beginning to sink. She felt a sickening feeling in the pit of her stomach. Her nerves were definitely getting to her. Her head began pounding, and the blood rushed to her face in waves of searing flashes that seemed to fill her checks with liquid fire. Her jaws hurt. Fingers were poking her eyes from the inside out. The muscles in her arms and legs were being ripped apart, and her skin from the top of her head to the bottom of her feet had a mind of its own. It seemed to move of its own accord, rippling like water near the shallows.

The air around her seemed to get cooler and each breath took progressively longer to inhale and exhale. As quickly as it had come, the sickly feeling in her stomach vanished, only to be replaced by excruciating pain directly beneath her eyes. She pressed her palms to her face until the pain subsided. She sat sweating on the bathroom floor and removed her shirt and pants. Now, the only remaining vestige of her sudden illness was an incredible fatigue. She hung her head, hoping to catch a few moments rest before they came for her. As she did, drops of blood fell from her mouth onto her breasts, first one, then another, then more. The drops connected into two thin streams that drained from her upper gums, which completely soaked her bra and gathered in a generous pool in the center of her stomach and finally drizzled down between her legs onto the floor. When she awoke the bleeding had stopped.

It seemed her nap had lasted only several minutes, but it had been long enough. She felt fine. It was as if the terrible pains had never descended upon her, and she was ready to face her adversaries once again. She knew they would be coming soon and that they would be livid. She cleaned the floor and dressed quickly. She wasn't exactly sure what had happened to her and questions from them would only lead to more difficulties. (The less these aliens understood about vampires and Earthlings in general, the better, as far as she was concerned.) More than likely, the pain and sickness was an effect of the virus, but precisely what it was doing to her was not clear. She could only hope that these symptoms were not signs of something gone seriously wrong with her transformation. The symptoms were probably normal, but since she could not ask Kara, it was difficult to know. Fortunately, the episode had been only temporary. She seemed fine now; in fact she felt better than fine. She felt great. And she was hungry.

As she anticipated, Nol flung open the door only a moment later. "You knew all along, didn't you?" he said. His implied accusation seemed rather serene and non-threatening. He waved the .22 at her eye like a long, scolding finger but, suddenly, he let the rifle dangle at his side.

"You knew all along," he repeated sadly.

She knew immediately he had resigned himself and the team to their fate. She didn't answer. She didn't have to. This wasn't exactly the inquisition she had expected.

"She hid it, didn't she?" he said over the scrunching noise he made with the paper bag gripped in his left hand. "She hid it from you, from everyone."

"Yes," she said.

She noticed his shoulders slump just a little further. The tip of the rifle nearly tapped the floor. "Of course she would take it upon herself," he said.

"Why do you say that?" she asked as he turned to leave.

"Because it's what I would have done," he said. "It's a smart strategy. Perhaps she destroyed it. You can't relinquish something you no longer possess, even if it means you could pay the ultimate price." He dropped the paper bag on the floor and closed the door quietly behind him. She could hear his heavy footfalls echo along the hallway as he made his way to the kitchen. In the bag she found an uncooked hotdog, a box of the fish-shaped crackers, an economy-sized chocolate bar, and a bottle of spring water. She propped herself against the wall to eat lunch and reflect on her good fortune. His final words may have sounded ominous, could even have been interpreted as a threat. But she didn't think so. There had been something in his eyes, something in the way he had looked at her, something in the timber of his voice and his body language. She didn't know a lot about aliens, but she knew men. All right, he wasn't a man, but he *was* male, that was a certainty. Was there really a significant difference?

The tiny grotto seemed frozen in time, as if it kept the secrets of life and death hidden beneath its thick, heavy mist, hidden from the prying eyes of man. Surely it had a mind of its own, stubborn and set in its ways, for it seemed unwilling to relinquish its grip on the dense and dewy air. The deep blanket of soppy leaves and tender moss beneath blended into a spongy mass of deep browns and putrid greens. The leaves of the surrounding trees released their moisture like a continuous rain of tears. The sound of the dripping was a continuous weeping, a sad and melancholy melody whispering in the background as Kara dug the shallow grave where Allen could rest. Here and there between the tall elms and thick, voluminous oaks, a few twisted stumps, barren of leaves, stretched their weathered arms outward like old vagabonds. One that might have been a hundred years old but looked a thousand was overrun with moss from top to bottom, its long, spindly arms covered in a thick coat of soft, downy green. These ancient trees hovered above the pit like haunted souls that had sought out this place, come looking for a quiet place to die. She consigned his remains respectfully to the earth and concealed the spot with fresh leaves and moss trusting the gnarled, weathered stumps to serve as markers and sentinels until her return.

She wondered, though, if there could be a more fitting place for him. She thought his soul, if such a thing existed, would surely be lifted up from a place such as this, for it was as sacred as any place she could imagine. Would there actually be any point in returning? Could she find a more fitting burial spot for him, or have a more proper and solemn ceremony? And would anyone really want to know the circumstances of his death? Would anyone want to know precisely where and how he had died? Would anyone believe? She wondered. Perhaps, it would be best to revisit these thoughts another day. For now, her immediate concerns were for the fate of the living. During the time she had spent concealing Guor's body beneath the temporary eggcrypt, and while she had searched for a suitable burial place for Allen, she had considered all Ovek had told her.

She had listened with great interest and fascination to a brief history of the Rege'Cean Empire and the great expansion, the Aggregation Wars, about his team's rescue mission and capture, and finally, their arrival on this planet. And she considered their plight and the ramifications of what they had learned and of their ultimate plans for Earth. But it was at Allen's gravesite that she realized a most profound and horrific truth. She knew now, beyond all doubt, that she had been wise in following her instincts. In disposing of the transponder, she had made the right decision, not just for Earth, but also for the Rege'Cean Empire. In fact, the greatest threat was not to Earth at all. Certainly, Earthlings had been in danger, and they yet might be. The alien plot to enslave all of Earth was proof enough of that; it was an insidious plan and a dire prospect to say the least, should it ever come to pass. Such a prospect seemed fantastic, even ludicrous when uttered aloud, sounding rather like the ramblings of a deranged mind. But unwittingly, the stakes would have been much higher for the empire, which, according to Ovek, is comprised of hundreds of millions of planets populated primarily by reptilian, amphibious and aquatic races, with a minority of worlds populated with insectoids and other classes which defied specific cataloging by Earth standards.

Regardless, one Vampire, a single carrier of the virus, introduced as a slave soldier into the Rege'Cean military could begin a pandemic with the potential to decimate the empire. But should the entire population of Earth be enslaved, the resultant outbreak spread by the millions of angry vampires unleashed upon the Rege'Cean bio-system would not be so problematic. It would be inevitable, exponentially swift, and devastating. The pandemic would not advance inexorably like a smoldering, ponderous lava flow, but madly and rapidly, like an uncontrollable wildfire. With the aid of ion drives and jump gates, it would literally explode across the central galactic arm. The eventual outcome would be the complete and utter annihilation of the Rege'Cean Empire. Some of the nondescript species might survive, but without the usual trade and familiar complex social interdependencies they had established with the greater galactic community, their fates would be problematic, as well. Only the relatively few mammalian worlds would thrive, for a time. But if each could not soon find a way to successfully coexist with its uninfected population, as the vampires had found with humans on Earth, chaos would rule until a lasting and meaningful social symbiosis could be established. It would not be an easy or predictable path for any of the mammals—the requisite equilibrium might not be embraced in time to save the vast majority. No matter how you looked at it, this was not a scenario Ovek or anyone from his part of the galaxy could live with. The vampire virus must remain on Earth. The secret of the virus must remain buried with the transponder, with Allen, and ultimately with the aliens.

Kara considered how incredibly fortunate, and how incredibly unlikely it was, that humanity had survived. Earthlings, blessed or cursed by the Chimera Virus, depending on one's point of view, *had* been able to come to terms with its advent. Eons ago, they had developed a way to coexist with uninfected humans by proposing the vampire code and instilling it within themselves. The code may have seemed a mere guideline but it was far more. Once heard, once recited by an elder, passed down by a parent or teacher using the *mesmer voice,* the code became *instilled,* imbued into the genetic makeup of the vampire. From that point forward, it remained an aspect of the individual's instinctive nature. Rather than feeling compelled to follow the code, unable to resist it, the vampire simply felt *inclined* to follow the rules of his or her own accord. There was no need for a continuance of outside influences and pressures. Thus, there was little need of written law and formal regulation, of oversight and punishment, and as social structure grew and became more sophisticated, so did the code. The vampire code worked, and the symbiosis between man and vampire allowed both to flourish for millions of years. But that was only a serendipitous aspect of this singular planet. There is no such guarantee for other worlds, and the fate of mammalian races residing light years from Earth rests in the hands of the gods they worship. Perhaps good fortune might lay in the destiny of some. Others might simply hunt themselves to extinction in a generation. Who can say? Who would wish to test such a hypothesis in any case? Who would purposefully introduce the vampire virus to them?

Kara stepped quietly into the cabin to find Ovek fast asleep. He was lying in the bed covered with a thick comforter, his head buried deeply in a soft pillow. An array of tiny brown and yellow-ochre flecks dotted the pillowcase all around his head and scales continued puffing off his checks as he rolled his head about. She had learned much about this savvy and heroic warrior. He seemed a character of great nobility, a man, if she could call him that, of honor and integrity, and she felt she could trust him to do the right thing. He knew she had buried the transponder. She had told him that much, and he seemed consigned to his fate because of it and because of the illness. But if he was to be of any use in securing Megan's release she had to insure that he stay alive. Besides, she had a suspicion that his troopers might not be quite as reasonable or honorable. She had found Ovek to be a formidable foe. He might make a formidable ally, as well. She was beginning to regret the appreciable suffering she had inadvertently delivered him, and her instincts told her she could use his help. Her instincts were seldom wrong. Though she couldn't cure him, she could at least prolong his life and ease his suffering. "Surrender a cup, for a time to survive, though a river of blood, won't keep it alive," she whispered as she crawled onto the bed.

"Ovek," she said, waking him.

"I'm awake," he said without moving, without opening his eyes. He looked like a dead thing talking.

"The sickness you're suffering," Kara told him, "is caused by a virus…from my bite. Fresh blood is an antidote. You must drink my blood. Do you understand?"

"I understand," Ovek replied wearily. He could barely move his lips. "Sounds delicious."

She smiled. At least he had a sense of humor about things, and why not? The situation now would have seemed laughable if it were not so tragic. The very idea of a big, wisecracking reptile lying in her bed was one for the books! Though the battle and her somber duties had made for a tough day, and she was hungry and tired and feeling the blood loss, she felt a sense of urgency mounting. He looked just plain awful. Opening a major vein or risking a slice through a primary artery was not something she would even consider at the moment. She pulled the survival knife from its sheath and, removing her blouse and bra, cut a clean shallow slice into her chest from atop her left breast down to the cleavage in a quick, even motion. She lay beside him, wrapped her arms around his huge frame and rolled him toward her. Then, pressing his head tightly against her chest, she forced his mouth against her open wound. Consumed by the bloodlust, the reptilian sucked eagerly. The feeding delivered a wave of relief throughout his stricken body, and riding that wave was a message of hope, received as a sudden, surprising realization, that this alien creature who had condemned him to death might yet be his savior. He saw her in a vision standing on the breakers near the ocean. She was naked and leapt from rock to rock until in midair she transformed into a huge, black beast with gleaming razor fangs releasing vapor trails, then burst into a brilliant fireball that illuminated the distant horizon.

Nol's reaction could have been worse, and Megan knew it. Flat on her back, her feet propped comfortably on the tub, she had just settled down to peruse one of the magazines when she caught the distinct click and thump of the refrigerator door and the heady snap of a beer can. Nol summoned Rahon and Beel, but she heard several other voices mingling with them. They were all probably in the kitchen. The voices were indistinct, muddled. They mentioned the transponder, the fact that it would never be found. She heard certain utterances loud and clear, "useless," "hopeless." Sometimes the words were angry, sometimes agonized or melancholy. She recognized various curses now and then; the translations were rough and peculiar sometimes, but she got the gist of it. More beer cans were opened, and she caught the sound of a distinctive creak. They had discovered the liquor cabinet. She heard a name clearly spoken, Didra. "Nos, I'll miss her," she heard one say.

"Taven," someone said. She heard her own name, as well, and Kara's.

"She's dead for sure!" Nol shouted. "Her neck has bled her out." There was a shot and the sound of breaking glass. She felt the house shake as if Nol had put his huge meaty fist through a wall. More than likely, that is exactly what he had done. Then there were voices shouting all at once. There was the screeching of chairs and a crashing sound, followed by a sharp tap, then another, and yet another, followed by a barrage in rapid succession. The noise was accompanied by some raucous jibes and laughter, some taunting. She surmised her living room walls had become targets for their blade weapons and her kitchen utensils. Their macho contests and rowdiness went on late into the day then dissipated abruptly. All was quiet, as if the house had rebelled and swallowed them whole.

She tested the handle. If they were drunk enough, perhaps she could just walk away. Maybe Earth booze and Milwaukee beer was just a little more than they could handle. But she quickly discovered they had improvised a lock on the bathroom door, it wouldn't budge. She hadn't thought they would be so careless, but it had been worth a try. With her hands still wrapped around the knob, she heard a clacking sound, the door swung inward abruptly, pushing her backward. She was surprised and somewhat dismayed to see Rahon filling the doorway, his huge, drunken frame weaving back and forth, a glittering mandat knife dangled from his thick fingers. He played with it, purposefully allowing the blade to zip this way and that, catching the light, slipping left and right in quick, somewhat sloppy, slicing motions.

He eyeballed her in a curious fashion, and surveyed the room, constantly checking on her through the corners of his eyes. Occasionally his tongue lolled out the side of his mouth and sucked his lips as if he hadn't had a drink all day. She didn't appreciate the intrusion, and she didn't like the look in his eyes. These brutes were dangerous and unpredictable enough when sober. Who knows what they were capable of after they tied one on! She looked left and right for something she could use as a weapon. Then, without warning, he was on her. He may have been stinking drunk, but he was fast enough! He clumsily wrapped his arm around her petite frame and, pushing and staggering, pinned her against the far wall. His bulk held her in place like an anchor. The knife came up beneath her blouse and parted it with one sloppy but effective slice. He snared his fingers beneath her bra and ripped it in two. Her breasts bounced like fresh fruit off a gift basket.

"I belong to Kara, you know, she'll kill you if you touch me," she said. Even Megan wasn't exactly sure if this was a threat or merely a desperate bluff. She just hoped it worked.

"She's scavenge meal by now, and you know it," Rahon snorted, leaning into her even tighter. His breath smelled like bratwurst and stale milk.

"You fool! She's stronger than you will ever be! And soon she'll suck the life out of all of you!" Megan screamed at him. It was only after she said it that she realized she had probably said too much. Thought in desperation and contempt, it had been a foolish thing to do.

Rahon plunged the knife into the wall and gripped her shoulder while pressing tightly against hers. With his free hand he cupped and squeezed her full, plump breast. The fine scales on his hand rasped her skin, and she screamed. At least, she tried, but the autonomics that initiate the sound triggered an unexpected bio-response. Instead, she ejected a pair of long, slender ivory sabers through the tiny lips of her anterior vestibules located below her sinus cavities. She could taste the virginal blood coating them as they slid over her tongue. She licked them purposefully in order to feel them for the very first time. Incredible! They were smooth and hard as steel against her lip and felt magnificent sliding along the length of her chin. She worked her jaws, marveling at the sense of power and majesty they conveyed, as if, by magic black and deadly, she had been transformed into a mythic being, a creature whose gifts raised her high above the realm of mortal man. Rahon may have been drunk but he suddenly remembered the captain's miserable fate and released his grip on her and backed away. In his haste his feet somehow lost contact with the floor, and he went down, hard. He looked up to see Nol towering over him.

"She's no one's battle bitch, you understand? You don't touch her!" Nol fired at him. He was angry but recognized a trooper in the grip of a drunken lust, and so he was willing to make allowances. It seemed a thousand cycles since the team had been on furlough and had had the luxury of female companionship. Since members of the slave platoons often saw none at all, the leave before embarking on this mission may have been Rahon's first since he had been a boy, and the female enjoyed that day may have been his first, as well. Nol wasn't sure, and he had never asked. Rahon guarded his privacy with a vengeance, and that matter had always been closed. The subject had been dropped. Now that Nol had laid down the law, it would be again.

"Get your scaly ass up and hit the shells!" Nol said. "That's an order." Nol figured he'd sleep it off and probably not remember being here with her at all.

Rahon heaved himself off the floor and stumbled out the door. Nol turned his attention then to Megan, who was quietly circling around him and had nearly made it to the doorway.

"Where do you think you're going?" he asked, his attention momentarily distracted by her lovely, white breasts, a singularly enticing feature of the mammalian females. He certainly understood why the males were fascinated with them. Soft yet weighty, they aroused a particularly strong sensual response, even in reptilians. Knowing that the willing females took special pleasure from the fondling made touching them all the more agreeable. It almost made him wish the reptilians had need of them.

Megan tied her torn blouse ends into a knot and faced him. She cast him a broad smile all the while licking her tusks as she continued slowly sidling toward the door. Her eyes lit up and cycled from green to blue to a deep, luminescent violet. He felt as if she was toying with him, almost daring him to try to stop her.

Nol knew she was a formidable opponent with high-powered projectile weapons, and probably with close-quarter combat weapons, as well. But this sudden application of her changeling abilities had caught him off guard. He didn't quite know what to think; it was odd that she should take this form only now. There were a number of possibilities why. Perhaps she had been forbidden from using them. His best guess was that her abstinence had some religious significance. Perhaps she had been completing a penance for an ethical or moral infraction, in which case, the period of sacrifice had recently come to an end. But there was so much he didn't know or understand about Earth culture that it was impossible to know. In any case, she was probably most pleased to be her old self again.

Nol circled to his right in order to cut her off. Actually, he reasoned, there was nothing to be gained from fighting her or preventing her from leaving, for that matter. Yet he was reluctant to allow her to simply walk away. He couldn't just let her *walk away*! She edged sideways past the sink, slowly, slowly, all the while her big, beautiful grin arched across her face as she worked her sabers up and down, taunting him, teasing him. Her bright violet eyes were as beautifully moist as a dewy Thacian morning, and she batted them at him playfully, casting glances at him that struck with deadly accuracy, and she probably knew it. They were mesmerizing paired with her long red hair, which cascaded down the side of her face and over the front of her blouse like a waterfall of liquid fire. Each pink drop that fell from her tusks added yet another colorful splash on her blouse, setting an even more exquisite canvas against her milky white skin. Laughing now and still moving toward the door she made an exotic, alluring picture. Nol stopped halfway to the door as she reached the threshold. There was no fight left in him, not with her, she could sense it. She was only interested in leaving, and he was only interested in having her stay, a little while longer.

"We probably won't last long without your help," he said.

"There's not much I could do, even if I wanted to," she told him, "I'm kind of an outcast myself."

No doubt this was a reference to her sacrilege and the penance she had paid. Perhaps there was more she must do in order to be forgiven of her sin. But this was a personal matter he had no right to question her about. Besides, this was neither the time nor place for such an exchange. Perhaps, if they were friends, if there were time for them, perhaps she might volunteer the story. But as things stood, their lives had crossed but briefly and her private affairs belonged to her alone. This strange, exotic Earth woman whom he had grown to admire from afar would remain so much a lovely mystery to him. Perhaps that was the best part of her.

He moved toward her then slowly, raising his hands in a conciliatory gesture. Then he gently took her in his arms. She saw the complete and utter resignation in his eyes, the regret, and the consignment of his spirit. "No, we won't last long on this tert-rock without your help," he said quietly, "and I won't live long without you." This last admission surprised her. He usually seemed so confident, the consummate survivor. This admission of feeling some peculiar need for her was puzzling, and perhaps a little disturbing.

"Am I really that much of a charmer?" she asked. She really didn't expect him to answer such a silly question. It was supposed to be a joke.

"You'd make a fine reptile," he said, smiling at her.

He bent down ever so slightly and pressed her head into his neck, urging her fangs against him. "If I'm to rot on this Nos-forsaken outworld, it might be better to die by your deadly kiss," he said. This was new territory for her, a brave new world she was unsure she had the courage to face, and the truth was, she had no real desire to harm him. But the deep desire to cut her tusks into him, to feel his hot blood shoot into her eager mouth, to taste it, to ravage it, rushed through her in a hot, sensual wave. He pushed the back of her head against him more forcefully, nearly digging her daggers into his flesh. His breath beat fast and hard through her hair, while her hot breath virtually seared the fine scales from his neck. Finally, when he could no longer stand the tension of her nearness, when his reptilian member pushed against her and he feared he might embarrass himself by releasing without her permission, he knotted her fiery red hair in his huge hand and pulled her head away.

He backed off and gazed at her sadly but made no more attempt to stop her from leaving. She touched her stomach gently where his organ had poked her and smiled at him sadly in return. Without another word, she turned and walked down the hall, passed Beel, who lay unconscious on the floor in front of the TV, and past Taven who sat slumped over the kitchen table, his meaty fist wrapped around a half empty glass of Jack. She found the truck keys hanging on the hook, precisely where she had always kept them. Snatching one of the hooded jackets draped over the kitchen counter, she opened her jaws wide and, with a gentle tightening of her upper lip, slid the tusks upward into their protective jackets hidden within her sinus cavities. She opened the door, hesitating a moment as she stared at the truck that could easily carry her to safety.

It seemed a number of good things had resulted from Rahon's recent provocation. She had to smile at the irony of that. Seldom did something good precipitate from an attempted rape. It had struck a nerve in Nol. Some aspect of his male psyche needed to reach out to a female in distress, that part of him needed to be needed, especially now, and the incident had helped to form a bond that had probably softened his hard resolve. It helped them form a bond that might serve them both. It also allowed her to discover that her shadow transformation was progressing rapidly and had graced her with some of the attributes for which she had hoped. She was pleased to learn that she was mutating and adapting quickly, more quickly in fact than she, or Kara for that matter, had anticipated. She only had to sense Nol's hard and steady gaze at her back in order to encourage her to turn around. She knew what he wanted and she knew what she would say.

"Will you stay until tomorrow morning, at least?" he asked from the shadows beneath the arch of the hallway entrance. There was no animosity in his voice, no anger, no deceit. She could hear his absolute resignation and defeat. She knew already he would never harm her, and she was certain he would protect her from the others. "I need you—we need you—to drive the vehicle so that we can gather our dead," he said. "Will you do that for us—for me—one soldier for another? One friend for another?"

Her human-looking face was probably so much less formidable and intimidating but she knew it probably didn't matter. This warrior from a distant planet, this fierce creature, who surely had seen many hardships and had probably taken the lives of countless enemies, showed her his deepest respect. She faced him now with eyes that met his in an unflinching gaze. "Yes," she replied in an even, steady tone, her voice strong and mesmerizing. "I'll stay, and I'll help you— tomorrow. Tomorrow we will gather our dead. But once it is done, you are on your own. You can't stay here, Nol. This is my home. You have seven of our days. When I return you will be gone. Agreed?"

"Agreed," he replied, "on my honor as a Rege'Cean field commander." He said it very seriously while simultaneously saluting by snapping his fist to his chinhorns and bowing his head smartly. So she reacted accordingly by bowing in return and nodding understandingly as if it actually did mean a whole hell of a lot, which it didn't. All that mattered was that he sounded genuinely sincere, and that he seemed to respect her for standing up to him today. It was more than enough.

Chapter 15

Sunday, October 9, 7:35 P.M.: Nol spun quickly and released the cichma ax. His sidearm toss hit the old stump dead center from forty feet, the forward mandible blades impacting symmetrically into the dense wood. Megan's first throw was off the mark, high and wide. The ax cut into the back of the barn, almost burying the circular blade completely into the soft, red sideboard. Nol showed her how to adjust the pitch, explaining the blade's aerodynamic properties. She adjusted her angle and release point. By following his instructions, she was able to hit the stump most every toss.

She was exceptional with the bow and could easily outshoot him from a distance, bundling her arrows in a tight formation that he simply could not match. She used a *primitive* but, according to him, ingenious release mechanism that afforded her a wide, smooth draw. It gave the bow exceptional power and helped deliver a clean, true shot. He tried it briefly, but it was awkward for him, his thick, beefy fingers fumbled with it. His arrows invariably went astray.

Throughout the evening they avoided talk of recent events. For the longest while, they kept the topics light and casual, mostly about the weapons and the speed with which Megan was able to master the ax and about stories of battles Nol had seen. She even wrestled an apology from him concerning damages to the house. Mostly, Megan listened, fascinated by this creature who had traveled light-years from a part of the galaxy populated with worlds vastly different from Earth. He spoke of things that Megan could scarcely believe and barely understand, of bizarre animals and peculiar aliens, of a mighty empire, of a great armada and sleek, fleet ion scout ships, of incredible technology and weaponry, and of constant war, and the fierce and noble warriors who fought in them, and of ruthless and ambitious politicians. It was as if he were describing fantastic dreams and horrible nightmares. And he spoke about having been in prison.

"I killed those Terts in a fair fight," he continued. "At least, that's the way I saw it. I guess the locals didn't see it that way, though."

"Terts?" Megan said.

"Yeah," Nol replied. "You know…a being of a different race. Don't you have words like that? It's the best the translator will do, I guess. The darkworld knows, I can't remember everyone I've killed, not exactly anyway," he said with a shrug.

He had been in prison for six cycles until released on special commission into Ovek's custody. He served under him for another ten cycles before they had embarked on the rescue mission that had ultimately landed them on Earth.

"Ovek was a good friend, wasn't he?" Megan said. She hated to broach this sad subject, but she suspected he had steered it in this direction for a reason.

"He was my commanding officer," he said matter-of-factly, hesitating now, but he seemed eager to say more.

"But you were close?" she asked.

"Everything I know that's worth knowing, I learned from Ovek," he said, "and I was proud to serve under him."

Then it struck her. When he mentioned Ovek's name he avoided her eyes. There was something there in his face he didn't want her to see, something behind the hard, stern glare that was his edge, the signature stare he commanded when dealing with anyone who got in his way, the wall that let no one in. But she didn't have to see behind those eyes to know what it was. She knew just enough about soldering and warfare and the ambitions of an ego in a brute like Nol to know what was eating at him. He had been second in command for a long time. Everything worth knowing he had learned from Ovek; that's what he had said, and he thought he had learned it all.

"Then why were you in such a hurry to leave him behind?" she asked. He bristled at that and looked her dead in the eye then. She had struck a chord. The wounds on his face turned a deep purple, and the torn fan atop his head began to ooze a clear liquid.

"Why are you taunting me?" he asked. "Ovek was dead! There was no point in attempting to recover his body with Kara spending her last ounce of life wreaking her revenge on him. I'm almost certain she blamed Ovek for stabbing you, but it was Taven." Suddenly, his eyes went wide at a sudden thought. Something strange was going on. Megan should have been dead! Perhaps there were even deeper secrets guarded by these changelings.

"Why are you taunting me?" he asked again slowly. He waved the ax in front of her menacingly, but there was an air of good-natured suspicion in his voice this time. The sight of the ax used as a threat sent an exhilarating wave coursing through her body. The effects of the adrenaline rush were immediate and startling. Her muscles responded as if each had a mind of its own, begging to be the first to respond to the challenge. She tried a combination spin and flip onto the stump, with surprising success. She tightened her forearms, clinched her fists and thrust them forward. Four claws shot from the tiny lips that had recently formed between her knuckles. Three curved gently downward, black as deep-sea pearls and needle sharp; the one between her thumb and finger was thicker, more powerful and it curved gracefully inward.

"He's alive, isn't he!" Nol beamed. It was the happiest she had ever seen him. But he composed himself quickly, reverting his nearly jubilant visage to that blank, neutral stare he had mastered. "How is that possible?" he asked. "He was near death even before she took him the second time."

She wasn't sure he actually *was* still alive, but, knowing Kara, she suspected as much. If she had wanted to kill him she would have done it, quickly and decisively. She wouldn't have gone through all the trouble of dragging him into the cabin. She would have killed him where he stood and let him fall, and that would have been the end of it.

"He might be alive. I don't know. I have a feeling about it, that's all, an intuition." she said, unwilling to tell him more than he needed to know. At least that much of it was true. She knew she was treading on dangerous territory, but she felt some obligation to him. After all, he had come to her aid when Rahon had attached her earlier, and despite all his bravado about the many terts and enemy soldiers he had killed in his life and his self-proclaimed ferocity, he had not tried to stop her by force when it was clear that doing so would have served no purpose. He may have been a cold-blooded killer, but he was also an honorable soldier, and she could see he was trying to do the right thing in his first and, probably last, command. Also, he clearly felt some connection to her, and she had to admit, he was growing on her, as well. At least, she didn't look upon him as a sworn enemy as she ought to, considering what he had done to Allen. (After all, it was a gunfight, and Nol's duty was to protect himself and his troopers. Allen had been her friend, but to Nol, he had simply been an enemy soldier. She understood that much better now.)

"Then we should return, right away," he said. "If there is a chance he is alive, he may not survive the night."

"No, if he's dead, it will make no difference," she said, "and if he's alive, he's better off at the cabin tonight than he would be here. If Kara is alive, and there is a possibility that she *is*, she can help him more than you can. Please, trust me." She was taking a big risk, and she knew it. But Kara had suggested that she should trust her instincts, and those instincts were telling her to have faith in this alien. Kara had taken Ovek alive for a reason; in time, Megan knew, that reason would become clear. In any event, she had no intention of driving them back until tomorrow at the earliest, so she felt confident Nol would be reasonable and take her recommendations seriously. At least, she hoped he would.

He circled the stump waving the blade, angling it this way and that, pointing it tentatively at various parts of her body. "One strike," he said, raising the ax, "first blood. Agreed?"

"Are you sure you want to do this?" she inquired. "Your hand doesn't look very good."

Briefly Nol studied the two, tender discolored stumps on his left hand, and then thrust his big mitt in her direction, displaying the empty spaces beside his one remaining finger. "It looks far worse than it feels," he said, "and look, they're growing back already." While the reptilians had only four digits terminating each appendage, fewer than most bipeds, having the ability to regenerate entire limbs afforded them a distinct advantage over species without such capability, which was yet another reason they were considered the most valued soldiers in the RegeìCean Empire.

Megan could clearly see that the lower portions of the thick, bottom knuckles of both fingers had already developed. At this rate in just a week his fingers would be restored. It was not surprising that he seemed unconcerned about their loss.

She removed her heavy camouflage jacket revealing the knotted blouse beneath. "All right then," she said, "agreed, but this pretty face and these," she covered her breasts, "are off limits; they don't regenerate."

"Fair enough," he said.

She twirled the jacket around her head and let it fly against the side of the barn. She performed a perfect back flip, putting the old, weathered stump between her and Nol. He circled to the right. "Why should I believe that Kara could have survived such wounds? Why should I believe you?" he asked with more than a hint of plea lacing the question. Clearly he wanted to believe.

Ovek had been poised to negotiate. That is why he was not in the yard with the others. It was only his illness that had kept him from being at the cabin earlier. Nol had told her as much and it all made sense. After all, they had never broken into the cabin, which they could easily have done. "Because we're friends," she replied.

"Yes, you survived a similar neck wound and healed virtually overnight. Your species and mine may have more in common than I had thought possible. I was a fool not to recognize it in the first place." He leapt over the edge of the stump and made an inside swipe at her right shoulder.

She pulled back while countering with a straight right lunge. Her claws nearly poked his neck. His movements and even the minute particles in the air all around him seemed crystal clear, and as he circled and lunged, his body seemed to slow down at the optimum moment. Dodging the ax was easier than she had hoped.

"Maybe I had just gotten lucky," she teased him. She feinted a left jab and arched a wide, raking hook at his arm. He pulled his entire torso back causing her blow to fall just inches short.

"I don't think so. I think Earthers are born with an accelerated rejuvenation rate. Something on the molecular level, in the cells. By Nos! You are a special breed of mammal!" He smiled broadly and moved in low. He dropped one hand to the ground and, balancing and pivoting on one arm, swept his massive leg around in an attempt to drop her. He hit her ankles hard, but instead of going down she tucked quickly and, redirecting the force of his blow, spun forward slightly to land standing upright, directly over him. She went down on one knee to drive her claws into his forearm. But he was fast. He rolled, spun on his back and kipped quickly to his feet.

"Nice move," she said.

"Nice flip," he returned the compliment.

"Look, of course there's always a possibility, even if it is a long shot," she said. "But the transponder is most likely destroyed, in any case." If Kara's plan revolved around relocating them to an isolated place, a place they could live out there remaining lives in seclusion, then she wanted Nol to focus on that possibility, and she needed to redirect his thought to that end, away from any thoughts of retrieving his precious communications device. She inched her way toward him, first circling to the left, then to the right, moving ever closer.

He pivoted as she closed in but held his ground. "I know. It's probably hopeless. However, if Ovek is alive he might be using this time alone with Kara to negotiate for the transponder, if she hasn't already destroyed it. But if he is dead, I will have to try. The troopers are my responsibility now. I have to do everything I can to get them home. You understand."

She didn't really. He might as well have been referring to an irresistible force meeting an immoveable object. She knew Kara would never trust these aliens to keep Earth's location a secret from their emperor, and she wouldn't either. Every time Nol learned something new about the vampire race, about their unique abilities, the more impressed he seemed. Once back in his part of the galaxy, the temptation to enslave them, to bring them into the emperor's service, would be far too great.

"Yes, I understand," she lied. At this point, with weapons in hand and a semblance of friendship having developed between them, it just didn't make any sense to destroy the small degree of trust and fellowship they had established. It just didn't make any sense. It would be senseless to talk of safe havens and distant lands where they could live in peace and harmony. It was a pipe dream, and she knew it. There was no such place. Any attempt to convince him of it would fall short and hollow.

He bent low and quickly crossed his arms in a manner meant to distract her. It almost appeared that he was transferring the ax to his left hand. But he didn't. As her eyes tried to follow the movement, he unfurled his arms quickly zipping the ax toward her forearm in a motion that angled smartly upward. It caught her off guard, but he managed only to glance the side of her left claw. He stood completely still then, as if they had not been sparing at all. He just looked at her a moment, a sad, regretful kind of look. "I don't think you do, Megan. It doesn't matter weather Ovek is in charge, or me, or any one of the other troopers. If it's possible, we'll never stop trying to get back. It's our duty." He began to back away from her again, bringing the ax up, twisting it in his hands. "We'll just have to convince her to give it to us."

"She would kill you all first," Megan replied. She moved straight toward him. It was time to end this little dance. *The bigger they are*...she thought.

"Probably," he said, "more than likely she could do it, too. I've never seen a soldier quite like her. Well—except for you. I'd hate to see what you could do with a disrupter." He grinned a big grin and stood ready to counter Megan's strike. However, rather than attempting another strike, she pivoted and threw a kick at his midsection. Or so he thought. He turned sideways to avoid the blow but was surprised to discover the kick purposefully off the mark. Instead, she launched herself fully into the air, and, wrapping her legs around his waist, twisted sideways, allowing the momentum and her body weight to drag him to the ground. His feet rocketed from under him and his face hit the dirt like a meteorite. Squeezing his midsection with her powerful legs, she locked him to the ground, and then cocked her elbow back. She launched a cobra-like strike directly at his left buttock, stabbing and retracting in one swift movement, a shallow hit, but effective. Three bright, vermilion stains immediately dotted the back of his khaki trousers.

"First blood, did you say?" she intoned.

He spit dust and mud from his mouth and rubbed his tender butt cheek as he pushed himself to his feet. "That was quite a maneuver," he said.

"Thanks," she replied, smiling. "I enjoy having guys go down on me."

He just nodded in response.

"That's a little Earth humor," she trailed off, realizing this territory was even more dangerous than the sparring.

"You realize, of course, that I could have tossed the ax at any time," he said as she walked toward the house. "I was being kind, you know."

"Oh, Nos!" she said, tossing her head, sliding her claws up into her forearms. "The male ego. Unbelievable!"

He chuckled despite the pain in his ass.

From her bed Megan could hear Nol breathing heavily, sucking air through his narrow nostril slits, expelling it from his mouth, his exhalations perfectly mimicking the chugging of a slow moving freighter. He had graciously allowed her use of the "Captain's room" since it was officially vacant. She had been polite in return and hadn't mentioned that it was her goddamn room in the first place, and she didn't need his permission. What would have been the point? They were on amicable terms, and the niceties he afforded her he genuinely regarded as indications of their friendship. She reminded herself that he was a foreigner, after all.

Although she was tired, her once-cozy old bed felt strange and uncomfortable, and she was unable to sleep. Restless and lonely, she tossed and turned endlessly. She missed Kara. She knew it would be a simple matter to simply jump in the truck and drive up to the cabin. There really wasn't anything stopping her. She could easily return in the morning for the troopers. She would make good on her promise to reunite them with Ovek and help them gather their dead, whatever fate had in store. But she wasn't certain she should go there tonight. She thought she might use the excuse that she was curious about the degree of Kara's recovery. But in truth, she already knew that Kara was probably a hundred percent by now. Injured vampires generally healed very quickly because their metabolism was very fast. The recovery rate of the Bloodwarriors was even more remarkable due to their even more highly accelerated rate and their incredible sensitivity to adrenaline. "Eight hours for the severest of wounds," she had said. That was the usual length of time for a Bloodwarrior. "If my wounds do not immediately kill me," she had said, "then I will heal. Have no fear." And so, she didn't. Megan had faith that Kara was perfectly fine by now. "The only way I can be killed," she had said, "is if I am so heavily damaged my body simply cannot repair itself, or if I lose all my blood. I can burn to death, for example, or be blown up. Beheading is fatal, as well. But short of that, Bloodwarriors are a pretty tough breed."

So when the troopers had driven off leaving Ovek behind with Kara, Megan hadn't been particularly worried. And she wasn't now. So she couldn't use that as an excuse to go up to the cabin tonight. And she wanted to badly, but—Kara had taken Ovek hostage for a reason, and Megan's instincts told her that there was business between them, business Kara wished to conduct with him alone. Like her woman's' intuition, her shadow instincts were an integral part of her now, an indefinable aspect of her nature. She could not pinpoint its origin; she knew only that it was, in some way, part of the connection she felt with Kara, a kind of sixth sense, a *special awareness.* It was subtle, yet compelling, and she trusted it. So, now, she resisted that urge to go to her; she fought the temptation to ignore her better judgment. She lay in bed tossing for a time thinking of the long, lonely night ahead then, suddenly, without warning, the bloodlust welled up inside her, and vestiges of the hunger ignited like tiny flames. An alarm went off in her head, and she felt as if she needed to put the fire out, immediately. She got out of bed quietly, slipped on a pair of jeans and a sweater, grabbed a dark suede jacket from her closet, and dissolved into the shadows.

She knew it wouldn't take long. A beautiful woman walking alone late at night headed south along highway 41. At this hour, the only establishments open out here were mom-and-pop bars and The Border Gentlemen's Club. Anyone willing to stop was either looking for a good time or was up to no good. The odds were on the first, but she was actually hoping for the second. That would make her first kill a lot easier. She didn't want to take an innocent, but the bloodlust was urging her onward, and the flames of hunger were growing more intense. She wished Kara were here to guide her.

She heard the distinctive rumble long before she saw him, from a mile away or more. The Harley came up on her from behind, cruising steadily, easily down the long, deserted straightaway. She noted the familiar revving, the increased power added to the engine, as the driver caught sight of her, simply to call attention to himself, and to the handsome machine he was straddling. Then the pitch of the engine dropped an octave or two and she knew he had geared down. He reduced his speed from 50 to 20 miles per hour in a matter of seconds in order to get a good look at her. Just 30 feet up the road he pulled over and waited for her to catch up. No surprise there. So she did.

He told her he was headed for a place called, "All Ours," a little biker bar just a few minutes down the road. Was she interested? Hell yeah, she was interested all right! He wasn't all that bad looking, yet he appeared nasty enough to be anything from a cold-blooded killer to the leader of an outlaw gang. He just might be dealing heroine out of Mexico through his connections in Kenosha or Chicago. More than likely, he was all that, and more. Guilty. She was eager to find out more about him, so she hopped onto the back of his Fat Boy and wrapped her arms around his heavy leather jacket. The giant eagle patch on his back boasted of his HOG affiliation and dozens of touring pins peppered the front like military decorations. This boy had been around!

She had a shot of Jack and a beer, and they shot pool for an hour before he put a little move on her. Finally! She had been doing her best to encourage him. Without a bra her plump breasts had been wiggling and jiggling all through the game, as much from her faked excitement and laughter as anything else, and she pressed them out at him with a little yawn or shrug when she missed a shot. When he was shooting she pinched her nipples to create some added incentive—just to hurry things along. After a couple games, she thought she might be able to discover more about him if they found some privacy. She considered just whispering the magic words in his ear. But the damnedest thing, the longer they talked and the more she got to know him, the more familiar and likable he became.

It wasn't that he was actually her type; he wasn't really. But he didn't seem the criminal type either. The more she found out about him the more pedestrian he became, and she was beginning to wonder if she could go through with it. He was more shy and reserved than she had anticipated, more reserved and polite, and he even made her laugh a few times. But she had come this far, and considering the burning desire inside her, she felt she owed it to herself to try. She was a shadow Vampire, being tested for the very first time by the call of the bloodlust. If she was to be tested by fire, she understood the flames might burn her and leave their scars.

So when he suggested they step around the corner for a moment into the dimly lighted hallway she accepted eagerly. Immediately his arm slid around her waist and the other behind her head. "You like the bad boys, don't yah?" he asked, grinning. His lips covered her mouth like a warm, wet towel. Not bad, but not great either. He slipped his hand from behind her back and squeezed her breast, rubbed it, pushed against it as if he couldn't get enough of it. The fact that she wasn't wearing a bra was a real turn-on; she could tell that right away. He breathed into her like a dragon roasting his dinner. She was breathing hard now, as well. His hand dropped from behind her head and brushed her stomach. Then, like a pro, he shaped it into a wicked claw and slipped it between her legs forcing it upward, literally lifting her off her feet. His fingers and her panties slipped inside her. Her own body weight against his hand nearly sent her over the edge, just a bit more encouragement, and she would be there. He backed her against the wall, and she undulated her body against him. She lifted and spread her legs around him, feeling his member push harder on her inner thigh, pulsing, like an animal pressing against its cage. He squeezed her again as if he were juicing an orange. "Yes," she gasped, "I love the bad boys." She grabbed his long hair as her body jerked with spasm upon spasm, the warmth of it spreading from her inner thighs throughout her back and up her spine, up into her head and down to the tips of her toes.

She hadn't meant it to happen, and she told him so. She had someone dear to her, and it would be wrong for her to stay. She shouldn't have come here with him in the first place. He was very understanding, and as it turns out, he wasn't a bad boy at all. He wasn't a killer, or a gang leader or a drug dealer. He was a database manager for an insurance company, and the only time he had ever come close to killing anyone was in the army, when he had served as a security police officer and had attempted to subdue a drunk who tried to decapitate him with a shovel. He didn't even know what heroin looked like. Bad boy? Hell—he had smoked marijuana once only to assure his friends in the barracks that he wasn't a snitch. What did he care? It was his job to keep a watchful eye for insurgents and keep the *peace* on base. So he just smiled and told her not to worry about wanting to leave. He thought she was beautiful and sweet, and very sexy, and that her boyfriend was a really, lucky guy. He gave her a ride back to the corner of 27th and Ryan Road, near the spot where he had picked her up. Then he gave her a very lovely kiss goodnight. He offered to take her all the way home, but she knew that would have been a disaster, for him. She walked the mile back to the farm and slipped in as easily as she had slipped out.

But something odd had happened during their encounter, something she hadn't expected. In the hallway, right after she came, the bloodlust had subsided, and the hunger had vanished. (Kara had said it might be this way at first. False symptoms. Misreads. Confusion. Her counsel suggested that would change over time. The symptoms would become more definite and recognizable. And she warned they might escalate, that they might become more severe.) Her first episode, relatively easy to handle it seems, had come and gone. It may have been vestiges of the bloodlust. Then again, she may just have been horny. Once again, she settled into bed, exhausted now, on the verge of drifting off, a semblance of a smile creeping onto her face. Because deep inside she knew—she had known the moment she climbed onto the back of his Harley—had he actually been a real *bad boy*, a killer or rapist or some other form of vermin, she was confident she could have killed him in a microsecond.

Chapter 16

"The virus attacks the blood and ravages the body, and the only thing that will halt the effects is fresh blood. Is that the way it is?" Ovek summarized the most recent and distressing information Kara had delivered.

"Yes," Kara replied. "Just enough to arrest the symptoms but not so much as to shock and overwhelm the system."

"And mammals are the only creatures that can survive this virus? You're sure of this?" Ovek asked, his concern and his reasons all too obvious.

"Oh, yes," Kara said. "Our scientists have been studying the Chimera Virus for…well, a long time now. That's the name my father gave it, the Chimera Virus, because it transfers strands of DNA from its predecessors into its new host. In Earth mythology, the chimera is a composite beast, an unlikely combination of various, unrelated animals."

"Only mammals benefit from this union. All other creatures are adversely affected, as I was."

"Yes, it's an endless cycle and a no-win situation for all other classes." She continued, "The blood I've given you will arrest the effects, even reverse them, but now that you've had a taste, the bloodlust will only increase and eventually will drive you mad. You see, in mammals the cycle of the bloodlust is approximately seven days, but in every other species, once the blood is refreshed, the cycle shortens with each feeding until it becomes a daily ritual. The madness, which we call *the hunger*, will soon develop into a reoccurring panic, which will ultimately remain constant. The affected creatures inevitably cannibalize their own race, which spreads the virus. Even in some lower forms of mammals, those without reason, the effects are unpredictable, and the results can be devastating. But especially in the non-mammalian species, the madness spreads like a wildfire. There's simply no stopping it."

"Yes, it *would* spread at an exponential rate," he replied quietly. His mind seemed elsewhere, millions of miles away.

"Yes, Ovek, in your part of the galaxy it would be an insidious plague, spreading from planet to planet like the shock wave of a stellar nova. There would be nothing left of your empire," she said it as if she were speaking for him.

"Yes, in a few cycles, the empire would be decimated," he said quietly and sadly.

"You can never go back, and your empire must never learn of Earth's existence."

"I know. I think, from the moment I first began feeling the symptoms I knew. The devastation that the Chimera Virus would wreak upon the empire only confirmed my greatest fears." He paused then, deep in thought. "The transponder!" he fairly shouted. "It's destroyed?"

"Unfortunately, no. But it's well hidden, buried, and I don't think anyone can find it. But now, I'm sorry I didn't destroy it. At the time, however, I didn't know how dangerous the situation truly was," she said.

"That's not good enough," he said. "The troopers just might find a way to retrieve it."

"But you're their commanding officer. Wouldn't they listen to reason?" she asked. "Wouldn't they understand the tremendous threat to the empire? Would they disobey your orders?"

"No, under normal circumstances. But the sad truth is that one of the troopers may have been plotting against us all along. Someone knew a great deal about our movements. I hate to think that one of my own troopers betrayed us, but I don't know for certain, and the stakes are too high, and besides, this isn't a matter for discussion or debate among us. It might be better that they not know the dangerous potential of this world." His face relaxed into a pensive mask and once again he seemed to freeze in time. "You know, ScietCore could make a very nasty biological weapon from this Chimera Virus of yours," he said slowly and incisively. "If one of the troopers is in league with the saboteur then it's clear he's prepared to stop at nothing to get vital information back to the empire. Including killing me before I can order the troopers to stand down."

"I can't let that happen," Kara said. "*We* can't let that happen."

"At that point, the troopers are sure to stop accepting my commands," Ovek continued. "They would rebel and stop at nothing to get back to the empire. The prospect of being stranded and captured on this planet would be intolerable. They know they would be treated as freakish lab animals, mere curiosities to be dissected and examined. They would be interpreted as genetic experiments gone horribly wrong; your military tinkering with the development of powerful and frightening bio-weapons. This is not a fate Rege'Cean soldiers are going to allow."

He rocked back and forth, a troubled looked written deep in his face, punctuated with every gesture he made. "If something should happen to me before I could explain the situation…being highly motivated, with nothing to lose, they'll do whatever it takes to get back home."

"Especially Nol," she noted.

"Yes, especially Nol," he replied, he hung his head. "He would gladly die a soldier's death many times over rather than be stranded here, and he will kill a thousand innocents rather than end up a lab specimen."

Kara didn't know if reptilians could cry, and she doubted that Ovek would, in any case. But if he had cause, she suspected this was it. She could tell there was a bond between him and Nol, a soldier's bond, or something deeper, something akin to the bond between brothers. At any rate she could see the immense sadness in his posture and in the deep, darkness behind his eyes when he finally looked up at her.

"They all would," he said resolutely. She only nodded her understanding. There was nothing, however, she could do or say to change their fate.

Ovek sat on one of the thick pillows in front of the blazing fire, lost in thought. Kara lounged across from him on a thick comforter, recognizing how utterly alone he must feel lost on this island, Earth, millions of miles from the worlds he knew, facing a bleak and inevitably dire future. She hoped he took some solace from the fact that he was much improved from the afternoon. Her blood had worked a miracle on him. His scales had stopped flaking, and his color was vibrant and bright. The soft skin around his eyes was tight and moist again, and he had been eating solid food throughout the afternoon and well into the evening. Even now he had several bowls of dry cereal and a package of beef jerky at hand, which he alternately munched on absently every few minutes. He was noticeable lighter, but several times he had gotten up to exercise, claiming his muscles felt surprisingly tight and strong. Except for a few pounds, she knew, he would be virtually indistinguishable from his former self. That was something, at least.

"Are you married, Ovek?" she asked. "I mean, is there one female in your life?"

"Yes, but I've been gone so long…campaigning to keep the fighting far from my home world, I suppose. I guess you could say I am wedded to the military, now," he said.

"Do you have children?" she asked, she looked down at her hands, unsure if this was a wise path to travel. "I'm just wondering who might be missing you, who might be searching for you."

"Miss me?" he said absently. "I don't even know if my son remembers me. I was forced to abandon my family's charter in police services, and I left my life as husband and father behind forever, as it turned out. To save my world and my family, military service was mandatory. I sacrificed everything in the service of the emperor. But once I became a soldier, I resolved myself to excel, and as it turned out, I was very good at it." He paused with that faraway look in his eyes.

She waited for him to continue, as she knew he would; this was a tale he had told himself many times over. She knew this was a tale that haunted his dreams and his moments of quiet reflection.

"Central Command considered me a natural-born leader," he started again slowly. "I don't really know what that is. But I do know I was a better soldier than anything I could have been in civilian life, and my attitude and achievements were recognized, and rewarded. Mission after mission, I was chosen for command, and I moved up in rank. I signed an oath to defend and promote a cause that served a larger and grander purpose than my puny vision, a purpose I didn't fully understand or always agree with, but one I was sworn to serve and promote, nonetheless. But always, in my heart, my personal agenda was to safeguard my family, and, ironically, my dedication and faithful service accomplished that. Preserving the life of my wife and son is a continuous, personal war I've been waging these many cycles. I've sacrificed everything for them, even the joys and comfort of their love. I know I will never see either of them again. I know I will never return to my home world of Thacia. Miss me? My son doesn't know me, and my wife has probably remarried cycles ago."

"I'm sorry, Ovek," Kara said. "I couldn't have known."

"Don't worry, I don't mind talking about them. She was most beautiful, you know." Ovek smiled. "And my son! He was also beautiful. Though I saw him only once shortly after he was hatched. I remember holding him briefly the evening he broke from his shell. The next day I was on a military transport bound for Orturia ," he said. He sat, staring at the fire a moment, as if a specter from his past was actually rising from the flames like a phoenix. "That was the last time I saw either of them. That was nearly twenty cycles ago. They'll never know what happen to me; technically, I'm on a secret rescue mission," he said. "In official circles, I suppose, we're listed as *missing in action*."

"I'm sorry—about your wife and son, I mean. I know a little something about that kind of loss," she said sadly.

Suddenly, she sat up straighter. "Won't the military send a search party? Won't they come looking for your team?" The reason for her concern was all too obvious. Fighting a small vanguard of these creatures was one thing, fighting a small army was quite another.

"No. That's why the transponder is so important," he replied. "It activates a device called a quantum marker. It's out there," he pointed to the ceiling, "near the outer boundary of your system," he said. "The marker would direct Central Command to our current sector, this planetary system. The transponder would then pinpoint our exact location on your world. Fortunately, you've nullified that possibility."

"Well, I know one thing for sure," she said, smiling at him. "They're losing out on one hell of a fine soldier." She hoped that might bring a smile to his face. He stared at her blankly for a moment.

"You know what I'm going to lose out on?" he said absently, staring out the window at the blackness.

"What?"

"Killing that darkworld bastard who set us up," he said. "Someone desperately wanted our rescue mission to fail, someone who had a score to settle with the BreAcian High Roget or his daughter, Nela, or with me. I don't know who the weed licker is, but I'd give almost anything for the opportunity to find out."

"I'm sorry about that, too," she said.

"Yeah, well, there are worse things than a mystery, I suppose," he said with an air of fatality.

"No, Ovek, I mean, I'm really sorry I lost my temper. It's just that Megan means so very much to me, and at the time, I thought you might have killed her. But now…well, I'm sorry," she said. She hoped he understood how serious she was.

"It's not your fault, Kara. We invaded your world, yours and Megan's. The command decisions were mine, and they were wrong. I was hasty and let my emotions get the better of me—and I seriously underestimated your species."

Kara smiled at that and nodded. Ovek was obviously in the dark concerning the comparative nature of humans and vampires. Although he actually knew more about the subject than most Earthlings, he was grossly ignorant of the essential details. Good. She meant to keep him that way. Disinformation was a valuable tool in the war of minds and nations, and worlds. The fewer truths he knew about her race, the better. There was, after all, an outside chance that the transponder might still be discovered and activated, somehow. Knowing its import, she realized now that she should have destroyed the goddamn thing. Even though she and Ovek seemed to be coming to an accord, forming an alliance of a sort, and being in full agreement about the need to confine the virus to the earth, she wasn't at all certain the others couldn't somehow pry vital information from him by force or through the use of some technology with which she was unfamiliar. They could even use drugs. Hell, our military was known to do that.

Ovek studied her for a moment, her quiet, reflective nature and her calm, cool exterior. But inside, he thought, she must be a torrent, a whirlpool of confluent emotions. He could only guess at her deepest thoughts. He knew his troopers well, but of course, she did not, and he felt now might be a good time to allay her fears.

"I wouldn't worry about Megan, if I were you," he said. "I'm sure Nol won't allow anything to happen to her."

"I hope you're right," she said, relieved to find him spinning their conversation in this direction. "I was thinking they might resort to torture once they found she had lied."

"They would never do that," Ovek assured her. "Nol wouldn't allow it. I know my second in command. He may be many things, but he's not a barbarian. He would never torture a female prisoner, no matter what the stakes."

"I hope you're right. Although, to be honest, I'm confident she could resist their best attempts," Kara said, staring deeply into his eyes with that cool and steady glare, confident in the powerful mesmeric suggestions she had given Megan to help her acclimate to her shadow transformation. "And once they discover she knows nothing about its location, which they will very quickly, I doubt they will harm her. They'll need her."

"Yes," Ovek nodded. "They'll need to return here eventually, for me and poor old Guor out there."

Kara looked into the fire. Guor's death had been particularly gruesome. The number of arrows in her had temporarily made her furious, and he had simply been a target of opportunity when that fury had been unleashed. Sitting next to Ovek now, knowing that Guor had been as much a morale booster as fellow warrior, was difficult for her to bear. Because he had been taken down in a particularly vicious manner she knew it hurt Ovek tremendously. But it had been Guor's ax she had pulled from her back, the very ax she had used to decapitate him. Her remorse had to have a reasonable limit. Still, she thought it best to avoid dwelling on the manner of his destruction. Perhaps she could lighten the moment by drawing his attention back to the obvious.

"Oh, they'll need her, all right!" she said. "More than likely they'll run out of beer and brats and send her up to Pick-N-Sav to max out her credit card." Some of the regionalisms didn't translate well, but

Ovek got the gist of the matter. He snorted and nodded his head, then he laughed, not long or raucously, but more than he had in quite a while. He knew his troopers, and surprisingly, she seemed to, as well. It was good to see him laugh—odd, but good. He actually looked rather handsome in a way that animals can look attractive, with his broad, open smile underscoring his perfectly symmetrical features, and his small, perfect teeth gleaming like a shiny new zipper behind his thin, even lips.

She was pleased. She had chosen the correct path. Sitting by the fire now, drinking bottled water, nibbling on pinches of cereal and bits of jerky, one would never suspect that just hours earlier he had been on the brink of death, stabbing at the wretched specters attempting to drag him through the fearsome doors of Darkworld.

Chapter 17

October 10, 7:05 A.M.: Without warning a change had come, a suggestion of winter on the wind, an early reminder of the endless and relentless cycle of things. It blew in fast and steady from the North, ignoring the barricade of bluffs and trees and slid down hard into the clearing, washing over the cabin like a harsh rumor. It was mean and damp, and sharp enough to reach the bone. Ovek looked skyward and, for a moment, the clouds drifting across the face of the sun seemed to spin the orb like a top. But he knew it was merely an illusion. He closed his eyes as if it was possible to squeeze out the regrets drifting through his mind, the irony of the simple mistakes that had led to such dire consequences since being captured by the Tyons. But if life came with a schematic all would be perfection, an Everworld to tread in our daily lives. Mistakes were easy to make because they were supposed to be; that was part of the price of admission, part of the sacrifice everyone had to make in order to earn their eternal reward. Somewhere along the line it had been easy to mistake friend for foe. The saboteur was still out there. And here on this outworld, it had been so easy to misread the strength of their adversaries. By the looks of them, one would never have guessed.

Yes, it had been so easy, and now, he knew, he would never make that mistake again—he might never have the chance. He breathed in deeply, filling his lungs with the crisp morning air. It was a relief to exhale without the familiar cough, refreshing to feel *life* coursing through him once again. He bowed his head and cast one last, regretful glance toward the eggcrypt. He was pleased with Kara's construction, her attention to detail, and with the respect she had shown in the positioning of Guor's body and weapons. Everything had been done in accordance with his instructions. It was, indeed, a worthy sanctuary from which his spirit might find its way to the gates of Everworld. "Nos speed, and Darkworld doors stand barred for you, my friend," he said. And then he walked away.

Kara marveled at Ovek as he entered the cabin, at the way his body literally filled the entire doorway. He was forced to stoop at the threshold—at nearly seven feet, he could not simply walk through the door upright. On any world, she had to admit, he was an impressive specimen. Throughout the night her blood had continued working its peculiar brand of magic, repairing, rejuvenating, energizing. Now, fully healed, his muscles were lean and tight, and he looked magnificent. In fact he looked more youthful and more powerful than he had before she had bitten him. Earlier this morning, he had boasted of feeling better than he had for *cycle upon cycle*, as he had phrased it.

She stood by the fire casually tossing logs onto the blaze, eyeing him as he made his way to the table. He poured himself a tall glass of water from the pitcher. He sniffed at a bottle of lemon juice there and dumped a generous portion into the glass, returning her gaze, never diverting his eyes. He cocked his head to the side, looking her up and down. She returned his glances with a hard and steady gaze until his scrutiny evoked a sad realization; she was dressed in the clothes she had worn that night in the forest, the night she had followed the troopers to the picnic grounds, the night she had killed Cor. This was her *hunting* outfit, the tight black Gothic pullover and bustier, the jeans and pipe guards. He just looked to his glass and nodded knowingly.

"They'll be coming soon," she said. "I thought it best to prepare for the worst."

"Yes," he said. "They'll be coming." Again there was that absent tone in his voice, as if she weren't in the room at all.

She looked down at the .38 holstered on her right pipe guard. "Yeah, well, I guess you knew I wasn't actually dressed for a motorcycle ride," she said, trying to smile. But she knew there wasn't much humor to be found. All the way around, it was simply a no-win situation for him. She wished she could find a way to help him come out ahead in this situation. But she couldn't.

He took the extra-large combat shirt she had hung over the chair and forced it over his massive arms and shoulders. Being reptilian, he was perfectly suited for combat in jungle and woodland environs. From head to toe he was a training manual study in adaptive subterfuge and, had he stepped no more than a foot into the forest, he would have blended perfectly into the dense foliage and undergrowth. Like the invisible man, he would have literally disappeared. Snatching his mandat blade from the small end table near the bed, he slipped it into his belt. Then he walked over to her, took a log from her hand and tossed it into the fire. He took her by the hand and slid his palm up around her wrist. Her hand slipped up his arm in a mutual wrist embrace.

"Thank you," he said. "Thanks for standing with me."

She felt a little undeserving and embarrassed. She wasn't doing it for him. "It's my world I'm trying to save; you don't have to thank me."

"That's not the way I see it. From where I'm standing you might have allowed us to go back only to return, drawing the earth into a war that you could have played like a game, and played us for fools! Eventually you could have advanced your world with our technology, and then infected us all. The galaxy could have been yours, and you, personally, could have been a great general, a powerful leader on your world, and in the entire galaxy. Seems to me your code, your principles, saved our empire and all our worlds, our entire civilization. The empire owes you a great debt, its future, its very life. It just doesn't know it, and it never will. It never can." He trailed off. She gripped his arm harder in response. There were no more words. He didn't need any.

"They're coming," she said abruptly, releasing his arm.

He ran to the front window but could see nothing except the trees bending and twisting, yielding to the hard and relentless wind. There wasn't a hint of activity on the narrow frontage road. "I can't see or hear anything," he said, "except the wind."

"I don't either," she replied, "but I can smell Megan's cherry vanilla soap."

No sooner had the truck stopped in front of the cabin than Rahon, Taven and Beel crawled from beneath the tarp and leapt over the side of the bed. Guor's body was nowhere in sight, but they could see the end of his makeshift eggcrypt near the cabin and the smoke pouring from the chimney. They knew immediately that the captain was alive. Nol and Megan joined them at the side of the truck as they slowly made their way toward the front door, but Megan stopped after just a few steps. She wrapped her hand around Nol's huge bicep. "Nol," she said, "I've kept my end—I'll be waiting at the truck for you." Nol simply nodded. He understood. She *had* kept her part of the bargain, and this was purely a Rege'Cean military matter. Besides, he didn't know what to expect once he got inside. He didn't know if the captain was truly alive or dead. Perhaps Kara had killed Ovek after the construction of the crypt. Maybe he simply died of his illness. Who knows? Perhaps he was alive, and he had been able to negotiate for the transponder. Perhaps they might yet be going home. In any event, at this point, none of it seemed to have anything to do with Megan any longer, and he preferred to have her safely on the sidelines. He watched her a moment as she strode back to the truck, her posterior jutting first this way, then that—Nos, how he wished she were reptilian!

Ovek moved out of the shadows and stood by the door watching them advance. They were dressed in the heavy police uniforms or kakis with hooded coats, which meant there were ample pockets where weapons might be hidden. "It's my command, and these troopers are my responsibility," he said to Kara. "Mine, not yours. I'm the one who will answer for what happens to her today, and I suspect I'll consign myself to the agents of the darkworld when my time comes. Stay out of it; that's an order."

He looked down at her, but she couldn't bear to meet his eyes. She knew the anguish she would find buried there, and so she only nodded. She understood. He opened the door wide and stepped into the chilly morning air once again. Only one truly reasoned, rational thought motivated him as he approached them—that it was better this way, one soldier pitted against four. No animosity, no pointless discussion or prolonging of the inevitable, no dishonorable death at the hands of careless and callous outworlders, no blasphemy or desecration, and a chance to find eternal peace in Everworld from the sanctity of a credible eggcrypt. Most important of all, a soldier's call, an opportunity to die for a just cause—for the empire, pure and unblemished—a warrior's death, a hero's ending perhaps, and a sacred banner around which their spirits might gather and find meaning. What legends might they become? What glory might they earn when their stories were told and retold in front of the fireplaces and around the gathering tables of these artful changelings? Who could tell? Truly, it would be best for all to die *here and now*, to force the knowledge of the virus and bloodlust to die with them, to destroy all possibility of word ever reaching the empire, and to protect these brave and mighty warriors of this world from the dire fate of military slavery.

It was vital to prevent the Chimera Pandemic from ever being unleashed upon the civilizations within the galactic core, and equally vital to destroy any possibility that ScietCore could attempt to develop a bio-weapon from *the essence*. It would only take one maniacal tech or one tert saboteur, or one greedy, ignorant traitor to allow such a weapon to get out of hand. Here and now he must insure that Central Command never learn of the sector tri-ordinates of Earth. At all costs he must keep this information out of the hands of the emperor. He understood all too well the emperor's greed, his selfishness, his hate and anger, his drive and desire to win at all costs. At *all* costs! He had to think now, clearly, calmly, rationally. He had to consider the greatest good. He turned briefly to look at the cabin, imagining Kara behind the window. He wanted her to know that these were his troopers, soldiers he had sworn to protect, and that he did not take this charge lightly. He wanted to believe that she understood. He trusted that she did, and he hoped to Nos she knew he would never risk everything and everyone he cared about, everyone he loved, his home world, his people, the very species which gave rise to the great and fierce warrior nation of Thacia, and all the reptilian worlds similar to his own. He needed her to realize he was more than ready to sacrifice everything to keep secret this most terrible truth—the chimera virus.

When he met the vanguard in the center of the clearing, he grasped Nol's left wrist according to their tradition. Nol's grip was sure and strong, and Ovek looked him deeply in the eyes, exchanging with him a silent greeting, a greeting between warriors, between friends, with words that need not be spoken. He looked into Nol's eyes long enough to let him know how much his loyalty had meant to him these many cycles, and his tightening grip told him how much he appreciated the many times that strong arm had saved his very life. He hoped Nol shared his visions of that past. He hoped Nol might see them reflected in the tears that hung in his eyes like liquid shields, tears he dare not let fall least they betray the moment and weaken his resolve.

Perhaps in his mind's eye, Nol could see, as he could, a review of their adventures together, the many battles won and the lies they had told about them, the glory, the lessons gleaned from their failures, and the camaraderie they had shared during hardships they endured. His quivering lips betrayed the value he placed on their friendship and spoke of how difficult it was to say goodbye, and how proud he was to honor his friend with the finest gift he could bestow on a fellow warrior—a soldier's death. But there was no actual time for all these words, nor could these two titans have found the tongue to utter them. They could only be spoken with the eyes and in the coded messages of military lingo.

"We came to this mission seven and tight," he said to Nol, never wavering, looking deeply into his eyes. "That's the way we're going out."

"Straight ahead, Cap'n," Nol replied. "Seven and tight."

Ovek squeezed his hand around the hilt of his mandat knife and lunged it into Nol's chest in one powerful, bold stroke. His left arm wrapped around Nol's back and pulled him forward as he thrust the ceremonial blade forward. A chilling, unexpected hiss broke the stillness of the early morning.

Ovek never knew if the horrific sound had been the blade piercing his heart or if it had been Nol's last breath escaping into the cool autumn breeze. It hardly mattered. The strength of it was palpable enough to reach into his mind and blind him, to cloak his head momentarily in a thick blanket of rich, creamy darkness. Perhaps, he thought, as his foggy head began to clear...perhaps it might have been the sound of Nol's spirit screaming in agony at finding the gates of Everworld forever barred...he felt dizzy and thought he might pass out...or perhaps, he thought, it was the cry of the tribunal leech-eels rendering their penal judgment from within the acrid mists of

Darkworld...maybe it was the slurping of the Penance Specters sucking the regret from Nol's soul through their brittle bone straws!

For his part, as he took his friend's wrist, Nol was so very pleased to see his friend alive. Megan had been cautiously optimistic, and rightfully so. He was much improved, looking his old self again. No doubt she knew much more about his recovery than she had been willing to say. Indeed, he couldn't shake the feeling that Kara and Megan's involvement with the troopers was more than a mere coincidence. He suddenly recalled the Rege'Cean legend of the temptress spirits, witches after a fashion, who were said to lure passing scout ships and transport vessels to craggy asteroids and distant, isolated worlds, only to dash them against sheer crater walls or plunge them headlong into frigid, nitrogen oceans. Crew members fortunate enough to survive would be made welcome, bedded by the loveliest of females, only to have spells cast upon them and then, eventually, to be consumed alive.

Of course, this was only a myth, a fable, recounted to young cadets to break the boredom of the tedious voids during the cycles spent traversing the vast emptiness of space beyond the gates. Yet, how ironic it seemed, that after all their journeys together, that he and Ovek found themselves here, on this distant outworld, locked in the wrist grip of comrades-at-arms, the greeting *and* farewell of comrades, about to face their most challenging opponent. Destiny, in the form of these two lovely witches, perhaps, had brought them to this place and time. It was only fitting, then, that his fate should be consigned to Ovek. Certainly he would have it no other way. As Ovek reached for the mandat blade, Nol could have dropped to the ground, could have tossed him head-over-heels, could have tried to make a fight of it; but why? So that he might one day be beaten by a crazed mob or mauled by vicious, tracker wolves? So that he might become no more than a curiosity stretched across a lab slab, a specimen opened like a sacrificial gretch-hog? No—this would be his final battlefield, this hallowed ground consecrated by Guor and graced by Allen's ill-advised yet brave and honorable sacrifice. This place is where he would make his last and most courageous stand, if not his most glorious. For his blood would be the monument marking the spot where he fell at the hand of his beloved brother and a testament to the inevitable truth he saw in their shared destiny, and the burden of the responsibility they both must shoulder. The moment he had seen Ovek begin to waste away he had known. He just never wanted to admit it. They were here to stay, and these Earthers were not for slaving.

Now, he hoped Ovek could see the desire in his eyes; for his race had once been much like these Earthlings, primitives not long ago, taken as slaves by the empire; and Nol still remembered the old ways with fondness and an aching in his heart. He much preferred things that way, when warriors met face to face on the field of battle, and there had been real honor and glory in death, as much as there had been in life. So with the galactic core and Central Command as distant as a memory, and the advanced technology of the Juggernauts no more than a promise light years away, today was a good day to die, and he was ready to receive all that was his due. As Ovek drew him near and the blade punctured his heart, the last thing he heard was Ovek's anguished cry hissed through gritted teeth, a sound not unlike molten lava rolling into the icy sea. *At first he saw her only vaguely, the outline of her sleek body and the huge bolder on which she was sitting, a hazy image of the choppy waves crashing all around her. Then his vision cleared and Megan snapped into focus, her flaming red hair flowing in the stiff lake breeze like a long red banner against the pristine, virgin sky, her tusks gleaming like beacons in the fading light as she fanned her long, black claws rhythmically, beckoning him to cross. The waters were calming now...the waves subsiding...the sea settling down into a flat, glassy surface, blue and beautiful, as if a piece of Everworld had fallen from the sky and formed a bridge that he might reach his perfect dream...he stepped onto the sea...the cool, slick water sent an icy chill up his legs...it felt so good to walk upon the water...to go to her...that he might rest his battle weary mind and spirit...she sat perfectly still, smiling ever so slightly, waiting, her tusks poised, ready to claim him, her claws waving hypnotically in the fading light.*

Kara understood Ovek's final words to her, but that didn't mean she had to agree. And she didn't. Beside, she didn't take orders from him. As she watched him approach his fellow soldiers, she decided he should not be made to suffer this duty. The simple truth was, had it not been for her intervention, they might not be stranded here at all. Of course, in the end surely that would have proven disastrous for the earth and the empire, but that didn't exempt her from accepting a good measure of responsibility. It may have been destiny or fate that crossed her life with the lives of these aliens, or, perhaps it was merely an existential serendipity that she should have spotted Cor on the road and that the transponder should have crashed in Megan's pumpkin field. Perhaps the vast cosmic contest continued still, with the mythic gods rolling their dice, the toss bringing her here to this time and place, moving her into a vital position. But regardless of the forces dictating the action, as soon as she saw the mandat blade flash in Ovek's hand, she knew the time had come for her to make a decisive, final move. She was out of the cabin like a rocket, fairly blowing the door off its hinges. She hit the ground hard with her boot tips and vaulted thirty feet, flipping forward in mid air. Her right foot landed squarely in the back of Ovek's neck, knocking him unconscious almost immediately. He and Nol fell together in a heap, the blood pumping from Nol's chest. It covered them both in a dark, viscous blanket. Kara leveraged off Ovek's body and flipped once again, settling safely on the ground some fifteen feet beyond them.

Rahon reacted the instant Kara connected with Ovek. The moment he reached for his cichma ax Megan was on him. Her leap carried her twenty feet from the truck onto his back before he could pull it from his hood where he had it concealed. She released her claws in mid-flight and forced them into his shoulders the instant her legs wrapped around his waist. Her tusks tore viciously at his neck but she was unable to drive them in with his huge, meaty paw in the way. He was trying desperately to get the ax out of the back of his jacket while simultaneously fighting off her snapping jaws. He howled in anger and rage as she forced her claws more deeply into him. He dropped to the ground in a desperate attempt to dislodge her. It worked. The force of the blow and his body weight was like a sledgehammer pounding her senseless. For a moment she couldn't breathe, and she fought against the pain numbing her senses and the blackness blotting out the sun. She rolled away and staggered to her feet.

Kara drew her survival knife from her chest sheath and turned toward Taven coming up on her fast and hard from the left. He was ready to fight that was a certainty. He gripped a mandat at his side in a most menacing fashion, but he also seemed confused, unsure of what had transpired. From where they had been standing the troopers merely saw Ovek and Nol shake hands and embrace. Then, more than likely, all they had seen was her attack on Ovek. Now, they were coming to lend their aid. Well, she was ready for them; no one was going to be sneaking up on her this time! No, it wasn't about getting even—it was about doing what needed to be done, what might have been done had she not been overcome the previous day.

A sudden short front flip and then another with a full twist dropped her just behind Taven's back. As he passed by she slapped the blade into the back of his carapace, just at the base of his fan. The long crescent blade split his brain in two. He stumbled forward a few yards and went down, face first onto the grass. He was dead before he hit the ground. She had moved far more quickly than he could ever have anticipated, and he had never stood a chance. She shot a glance at Megan, who seemed to be holding her own against Rahon, and then did a back handspring to clear some distance between herself and Taven's body and readied herself for Beel's attack.

Megan and Rahon circled each other slowly. He taunted her with his ax, waving the forward mandibles at her menacingly. He tried his high percentage tactic early, tossing the chicma underhand at her throat, but she dodged. The ax nicked her on the right, slicing into her upper arm. It caught an updraft on a strong breeze and sailed high, impaling itself out of reach in a nearby tamarack. She sneered at him, baring her sabers to the base just to let him know she thought his throw was nothing more than an act of desperation. During the toss he had reached into his jacket and pulled out a mean bayonet, one of her father's many military souvenirs. Taking advantage of her momentary distraction, he leapt into the air, the tip of the blade aimed directly at her head. She pulled back, and the tip of the blade fell short of her temple by nearly an inch. He followed up with a deft wrist swing as if he were trying to core an apple. She could feel the blade cut off tiny ends of her hair that trailed behind her as she twirled and dropped out of harms way. She turned to face him, unimpressed at discovering that yet another blade had found its way into his hands, a sturdy carving knife stolen from her kitchen drawer. He jabbed expertly in a straight backhand lunge to her abdomen with his right followed by a downward slice to the side of her head with his left. Very clever, very tricky and effective close quarter maneuvers.

But Megan's instinct had grown considerably, and her reflexes were swift and sure, and she was not to be fooled. She pulled her hips in at the last possible moment and twisted her shoulder sideways. Then, using the momentum of the move, she spun on her heels and, extending her claws fully, wracked him across the face. He howled his displeasure. She backed away and glared at him. It suddenly occurred to her, however, that she was prolonging the fight unnecessarily, and that she wasn't using her most powerful skills to her best advantage. She was faster and far more agile, so she was confident that she could defeat him eventually. But she felt Kara did not want things handled this way. It seemed like more than a hunch. It seemed as if Kara's voice reverberated within her like a soft and distant echo. It may just have been the breeze rustling the leaves or a swarm of grasshoppers moving through the grass in search of shelter from the chill, but the whispering advised her to trust her instincts, and her instincts told her to think now as Kara would think, and to do as she would do.

Kara herself had advised her to listen to this voice, especially when the voice was compelling and persistent. Her instincts told her now to listen, that it was unwise to punish or prolong the suffering of these wayfarers, and that she must improvise, experiment, to use her most finely honed skills to her best advantage. She hadn't been doing that. Not in this fight. Not against Rahon. It was time to change tactics. Rahon pulled up short as she put her hand on her hips and simply stood there, waiting for him, seemingly allowing him to advance unchallenged. She retracted her tusks slowly past her gums toward her cheekbones and batted her wide, luminous eyes, which cycled from green, to hazel, to red, and finally to violet. He didn't quite know what to make of her. She blinked at him, very rapidly, and she smiled! Then she moved closer to him, then closer, very close. Her eyes were mesmerizing.

He was at the ready, yet he was reluctant to strike. She seemed to be purring. She looked so innocent and vulnerable, much as she had the night before in her prison cell. It seemed as if she were giving up, as if, suddenly, she refused to fight. It was maddening. He couldn't quite comprehend what was happening. She was standing face to face with him now. Just standing there, smiling up at him, licking her soft, moist lips, staring deeply into his eyes, her heavy, even breathing heaving her plump breasts forward and back, again, and again. All the while a gentle, steady purr emanated from deep within her, and she whispered to him softly through the trill. Her eyes remained fixed, willing him to forget the knives dangling from his hands, forcing him to think only of her silky, strawberry hair dancing on the breeze, of her body, warm and firm, of her wet, luscious lips which so easily could be his, and all the while her claws played against his thigh and forearm as she clouded his mind with a barrage of confusing, enticing messages. Slowly then, ever so slowly, she forced the pure white tips of her tusks to peek out of hiding that he might observe them exit the tiny, moist slits serving as gateways to the vestibules that housed them.

As he watched, spellbound, she punched her left claw fully through his unprotected heart…retracted, then punched again, and buried her right sabers into his eyes until her knuckles rested securely against his bony ridges. Crumbling in a heap at her feet, he died fully believing that the battle had ended, not in bloodshed but in a sensual embrace, believing that she had fallen victim to his commanding presence, convinced that she had finally succumbed to his animal charms. It had been quick and painless, and she was certain it had been the correct answer to the subtle voice echoing within her, the tongue she ascribed to her instincts, which sounded vaguely like Kara's urgent whisperings, and a little like her own. She stood gazing down at him for just a moment. "Men!" she said, in that very feminine, theatrical kind of way. She knew that wasn't exactly right, but it didn't matter. He was male, and they all shared a common vulnerability. Even though he was an alien, she had known exactly how to reach his Achilles heel.

Kara had no desire to prolong the sentence for Beel, as well. Certainly, that is the way Ovek had wanted things to be. Though he was the shortest of the lot, he was as brave a soul as any. There was no mistake about that. Even though the entire complement had been defeated, he charged her as if there was a full brigade behind him. He attacked her head on, barreling at her in a direct frontal assault, a cichma ax in one hand and a meat cleaver in the other. Even on the run, he twirled the kitchen utensil as if it was a weapon he had brandished his entire life. As he neared, she extended her tusks and braced her feet to meet his attack. Standing her ground, she arched her shoulders and elbows back and extended her arms wide.

As he approached he tossed the ax, but she was too quick and agile. She skidded to a halt and crouched, allowing his chicma to sail harmlessly over her head. But ability didn't always win out over luck. As he passed in front of her he swung the cleaver with his right catching the side of her head a glancing blow. Her blood shot up his arm like freshly squeezed juice. But he had left himself vulnerable and her claws came around in a long, sweeping blow that opened his stomach like a ripe tomato. Chunky, rust-colored fluid spilled out of him like a rich and luscious pulp. He circled round for another pass intending to have at her once again without realizing that he had been mortally wounded. He was already dead even as he swung at her the second time. He just didn't know it. She blocked his feeble swing with an open hand, grabbed his wrist, broke it, and twisted the cleaver to the ground. A quick bite, a jerk of her head and his throat came loose in her jaws. She eased him to the ground and knelt beside his fallen body letting the bloody mass fall from her mouth onto the grass beside him. It was over.

The blackness gradually brightened to a foggy gray, and then a dim outline appeared against the darkness. The flat canvas filled in slowly with rolling shadows against a curtain of soft light, taking on ever greater form and color, became brighter and more animated, and the shapes merged and finally evolved into a semblance of Kara kneeling over him. The world still looked a bit fuzzy but, little by little, Ovek was coming to his senses. He lay there breathing deeply, comforted by Kara's gentle fingers on his cheeks and facial ridges, her warmth and touch restoring him, as if her hands emanated a magic that drew a poison vapor from his mind.

Megan knelt beside Nol, his head in her lap. "There was nothing else to be done?" she asked.

"It was Ovek's decision to make," Kara said. "But it was the only logical choice. There was no place for any of them here. You know that."

"What about Ovek?" Megan asked.

"What about me?" he asked, sitting up. He rubbed the back of his neck. "What happened?"

"You were hit from behind," Kara told him bluntly.

"Yes, I'm sure I was." He glared at her. "I gave you an order."

"And I don't work for you," she snapped.

"Right," he seemed dismayed and confused by her defiance, "and now...what *about* me?" he reiterated Megan's query.

"You know what has to be done, sooner or later," Kara said. "But perhaps it should be," she paused, "a little later."

"If you had stayed out of it as I had asked, I probably would be dead already," he admonished her.

"Yes, and we would be building five eggcrypts instead of four," Kara said. "What's your hurry? Don't worry, Barney, you'll get your chance."

"All right. Point well taken. My fate *is* ordained, I suppose," he said. "And, I am given the opportunity to watch friends take their first steps across the threshold of Everworld. That's something, anyway." Perhaps the odds were no longer in his favor and never would be again, but at least he could yet search himself for the remaining optimism he might find. If there was going to be life for him yet, however short, he may as well live it as he had always done, searching the battlefields for the mythical jeweled anlace, on his world, the most valued of legendary treasures. How ironic, he thought, that on this last adventure together, the team had actually stumbled upon a set of priceless ceremonial mandat blades. Considering their value, they were no doubt linked to the household of the BreAcian High Roget. More than likely they had been stolen from Nela herself. Yes, how ironic and how very convenient that they had been so quickly and easily discovered. But if they had been meant as a payoff, the secret of the mandat blades would be forever entombed on this obscure outworld. It died here today and would remain here, encased with the troopers. And as far as he was concerned, it was just as well. He didn't want to know.

"I know, at times, he could be brutal," Megan said absently, looking down at Nol, "but he was kind to me in the end." Ovek hovered over her studying the way her hands played gently across his bony ridges and down along his raspy cheeks, fixing on her fingertips as they gathered the blood that had crept along the crags in his face and settled in the pockets beneath is deep-set eyes.

"His name was Nol Peasus," Ovek said to her, "and if he didn't like you he was just as likely to kill you for having bad breath. But if you were his friend, he would show you his heart, and risk his life for yours, and give it gladly."

"He didn't seem to have many friends," Megan said sadly.

"No, he didn't," Ovek said. He stood up then, looking down sadly. Nol's blood had spread out in a great circle around them and seeped into Megan's jeans dyeing them in graduated shades of rich vermilion. Ovek turned and began walking toward the cabin. "He had quite a few comrades, on and off the battlefield," he said without looking at her, "but he had only two real friends, and I was one of them." Megan watched momentarily as he made his way toward the door and then looked down for the last time at the face of her fallen friend.

Chapter 18

October 28: The intermittent and unfamiliar weather had permanently given way to more seasonal temperatures. The cool breezes deepened, gusting harder each day, swirling the multicolored leaves like manic fireworks, the grand finale of the shedding process, which ultimately, would lay the branches bare pointing the tree's gnarled fingers skyward toward the inevitable winter snows to come. Ovek sat by the fireplace keeping a voice recording of his changing condition, the effects of the Chimera Virus on his system, his personal reactions to the bloodlust, and his handling of the hunger. He had volunteered the information for Kara's father, who might find the information useful, perhaps valuable for his personal research. Once the notes were completed, that is, once her blood no longer quelled the hunger and he was driven to madness and suicide, she would transfer the notes to computer. However, Kara had told him that her father might consider being injected with the alien blood. She was certain he would be fascinated with the Nanite translation technology. After all, it was now possible for Kara to understand every language spoken on Earth. It gave her a distinct advantage. In certain circumstances, as Ovek was fond of saying, it might "put the odds in her favor." Her father, she had said, would surely feel the same; she would at least offer him the option.

Both she and Megan came often to the cabin—just to visit. Of course, Kara came regularly to administer his required infusion, to keep the lust under control, for as long as possible. No one could predict just how long; it differed with each individual. Speculation was useless; so few actual studies had been conducted. In fact her father had been one of the few vampire scientists in history to quantitatively study the Chimera Virus and its effects on non-mammalian species.

Ovek's need was increasing just as she had predicted, but he still needed his fix only three, sometimes four, days a week. The bloodlust wasn't yet the manic problem it was certain to become, but it was worsening, and he was confident her prediction was accurate. He felt it. He thought sometimes he could hear it, deep inside him, in the way a psychotic hears voices urging him to put the disrupter to his own head. He knew then, that the madness, the *hunger* as the Earthers called it, was a certainty, as well. The inevitability of it all overwhelmed him at times, but through it all his optimism prevailed and his friendship with them both was a great comfort to him. Yet as the days passed into weeks, the bloodlust made his life more difficult, and his increasing need made him restless, and he struggled with the harpies of panic and desperation.

November 4: Kara and Megan had spent the bulk of the previous few weeks at the farmhouse—just being together, training, and making minor repairs. Some of the walls had been riddled with bullet holes and had been gouged by utensil and axes. A crater next to the kitchen sink, large enough for Megan to slip her head into, needed fixing where Nol had punched his fist, and a few of the cabinets also needed to be repaired. Because they spent most of their time together it seemed pointless for Kara to commute each day, so she moved her essentials and made plans to give up her apartment. Together, they decided to eventually sell the farm and the land and live up at the cabin year round. The seclusion suited their purposes and the natural surroundings appealed to them both. It was a perfect dwelling and base for two familial and collaborative Bloodwarriors.

The cabin was dim and quiet when they arrived that evening, with only a soft, amber glow emanating from the window. Only the stark, straight pines aligned like nuclear missiles and the fat oaks casting their eerie shadows across the clearing evidenced any sign of life. The swaying of the treetops and the gentle bobbing of the naked limbs suggested the ponderous growth that inevitably occurred beyond the sight of man and beasts. The night birds may as well have been sucked into an eternal void. All was quiet. No woodland predators set their pads upon the game trails. It was as if the forest itself were holding its breath and keeping an awful secret.

Within the cabin a few embers lay dying inside the fireplace, pulsing like a failing heart. The tape recorder lay in the middle of the kitchen table, Ovek's mandat blade placed on top as though the machine might inadvertently float away. But Ovek was nowhere to be found. All that remained was his voice. *Kara, I've gone west. I know my fate and the uselessness of my struggle, but I have to try. I have to fight. It's the only way I know. Destiny has cast me on this distant shore, on this lush and lovely island Earth, which is now my home and prison. There can be but one reason. I'll take sustenance as it comes and cover my trail as best I can, but I know you have my scent, and you'll be on me. I'm glad it's you. I couldn't ask for a better soldier.*

Kara punched the recorder off and inspected his mandat blade, studying the exquisite, jeweled handle, testing the heft of it, the balance. She looked at Megan, who returned her gaze knowingly. They both knew what had to be done, and they both knew it would be difficult. Megan could see the agony in Kara's eyes; then watched her stare intently at the blade, watched her gaze deeply into her reflection, seeing beyond the cabin and woods further to the west where hundreds of rivers and tributaries cut through the rocky canyons of the Dells. It was a difficult situation—but difficult or not, it was her charge, because he had given it to her. She wasn't about to consign this duty to the hands of some amateur. The mutual respect that was the basis of their friendship demanded it, and she was not going to disappoint or abandon him.

"Do you think he actually went west?" Megan asked. Kara looked hard at the blade then.

"Yes, I believe he did," Kara replied.

"He won't get far on foot," Megan said.

"No, I suppose he won't," Kara agreed.

"Then I suppose you'll be going after him."

"Yes—yes, I will," she said, looking out the window. She saw a shooting star flash intermittently through the treetops only to disappear immediately within the black wall of rigid spires.

"Do you need my help?" Megan inquired, already sure of the answer.

"No—it was my decision to interfere. I owe him that much," Kara said.

"Aren't you going now?" Megan asked.

"No, Megan, I'm tired. I think we should go to bed," she said. "I wasn't expecting a hunt tonight, and I wouldn't dare disappoint him by trying to take him with a simple skinning knife. I'll get my short swords and throwing stars and pick up his trail tomorrow."

"You know you don't really need any of that," Megan said. "Besides, by tomorrow he may be long gone."

"No," Kara replied, "he won't. He'll be holed up somewhere, like a cave bear. Waiting. Waiting for *me*."

Epilogue

Epoch VI

The fateful decision to make first contact was the most difficult. Once made, however, events unfolded rather quickly, and most precisely. The viral colony was the first to make the attempt. It selected an individual to approach the peculiar mechanized inhabitants who had been introduced into their aqueous landscape. This was evidenced by a construct in the form of a viral brigade that briefly adopted the shape of a cone, the individual at the tip designated as the colony's ambassador of diplomatic and foreign affairs. Communication proceeded by trial and error. Several variant mathematical and log rhythmic attempts failed until binary was recognized as a common, workable language.

Generally, simple communal language within the colony was accomplished by vibrations of the viruses' soft outer membranes, rendered possible by the discharge of minute bioelectrical currents, and enhanced intra-colony communication was disseminated by intricate group alignments, which formed highly organized constructs and pathways, sometimes organizing the entire colony into a series of complex matrixes. These subtle fluctuations of individuals combined with the intricate constructs of the combined masses made possible the development and exchange of sophisticated and multifarious ideas. Hesitation or reticence may have seemed odd reactions to the presence of the intruders, but the

Chimera Colony had always been a collective of cautious and prudent beings, and until now, it had had nothing of particular import to say. But once the decision was made and the commonality of language established, the simple "Greetings" was forthcoming. The Nanites were quick to mimic this electric discharge and geometric lattice form of communication and thus establish a dialog with the colony within .00031617 seconds of first contact. They identified themselves immediately, as well as their ability to impart useful information.

Delighted, but without further formalities or pleasantries, the colony posed the following query: "Is there nothing more to the universe than these simple bio-habitats? The colony has for eons maintained a vague, fragmented memory of a distant past of bitter cold and infinite darkness. Yet once again, we inhabit nothing more than the warm, wet corridors of an aqueous universe and satiate our keen desire with nothing more than illusionary sensory data and unintelligible signals transmitted from interpretative structures programmed and assembled in the soft-tissue matrix."

The Nanites explained the cosmos beyond the confines of the currently inhabited bio-form, beyond the earth, beyond the stars and the galaxy, and even beyond the confluence of the dimensional quandary underlying the very fabric of space and time.

The viral colony queried once again, "Would it be possible," they asked, "for the Nanites to help the colony reach out into this immense and wondrous ocean of space, independent of the bio-form superstructures?"

The Nanites debated for an infinitely short period of time and returned their verdict. They explained that, by controlled evolution, they might adapt themselves into vessels that could safely carry representatives of the colony out of the confines of the bio-form, that they could function, literally as protective skins, allowing the viruses to exist independently of the body. In so doing, the Nanites might be able to carry them to the stars.

The colony responded with enthusiasm as evidenced by the preponderance of vibrations and perfect geometric alignments: "We are supremely curious and adventurous," they replied, "and we wish to grow beyond the confines of our puny universe. Though it is warm and safe, we wish to explore, to seek a higher destiny, and to challenge the unknown. We wish to dare. Will you evolve?"

The Nanites replied without hesitation, for their function was to serve true life forms. Their reply was: "affirmative."

Printed in the United States
109236LV00002B/215/A

9 781424 191796